WITHOUT DOGMA

WITHOUT DOGMA.

A NOVEL OF MODERN POLAND

BY

HENRYK SIENKIEWICZ,

AUTHOR OF "WITH FIRE AND SWORD," "THE DELUGE," ETC.

TRANSLATED FROM THE POLISH BY

IZA YOUNG.

"A man who leaves memoirs, whether well or badly written, provided they be sincere, renders a service to future psychologists and writers, giving them not only a faithful picture of the times, but likewise human documents that can be relied upon"

Fredonia Books
Amsterdam. The Netherlands

Without Dogma

by
Henryk Sienkiewicz

ISBN: 1-58963-301-6

Reprinted from the 1893 edition

Fredonia Books
Amsterdam, the Netherlands
http://www.fredoniabooks.com

In order to make original editions of historical works available to scholars at an economical price, this facsimile of the original edition of 1893 is reproduced from the best available copy and has been digitally enhanced to improve legibility, but the text remains unaltered to retain historical authenticity.

PUBLISHERS' PREFACE.

IN "WITHOUT DOGMA" we have a remarkable work, by a writer known only in this country through his historical novels; and a few words concerning this novel and its author may not be without interest.

Readers of Henryk Sienkiewicz in America, who have known him only through Mr. Curtin's fine, strong translations, will be surprised to meet with a production so unlike "Fire and Sword," and "The Deluge," that on first reading one can scarcely believe it to be from the pen of the great novelist.

"Fire and Sword," "The Deluge," and "Pan Michael" (now in press) form, so to speak, a Polish trilogy. They are, first and last, Polish in sentiment, nationality, and patriotism. What Wagner did for Germany in music, what Dumas did for France, and Scott for all English-speaking people, the great Pole has achieved for his own country in literature. Even to those most unfamiliar with her history, it grows life-like and real as it speaks to us from the pages of these historical romances. Only a very great genius can unearth the dusty chronicles of past centuries, and make its men and women live and breathe, and speak to us. These historical characters are not mere shadows, puppets, or nullities, but very real men and women, our own flesh and blood.

His warriors fight, love, hate; they embrace each other; they laugh; they weep in each other's arms; give each other sage counsels, with a truly Homeric simplicity. They are deep-versed in stratagems of love and war, these Poles of the seventeenth century! They have their Nestor, their Agamemnon, their great Achilles sulking in his tent. Oddly enough, at times they grow very familiar to us, and in spite of their Polish titles and faces, and a certain tenderness of nature that is almost feminine, they seem to have good, stout, Saxon stuff in them. Especially where the illustrious knights recount their heroic deeds there is a Falstaffian strut in their performance, and there runs riot a Falstaffian imagination truly sublime.

Yet, be it observed, however much in all this is suggestive of the literature of other races and ages, these characters never cease for a moment to be Poles. Here is a vast, moving panorama spread before us; across it pass mighty armies; hetman and banneret go by; the scene is full of stir, life, action. It is constantly changing, so that at times we are almost bewildered, attempting to follow the quick succession of events. We are transported in a moment from the din and uproar of a beleaguered town to the awful solitude of the vast steppes, — yet it is always the Polish Commonwealth that the novelist paints for us, and beneath every other music rises the wild Slavic music, rude, rhythmical, and sad.

There is, too, a background against which these pictures paint themselves, and it reminds us not a little of Verestchagin, — the same deep feeling for nature, and a certain sadness that seems inseparable from the Russian and Lithuanian temperaments, tears following closely upon mirth. At times, after incident upon incident of war, the reader is tempted to exclaim, "Something too much of this!" Yet nowhere, perhaps, except from the great canvases of Verestchagin, has there ever come a more awful, powerful plea for peace than from the pages of "Fire and Sword."

In "Without Dogma" is presented quite another theme, treated in a fashion strikingly different. In the historical novels the stage is crowded with personages. In "Without Dogma," the chief interest centres in a single character. This is not a battle between contending armies, but the greater conflict that goes on in silence, — the battle of a man for his own soul.

He can scarcely be considered an heroic character; he is to some extent the creature of circumstances, the fine product of a highly complex culture and civilization. He regards himself as a nineteenth-century Hamlet, and for him not merely the times, but his race and all mankind, are out of joint. He is not especially Polish save by birth; he is as little at home in Paris or at Rome as in Warsaw. Set him down in any quarter of the globe and he would be equally out of place. He folds the mantle of his pessimism about him. Life has interested him purely as a spectacle, in which he plays no part save a purely passive one. His relation to life is that of the Greek chorus, passing across the stage, crying "Woe, woe!"

Life has interested, entertained, and sometimes wearied him. He muses, philosophizes, utters the most profound observations upon life, art, and the mystery of things. He puts mankind and himself upon the dissecting-table.

Here is a nature so sensitive that it photographs every impression, an artistic temperament, a highly endowed organism; yet it produces nothing. The secret of this unproductiveness lies perhaps in a certain tendency to analyze and philosophize away every strong emotion that should lead to action. Here is a man in possession of two distinct selves, — the one emotional, active; the other eternally occupied in self-contemplation, judgment, and criticism. The one paralyzes the other. He defines himself as "a genius without a portfolio," just as there are certain ministers-of-state without portfolios.

In such a character many of us will find just enough of ourselves to make its weaknesses distasteful to us. We resent, just because we recognize the truth of the picture. Leon Ploszowski belongs unmistakably to our own times. His doubts and his dilettanteism are our own. His fine æsthetic sense, his pessimism, his self-probings, his weariness, his overstrung nerves, his whole philosophy of negation, — these are qualities belonging to this century, the outcome of our own age and culture.

If this were all the book offers us one might well wonder why it was written. But its real interest centres in the moment when the cultivated pessimist "without dogma" discovers that the strongest and most genuine emotion of his life is its love for another man's wife. It is an old theme; certainly two thirds of our modern French novels deal with it; we know exactly how the conventional, respectable British novel would handle it. But here is a treatment, bold, original, and unconventional. The character of the woman stands out in splendid contrast to the man's. Its simplicity, strength, truth, and faith are the antidote for his doubt and weakness. Her very weakness becomes her strength. Her dogmatism saves him.

The background of the book, its lesser incidents, are thoroughly artistic, its ending masterly in its brevity and pathos; here again is the distinguishing mark of genius, the power of condensation. The man who has philosophized and speculated now writes the tragedy of his life in four words: "Aniela died this morning." This is the culmination towards which his whole life has been moving; the rest is foregone conclusion, and matters but little.

One sees throughout the book the strong influence that other minds, Shakespeare notably, have produced upon this mind; here its attitude is never merely pessimistic. It does not criticise them, it has absorbed them.

One last word concerning this novel. It does not seek to formulate, or to preach directly. Its chief value and the keynote to its motive lie in the words that Sienkiewicz at the beginning puts into the mouth of his hero: —

"A man who leaves memoirs, whether well or badly written, provided they be sincere, renders a service to future psychologists and writers, giving them not only a faithful picture, but likewise *human documents* that may be relied upon."

A *human document* — the modern novel is this, when it is anything at all. If Mr. Crawford's canons of literary art are true, and we believe they are, they give us a standard by which to judge; he tells us that the heart in each man and woman means the whole body of innate and inherited instincts, impulses, and beliefs, which, when quiescent, we call Self, when roused to emotional activity, we call Heart. It is to this self, or heart, he observes, that whatever is permanent in the novel must appeal; and whatever does so must live and find a hearing with humanity "so long as humanity is human." If this be a test, we cannot doubt as to what will be the reception of "Without Dogma."

A few words concerning the novelist himself. The facts obtainable are of the most meagre kind. He was born in 1845, in Lithuania. The country itself, its natural and strongly religious and political influences, its melancholy, seem to have left their strong, lasting impression upon him. He has a passionate fondness for the Lithuanian, and paints him and his surroundings most lovingly.

His student days were spent at Warsaw. He devoted himself afterward to literature, writing at first under a pseudonym. He does not seem to have won immediate recognition. He spent some years in California; a series of articles published in this connection in a Polish paper brought him into notice.

In 1880, various novelettes and sketches of his production were published in three volumes.

In 1884 were given to the Polish public the three historical novels which immediately gave their author the foremost place in Polish literature. It is a matter of pride that the first translation of these great works into English is the work of an American, and offered to the American public.

He is a prolific writer, and it would be impossible

to attempt to give even the names of all his minor sketches and romances. Some of them have been translated into German, but much has been lost in the translation.

Sienkiewicz is still a contributor to journalistic literature. He has travelled much, and is a citizen of the world. He is equally at home in the Orient or the West, by the banks of the Dnieper, or beside the Nile. Probably there is scarcely a corner of Poland that he has not explored. He depicts no type of life that has not actually come under his own observation. The various social strata of his own country, the condition of its peasantry, the marked contrast between the simplicity of that life and the culture of the ecclesiastic and aristocratic bodies, the religious, poetic, artistic temperament of the people,—all these he paints in a life-like fashion, but always as an artist.

So much of the writer. Of the man Sienkiewicz there is little to be obtained. Like all great creative geniuses, he is so completely identified with his work that even while his personality lives in his creations it eludes them. He offers us no confidences concerning himself, no opinions or prejudices. He does not divert the reader with personalities. He sets before us certain groups of men and women, whom certainly he knows and loves, and has lived among. He sets them in motion; they become living, breathing creations; they assume relations in time and space; they speak and act for themselves. If there be a prompter he remains always behind the scenes. Admire or criticise or love the actors as you will, you cannot for a moment doubt that they are alive.

This is the supreme miracle of genius,—the fine

union of dramatic instinct, the æsthetic sense, and an intense, vital realism; not the realism of the cess-pool or the morgue, but the realism of the earth and sky, and of healthy human nature. We are inclined to believe that Henryk Sienkiewicz has answered an often discussed question that has much exercised the keenly critical intellect of this age. One school of thought cries out, "Let us have life as it is. Paint anything, but draw it as it is. Let the final test of all literary works be, 'Is it real and true?'"

To the romantic school quite another class of ideas appeals; to it much of the so-called realistic literature seems very bad, or merely "weary, stale, flat, and unprofitable." The profoundest utterances of realism do not impress it much in themselves. It insists that art has something to say to literature, that in this field as elsewhere holds good the law of natural selection of types and survival of the fittest.

While each school has its down-sittings and uprisings, its supporters and its critics, neither school has yet exhausted the possibilities of literature. The novel's aim is to depict Life, and life is neither all romance nor all realism, but a curious mixture of both. Man is neither a beast nor a celestial being, but a compound. Though he can crawl, and may have clinging to him certain brute instincts that may be the relics of his anthropoidal days, he has also, thank God, divine desires and discontents, and certain rudimentary wings. And neither school alone is competent to paint him as he is. The author of "La Bête Humaine" fails as completely as the visionary À Kempis. Neither realism nor romance alone will ever with its small plummet sound to its depths the human heart or its mystery; yet from the union of the two much perhaps might come.

We believe that just here lies the value of the novels of Henryk Sienkiewicz. He has worked out the problem of the modern novel so as to satisfy the most ardent realist, but he has worked it out upon great and broadly human lines. For him facts are facts indeed; but facts have souls as well as bodies. His genius is analytic, but also imaginative and constructive; it is not forever going upon botanizing excursions. He paints things and thoughts human.

The greatest genius assimilates unconsciously the best with which it comes in contact, and by a subtle chemistry of its own makes new combinations. Shakespeare, Dante, Goethe, and the realists, as well as all the forces of nature, have helped to make Henryk Sienkiewicz; yet he is not any one of them. He is never merely imitative. Originality and imaginative fire, a style vivid and strong, large humor, a profound pathos, a strong feeling for nature, and a deep reverence for the forms and the spirit of religion, the breath of the true cosmopolitan united with the intense patriotism of the Pole, a great creative genius, — these are the most striking qualities of the work of this modern novelist, who has married Romance to Realism.

WITHOUT DOGMA.

ROME, 9 January.

SOME months ago I met my old friend and school-fellow, Jozef Sniatynski, who for the last few years has occupied a prominent place among our literary men. In a discussion about literature Sniatynski spoke about diaries. He said that a man who leaves memoirs, whether well or badly written, provided they be sincere, renders a service to future psychologists and writers, giving them not only a faithful picture of the times, but likewise human documents that can be relied upon. He seemed to think that most likely the novel of the future would take the form of diary; finally he asserted that anybody who keeps a diary works for the common good, and does a meritorious thing.

I am thirty-five, and do not remember ever having done anything for my country, for the reason, maybe, that after leaving the University, my life, with slight intervals, was spent abroad. This fact, so lightly touched upon, has given me, in spite of all my scepticism, many a bitter pang; therefore I resolved to follow my friend's advice. If this indeed means work, with some kind of merit in it, I will try to be of some use in this way.

I intend to be perfectly sincere. I enter upon the task, not only because of the above-mentioned reasons, but also because the idea pleases me. Sniatynski says that if a man gets accustomed to put down his thoughts and impressions it becomes gradually one of the most delightful occupations of his life. If it should prove the contrary, then the Lord have mercy on my diary; it would snap asunder like a string too tightly drawn. I am ready to do much for my community; but to bore myself for its sake, oh, no! I could not do it.

Nevertheless, I am resolved not to be discouraged by first difficulties, and shall give it a fair trial. "Do not adopt any style; do not write from a literary point of view," says Sniatynski. Easier said than done. I fully understand that the greater the writer, the less he writes in a purely literary style; but I am a *dilettante*, and have no command over any style. I know from experience that to one who thinks much and feels deeply, it often seems that he has only to put down his thoughts and feelings in order to produce something altogether out of the common; yet as soon as he sets to work he falls into a certain mannerism of style and common phraseology; his thoughts do not come spontaneously, and one might almost say that it is not the mind that directs the pen, but the pen leads the mind into common, empty artificiality. I am afraid of this for myself, for if I am wanting in eloquence, literary simplicity, or picturesqueness, I am not wanting in good taste, and my own style might become distasteful to myself, and thereby render my task impossible. But this I shall see later on. I begin my diary with a short introductory autobiography.

My name is Leon Ploszowski, and I am, as I said before, thirty-five years of age. I come from a wealthy family which has been able to preserve its fortune. As to myself I shall not increase it, and at the same time I am not likely to squander it. My position is such that there is no necessity for me to enter into competition with struggling humanity. As to expensive and ruinous pleasures, I am a sceptic who knows how much they are worth, or rather, knows that they are not worth anything.

My mother died a week after I was born. My father, who loved her more than his life, became affected with melancholia. Even after he recovered from this, at Vienna, he did not wish to return to his estates, as the memories associated with them rent his very soul; he left

Ploszow under the care of his sister, my aunt, and betook himself in the year 1848 to Rome, which, during thirty-odd years, he never left once, so as to be near my mother's tomb. I forgot to mention that he brought her remains to Rome, and buried her on the Campo Santo.

We have our own house on the Babuino, called Casa Osoria, from our coat of arms. It looks more like a museum than anything else, as my father possesses no mean collections, especially from the early Christian times. In these collections his whole life is now absorbed. As a young man, he was very brilliant in appearance as well as in mind; his wealth and name added to this, all roads were open to him, and consequently great things were expected from him. I know this from his fellow-students at Berlin. He was deeply absorbed in the study of philosophy, and it was generally believed his name would rank with such as Cieszkowski, Libelt, and others. Society, and his being a favorite in female circles, diverted him somewhat from scientific studies. In society he was known by the nickname of "Leon l'Invincible." In spite of his social success he did not neglect his philosophical researches, and everybody expected that some day he would electrify the world with a great work, and make his name illustrious. They were disappointed in their expectations.

Of the once so beautiful appearance there still remains up to this day one of the finest and noblest heads. Artists are of the same opinion, and not long ago one of them remarked that it would be difficult to find a more perfect type of a patrician head. As to his scientific career, my father is and remains a cultured and gifted nobleman-dilettante. I almost believe dilettantism to be the fate of all Ploszowskis, to which I will refer later on, when I come to write about myself. As to my father, there is in his desk a yellow manuscript about Triplicity in Nature. I perused it, and it did not interest me. I only remember a comparison between the transcendental belief of Christianity in the Father, the Son, and the Holy Ghost, and the natural triplicity of oxygen, hydrogen, and ozone, with many other analogous triplicities from absolute truth, goodness, and beauty, to the syllogism of the minor premise, the major premise, and the conclusion, — a quaint mixture of Hegel and Hoene-Wronski, and utterly useless. I am quite convinced that my father did not intend to have it published, if only for the reason that speculative philosophy had failed in him even before it was set aside by the world. The reason for this failure was the death of my mother. My father, who in spite of his nickname, "Leon l'Invincible," and reputation of conqueror of hearts, was a man of deep feelings and simply worshipped my mother, put many terrible questions to his philosophy, and not obtaining either answer or comfort, recognized its utter emptiness in the presence of a great sorrow. This must have been an awful tragedy of his life, since it almost shattered its foundations, — the brain and heart. His mind became affected, as I said before, and when he recovered he went back to his religious convictions. I was told that at one time he prayed night and day, knelt down in the street when he passed a church, and was carried away by his religious fervor to such an extent that he was looked upon by some as a madman, by others as a saint. It was evident he found more consolation in this than in his philosophical triplicities, for he gradually calmed down and began to lead a more rational life. His heart, with all his power for affection, turned towards me, and his æsthetic bent found employment in the study of early Christianity. The lofty, restless mind wanted nourishment. After his first year in Rome he took up archæology, and by dint of hard study acquired a thorough knowledge of the antique.

Father Calvi, my first tutor and at the same time a great judge of Roman antiquities, gave him the final impulse towards investigation of the Eternal City. Some fifteen years ago my father became acquainted and subsequently on terms of friendship with the great Rossi, in whose company he spent whole days in the catacombs. Thanks to his extraordinary gifts he soon acquired such consummate knowledge of Rome as to astonish Rossi himself. Several times he began writing treatises on the subject, but never finished what he had begun. Maybe the completion of his collections took up too much of his time, but most likely the reason he will not leave anything behind him except his collections is that he did not confine himself to one epoch or any specialty in his researches. Gradually mediæval Rome began to fascinate him as much as the first era of Christianity. There was a time when his mind was full of Orsinis and Colonnas; after that he approached the Renaissance, and was fairly captivated by it. From inscriptions, tombs, and the first traces of Christian architecture he passed to nearer times; from the Byzantine paintings to Fiesole and Giotto, from these to artists of the fourteenth and fifteenth centuries, and so on; he fell in love with statues and pictures; his collections certainly increased, but the great work in Polish about the three Romes remained forever in the land of unfulfilled intentions.

As to these collections my father has a singular idea. He wants to bequeath them to Rome under the condition they should be placed in a separate gallery named after him, "Museum Osoria Ploszowski." Of course his wishes will be respected. I only wonder why my father believes that in doing this he will be more useful to his community than by sending them to his own country.

Not long ago he said to me: "You perceive that scarcely anybody there would see them, and very few derive any benefit, whereas here the whole world can study them, and every individual that benefits thereby carries the benefit to other communities." It does not befit me to analyze how much family pride and the thought of having his name engraved in marble in the Eternal City has to do with the whole scheme. I almost think that such must be the case. As to myself, I am perfectly indifferent where the collections are to remain. But my aunt, to whom by the bye I am shortly going to pay a visit at Warsaw, is very indignant at the idea of leaving the collections out of the country, and as, with her, thought and speech go always together, she expresses her indignation in every letter. Some years ago she was at Rome, and they wrangled every day over the matter, and would have quarrelled outright had not the affection she has towards me subdued her temper.

My aunt is older than my father by several years. When my father, after his great sorrow, left the country, he gave up the Ploszow estate to her, and took instead the ready capital. My aunt has managed the property for thirty years, and manages it perfectly. She is of a rather uncommon character, therefore I will devote to her a few lines. At the age of twenty she was betrothed to a young man who died in exile just when my aunt was about to follow him abroad. From that time forth she refused all offers of marriage and remained an old maid. After my mother's death she went with my father to Vienna and Rome, where she lived with him, surrounding him with the tenderest affections, which she subsequently transferred to me. She is, in the full meaning of the word, *une grande dame*, somewhat of an autocrat, haughty and outspoken, with that self-possession wealth and a high position give, but withal the very essence of goodness and kindliness. Under the cover of abrupt manners she has an excellent and lenient disposition, loving not only her own family, as for instance my father and myself and her own household, but mankind in general. She is so virtuous that really I do not know whether there be any merit in it, as she could not be otherwise if she tried. Her charities are proverbial. She orders poor people about like a constable, and tends them like a Saint Vincent de Paul. She is very religious. No doubts whatever assail her mind. What she does, she does from unshaken principles, and therefore never hesitates in the choice of ways and means. Therefore she is always at peace with herself and very happy. At Warsaw they call my aunt, on account of her abrupt manners, *le bourreau bienfaisant*. Some people, especially among women, dislike her, but generally speaking she lives in peace with all classes.

Ploszow is not far from Warsaw, where my aunt owns a house in which she spends the winter. Every winter she tries to inveigle me there in the hope to see me married. Even now I received a mysteriously worded missive adjuring me to come at once. I shall have to go, as I have not seen her for some time. She writes that she is getting old and wishes to see me before she dies. I confess I do not always feel inclined to go. I know that my aunt's dearest wish is to see me married, therefore every visit brings her a cruel disappointment. The very idea of such a decisive step frightens me. To begin a new life when I am so tired of the old one! Finally, there is another vexatious element in my relations with my aunt. As formerly my father's friends looked upon him as a genius, so she persists in regarding me as one exceptionally gifted, from whom great things are to be expected. To allow her to remain of this opinion seems an abuse of her good faith; to tell her that nothing is to be expected from me would be a more likely conclusion, but at the same time inflict upon the dear old lady a cruel blow

To my misfortune many of those near me share my aunt's opinion, and this brings me to the point of drawing a sketch of my own character, which is by no means an easy task, as my nature is rather a complicated one.

I brought with me into the world very sensitive nerves, nerves perfected by the culture of generations. During the first years of my childhood I remained under the care of my aunt; after her departure, according to the custom of our country, a nursery governess was engaged for me. As we lived in Rome, among foreign surroundings, and my father wished me to be well grounded in my own language, he engaged a Polish governess. She is still with us as housekeeper at Babuino. My father also bestowed some pains upon me, especially after my fifth year. I used to go to his room to talk with him, and this developed my mind prodigiously, too much so perhaps for my age. Later on, when his studies and archæologic researches took up his whole time, he engaged a tutor, Father Calvi. This was an old man, with a mind and faith exceedingly serene. He loved art beyond everything. I believe religion even reacted upon him through its beauty. In the galleries before the old masters, or listening to the music in the Sistine Chapel, he lost himself altogether. There was nothing pagan in these feelings, as they were not based upon sybaritism or sensual enjoyment. Father Calvi loved art with the pure, serene feeling as maybe a Da Fiesole, a Cimabue, or Giotto loved it. And he loved in all humility, as he himself had no gifts that way. I could not say which of the fine arts he loved best, but I believe he leaned mostly towards harmony, which responded to the harmony of his own mind.

Whenever I think of Father Calvi, I am reminded at the same time of the old man that stands beside Raphael's Saint Cecilia listening intently to the music of the spheres.

Between my father and the priest sprang up a friendship which lasted unto the latter's death. It was he who confirmed my father in his archæologic researches, especially about Rome. There was another bond between these two, — their love for me. Both considered me as an exceptionally gifted child, and of a God knows what promising future. It strikes me at times that I formed for them a kind of harmony, — a rounding of and completion to the world in which they lived; and they loved me with the same absorbing passion with which they loved Rome and its antiquities. Such an atmosphere, such surroundings, could not fail to impress my mind. I was brought up in an original way. With my tutor, — sometimes with my father, — I visited galleries, museums, villas, ruins, catacombs, and the environs of Rome. Father Calvi was equally sensitive to the beauties of nature and to those of art, and taught me at an early age to understand poetic melancholy. The Roman Campagna, the harmony of the arch-line on the sky of the arches in the ruined aqueducts, the fine tracery of the pines, — I understood all this before I could read or had mastered the first rudiments of arithmetic. I was able to set English tourists right to whom the names of Carracci and Caravaggio caused confusion. I learned Latin early and without effort, from being familiar with the Italian language. I gave my opinion about Italian and foreign masters, — which, however unsophisticated, made both my father and my tutor look at each other in astonishment. I did not like Ribera, — there was too great a contrast of color in his pictures, and he frightened me a little; but I liked Carlo Dolce. In short, my tutor, my father, and his friends considered me a very prodigy; I heard myself praised, and it flattered my vanity. But, all the same, it was not the healthiest of educations; and my nervous system, developed too early, always remained very sensitive. It seems strange that these influences were neither so deep nor so lasting as might have been expected. That I did not become an artist is owing, may be, to a lack of gifts that way, — although my drawing and music masters opined differently; but how was it that neither my father nor the priest was able to imbue me with that love of art for art's sake? Have I a feeling for art? Yes. Is art a necessity of my life? Yes, again. But they loved it; I only feel it as a *dilettante;* it is a necessity in so far as it complements every kind of pleasant and delightful sensation. It is one of my delights, but not an all-absorbing passion; I should not like to live without it, but could not devote my whole life to it.

As the schools at Rome left much to be desired, my father sent me to a college in Metz, where I carried off honors and prizes with very little effort. A year before the last term, I ran away to join Don Carlos, and with Tristan's detachment wandered for some time about the Pyrenees; until my father, with the help of the consul in Burgos, found me, and I was sent back to Metz to be duly punished. The penalty was not a heavy one, as my father and the teachers were secretly proud of my escapade. A brilliant success at the examinations quickly earned me a full absolution.

Among my schoolfellows, whose sympathies were naturally with Don Carlos, I henceforth passed as a hero; and as I was at the same time one of the foremost pupils, my position as the first at school was beyond dispute. I was growing up with the conviction that later on, in a larger sphere, it would be the same. This opinion was shared by my teachers and schoolfellows; and yet the fact is that many of my schoolfellows who at one time would not have dreamed of competing with me, occupy to-day in France high places in literary, scientific, and political spheres; whereas I, had I to choose a profession, should feel considerably perplexed. My social position is excellent. I possess independent means from my mother's side, shall inherit my father's fortune in time to come, and administer the Ploszow estate more or less wisely, as the case may be; but the very limitation of the work excludes all hope of distinguishing myself in life, or playing any prominent part in it.

I shall never be a great administrator or agriculturist, for though I do not mean to shirk my duties, I could not devote my whole life to them, — for the simple reason that my aspirations aim much higher. Sometimes I ask myself whether we Ploszowskis do not delude ourselves as to our abilities. But if such were the case, the delusion would be only personal; other people, strangers, could not be deceived in the same way. Besides, I know that my father is an extraordinarily gifted man. As to myself, I will not enter more fully on the subject, as it might appear mere boastfulness; nevertheless I have the conviction that I could be something infinitely greater than I am.

For instance, at Warsaw (my father and my aunt

wished me to enter the university there) Sniatynski and I were fellow-students. We both were drawn towards literature, and tried our hand at it. I do not say I was looked upon as the more gifted of the two, but the truth is that my work then was considered better and more promising than Sniatynski's. Sniatynski has for some years past occupied a prominent position in literature, and I am still the greatly promising Pan Ploszowski, of whom here and there people are wont to say: "If he would only take up something!"

Ah! there is the rub, — "if he would!" But they do not seem to take it into account that one has to know how to will. I thought sometimes that if I had no means of subsistence I should have to work. Certainly I should have to do something in order to earn my bread; but even then I am firmly convinced I should not derive the twentieth part of advantage from my capacities. Besides, such men as Darwin or Buckle were rich; Sir John Lubbock is a banker; most of the known men in France are in easy circumstances. This proves that wealth is not a hindrance, but rather a help towards attaining a proper standing in the chosen field of labor. I confess that, as far as I am concerned, it has done me some service, as it preserved my character from many a crookedness poverty might have exposed it to. I do not mean by this that I have a weak character, — although struggle for existence might have made it stronger; but still I maintain that the less stony the road, the less chance of a fall. It is not owing to constitutional laziness, either, that I am a nullity. I possess alike a great facility for acquiring knowledge, and a desire for it; I read much, and have a good memory. Perhaps I could not summon energy enough for a long, slow work, but the greater facility ought to serve instead; and besides, there is no urgent necessity for me to write encyclopedias, like Littré. He who cannot shine with the steady light of a sun might at least dazzle as a meteor. But oh! that nothingness of the past, —

the most probable nothingness of the future! I am growing peevish — and tired; and will leave off writing for to-day.

ROME, 10 January.

Last night, at Count Malatesta's reception, I heard by chance these two words: "l'improductivité Slave." I experienced the same relief as does a nervous patient when the physician tells him that his symptoms are common enough, and that many others suffer from the same disease. I have many fellow-sufferers, not only among other Slavs, a race which I know but imperfectly, but in my own country. I thought about that "improductivité Slave" all night. He had his wits about him who summed the thing up in two words. There is something in us, — an incapacity to give forth all that is in us. One might say, God has given us bow and arrow, but refused us the power to string the bow and send the arrow straight to its aim. I should like to discuss it with my father, but am afraid to touch a sore point. Instead of this, I will discuss it with my diary. Perhaps it will be just the thing to give it any value. Besides, what can be more natural than to write about what interests me? Everybody carries within him his tragedy. Mine is this same "improductivité slave" of the Ploszowskis. Not long ago, when romanticism flourished in hearts and poetry, everybody carried his tragedy draped around him as a picturesque cloak; now it is carried still, but as a jaegervest next to the skin. But with a diary it is different; with a diary one may be sincere.

ROME, 11 January.

The few days which remain to me before my departure I will use in retrospects of the past, until I come to note down day after day the events of my present life. As I said before, I do not intend to write an autobiography; who and what I am, my future life will show sufficiently. I should not like to enter into minute details of the past, — it is a kind of adding number to number, and a summing up. I always hated the four rules of arithmetic, and especially the first. But I want to have a general idea of the total, so as to have a clearer view of myself. Therefore I go on with the mere outline.

After having finished my studies at the university I went to an agricultural school in France. The work there was easy enough, but it had no special attraction for me. I did it as one who knows that this special branch of knowledge will be useful to him, but at the same time feels that he lowers himself to it and that it does not respond either to his ambition or his faculties. I derived a twofold gain from my sojourn there. Agriculture became to me familiar enough to protect me from being cheated by any agents or bailiffs, and it strengthened my frame so that it could withstand the life I later on led in Paris.

The years following I spent either in Rome or in Paris, not to mention short stays at Warsaw, where my aunt summoned me now and then in order to introduce me to some special favorite of hers with a view to matrimony.

Paris and its life attracted me greatly. With the truly excellent opinion I had then of myself, with more confidence in my intelligence and the self-possession an independent position gives, I still played a very unsophisticated part on this scene of the world. I began by falling desperately in love with Mademoiselle Richemberg of the Comédie Française, and absolutely insisted upon marrying her. I will not dwell now upon the many tragicomic imbroglios, as I am partly ashamed of those times, and partly inclined to laugh at them. Still later on it happened that I took counterfeits for pure gold. The French women, and for the matter of that, my own countrywomen, of whatever class and in spite of all their virtues when young, remind me of my fencing lessons.

As the fencer has his hour of practice with the foils so as to keep his hand in, so women practise with sentimental foils. As a mere youth, fairly good looking, I was sometimes invited to a passage of arms, and as I took the matter seriously, received many a scratch. They were not mortal wounds and healed quickly. Besides, everybody has to pay for his apprenticeship in this world, especially in a world like that. My time of probation was, comparatively speaking, a short one. Then came a period one might call "la revanche." I paid back in the same coin, and if now and then I was still taken in, it was with my eyes open to the fact.

Myself of a good social standing, I came to know all shades of society, from the old legitimist circles, where I was not a little bored, to the new aristocracy created by the Bonapartes and the Orléanists, representing the society, perhaps not of Paris, but let us say, of Nice. Dumas the Younger, Sardou, and others, take thence their counts, marquises, and princes, who, without historical traditions, have titles and money in plenty, and whose principal aim is to enjoy life. I frequented their salons mostly for the sake of their female element. They are very subtle, the women there, with highly strung nerves always in search for new pleasures, fresh sensations, and truly void of any idealism. They are often as corrupt as the novels they are reading, because their morality finds no support either in religion or tradition. But it is a brilliant world all the same. The hours of practice with the foils are so long there that they look more like days and nights, and the weapons are dangerous sometimes, as they are not blunted. There too I received a few painful lessons until I got my hand in. It would be a sign of mere vanity and still more of bad taste to write about my successes, and I will only say this, that I tried to keep alive the tradition of my father's youth.

The lowest circles of this world slightly merge into the higher sphere of the great *demi-monde.* This *demi-monde* is far more dangerous than appears on the surface because it is not in the least commonplace. Its cynicism has a certain air of refinement and art. If I did not leave many feathers there it must be because my beak had acquired a certain curve and my claws had grown. Generally speaking of the life in Paris, a man who has passed through that mill feels rather exhausted, and what then of such as I, who leave only to go back again? It is only later on in life we begin to understand that triumphs like these are somewhat like the victories of Pyrrhus. My naturally strong constitution withstood this life, but my nerves are somewhat shattered.

Paris, though, possesses one superiority over other centres of civilization. I do not know of any other city in the world where the elements of art, science, and all kinds of human ideas seem to float in the air to be assimilated by the human brain. Almost unconsciously it imbibes not only the newest ideas in the sphere of intellect, but also loses some of its onesidedness, broadens out, becomes more civilized. I say again, civilized, because in Italy, Germany, and Poland, I met with brains and powerful brains too, but who would not recognize any light but their own, so onesided and barbarian that for one who did not want to sacrifice his own opinions, intercourse from an intellectual point of view was simply impossible.

In France and still more in Paris, similar manifestations have no existence. As a running stream smoothes and polishes the pebbles, rubbing them against each other, so the swift current of life rubs off the angles from the human mind. It is obvious that under such influences my mind became that of a civilized being, that can make due allowance for other people's opinions; I do not utter peacock cries when I hear of anything opposed to my views or something utterly new. It may be that such leniency and tolerance of all opinions leads finally to indifferentism and weakens the active principle in the human mind, but I could not be different now.

A certain mental current got hold of me and carried

me along. If the social circles, salons, boudoirs, and clubs took up a considerable part of my time, they did not occupy it altogether. I made many acquaintances in the literary and artistic world, and lived their life, or rather I live it still. Prompted by innate curiosity I read very much, and as I have the faculty of assimilating what I read, I may say that I derived considerable benefit from it and am able to keep step with every intellectual movement of the time.

My consciousness of self is highly developed. At times I feel inclined to send that second self to the devil, that self which does not permit yielding to any sensation, but is always there, searching, criticising every action, feeling, delight, or passion. "Know thyself" may be a wise maxim, but to carry about one's self an ever watchful critic deadens the feeling, dividing as it were your soul in two parts. To exist in a state of mind like this is about as easy as for the bird to fly with one wing. Besides, self-consciousness too much developed weakens the power of action. But for this, Hamlet would have made a hole in his uncle in the first act, and with the greatest composure taken possession of the throne.

As far as I am concerned, it sometimes protects me or saves me from heedless slips, yet more often tires me, preventing absolute concentration upon one point of action. I carry within me two beings, — the one that protests and criticises, the other leading only half a life, losing gradually all power of decision. I am afraid I shall never free myself from that yoke; on the contrary, the more my mind expands, the more minute will be the knowledge of self, and even on my deathbed I shall not leave off criticising the dying Ploszowski unless disease has fogged my brain.

I must have inherited from my father a synthetic mind, because I always try to generalize matters, and for that reason science attracts me more than philosophy. In my father's time philosophy embraced no more nor less than the whole universe and all being; consequently it had a ready answer for all questions. In our times it has become rational in so far as to confess that it has ceased to exist in the old meaning of the word, and remains only as a philosophy of special scientific branches. Truly, when I come to think of it it seems that the human mind too has its tragedies, and it began by confessing its own powerlessness. As I write a personal diary I will treat these matters from a personal point of view. I am not a professed philosopher, because I am nothing by profession; but as a thinking being I am interested in the new philosophic movement; I have been and am under its influence, and have a full right to speak about what entered the composition, and contributed to the creation, of my moral and intellectual being.

To begin with, I note down that my religious belief I carried still intact with me from Metz did not withstand the study of natural philosophy. It does not follow that I am an atheist. Oh, no! This was good enough in former times, when he who did not believe in spirit, said to himself, "Matter," and that settled for him the question. Nowadays only provincial philosophers cling to that worn-out creed. Philosophy of our times does not pronounce upon the matter; to all such questions it says, "I do not know!" and that "I do not know" sinks into and permeates the mind. Nowadays psychology occupies itself with close analysis and researches of spiritual manifestations; but when questioned upon the immortality of the soul it says the same, — "I do not know;" and truly it does not know, and it cannot know. And now it will be easier to describe the state of my mind. It all lies in these words: I do not know. In this — in the acknowledged impotence of the human mind — lies the tragedy. Not to mention the fact that humanity always has asked, and always will ask, for an answer, they are truly questions of more importance than anything else in the world. If there be something on the other side, and that something an eternal life, then misfortunes and losses on this side are as nothing. In this case we might exclaim with Hamlet: "Nay, then, let the devil wear black, for I'll have a suit of sables."

"I am content to die," says Renan; "but I should like to know whether death will be of any use to me."

And philosophy replies, "I do not know."

And man beats against that blank wall, and like the bedridden sufferer fancies, if he could lie on this or on that side, he would feel easier. What is to be done? Are we to abuse philosophy that, instead of building up new systems which, like a house of cards, fall at a touch, it has confessed its impotence, and begun to search for and classify manifestations within reach of the human intellect? Methinks that I and everybody else has a right to say: "Philosophy, I am struck by your common sense, admire your close analysis; but with all that, you have made me supremely wretched. By your own confession you have no answer for a question, to me of the greatest importance, and yet you had power enough to destroy that faith which not only cleared up all doubts, but soothed and comforted the soul. And do not say that, since you do not lay down the law, you permit me to adhere to my old beliefs. It is not true! Your method, your soul, your very essence is doubt and criticism. This, your scientific method, this scepticism, this criticism you have implanted in the soul till they have become a second nature. As with lunar caustic, you have deadened the spiritual nerves by the help of which one believes simply and without question, so that even if I would believe I have lost the power. You permit me to go to church if I like; but you have poisoned me with scepticism to such a degree that I have grown sceptical even with regard to you, — sceptical in regard to my own scepticism; and I do not know, I do not know. I torture myself, and am maddened by the darkness."

ROME, 12 January.

Yesterday I allowed myself to be carried away by my writing. But all the same it seems to me that I laid a finger upon the rottenness of my soul and that of humanity. There are times when I am indifferent to these questions; then again they seem to tear at me without mercy; all the more as those are matters kept within the privacy of the soul. It would be better to put them aside; but they are too important for that. We want to know what we are to expect, and arrange our life accordingly. I have tried to say to myself: "Stop, you will never leave that enchanted circle; why enter it at all?" I have every qualification to render myself a well-satisfied, cheerful animal; but I cannot always be satisfied with that. It is said the Slav temperament has a tendency towards mysticism. I have noticed that our greatest writers and poets end by becoming mystics. It is not surprising that lesser minds should be now and then troubled. As to myself I feel obliged to take notice of those inward struggles in order to get a faithful image of myself. Perhaps I feel also the want of justifying myself before my own conscience. For instance, with the great "I do not know" before me, I still observe the regulations of the Church; yet do not consider myself a hypocrite. This would be the case if, instead of the "I do not know," I could say "I know there is nothing." But our scepticism is not an open negation; it is rather a sorrowful, anxious suspicion that perhaps there is nothing, — a dense fog around our minds that stifles the breath and hides from us the light. I therefore stretch out my hands towards that sun that maybe shines beyond the mist. I fancy that not I alone am in that position, and that of all those who go to church and mass on Sundays the prayers might be condensed in these words: "O God! lift the mist!"

I cannot write coldly or dispassionately about all this. I keep religious observances for the simple reason that I long to believe, and since the sweet teaching of my childhood tells me that faith is a gift of grace, I am waiting for that grace. I am waiting that it may be given unto me; that my soul may believe unquestioningly, even as it believed in childhood. Those are my motives; no self-interest prompts me; it would be much easier to be a cheerful, contented animal. Since I am justifying my outward semblance of piety, I have some other less noble and more practical reasons. From the days of my childhood I have been accustomed to keep certain rules, and they have grown into a habit. Henry the Fourth said Paris was well worth a mass; so say I that the peace of those nearest is worth a mass; people of my class, as a rule, observe religious prescriptions, and I should protest against the outward symbols only in such a case if I could find something more conclusive to say than "I do not know." I go to church because I am a sceptic in regard to my own scepticism. It is not a comfortable feeling, and my soul drags one wing along the earth. But it would be much worse with me if I always pondered over these questions so earnestly as I have done while writing these last pages. Fortunately for me this is not the case. I have mentioned already that at times I am indifferent to them. Life carries me along, and although in the main I know what to think of its hollow pleasures, I give myself up to it altogether, and then the moral "to be, or not to be" has no meaning for me. A strange thing, about the power of which not much has been said, is the influence of social suggestion on the mind. In Paris, for instance, I feel happier not only because the continual mill deafens me, — I am swallowed up by the surging masses, and my mind is diverted by tricks of the fencing ring, — but also because the people there, without being conscious of it, live as if it were worth their while to put all their energies into this life, and as if beyond there was nothing but a chemical process. My pulse begins to beat in unison with theirs; I feel myself in harmony with my surroundings; amuse myself or bore myself, conquer or am conquered, but enjoy a comparative rest.

ROME, BABUINO, 13 January.

I have only four days left before my departure, and will now sum up what I said about myself. I am an individual rather worn out, very sensitive, and of a highly nervous temperament. I have a strongly developed consciousness of self, seconded by comparative culture, and taken altogether, may consider myself an intellectually developed being.

My scepticism debars me from all firm convictions. I look, observe, criticise, sometimes fancy I get hold of some essential truth, but am ready always to doubt even that. I have already said all that was necessary in reference to religion. As to my social creed I am a conservative so far as a man in my position is bound to be, and so far as conservatism suits me. No need to mention that I am far from considering conservatism as a dogma, which no one is allowed to touch or to criticise. I am too much civilized to take a party view of either aristocracy or democracy. I leave that as a pastime to those who live in the country, or in remote places where ideas, like fashions, are some ten years late. From the time when privileges were done away with, the question has been closed; but in remoter parts, where the world remains more or less stagnant, it has become not so much a question of principle as rather a question of vanity and nerves. In regard to myself, I like well-bred people, — people with brains and nerves, and look for them where they are most readily found. I like them as I like works of art, fine scenery, and beautiful women. From an æsthetic point of view, I possess refined nerves, — too refined, perhaps, owing to my early training and a naturally impressionable temperament. This æsthetic sensitiveness gives me as many delights as torments, and renders me one great service: it preserves me from cynicism or otherwise extreme corruption, and serves me instead of moral principle. I recoil from many things, not because they are wicked, but because they are ugly. From my æsthetic nerves I derive also a certain delicacy of feeling. Taken all in all, it seems to me that I am a man a little marred by life, decent enough though to say the truth, rather floating in mid-air because not supported by any dogma, either social or religious. I am also without an aim to which I could devote my life.

One word more about my abilities before concluding the synthesis. My father, my aunt, my colleagues, and sometimes strangers, consider them simply prodigious. I allow that my intellect has a certain glitter. But will the *improductivité Slave* scatter all the hopes invested in me? Considering all I have, or rather have not done up to this day, either for others or myself, I feel inclined to think that such will be the case. This confession costs me more than appears on the surface. My irony when I think of myself tastes bitter on the palate. There was something barren in the clay from which God formed the Ploszowskis, since on that soil everything springs up and grows so luxuriously, yet produces no fruit. Truly, if with this barrenness, this powerlessness to act, I possessed the abilities of a genius, it would be a strange kind of genius, — a genius without portfolio, as there are ministers of state without portfolio.

This definition, "a genius without portfolio" seems to fit me to perfection. I shall take out a patent of invention for the word. But the definition does not apply to me alone. Its name is legion. Side by side with the *improductivité Slave* goes the genius without portfolio; it is a pure product of the Slav soil. Once more I say its name is legion. I do not know another part of the world where so much ability is wasted, in which even those who bring forth something give so little, so incredibly little, in comparison with what God gave them.

ROME, BABUINO, 14 January.

Another letter from my aunt urging me to come. I am coming, I am coming, dear aunt, though God knows I am doing it out of love for you; otherwise I should greatly prefer to remain where I am. My father seems not well; from time to time he feels a strange numbness on the whole of his left side. At my urgent entreaties he has seen a physician, but I am quite sure the physic he received is safely stowed away in a cupboard, according to an old custom he has. Once he opened the mysterious receptacle and showed me a whole collection of bottles, pill-boxes, and powders, saying: "For mercy's sake! this would kill a strong man, let alone a sick one." Up to now, this quaint way of looking upon medicine has not done him any harm, but I am troubled about the future. Another reason for my unwillingness to go is my aunt's plan of campaign. Of course she is anxious to see me married. I do not know whether she has anything definite in view. God grant I may be wrong; but she does not deny the intention. "About an eligible *parti* like you," she writes, "there will be at once a war of the roses, you may be sure of that." I am tired and do not wish for any war, and least of all to end it like Henry VII. by a marriage. On the other hand, — I dare not tell my aunt, but may confess it to myself, — I do not like Polish women. I am thirty-five, and like other men that live much in society, I had my sentimental passages, among others, with Polish women, and from these encounters I carried away the impression that they are the most impossible and most wearying women in the world. I do not know whether, generally speaking, they are more virtuous than their French or Italian sisters; I only know that they are more pathetic. The very remembrance of it gives me a creepy sensation. I can understand an elegy over a broken pitcher when you behold the shards for the first time; but to go on with the same pathos over a much mended pitcher, looks more like a comic opera.

A pleasant rôle that of the listener, whom courtesy bids to take it seriously.

Strange, fantastic women with fiery imagination and cold temperaments! In their sentiments there is neither cheerfulness nor even simplicity. They are in love with the outward forms of love, caring less for its intrinsic value. With French or Italian women after the first skirmishes, you may be sure of your "ergo." With a Pole it is different. Somebody said that if a man is mistaken and says two and two makes five, you may be able to set him right; a woman says two and two is a lamp, and you come against a blank wall. In a Polish woman's logic two and two may be not four, but a lamp, love, hatred, a cat, tears, duty, scorn; in brief, you cannot foresee anything, calculate upon anything, or guard against anything. It may be, after all, because of these very pitfalls that their virtue is better guarded than that of other women, if only for the reason that the beleaguering forces get mortally tired. But what struck me, and what I resented most, is that those pitfalls, barricades, and the whole array of defence are not so much erected for the repulse of the enemy as to give them the sensation of warfare. I spoke of this in a roundabout way with a clever woman only half a Pole, for her father was an Italian.

She listened to me for a while, then said at last: —

"It seems to me you are very much like the fox looking at the dovecote. He does not like, and it makes him wroth, to see the doves dwelling so high, and unlike the hens, always on the wing. All you have said tells in favor of Polish women."

"How do you make that out?"

"The more a Polish woman seems intolerable as somebody else's wife, the more desirable she is to have for one's own."

She had driven me into a corner, and I could not find an answer. Perhaps she is right, and I look upon it from a fox's point of view. There is also not the slightest doubt that if I were to marry, especially a Pole, I not only should search for her among the high flying doves, but I should choose a perfectly white one.

But I am like the chickens when asked in what sauce they would like to be served; I do not want to be dished up at all. Now, to return to my grievance against you, dear ladies, you are before everything in love with love, and not with the lover. Every one of you is a queen in her own rights, and in this you differ from other women; every one seems to confer a boon and a favor in permitting herself to be loved; none agrees to be only an addition or completion of a man's life, who, besides matrimony, has some other aims in life. You want us to live for you, instead of living for us. Last, but not least, you love your children more than your husband. His final fate is that of a satellite turning forever round in the same orbit. I have seen this and noticed it very often in a general way; but now and then there happens to be found a pure diamond too among the chaff. No, my queens and princesses, permit me to worship you from a safe distance.

Fancy putting aside all other aims, all ideals, in order to burn incense every day at the shrine of a woman, and that woman one's own wife. No, dear ladies, that is not sufficient to fill a man's life.

Nevertheless, that second self sometimes mutters, "And what else is there for you to do? If, anybody it is you who are fittest for the sacrifice, for what are your aims or your intentions? No! the deuce and all! To change the whole tenor of one's life, renounce old habits, comforts, pleasures, it must be a great love, indeed, that could induce me to such a venture. Marriage means a most amazing act of faith in a woman, I could never summon courage enough to commit. No, most decidedly, I do not wish to be served up in any sauce whatever."

WARSAW, 21 January.

I arrived here to-day. I broke my journey at Vienna which made it less tiring, but my nerves do not let me sleep, so I take up my journal which has grown as a friend to me. What joy there was in the house at my arrival, and what a dear, kind soul that aunt of mine is! I do believe she is awake now for very joy. She could scarcely eat any dinner. When in the country at Ploszow, she is continually wrangling with her land-agent, Pan Chwastowski, a burly old nobleman who does not give in to her one whit. Sometimes their disputes reach to such a pitch that a catastrophe seems imminent; then suddenly my aunt relaxes, falls to with an appetite and eats her dinner with a certain determination. To-day she had only the servants to scold, and that was not sufficient to give her an appetite. She was in capital spirits though, and the loving glances she bestowed on me beggar description. In intimate circles I am called my aunt's fetich, which makes her very angry.

Of course my fears and presentiments have not deceived me. There are not only plans, but also a definite object. After dinner my aunt is in the habit of walking up and down the room, and often thinks aloud. Therefore, in spite of the mystery she deems fit to surround herself with, I heard the following monologue:—

"He is young, handsome, rich, intelligent; she would be a fool if she did not fall in love with him at once."

To-morrow I am to go to a picnic the gentlemen are giving for the ladies. They say it is going to be a grand entertainment.

WARSAW, 25 January.

I am often bored at balls. As a *homo sapiens* and an *éligible parti*, I abhor them; as an artist, that is, artist without portfolio, I now and then like them. What a splendid sight, for instance, that broad staircase well lit up, where, amid a profusion of flowers the women ascend to the ball-room. They all appear tall, and when not seen from below (because the training robes destroy the illusion) they remind one of the angels on Jacob's ladder. I like the motion, the light, the flowers, and the gauzy material which enwraps the young girls as in a soft mist; and then those shoulders, necks, and arms which released from the warm cloaks seem at once to grow firm and crisp as marble. My sense of smell, too, is gratified, for I delight in good perfumes.

The picnic was a great success. To give Staszewski his due, he knows how to arrange these things. I arrived together with my aunt, but lost sight of her in the entrance hall, for Staszewski himself came down to lead her upstairs. The dear old lady had on her ermine cloak she uses on great occasions, and which her friends call her robe of state. When I entered the ballroom I remained near the door and looked around. What a strange sensation when, after a long interval, one comes back to once familiar scenes. I feel I am a part of them, and yet I look at them and criticise them as if I were a stranger. Especially the women attracted my attention,— I must admit, fastidious as I am, that our society is very choice. I saw pretty faces and plain faces, but all stamped with the same well-bred refinement. The necks and shoulders, in spite of the softly rounded contours, simply reminded me of Sèvres china. There is a restful elegance, something daintily finished, in all of them. Truly, they do not imitate Europe,— they are Europe.

I remained there about a quarter of an hour indolently musing which of all these dainty damsels my aunt had chosen for me, when Sniatynski and his wife came up. I had seen him only a few months ago at Rome, and had known her, too, for some time. I like her very much; she has a sweet face and belongs to those exceptional Poles that do not absorb their husband's whole life, but surrender their own. Presently a young girl slipped in between us, and while greeting Pani Sniatynska, put out a small hand encased in a white kid glove and said: —

"Don't you know me, Leon?"

I felt slightly perplexed at this question, for indeed I did not know who it was that greeted me thus familiarly; but not wishing to seem rude, I smiled and pressed the little hand, saying, "Of course I do." I must have looked a little foolish because, presently Pani Sniatynska burst out laughing and said, "But he does not recognize you; it is Aniela P."

Aniela, my cousin! No wonder I did not recognize her. The last time I saw her, some ten or eleven years ago at Ploszow, she wore a short frock and pink stockings. I remember the midges had stung her about the legs, and she stamped on the ground like a little pony. How could I dream that these white shoulders, this breast covered with violets, this pretty face with the dark eyes, in short, this girl in the full bloom of maidenhood, was the same as the little wagtail on thin feet I had known formerly. How pretty she had grown; a fine butterfly had come from that chrysalis. I renewed my greeting very heartily. Afterwards when the Sniatynskis had left us she told me that my aunt and her mother had sent her to fetch me. I offered my arm and we went across the room.

All at once it burst in upon me. It was she, Aniela, my aunt had in her mind. That then was the secret, the surprise meant for me. My aunt always used to be fond of her, and troubled herself not a little over Pani P.'s financial difficulties. I only wondered why these ladies were not stopping with my aunt; but I did not ponder over it long; I preferred to look at Aniela, who naturally interested me more than the average girl. As we had to make our way to the other end of the room and the crush was great, I had ample time for conversation and scrutiny. Fashion this year has it that gloves should be worn halfway up the elbow, so I noticed that the arm which rested on mine had a slightly dusky shade, covered as it was with a light down. And yet she could not be called a brunette. Her hair is a light brown with a gleam of bronze. Her eyes are light too, but appear dark, shaded as they are by long eyelashes; the eyebrows, on the contrary, are dark and very pretty. The characteristic of this little head with the low brow is that exuberance of hair, eyebrows, eyelashes, and that down, which on the face is very slight. This at some future time may spoil her beauty, but at present she is so young that it points only to an exuberance of organism, and shows that she is not a doll, but a woman full of warm, active life.

I do not deny that, fastidious as are my nerves and not easily thrilled, I fell under a spell. She is my type exactly. My aunt, who, if she ever heard about Darwin would call him a wicked writer, has unconsciously adopted his theory of natural selection. Yes, she is my type. They have baited the hook this time with a dainty morsel.

An electric current seemed to pass from her arm into mine. Besides I noticed that she too seemed pleased with me, and that naturally raises one's spirits. My scrutiny from an artistic point of view proved highly satisfactory. There are faces that seem to be a translation from music or poetry into human shape. Such a face is Aniela's. There is nothing commonplace about it. As children are inoculated for small-pox so the upper classes inoculate modesty in their girls; there is something so very innocent in this face, but through that very innocence peeps out a warm temperament. What a combination! — as if some one said, "An innocent Satan!"

Unsophisticated as Aniela is, she is yet a little bit of a coquette, and quite conscious of her attractions. Knowing for instance that she has beautiful eyelashes, she very often drops her eyes. She has also a graceful way of lifting her head and looking at the person she is speaking to. In the beginning she was slightly artificial, from shyness I fancy, but soon afterwards we chatted together as if we had never been separated since those times at Ploszow. My aunt is highly amusing with her absentmindedness, but I should not care to have her for a fellow-conspirator. Scarcely had we approached the two elderly ladies and I exchanged greetings with Aniela's mother, when my aunt, noticing my animation, turned to her companion and said aloud, "How pretty she looks in those violets! It was, after all, a happy thought that he should see her the first time at a ball."

Aniela's mother grew very confused, and so did Aniela, and the truth began to dawn upon me why it was the ladies were not staying with my aunt. This had been Pani P.'s idea; she and my aunt had been plotting together. I suppose Aniela had not been taken into confidence, but thanks to female perspicacity could not help guessing how matters stood.

To put an end to the embarrassing situation I turned to her and said, "I warn you that I am not very proficient at dancing, but as they will carry you off any moment, will you grant me a waltz?"

Aniela for all answer handed me her tablets and said resolutely, "Put down as many as you like."

I confess that I do not like the rôle of a puppet pulled by a string, therefore I resolved to take an active part in the old ladies' politics. I took the tablets and wrote, "Did you understand that they want us to marry?"

Aniela read it and changed color. She remained silent for a moment, as if not trusting her voice, or hesitating what to say; at last she lifted her eyelashes and looking straight into my eyes she replied, "Yes."

It was now her turn to question me, not in words but with her eyes. I already knew I had made a favorable impression on her, and if she had an inkling of the truth her mind must needs dwell a good deal on me. I interpreted the look of her eyes thus: "I am aware my mother and my aunt want us to become acquainted, to know each other well. And you?"

Instead of an answer I put my arm around her waist, and lightly drawing her towards me, led her into the mazes of a waltz. I remembered my fencing practice.

A mute answer could not but stir up fancies in a girl's mind, especially after what I had written on the tablets. I thought to myself: "What harm is there if her fancy turns into my direction? As far as I am concerned I shall not go a step further than I intend, and if her fancy travels further I cannot help it." Aniela dances exquisitely, and she danced this waltz as a woman should, with a certain vehemence and self-abandon at the same time. I noticed that the violets on her breast rose and fell far quicker than the quiet step of the dance warranted. I understood that she felt agitated. Love is a law of nature, kept under control by a careful bringing-up. But once the girl is told that she may love this one or that, the chance is she will obey very readily. Aniela evidently expected that after I had been bold enough to write those few words I would allude to it further, but I kept aloof on purpose to leave her in suspense.

I wished also to look at her from a distance. Decidedly she is my type. Women of that kind have a special attraction for me. Oh, if only she were thirty, and not a girl they expect me to marry!

WARSAW, 30 January.

They have come to stay with us. Yesterday I spent all the day with Aniela. She has more pages to her soul than most girls at her age. On many of these pages the future will write, but there is room for many beautiful things. She feels and understands everything, and is an excellent listener, and follows the conversation with her large, intelligent eyes. A woman that can listen possesses one more attraction, because she flatters man's vanity. I do not know whether Aniela is conscious of this, or whether it be her womanly instinct. Maybe she has heard so much about me from my aunt that she deems every word I say an oracle. She is decidedly not without coquetry. To-day I asked her what she wished for most in life. She answered. "To see Rome:" then her eyelashes fell, and she looked indescribably pretty. She sees that I like her, and it makes her happy. Her coquetry is charming, because it comes straight from a delighted heart, and tries to please the chosen object. I have not the slightest doubt that her heart is fluttering towards me, as a moth flutters into the candle. Poor child! she feels the elders have given their mute consent, and she obeys only too willingly. I can watch the process from hour to hour.

Perhaps I ought to inquire of myself, "If you do not want to marry her, why are you trying to make her love you?" But I do not choose to answer that question. I feel at peace here, and restful! After all, what is it I am doing? I try not to appear more foolish or disagreeable or less courteous than I am by nature, that is all.

Aniela appeared to-day at breakfast in a loose sailor-dress, which only just betrayed the outline of her shape, and she looked bewitching. Her eyes were still full of dreaminess and sleep. It is something wonderful what an impression she is making on me.

31 January.

My aunt is giving an entertainment in honor of Aniela. I am paying visits and leaving cards right and left. I called upon the Sniatynskis, and sat with them for a long time, because I feel there at home. Sniatynski and his wife are always wrangling with each other, but their life is different from that of most other married people. As a rule, it happens when there is one cloak, each tries to get possession of it; these two dispute because he wishes her to have it, and she wants it all for him. I like them immensely, — it is so refreshing to see there is still happiness out of novels. With all that, he is so clever; as sensitive as a Stradivarius violin, and quite conscious of his happiness. He wanted it, and has got it. I envy him. I always used to like his conversation. They offered me some black coffee; it is only at literary people's houses one can get such coffee. He asked me what I thought of Warsaw after so long an absence. There was also some talk about the ball, especially from the lady's part. She seems to guess something about my aunt's plans, and wants to have one of her rosy fingers in the pie, — especially as she comes from the same part of the country as Aniela.

We touched personal matter very slightly, but had a lively discussion about society in general. I told him what I thought about its refinement; and as Sniatynski, though he criticises it himself mercilessly, is always greedy to hear its praises sung, it put him into capital spirits.

"I like to hear you say so," he remarked, "as you have so many chances to make comparisons, and are rather inclined to look at the world from a pessimist's point of view."

"I do not know whether what I just said does not lean that way."

"How do you prove that?" asked Sniatynski, quickly.

"You see, refined culture might be compared to cases with glass and china, upon which is written, 'Fragile.' For you, a spiritual son of Athens, for me and a few others, it is pleasant to be in touch with it; but if you want to build anything on such foundation, you will find the beams coming down on your head. Don't you think those refined *dilettanti* of life are bound to get the worst in a struggle with a people of strong nerves, a tough skin, and iron muscles?"

Sniatynski, who is very lively, jumped up and walked about the room, then rushed at me impetuously. "You have seen only one side of the picture, and not the best one, either; do not think there is nothing more to be seen. You come from abroad, and pronounce judgment upon us as if you had lived here all your life."

"I do not know what else there may be, but I know that nowhere in the world is there such a vast difference between the classes. On one side, the most refined culture, — over-refined, if anything; on the other, absolute barbarism and ignorance."

A long discussion followed, and it was dusk before I left them. He said if I came oftener to see them, he would show me the connecting link between the two classes, introduce me to men who were neither over-refined, ignorant, nor sickening with dilettantism, but strong men, who knew what they wanted, and were going straight for it.

When I was going away, Sniatynski called out after me:

"From such as you nothing good will come, but your children may be men; but you and such like must lose every penny you possess, otherwise even your grandchildren will do nothing useful."

I still think that on the whole I was right. I have taken special notice of this conversation, as this discrepancy has occupied my thoughts ever since my arrival. The fact is that between the classes there is a vast gulf that precludes all mutual understanding, and makes simultaneous efforts simply impossible. At least, I look upon it in that light. Sèvres china and common clay, — nothing between; one *très fragile*, the other, Ovidius's "rudis indigestaque moles." Of course Sèvres china sooner or later breaks, and from the clay the future may mould anything it likes.

2 February.

Yesterday my aunt's entertainment took place. Aniela was the cynosure of every eye. Her white shoulders peeping out from a cloud of muslin, gauze, or whatever it is called, she looked like a Venus rising from the foam. I fancy it is already gossiped about that I am going to marry her. I noticed that her eyes often strayed in my direction, and she listened to her partners with an absent, distracted expression.

Guileless child! she cannot hide the truth, and shows so plainly what is going on in her heart that I could not help seeing it, unless I were blind. And she is so humble and quietly happy when I am with her! I like her immensely, and begin to waver. Sniatynski is so happy in his home life! It is not the first time I have asked myself whether Sniatynski be more foolish or wiser than I. Of the many problems of life, I have not solved one. I am nothing; scepticism is sapping my whole system; I am not happy, and am very tired. He, with less knowledge than I, does useful work, has a good and handsome wife, the rogue! and his very philosophical principles, adapted to life, help to make him happy. No, it must be acknowledged, it is I who am the more foolish of the two.

The keynote of Sniatynski's philosophy is found in his dogmas of life. Before he was married he said to me: "There are two things I never approach with scepticism, and do not criticise: to me as a literary man, the community is a dogma; as a private individual, the beloved woman." I thought to myself then: "My mind is bolder, — it analyzes even that." But I see now that this boldness has not led me to anything. And how lovely she is, — that little dogma of mine with the long eyelashes! Decidedly, I am going the way I did not mean to go. The singular attraction which draws me towards her cannot be explained by the law of natural selection. No! there is something more, and I know what it is. She loves me with all the freshness of her honest heart, as I was never loved before. How different from the fencing practice of former years, when thrusts were dealt or guarded against! The woman who is much liked, and who in her turn loves, is sure to win in the end if she perseveres.

"The stray bird," says the poet Slowacki, "comes back to his haven of rest and peace all the more eagerly after the lonesomeness of his stormy flight. Nothing takes so firm a hold upon a man's heart as the consciousness that he is loved."

A few pages before, I wrote God knows what about Polish women; but if any one fancies that for the sake of a few written sentences I feel myself bound to pursue a certain course, he is vastly mistaken.

How that girl satisfies my artistic taste is simply wonderful. After the ball, came the pleasantest moment when, everybody gone, we sat down and had some tea. Wanting to see how the world looked outside, I drew back the heavy curtains. It was eight o'clock in the morning and a flood of daylight poured into the room. It was so perfectly blue, seen by the glare of the lamps, that it reminded me of the Capri grotto. And there stood Aniela, with that blue haze around her white shoulders. She looked so lovely that all my resolutions tottered and fell to pieces; I felt positively grateful to her for this glimpse of beauty, as if it were her doing. I pressed her hand more tenderly than I had ever done before when saying good-night to her.

"Good-morning, you mean, not good-night, — good-morning."

Either I am blind and deaf or her eyes and voice expressed: "I love you, I love you."

I do the same — almost.

My aunt looking at us gave a low grunt of contentment. I saw tears shining in her eyes.

To-morrow we leave here for Ploszow.

PLOSZOW, 5 February.

This is my second day in the country. We had a splendid drive. The weather was clear and frosty. The snow creaked under the runners of the sledge and glittered and sparkled in the fields. Towards sunset the vast plain assumed pink and purple shades. The rooks, cawing and flapping their wings, flew in and out the lime trees. Winter, the strong, homely winter, is a beautiful thing. There is a certain vigor in it, and dignity, and what is more, so much sincerity. Like a true friend, who, regardless as to consequences, hurls cutting truths, it smites you between the eyes without asking leave. By way of compensation it bestows upon you some of its own vigor. We were all of us glad to leave town, — the elder ladies, that their pet scheme might be brought to a climax by closer companionship; I, because I was near Aniela; she, maybe for the same reason, felt happy too. She bent down several times to kiss my aunt's hands, apropos of nothing, out of sheer content. She looked very pretty in a long, fluffy boa and a coquettish fur cap, from under which the dark eyes and the almost childish face peeped forth.

How young she looks.

I feel at home in Ploszow, it is so quiet and restful; and I like the huge, old-fashioned chimneys. The woods are to my aunt as the apple of her eye, but she does not grudge herself fuel; and big logs, which are crackling and burning there from morning until night, make it look bright and cheerful. We sat around the fire the whole afternoon. I brought out some of my reminiscences, and told them about Rome and its treasures. The three women listened with such devoutness that it made me feel ridiculous in my own eyes. From time to time, while I was talking, my aunt cast a searching glance at Aniela to see whether she expressed enough admiration. But there is too much of that already. Yesterday she said to me: —

"Another man might spend there his whole life and not see half the beautiful things you do."

My aunt added with dogmatic firmness, —

"I have always said so."

It is as well that there is not another sceptic here, for his presence would embarrass me not a little.

A certain dissonant chord in our little circle is Aniela's mother. The poor soul has had so many sorrows and anxieties that her cheerfulness, if ever she had any, is a thing of the past. She is simply afraid of the future, and instinctively suspects pitfalls even in good fortune. She was very unhappy in her married life, and afterwards has had continual worries about her estate, which is very much involved. In addition to all this she suffers from nervous headaches.

Aniela belongs to that category of women who never trouble themselves about money matters. I like her for that, for it proves that she thinks of higher things. For the matter of that, everything in her pleases and delights me now.

Tenderness grows on the soil of attraction by the senses, as quick as flowers after a warm rain. To-day, in the morning, I saw the maid carrying up her gown and boots; this moved me very much, especially the little, little boots, as if the wearing of them was the crown of all virtues in Aniela.

PLOSZOW, 8 or 9 February.

My aunt has taken up her usual warfare with Pan Chwastowski. This is such an original habit of hers that I must describe one of their disputes. The dear lady can evidently not exist without it, or at least not enjoy her dinner; Chwastowski, again, who, by the bye, is an excellent manager, is a compound of brimstone and saltpetre, and does not allow anybody to thwart him; therefore the quarrels sometimes reach the acute state. When entering the dining-room they eye each other with suspicious glances. The first shot is fired by my aunt while eating her soup.

"It is a very long time, Pan Chwastowski, since I heard anything about the winter crops, and Pan Chwastowski, instead of giving me the information, speaks about anything but what I want to know."

"They were very promising in autumn, my lady; now they are covered by a yard or two of snow,—how am I to know the state they are in? I am not the Lord Almighty."

"I beg of you, Pan Chwastowski, not to take the Lord's name in vain."

"I do not look under His snow, therefore do not offend Him."

"Do you mean to insinuate that I do?"

"Most certainly."

"Pan Chwastowski, you are unbearable."

"Oho! bearable enough because he bears a great deal."

In this or that way the screw goes round. There is scarcely a meal but they have some differences. Then my aunt at last subsides, and seems to wreak the remnants of her anger on the dinner. She enjoys a hearty appetite. As the dinner goes on she gradually brightens up and recovers her usual spirits. After dinner, I offer my arm to Aniela's mother, my aunt accepts Pan Chwastowski's, and presently they sip their black coffee in peace and perfect amity. My aunt inquires after his sons, and he kisses her hands. I saw those sons of his when they were at the university, and I hear they are promising young men, but great radicals.

Aniela used to get frightened at first at these prandial disputes, until I gave her the clue to the real state of things. So now when the first signal of battle is given, she looks at me slyly from under those long lashes, and there is a little smile lurking in the corners of her mouth. She is so pretty then I feel tempted to take her in my arms. I have never met a woman with such delicate veins on her temples.

12 February.

Truly a metamorphosis of Ovidius on the earth and within me! The frost has gone, the fine weather vanished, and there is Egyptian darkness. I cannot describe it better than by saying the weather is foul. What an abominable climate! In Rome, at the worst, the sun shines at intervals half a dozen times a day; here lamps ought to be lit these two days. The black, heavy mist seems to permeate one's thoughts, and paint them a uniform gray. My aunt and Pan Chwastowski were more intent than usual upon warfare. He maintained that my aunt, by not allowing the woods to be touched, causes the timber to spoil; my aunt replied that others did their best to cut down all the timber, and not a bit of forest would soon be left in the country. "I am getting old; let the trees grow old too." This reminds me of the nobleman of vast possessions who only allowed as much land to be cultivated as to where the bark of his dog could be heard.

Aniela's mother, without intending it, gave me to-day a bad quarter of an hour. Alone with me in the conservatory, she began telling me, with maternal boastfulness, that an acquaintance of mine, a certain Pan Kromitzki, had made overtures for Aniela's hand.

I had a sensation as if somebody tried to remove a splinter from my flesh with a fork. As the blue waves of light had stirred up within me a tender feeling for Aniela, — although it was no merit of hers, — so now the wooing of such a man as Kromitzki threw cold water upon the nascent affections. I know that ape Kromitzki, and do not like him. He comes from Austrian Silesia, where it seems they had owned estates. In Rome he used to say that his family had borne the title of count already in the fifteenth century, and at the hotels put himself down as "Graf von Kromitzki." But for his small, black eyes, not unlike coffee-berries, and his black hair, his head looks as if cut out from a cheese-rind, — for such is his complexion. He reminds me of a death's-head, and I simply have a physical loathing for him. Ugh! how the thought of him in connection with Aniela has spoiled her image. I am quite aware that she is in no way responsible for Kromitzki's intentions; but it has damaged her in my eyes. I do not know why her mother should think it necessary to tell me these details; if it be a warning, it has missed its aim. She must have some grand qualities, this Pani P., since she has managed to steer her life through so many difficulties, and at the same time educated her daughter so well; but she is clumsy and tedious with her headaches and her macaronism.

"I confess," she said, "that the alliance suited me. At times I almost break down under the weight of troubles. I am a woman with little knowledge of business, and what I acquired I have paid for with my health; but I had to think of my child. Kromitzki is very clever. He has large concerns at Odessa, and is at present engaged in some large speculations in naphtha at Baku, or some such place, 'que sais-je.' It seems there is some difficulty about his not being a Russian subject. If he married Aniela he might clear the estate; and as an extensive landowner he would have no difficulty in getting naturalized."

"What does Aniela say to this?" I asked impatiently.

"She does not care for him, but is a good and obedient child. I am anxious to see her married before I die."

I did not care to prolong the conversation, which irritated me more than I can tell; and though I understand well enough, if that match has not been arranged, it was Aniela's doing, yet I feel aggrieved that she should allow a man like that even to look at her. For me this would be a mere question of nerves. I forget, however, that others are not constituted like me, and that Kromitzki, in spite of his cadaverous face, passes among women as a good-looking man.

I wonder what his affairs are. I forgot to ask whether he is at Warsaw; most likely he is, as he goes there every winter. As to his business, it may be very magnificent, but I doubt whether it be on a solid basis. I am not a speculator, and could not for the life of me transact a stock-exchange affair; but I am shrewd enough to know it. Besides I am a close observer, and quick to draw conclusions. Therefore I do not believe in noblemen with a genius for speculation. I am afraid Kromitzki's is neither an inherited nor innate quality, but a neurosis driving him into a certain direction. I have seen examples of that kind. Now and then blind fortune favors the nobleman-speculator, and he accumulates wealth; but I have not seen one who did not come to grief before he died.

Capacities such as these are either inherited or acquired by early training. Chwastowski's boys will be able to do something in that way because their father lost by accident all his fortune, and they have to make a fresh start. But he who with ready capital, without commercial tradition or professional knowledge, embarks upon commerce, is bound to come to grief. Speculation cannot be based upon illusions, and there is too much of that in the speculations of our noblemen. Upon the whole, I wish Pan von Kromitzki every luck!

14 February.

Pax! pax! pax! The painful impression has vanished. What keen perceptions Aniela has! I endeavored to be cheerful, though I felt out of spirits, and I do not think there was any perceptible change in my behavior; yet she perceived a change at once. To-day, when we looked at the albums and were alone, — which happens pretty often, on purpose I suppose, — she grew embarrassed and changed color. I saw at once she wanted to say something, and did not dare. For a single moment the mad thought flashed across my brain that she was about to confess her love for me. But as quick as the thought, I remembered it was a Polish girl I had before me. A mere chit of a girl — I beg her pardon, a young princess, — would rather die than be the first to confess her love. When asked she gives her assent rather as a favor. Besides, Aniela very quickly corrected my mistake; suddenly closing the album she said in a hesitating voice: "What is the matter with you, Leon? There is something the matter, is there not?"

I began assuring her at once that there was nothing the matter with me, and to laugh away her perturbation; but she only shook her head and said: "I have seen that something was amiss these last two days. I know that men like you may be easily offended, and I have asked myself whether anything I might have done or said —" Her voice shook a little, but she looked straight at me.

"I have not hurt you, have I?"

There was a moment I felt tempted to say, "If there is anything wanting to my happiness it is you, Aniela, only you;" but a sudden terror clutched me by the hair. Not terror of her, but of the consequences that might follow. I took her hand, kissed it, and said in the most cheerful voice I could assume, "You are a good and dear girl; do not mind me, — there is nothing whatever the matter; besides, you are our guest, and it is I who ought to see that you are comfortable."

And I kissed again her hand, both hands in fact. All this could be still put down to cousinly affection, — human nature is so mean that the consciousness that there was still a door through which I could escape lent me courage. I call this feeling mean for the very reason that I am not responsible to anybody except to myself, and myself I cannot deceive. Yet I feel that even to myself I shall not give a strict account, because in so far as my relations to Aniela are concerned I am carried away by my sensations. I still feel on my lips the touch of her hand,— and my desires are simply without limit. Sooner or later I shall myself close that door through which I could still escape. But could I still escape? Yes, if some extraneous circumstances came to my aid.

In the meanwhile she loves me, and everything draws me towards her. To-day I asked myself, "If it is to be, why put it off?" I found a ready answer: "Because I do not want to lose any of my present sensations; the sudden thrills, the charm of the words unspoken, the questioning glances, the expectations. I wish to spin out the romance to the very end. I found fault with women that they preferred the semblance of love to love itself, and now I am quite as anxious not to lose any of its outward manifestations. But as one gets more advanced in years one attaches greater importance to these things; and besides, I am an Epicurean in my sensations."

After the above conversation with Aniela, we both recovered our spirits. During evening I helped her in the cutting out of lampshades, which gave me the opportunity to touch her hands and dress. I hindered her with the work and she became as gay as a child, and in a child's quick, plaintive voice called out, "Aunty, Leon is very naughty."

14 February.

Ill luck would have it that I accepted an invitation to attend a meeting at Councillor S.'s, who always tries to bring together representatives of all shades and opinions, and over a cup of tea and a sandwich to bring about a mutual understanding. As a man almost continually living abroad, I came to this meeting to find out what was going on in the minds of my countrymen and listen to their reasonings. The crush was very great, which made me feel uncomfortable, and at the same time happened what usually happens at large gatherings. Those of the same shade of opinion congregated in separate rooms to pay each other compliments and so forth. I was made acquainted with various councillors and representatives of the press. In other countries, there is a considerable difference between writers and journalists. The first is considered an artist and a thinker, the latter, a mere paragraph-monger — I cannot find a better word. Here there is no such distinction, and men of both occupations are known under the same collective name as literary men. The greater part of them follow both avocations, literature and journalism. Personally, they are more refined than the journalists I met abroad. I do not like the daily press, and consider it as one of the plagues sent down to torment humanity. The swiftness with which the world becomes acquainted with current events is equal to the superficiality of the information, and does not compensate for the incredible perversion of public opinion, as any one who is not prejudiced must perceive. Thanks to the daily press, the sense which knows how to sift the true from the false has become blunted, the notions of right and wrong have well-nigh disappeared, evil stalks about in the garb of righteousness, and oppression speaks the language of justice; in brief, the human soul has become immoral and blind.

There was, among others, also Stawowski, who is considered a leader among the advanced progressists. He spoke cleverly, but appeared to me a man suffering from a two-fold disease: liver, and self. He carries his ego like a glass of water filled to the brim, and seems to say, "Take care, or it will spill." This fear, by some subtle process, seems to communicate itself to his audience to such an extent that nobody dares to be of a different opinion. He has this influence over others because he believes in what he says. They are wrong, those who consider him a sceptic. On the contrary, he is of the temperament which makes fanatics. Had he been born a hundred years ago and been a judge, he would have sentenced people to have their tongues cut out for uttering blasphemy. Born as he is in the more enlightened times, he hates what he would have loved then; but essentially it is the same man.

I noticed that our conservatives crowded round Stawowski, not so much out of curiosity to hear what he said as rather with a certain watchful coquetry. Here, and maybe in other countries, this party has little courage. They looked at the speaker with insinuating smiles, as if they would say: "Although conservatives, nevertheless—" Ah! that "nevertheless" was like an act of contrition, a kind of submission. This was so evident that I who am a sceptic as to all party spirit, began to contradict Stawowski, not as a representative of any party, but simply as a man who is of a different opinion.

My audacity excited some astonishment. The matter in question was the position of the working-men. Stawowski spoke of their hopeless condition, their weakness and incapacity for defending themselves; the audience which listened to his words grew every minute larger, when I interrupted: —

"Do you believe in Darwin's theory, the survival of the fittest?"

Stawowski, who is a naturalist by profession, took up the challenge at once.

"Of course I do," he said.

"Then allow me to point out to you that you are inconsequent. If I, as a Christian, care for the weak and defenceless, I do so by the doctrine of Christ; but you, from a standpoint of a struggle-for-life existence, ought to see it in a different light: they are weak, they are foolish, consequently bound to succumb; it is a capital law of nature, — let the weaker go to perdition. Why is it you do not take it this way? please explain the contradiction."

Whether Stawowski was taken aback by the unexpected opposition, or whether he really had never put the two things together, the fact was that he was at a loss for a ready answer, grew confused, and did not even venture upon the expression "altruism," which, after all, says very little.

The hero of the evening worsted, the conservatives came over to me in a body, and I might have become the hero now; but it was getting late, I was bored, and wanted to get back to Ploszow. Gradually the others too began to disperse. I was already in my fur coat and searching for my eyeglasses, that had slipped between the coat and furs, when Stawowski, who evidently had found his answer, came up to me and said: —

"You asked why — "

I, still searching for the eyeglasses and rather put out, said impatiently: —

"Plainly speaking, the question does not interest me

very much. It is getting late and everybody is leaving; besides I can guess what you are going to say, therefore permit me to wish you good-night."

I fancy I have made an enemy of the man, especially by my last remark.

It was one o'clock when I arrived at Ploszow, and there a pleasant surprise awaited me; Aniela was sitting up to make some tea for me. I found her in the dining-room, still fully dressed, with the exception of her hair, which was done up for the night. From the intense delight I felt in seeing her thus unexpectedly, I perceived how deeply she had entered into my heart. What a dear girl she is, and how pretty she looks with the tresses coiled low down her neck. And to think that I have only to say the word and in a month or two I might have the right to undo those tresses and let them fall on her shoulders. I cannot think of it quietly. It seems past all belief that happiness should be so easy to get.

I began to scold her a little for sitting up so late, and she replied: —

"But I was not in the least sleepy, and begged mamma and aunty to let me sit up for you. Mamma would not allow it, said it was not proper; but I explained to her that we were cousins, and that makes all the difference. And do you know who took my part? — auntie."

"Dear aunt! You will take some tea with me, will you not?"

I watched her handling the cups with those deft, graceful fingers, and felt a desire to kiss them.

She looked at me now and then, but upon meeting my eyes her eyelashes drooped. Presently she inquired how I had spent the evening, and what impressions I had carried away. We spoke in a low voice, though the sleeping-rooms were far enough away to make it unnecessary. There was such confidence and heartiness in our intercourse as among relatives who are fond of each other.

I told her what I had seen and noticed, as one tells a friend. I spoke about the general impression the society of the country makes upon a man that has chiefly lived abroad. She listened quietly with wide-open eyes, happy to be thus taken into confidence. Then she said: —

"Why do you not write about all that, Leon? That I do not think of such things is not to be wondered at; but nobody else here has thoughts like these."

"Why do I not write?" I replied. "There are many reasons for it. I will explain to you some time; one of them is that I have nobody near me who, like you, says: 'Leon, why do you not do something?'"

After this we both became silent. I had never seen Aniela's lashes veil her eyes so closely, and I could almost hear the beating of her heart.

And indeed she had a right to expect me to say: "Will you remain with me always and put the same question?" But I found such a keen delight in skirting the precipice before making the final plunge, and feeling that heart palpitating almost in my hand that I could not do it.

"Good-night," I said, after a short time.

And that angelic creature gave not the slightest sign that she had met with a disappointment. She rose, and with the least touch of sadness in her voice, but no impatience, replied: "Good-night."

We shook hands and parted for the night. My hand was already on the latch, when I turned round and saw her still standing near the table.

"Aniela! Tell me," I said, "do you not think me a fantastic kind of man, full of whims and fancies?"

"Oh, no, not fantastic; sometimes I think you a little strange, but then I say to myself that men like you are bound to be different from others."

"One question more; when was it you thought me strange the first time?"

Aniela blushed to the tips of her ears. How pretty she looked with the pink flame spreading over her face and neck.

"No, I could not tell you."

"Then let me guess, and if I am right say yes. It is a single word."

"What word?" she asked, with increased confusion.

"Tablets. Yes, or no?"

"Yes," said Aniela, with drooping eyes.

"Then I will tell you why I wrote those words. First, because I wanted a link connecting us together, a little secret shared by both of us, and also —"

I pointed at the flowers the gardener had brought from the hot-house.

"You know flowers want light to bring out all their beauty, and I wanted plenty of light for our atmosphere."

"I cannot always follow you," she said, after a momentary silence, "but I trust you, yes, and believe in you."

We remained once more silent; I pressed her hand again, saying good-night. We stopped near the door, and our eyes met. The waters begin to rise and to rise. They will overstep their boundary any moment.

23 February.

The human being, like the sea, has his ebb and flood tides. To-day my will, my energy, the very action of life are at a very low tide. It came upon me without warning, a mere matter of nerves. But for that very reason my thoughts are full of bitterness. What right have I, a man physically worn out and mentally exhausted, to marry at all? Involuntarily the words of Hamlet come in my mind: "Get thee to a nunnery; why wouldst thou be a breeder of sinners?" I shall not bury myself within cloister walls. The future sinners will be like me, all nerves, oversensitive, not fit for any practical life, — in fact, artists without portfolios. But the deuce take it, it is not they, but Aniela I am thinking of. Have I a right to marry her, — to link that fresh budding life, full of simple faith in God and the world, to my doubts, my spiritual impotence, my hopeless scepticism, my criticism and nerves? What will be the result of it for her? I cannot regain another spiritual youth, and even at her side cannot find my old self; my brains cannot change, or my nerves grow more vigorous, — and what then? Is she to wither at my side? It would be simply monstrous. I to play the part of a polypus that sucks the life-blood of its victims in order to renew its own life! A heavy cloud weighs on my brain. But if such be the case why did I allow it to go so far? What have I been doing ever since I met Aniela? Playing on her very heart-strings to bring forth sweet music. And yet, what for me was "Quasi una fantasia" may prove to her "Quasi un dolore." Yes, I have played on that sensitive instrument from morning until night; and what is more, I feel that in spite of my self-upbraidings, I shall do the same to-morrow and the days following, for I cannot help it; she attracts me more than any woman I ever met, I desire her above all things — I love her!

Why delude myself any longer? — I love her!

What is to be done? Must I go away back to Rome? That means a disappointment and sorrow for her; for who knows how deeply rooted her feelings may be? To marry her is the same as to sacrifice her for myself, and make her life unhappy in another way. A truly enchanted circle! Only people of the Ploszowski species ever get into such dilemmas. And there is devilish little comfort in the thought that there are more such as I, or that their name is legion.

Whether the species be gradually dying out, as badly fitted for the struggle of life, remains to be seen; for in addition to an incapacity for life, there is ill luck as well. I might have met such an Aniela ten years ago, when my sails were not, as now, worn to shreds and patches.

If that honest soul, my aunt, knew how, with the best

of intentions, she brought me to this pass, she would be truly grieved. There was tragedy enough in my life, — the consciousness of utter failure, the dark mist in which my thoughts were straying; now there is a new, — to be, or not to be; but no, it is far worse than that!

26 February.

Yesterday I went again to Warsaw by appointment, to meet a certain Pan Julius Keo, on whose estates I lodged part of the capital I inherited from my mother. Pan Julius Keo wants to pay off the mortgage, and asked me to meet him at a fixed time; and I waited for him the whole day. The devil take their ways of managing any business in this country! He will make five other appointments, and not keep one. He is very rich, wants to get rid of the mortgage, and is able to pay it off any time; and yet — such is our way of transacting business.

From my own observations I long since came to the conclusion that in money matters we are the most flighty and unbusinesslike people in the world. I, who like to go to the root of matters, often pondered over this phenomenon.

According to my ideas, this is the result of the purely agricultural occupation of the people. Commerce was in the hands of the Jews, and these could not teach us accuracy; the cultivator of the soil is unreliable because the soil is unreliable, he is unpunctual because nature has no punctuality. Working in the soil, they gradually take some of its characteristics, which enters into their moral being, and in the course of time becomes an inherited defect.

The knowledge of cause and effect does not restore me to an equable temper. I had to tear myself away from Aniela for a whole day, and what is more, shall have to go through the some process a few days hence; but it cannot be helped. In my aunt's house I found visiting-cards from Kromitzki, — one for me and two for the elder ladies. I was afraid he might take it into his head to pay us a visit at Ploszow; to avoid that, I went out to leave my card on him. Unfortunately for me, he was at home, and I had to stay half an hour. He began his conversation by telling me that he had promised to call at Ploszow; to which I replied that we had gone there merely for a few days, and would be back in town almost immediately. He asked after Aniela's mother, and very guardedly after Aniela herself. He evidently wanted to impress me with the fact that he inquired as a mere acquaintance. I am so impressionable that even this gave me a twinge; how I loathe that man! I fancy the Tartars under Batu Khan must have played many pranks in what is to-day Austrian Silesia, when looting the country after the battle of Liegnitz. That those black eyes, like roasted coffee-berries, did not come from Silesian ancestors, I have not the slightest doubt.

He was exceedingly polite to me, because I am rich. It is true, he wants nothing from me, — I do not give him anything, and my being rich is of no advantage to him; but as a financier he worships money. We spoke about the difficulties in which Aniela's mother was and is still involved. According to Kromitzki, a great deal of her fortune might still be saved if she would part with the estate. Kromitzki looks upon the reluctance to part with ancestral lands as a mere fad. He said he might be able to understand it if she had the means to prevent it, but as the case stood it was mere sentimentality.

He is very talkative, and discussed at some length our national idiocy. Money was lying on the pavement, to be had for the picking up. His father, like other noblemen, had left scarcely any fortune; when all debts were cleared off there remained a paltry hundred thousand florins, and the world knew how he, Kromitzki, stood at present.

"If that business in Turkestan comes off. I shall be

able to wind up my affairs. The Jews and Greeks have made millions in the contract business; why should not we be able to do as well? I do not put myself as an example; but I say, why should we not? There is room for everybody, — why not go in for it?"

According to my opinion, Kromitzki has a certain aptness for business, but is foolish in a general sense. That we are shiftless, everybody knows that; and that here and there somebody makes a fortune by contracts, I can well believe; but the greater part of the people must work at home, and not look for millions from contracts in Turkestan.

May God save Aniela from an alliance with that man. He may have some good qualities, but he belongs to a different moral type. If there be a worse fate in store for her, ought I to hesitate any longer?

28 February.

The elder ladies seem uneasy that the affair is not going on as speedily as they had fancied; my aunt, who is of an impatient temper, must chafe inwardly not a little. But the expression of happiness on Aniela's face soothes them, and allays their fears. I can read in her eyes endless trust and thorough belief in me. She fills my thoughts so that I cannot think of anything but her. I desire her more and more, and do not want to play upon her feelings any longer, — I want her.

4 March.

This day has been to me of so much importance that I am obliged to muster all my calmness and self-possession to put down everything in its proper order. Nevertheless, I cannot contain myself. The die is cast, or as good as cast. I could not have gone on quietly, had I not put that down.

And now I can begin. Sniatynski and his wife arrived here towards noon, for an early dinner. He had to go back, as a new play of his is coming out at the theatre. However happy we may be in our rural seclusion, we are always delighted to see them. Aniela is great friends with Pani Sniatynska, and I suppose there will be an exchange of confidences. Pani Sniatynska guessed at the state of things, and tried to put her hand to the wheel, to make the cart go a little faster. She had only just arrived, when she said to my aunt: —

"How lovely and peaceful everything is here! No wonder the young people there do not pine after the dissipations of town."

We both, Aniela and I, understood perfectly well that Pani Sniatynska, calling us the young people, was not referring only to our age. Besides, she repeated the same thing several times during dinner: "the young people," "the young couple," as if making a pointed difference between us two and the elder ladies. But there was such real sympathy for us in the friendly eyes; such a pricking up of her little ears to hear what we were saying to each other; and the little woman looked so charming withal that I forgive her readily her good-natured meddling. I have arrived at such a state of infatuation that this coupling of our names rather gladdens than irritates me. Aniela too seemed to hear it with pleasure. In her efforts to please the Sniatynskis and the attentions she bestowed on them during dinner, she truly looked like a young bride, who receives dear visitors for the first time in her new home. At the sight of this my aunt's heart seemed to swell, and she said many kind and polite things to both Sniatynskis. I noticed a wonderful thing, which I should not believe had I not seen it with my own eyes. Pani Sniatynska blushes up to her ears when anybody praises her husband! To blush with pleasure when her husband is praised after eight years of married life! Surely, I committed an egregious mistake writing as I did about Polish women.

The dinner passed off very pleasantly. A married couple, like these two, are born matchmakers. The very sight of them sets people thinking: "If married life is like that, let us go and commit matrimony." I at least saw it for the first time in a quite different light, — not as the prose of life, a commonplace, more or less skilfully disguised indifference, but as a thing to be desired.

Aniela evidently read our future in the same light; I saw it in her eyes shining with happiness.

After dinner I remained in the dining-room with Sniatynski, who liked a quiet talk over a glass of cognac after his coffee. The elder ladies went to the drawing-room, and Aniela took Pani Sniatynska upstairs to show her some photographs of Volhynia. I questioned Sniatynski about his new play, the fate of which seemed to make him a little anxious. Our conversation drifted on to those times when we both tried our sprouting wings. He told me how afterwards, step by step, he had worked his way upward; how he had been full of doubts, and still doubted his power, in spite of having acquired a certain reputation.

"Tell me," I asked, "what do you do with your fame?"

"How do you mean what I do with my fame?"

"For instance, do you wear it as a crown on your head, or as a golden fleece round your neck? do you put it over your writing-desk, or hang it up in your drawing-room? I only ask as a man who has no idea what to do with it if he once obtains it?"

"Let us suppose I have won it; the man must be deuced ill-bred mentally either to wear the so-called fame as an ornament or to put it up for show. I confess that at first it gratifies one's vanity; but only a spiritual parvenu would find it sufficient to fill the whole life, or take the place of real happiness. It is quite another thing to be conscious you are doing good work; that the public appreciates it, and that your work calls forth an echo in other minds, — a public man has the right to feel pleased with that. But as to feeling gratified when somebody, looking more or less foolish, comes up and says: 'We are indebted to you for so much pleasure;' or, when a dinner does not agree with me, our daily press remarks: 'We communicate to our readers the sad news that our famous XX. suffers from a stomach-ache,' — pshaw! what do you take me for, that such a thing could give me satisfaction?"

"Listen," I said, "I am not inordinately vain; but I confess that, when people speak of my extraordinary talents, and regret that I make not a better use of them, it flatters me; and though I feel more than ever my uselessness, it gives me pleasure; humankind is fond of approbation."

"That is because you pity yourself, and in that you are quite right. But you are turning away from the question. I do not say that it would give one pleasure to be called an ass."

"But the public esteem that goes hand in hand with fame?"

Sniatynski, who is very lively and always walks about the room, sitting down on any table or chair, now sat on the window-sill, and replied: —

"Public esteem? You are wrong there, old fellow; there is no such thing. Ours is a strange society, dominated by a pure republican jealousy. I write plays, work for the stage; very good. I have gained a certain reputation; better still. Now, these plays excite the jealousy, — of another playwright, you think? Not at all; it is the engineer, the bank clerk, the teacher, the physician, the railway official, — in short, people who never wrote a play in their lives, — that envy you. All these in their intercourse will show that they do not think much of you, will speak slightingly of you behind your back, and belittle you on purpose, so as to add an inch or two to their own height. 'Sniatynski? who is he? Yes, I remember; he dresses at the same tailor as I.' Such is fame, my dear fellow."

"But it must be worth something, since people risk their lives for it?"

Sniatynski grew thoughtful, and replied with a certain gravity: —

"In private life it is worth something; you can make a footstool of it for the woman you love."

"You will gain a new fame by this definition."

Sniatynski rushed at me with lively impetuosity.

"Yes, yes; put all your laurels into a cushion, go to the dear one, and say to her: 'This for which people risk their lives; this which they consider supreme happiness, appreciate more than wealth, — I have got it, striven for it; and now put your dear feet on it at once.' If you do this, you will be loved all your life. You wanted to know what fame is good for, and there you are."

Further discussions were cut short by the entrance of Pani Sniatynska and Aniela. They were dressed for going out to the hot-houses. What an imp of mischief lurks in that little woman. She came up to her husband to ask his permission to go out, which he granted, insisting only that she should wrap herself up warm; she turned to me and said with a roguish smile, —

"You will let Aniela go, will you not?"

That Aniela should blush furiously was only natural, but that I, an old stager, a razor sharpened against the strops of so many experiences, should have betrayed so much confusion, I cannot forgive myself. But, putting on a semblance of self-possession, I went up to Aniela, and raising her hand to my lips, said: —

"It is Aniela who gives orders at Ploszow, and I am her humble subject."

I should have liked to take Sniatynski with me and join the excursion, but refrained. I felt a want to speak about Aniela, my future marriage, and I knew that sooner or later Sniatynski himself would broach the question. I gave him an opening after the ladies had left us by saying: —

"And do you still believe as firmly as ever in your life-dogmas?"

"More than ever, or rather, the same as ever. There is no expression more worn to tatters than the word 'love;' one scarcely likes to use it; but between ourselves, I tell you; love in the general meaning, love in the individual sense does not permit of criticism. It is one of the canons of life. My philosophy consists in not philosophizing about it at all, — and the deuce take me if for the matter of that, I consider myself more foolish than other people. With love, life is worth something; without, it is not worth a bag of chaff."

"Let us see what you have to say about individual love, — or better still, put in its place woman."

"Very well, let it be woman."

"My good friend, do you not perceive on what brittle foundation you are building human happiness?"

"On about as brittle a foundation as life, — no more nor less!"

I did not want to drift into a discussion of life and death, and pulled Sniatynski up.

"For mercy's sake, do not generalize about individual happiness. You chanced to find the right woman, another might not."

He would not even listen to that. According to his view, ninety out of a hundred were successful. Women were better, purer, and nobler than men.

"We are rascals all, in comparison with them!" he shouted, waving his arms and shaking his leonine mane. "Nothing but rascals! It is I who say it, — I, who study mankind closely, if only for the reason that I am a playwright."

He was sitting astride on his chair, attacking me, as it were, with the chairback, and went on with his usual impetuosity: —

"There are, as Dumas says, apes from the land of

Nod, who know neither curb nor bridle; but what are eyes given for but to see that you do not take to wife an ape from Nod? Generally speaking a woman does not betray her husband nor deceive him, unless he himself corrupts her heart, tramples on her feelings, or repulses and estranges her by his meanness, his selfishness, narrowness, and his miserable, worthless nature. You must love her! Let her feel that she is not only your female, but the crown of your head, as precious as your child and friend; wear her close to your heart, let her feel the warmth of it, and you may rest in peace; year after year she will cling closer to you, until you two are like Siamese twins. If you do not give her all that, you pervert her, estrange her by your worthlessness, — and she will leave you. She will leave you as soon as she sees nobler hands stretched out for her; she is forced to do it, as this warmth, this appreciation, are as necessary to her life as the air she breathes."

He charged me with the chairback as with a battering ram. I retreated before him until we had come close to the window; there he jumped up.

"How blind you are! In presence of such social drought, such utter absence of general happiness as stamps our time, not to grasp this felicity that is within reach! Shiver on the forum, and not light a fire at home! Idiotism can go no farther! I tell you plainly, go and get married."

He pointed through the window at Aniela, who with his wife was coming back from the hot-houses, and added: "There is your happiness. There it patters in fur boots on the frozen snow. Take her by weight of gold, by weight in carats rather! You simply have no home, not only in a physical sense, but in a moral, intellectual meaning; you have no basis, no point of rest, and she will give you all that. But do not philosophize her away as you have philosophized away your abilities and your thirty-five years of life!"

He could not have told me anything better, nobler, or

what chimed in more with my own desires. I pressed his hands and replied: —

"No, I will not philosophize her away, because I love her."

Upon this the ladies entered, and Pani Sniatynska observed: —

"We heard some disputes when we were leaving, but I see peace is restored. May I ask what you have been discussing?"

"Woman, madame," I said.

"And what was the result?"

"As you see, a treaty of peace sealed by a grasp of the hand, and something further may come of it in the course of time."

The sledge was already waiting at the door. The short day was drawing to its close, and they had to go back; but as the weather was calm, and the snow on the drive as smooth as a parquetted floor, we resolved, Aniela and I, to accompany them as far as the high-road.

And so we did. After having said good-by to our charming visitors, we went slowly homeward. It was already dusk; in the dim light I could still see Aniela's face. She seemed moved, perhaps had opened her heart to Pani Sniatynska, and even now hoped for the long deferred word. It was almost burning on my tongue; but, oh, wonder! I who never yet had lost all my self-possession, I who was used to play upon heartstrings, who at a fencing match of that kind, if not cleverly, at least with perfect composure guarded myself against the most masterly strokes, I was as deeply moved as a lad in his teens. What a difference from former sentiments. I was afraid I could not find words to express myself, — and remained silent.

Thus in silence we approached the veranda. The snow was slippery; I offered her my arm, and when she leaned on it I felt how all my desires were centred in her. The feeling grew so intense that it thrilled my nerves like electric sparks. We entered the hall. There was nobody there; not even the lamps were lit, the only light came in fitful gleams from the open stoves. In this half-light and in silence I began to relieve Aniela of her furs, when suddenly the warmth emanating from her body seemed to enter into my veins; I put my arm around her, and drawing her close to me I pressed my lips on her brow.

It was done almost unconsciously, and Aniela must have been greatly startled, for she made not the slightest resistance. Presently a footstep became audible; it was the servant with the lamps. She went upstairs, and I, deeply moved, entered the dining-room.

To every man who is ever so little enterprising, similar events occur in the course of life. I am no exception, but, as a rule, I always kept the mastery over myself. Now it was different. Thoughts and sensations whirled across my brain like leaves before a gale. Fortunately the dining-room was empty; my aunt and Aniela's mother were in the drawing-room, where I joined them after a while. My thoughts were so far away that I scarcely heard what they were saying to me. I felt restless. I seemed to see Aniela sitting in her room, pressing her hands to her temples, trying to realize what it all meant. Soon Aniela herself came down. I felt relieved, as I had feared she might not come down again for the evening. She had two burning spots on either side of her face, and eyes bright as if from recent slumber. She had tried to cool her face with powder; I saw the traces on her left temple. The sight of her moved me; I felt that I loved her deeply.

Presently she stooped over some needlework. I saw that her breath came and went irregularly, and once or twice I intercepted a quick glance full of unsettled questions and trouble.

In order to set her mind at rest I thrust myself into the conversation of the elder ladies, who were speaking about Sniatynski, and said: —

"Sniatynski considers me a kind of Hamlet, and says

I philosophize too much; but I am going to show him that he is mistaken, and that not later than to-morrow."

I laid some stress on the "to-morrow," and Aniela caught the meaning, for she gave me a long look; but my aunt, all unconscious, asked:—

"Are you going to see him to-morrow?"

"We ought to go and see his play, and if Aniela agrees we will all go to-morrow."

The dear girl looked at me shyly but trustingly, and said, with indescribable sweetness:—

"I will go with great pleasure."

There was a moment when I could scarcely contain myself, and felt I ought to speak there and then; but I had said "to-morrow," and refrained.

I feel like a man who shuts his eyes and ears before taking the final plunge. But I really think it is a costly pearl I shall find at the bottom of the deep.

CASA OSORIA, 6 March.

Yesterday I arrived at Rome. My father is not quite so bad as I had feared. His left arm and the left side of his body are almost paralyzed, but the doctor tells me his heart is not threatened, and that he may live for years.

7 March.

I left Aniela in doubt, expectation, and suspense. But I could not do otherwise. The day following the Sniatynskis' visit, the very day I was going to ask Aniela to be my wife, I received a letter from my father telling me about his illness.

"Make haste, dear boy," he wrote, "for I should like to see you before I die, and I feel my bark very close to the shore."

After the receipt of such a letter I took the first train, and never stopped until I reached Rome. When leaving

Ploszow I had very little hope to find my father alive. In vain my aunt tried to comfort me, saying if things were so bad he would surely have sent a telegram instead of a letter.

I know my father's little oddities, among which is a rooted dislike to telegrams. But my aunt's composure was only put on, at the bottom she felt as frightened as myself.

In the hurry, the sudden shock, and under the horror of my father's likely death, I could not speak of love and marriage. It seemed against nature, almost a brutal thing, to whisper words of love, not knowing whether at the same time my father might not be breathing his last. They all understood that, and especially Aniela.

"I will write to you from Rome," I said before starting; to which she replied: "May God comfort you first."

She trusts me altogether. Rightly or wrongly, I have the reputation of fickleness in regard to women, and Aniela must have heard remarks about it; maybe it is for that very reason the dear girl shows such unbounded confidence in me. I understand, and can almost hear the pure soul saying: "They wrong you, — you are not fickle; and those who accuse you of fickleness do not know what love means, and did not love you as truly and deeply as I love you."

Perhaps I am a little fickle by nature, and this disposition, developed under the influence of the barren, empty, worthless sentiments I met with in the world, — this might have dried up my heart and corrupted it altogether; in which case Aniela would have to pay for the sins of others. But I believe the case is not hopeless, and the blessed physician has not come too late. Who knows whether it be ever too late, and that the pure, honest love of a woman does not possess the power to raise the dead? Perhaps, too, the masculine heart has a greater power of recuperation. There is a legend about the rose of Jericho, which, though dry to the core, revives and brings forth leaves when touched by a drop of dew. I have noticed that the male nature has more elasticity than the female. A man steeped in such utter corruption that half of its venom would cover the woman with moral leprosy is able to throw off the contagion, and recover easily not only his moral freshness, but even a certain virginity of heart. It is the same with the affections. I have known women whose hearts were so used up that they lost every capacity of loving, even of respecting anything or anybody. I have never known men like that. Decidedly, love cleanses our hearts. Definitions like these sound strange from a sceptic's pen; but in the first place I have no more belief in my doubts than I have in any other kind of assertions, axioms, and observations which serve general humanity as a basis of life. I am ready to admit at any moment that my doubts are as far removed from the essence of things as are these axioms. Secondly, I am writing now under the influence of my love for Aniela, who, maybe, does not know herself how wisely she is acting, and how by that very trust in me she has secured a powerful hold on my affections. Lastly, whenever I speak of love, or any other principle of life, I speak and write of it as it appears to me in the present. What my opinion about it will be to-morrow, I do not know. Ah, if I but knew that whatever view I take or principle I confess would withstand the blasting scepticism of to-morrow or the days following, I would make it my canon of life, and float along with sails unfurled, like Sniatynski, in the light, instead of groping my way in darkness and solitude.

But I do not intend to go back now to my inner tragedy. As to love in general, from the standpoint of a sceptic in regard to the world and its manifestations, I might say with Solomon, "Vanitas vanitatum;" but I should be utterly blind did I not perceive that of all active principles this is the most powerful, — so powerful indeed that whenever I think of it or my eyes roam over the everlasting ocean of all-life, I am simply struck with amazement at its almightiness. Though these are known things, as much known as the rising of the sun and the tides of the ocean, nevertheless they are always wonderful.

After Empedocles, who divined that Eros evolved the worlds from Chaos, metaphysics have not advanced one step. Only death is a power equally absolute; yet in the eternal struggle between the two, love is the stronger; love conquers death by night and day, conquers it every spring, follows death step by step, throwing fresh grain into the gulf it creates. People occupied with every-day affairs forget or do not wish to remember that they are love's servants. It is strange when we come to think of it that the warrior, the chancellor of state, the cultivator of the soil, the merchant, the banker, in all their efforts, which apparently have nothing to do with love, are merely furthering its ends; that is, they serve the law of nature which bids the man to stretch out his arms for the woman. A mad paradox it would seem to a Bismarck if he were told that the final and only aim of all his endeavors is to further the love of Hermann and Dorothea. It seems even to me a paradox; and yet Bismarck's aim is the consolidation of the German empire, and this can be achieved only through Hermann and Dorothea. What else, then, has a Bismarck to do but to create by the help of politics and bayonets such conditions that Hermann and Dorothea may love each other in peace, unite in happiness, and bring up new generations?

When at the university I read an Arabian ghazel in which the poet compares the power of love to that of infernal torments. I forget the name of the poet, but the idea remained in my memory. Truly, love is the one power that lasts for all times, holds the world together, and creates new worlds.

10 March.

To-day I tore up three or four letters to Aniela. After dinner, I went into my father's room to talk with him about my aunt's plans. I found him looking through a lens at some epilichnions with the earth still adhering to them, he had received from the Peloponnesus. How splendid he looked in that light coming through stained windows in the large room full of Etruscan vases, statues more or less mutilated, and all kinds of Greek and Roman treasures. Among these surroundings his face reminded me of a divine Plato or of some other Greek sage. When I entered he interrupted his work, listened attentively to what I had to say, and then asked, "Do you hesitate?"

"No, I do not hesitate, but I am reflecting. I want to know why I want it."

"Then I will tell you this. I was once like you, inclined to analyze not only my own feelings but all manifestations of life. When I came to know your mother I lost that faculty at once. I knew one thing only, that I wanted her, and did not care to know anything else. Therefore if you have a like powerful desire, marry. I express myself wrongly, for if you wish it very much you will do it without anybody's help or advice, and be as happy as I was until your mother died."

We remained silent for some time. If I were to apply my father's words closely to my own case, I should feel small comfort. I love Aniela, there is no doubt; but I have not arrived yet at a state that precludes all reflection. But I do not consider this as a bad sign; it simply means that I belong to a generation that has gone a step farther on the way to knowledge.

There are always two persons within me, — the actor, and the spectator. Often the spectator is dissatisfied with the actor, but at present they both agree.

My father was the first to interrupt the silence.

"Tell me what she is like."

Since a description is an unsatisfactory way of painting a portrait, I showed my father a large and really excellent photograph of Aniela, at which he looked with the keenest interest. I was no less interested in the study of his face, in which I saw not only the roused artist, but also the refined connoisseur of female beauty, the old Leon *l'Invincible.* Resting the photograph on the poor hand half paralyzed, he put on his eyeglass with the right, and then holding the likeness at a longer or shorter distance he began to say: "But for certain details, the face is like one of those Ary-Schaeffer liked to paint. How lovely she would look with tears in her eyes. Some people dislike angelic faces in women, but I think that to teach an angel how to become a woman is the very height of victory. She is very beautiful, very uncommon looking. 'Enfin, tout ce qu'il y a de plus beau au monde — c'est la femme.'"

Here he fumbled with his eyeglass, and then added: "Judging by the face, or rather by the photograph (sometimes one makes mistakes, but I have had some practice), hers is a thoroughly loyal nature. Women of this type are in love with the whiteness of their plumage. God bless you, my boy! I like her very much, this Aniela of yours. I used to be afraid you might end by marrying a foreigner — let it be Aniela."

I came up close to him and he put his arm round my neck.

"I should like to see my future daughter before I die."

I assured him that he would certainly see her shortly. Then I unfolded my plans of bringing Aniela and her mother over to Rome. After a betrothal by letter I might expect as much, and the ladies would not refuse, if only out of consideration for my father. In this case the marriage ceremony would take place at Rome, and that very soon.

My father was delighted with the plan; old and sick people like to see around them life and motion. I knew that Aniela would be pleased with this turn of affairs, and let my thoughts dwell upon it with more and more pleasure. Within a few weeks everything would be settled. Such quick decision would be against my nature, but the very idea that I could exert myself if I wished raised my spirits. I already saw myself escorting Aniela about Rome. Only those who live there understand what a delight it is to show to anybody the endless treasures of that city, — a much greater delight when the somebody is the beloved woman.

Our conversation was interrupted by a visit from Mr. and Mrs. Davis, who come every day to see my father. He is an English Jew, and she an Italian nobleman's daughter who married him for the sake of his wealth. Mr. Davis himself is a valetudinarian, who took out of his life twice as much as his poor organization could bear. He is ill, threatened with softening of the brain, indifferent to everything that goes on around him, — one of those specimens of mankind one meets at hydropathic establishments. Mrs. Davis looks like a Juno; her eyebrows meet on her forehead, and she has the figure of a Greek statue. I do not like her; she reminds me of the leaning tower at Pisa,— leans but does not fall. A year ago I paid her some attentions; she flirted with me outrageously, that was all. My father has a singular weakness for her; I thought at times he was in love with her. At any rate, he admires her from a thinker and artist's point of view; for beautiful she is,— there can be no two opinions as to that, — and of more than average intelligence. Their conversations, which my father calls "causeries Romaines," are endless, and they never seem to get tired of them; maybe these discussions about life's problems with a beautiful woman appear Italian to him, poetical, and worthy of the times of the Renaissance. I very seldom take part in these conversations because I do not believe in Mrs. Davis' sincerity. It seems to me that her intellect is merely a matter of brain, and not of soul, and that in reality she does not care for anything except her beauty and the comforts of life. I have often met women who seem full of lofty aspiration; upon closer acquaintance it seems that religion, philosophy, art, and literature, are only so many items of their toilet. They dress themselves in either as it suits their style of beauty. I suppose it is the same with Mrs. Davis; she drapes herself in problems of life, sometimes in Greek and Roman antiquities, in the Divina Commedia, or the Renaissance, the churches, museums, and so forth. I can understand a powerful intellectual organism making itself the centre of the universe; but in a woman, and one who is bent upon futile things, it is mere laughable egoism and vanity.

I ask myself what makes Mrs. Davis so fond of my father; and I fancy I know the reason. My father, with his fine head of a patrician philosopher, and his manners reminding one of the eighteenth century, is for her a kind of *objet d'art*, and still more, a grand intelligent mirror, in which she can admire her own beauty and cleverness; besides, she feels grateful that he never criticises her, and likes her very much. Upon this basis has sprung up a friendship, or rather a kind of affection for my father which gradually has become a necessity of her life. Moreover, Mrs. Davis has the reputation of a coquette, and coming here to see my father every day, she says to the world: "It is not true; this old man is seventy, and nobody can suspect me of flirting with him, and yet I show him more attentions than to any one else." Finally, though she herself comes from an old family, Mr. Davis, in spite of his wealth, is a mere nobody, and their friendship with my father strengthens their position in society. There was a time when I asked myself whether these daily visits were not partly for my sake — and who knows? At any rate, it is not my qualities which attract her, nor any real feeling on her part. But she feels that I do not believe in her, and this irritates her. I should not wonder if she hated me, and yet would like to see me at her feet. I might have been, for she is a splendid specimen of the human species; I would have been, if only for the sake of the meeting eyebrows and the Juno shoulders, — but at a price she does not feel inclined to pay.

Soon after the arrival of Mr. and Mrs. Davis my father began a philosophical discussion, which, going from one question to another, concluded with an analysis of human feelings. Mrs. Davis made several very shrewd remarks. From the studio we went to the terrace overlooking our gardens. It is only the tenth of March, and here spring is at its best. This year everything is much advanced, — a fierce heat in the daytime, the magnolias covered with snow-white blossoms, and the nights as warm as in July. What a different world from that of Ploszow. I breathe here with all my lungs.

Mrs. Davis on the terrace with the moon shining upon her was beautiful as a Greek dream. I saw she was under the influence of that indescribable Roman night. Her voice was softer, even, and more mellow than usual. Perhaps even now she only thinks of herself, is impressed because it is herself who feels it, dresses herself in moonbeams, restfulness, and magnolia scent as in a new shawl or bonnet. But all the same the dress suits her splendidly. Were it not that my heart is full of Aniela, I should fall under the spell of the picture. Besides this, she said things which not many could have conceived.

All the same, whenever I am present at these *causeries Romaines* I have always a feeling that my father, I, such as Mrs. Davis, and generally speaking, all the people of the so-called upper classes do not live a true, real life. Below us something is always going on, something always happens; there is the struggle for life, for bread, — a life full of diligent work, animal necessities, appetites, passions, every-day efforts, — a palpable life, which roars, leaps, and tumbles like ocean waves; and we are sitting eternally on terraces, discussing art, literature, love, woman, strangers to that other life far removed from it, obliterating, out of the seven, the six work-days. Without being conscious of it, our inclinations, nerves, and soul are fit only for holidays. Immersed into blissful dilettantism as in a warm bath, we are half awake, half dreaming. Consuming leisurely our wealth, and our inherited supply of nerves and muscles, we gradually lose our foothold upon the soil. We are as the down, carried away by the wind. Scarcely do we touch ground, when the real life pushes us back, and we draw aside; for we have no power of resistance.

When I think of it I see nothing but contradictions in us. We consider ourselves the outcome and highest rung of civilization, and yet have lost faith in ourselves; only the most foolish believe in our *raison d'être.* We look out instinctively for places of enjoyment, gayety, and happiness, and yet we do not believe in happiness. Though our pessimism be wan and ephemeral as the clouds from our Havanas, it obscures our view of wider horizons. Amidst these clouds and mists we create for ourselves a separate world, a world torn off from the immensity of all life, shut up within itself, a little empty and somnolent. If this merely concerned the aristocracy, whether by descent or wealth, the portent would be less weighty. But to this isolated world belong more or less all those who boast of a higher culture,—men of science, literature, and art. This world does not dwell within the very marrow of life, but parting from it creates a separate circle; in consequence withers within itself and does not help in softening down the animalism of those millions which writhe and surge below.

I do not speak as a reformer, because I lack the strength. Besides, what matters it to me? Who can avoid the inevitable? But at times I have the dim presentiment of a terrible danger which threatens the cultured world. The great wave which will wash us from off the surface of the earth will carry off more than that one which washed away hairpowder and shirtfrills. It is true that to those who perished then it seemed that with them the whole civilization was perishing.

In the mean while it is pleasant to sit on moonlit terraces and talk in subdued tones about art, love, and woman, and look at the divine profile of such a woman as Mrs. Davis.

10 March.

Mountains, towers, rocks, the further they recede from our view, appear as a mere outline through a veil of blue haze. There is a kind of psychical blue haze that enfolds those who are removed from us. Death itself is a removal, but the chasm is so wide that the beloved ones who have crossed it disappear within the haze and become as beloved shadows. The Greek genius understood this when he peopled the Elysian fields with shadows.

But I will not enlarge upon these mournful comparisons, especially when I want to write about Aniela. I am quite certain my feelings towards her have not changed, but I seem to see her a long distance off, shrouded in a blue haze and less real than at Ploszow. I do not feel her through my senses. When I compare my present feelings with those I had at Ploszow, she is more of a beloved spirit than a desired woman. From a certain point of view it is better, as a desired woman might be even such a woman as Mrs. Davis; but on the other hand this is not one of the reasons that have prevented me from writing to Aniela. Doubtless that profile of Mrs. Davis which I still see before me is a mere passing impression. When I compare these two women my feeling for the other becomes very tender; and yet I leave her in cruel suspense and uncertainty.

To-day my father wrote to my aunt, setting her mind at rest as to his health, and I added a postscript from myself, sending kind regards to Aniela and her mother. I could not say much in a few lines, but I might have promised them a longer letter. Such a promise would have comforted Aniela and the elder ladies. I did not do it because I could not. To-day my spirits are at a very low ebb. My wish for another life, and my trust in the future have retreated into the farthest distance; I can see them no more, see only the barren, sandy wilderness. I cannot get rid of the idea that I can only marry Aniela if I can conscientiously believe that our union would lead to mutual happiness. I cannot represent it otherwise to Aniéla without uttering a lie; for I have none of that belief, and instead of it an utter hopelessness almost a dislike of life. She is ill at ease with longing and uncertainty, but I am worse, all the more so because I love her.

11 March.

Mrs. Davis, to whom, during our *causerie* on the moon-lit terrace, I unfolded my view as to the all-powerfulness of love, more or less as I have written it down, called me Anacreon, and advised me to crown my head with vine leaves, and then said more soberly, "If such be your opinions, why play the part of pessimist? Belief in such a deity ought to make any man happy."

Why? I did not tell her, but I know why. Love conquers death, but saves from it only the species. What matters it to me that the species be preserved, when I, the individual, am sentenced to a merciless, unavoidable death? Is it not rather a refined cruelty that the very affections, which can be felt only by the individual, should serve the future of the species only? To feel the throbbing of an eternal power, and yet to die, — that is the height of misery. In reality there exists only the individual; the species is an abstract idea, and in comparison to the individual, an utter Nirvana. I understand the love for a son, a grandson, a great grandson, — for the individual, in fact, that is sentenced to perish, — but to profess love for one's species one needs be insincere, or a fanatical sectarian. I can understand now how centuries after Empedocles there came Schopenhauer and Hartmann.

My brain feels as sore as the back of the laborer who carries burdens beyond his strength. But the laborer stooping to his work earns his daily bread and is at peace.

I still seem to hear Sniatynski's words. "Do not philosophize her away, as you have philosophized away your abilities and your thirty-five years of life." I know it leads to nothing, I know it is wrong, but I do not know how not to think.

13 March.

My father died this morning. He was ill only a few hours.

PELI, VILLA LAURA, 22 March.

Death is such a gulf, and though we know that all have to go thither, yet when it swallows up one of our dear ones, we who remain on the brink are torn with fear, sorrow, and despair. On that brink all reasoning leaves us, and we only cry out for help which cannot come from anywhere. The only solace and comfort lies in faith, but he who is deprived of that light gets well-nigh maddened by the impenetrable darkness. Ten times a day it seems to me impossible, too horrible, that death should be the end of everything, — and then again, a dozen times I feel that such is the case.

23 March.

When I arrived from Ploszow I found my father so much better that it never even entered my mind that the end could be so near. What strange twists there are in the human mind. God knows how sincerely I rejoiced when I found my father so much better than I had thought, and yet because throughout that anxious journey I had fancied him sick unto death, and already saw myself kneeling at his coffin, I was sorry for my wasted anxieties. Now the memory of this fills me with keen remorse.

How thoroughly unhappy is the individual whose heart and soul have lost their simplicity. Thus not less bitter, not less of a reproach, is the remembrance that at my father's deathbed there were two persons in me: one of them the son full of anguish, who gnawed his hands to keep back his sobs; the other the philosopher, who studied the psychology of death. I am unutterably unhappy because my nature is an unhappy one.

My father died with full consciousness. Saturday evening he felt a little worse. I sent for the doctor, that he might be at hand in case we should want him. The doctor prescribed some physic, and my father, according to his habit, disputed the point, demonstrating that the physic would bring on a stroke. The doctor calmed my fears, and said though there was always fear of another stroke, he saw no immediate danger, and that my father most likely would live for many years to come. He repeated the same to the patient, who, hearing of the many years to come, incredulously shook his head and said: "We will see." As he has always been in the habit of contradicting his doctors, and proving to them that they know nothing, I did not take his words seriously. Towards ten at night, when taking his tea, he suddenly rose and called out: —

"Leon, come here, quick!"

A quarter of an hour later he was in his bed, and within an hour he was dying.

24 March.

I am convinced that people preserve their idiosyncracies and originality to the last minute of their life. Thus my father, in the solemn dignity of thoughts at the approaching end, still showed a gratified vanity that he, and not the doctor, had been right, and that his unbelief in medicine was well founded. I listened to what he said, and besides, read his thoughts in his face. He was deeply impressed with the importance of the moment; there was also curiosity as to the future life, — not a shadow of doubt as to its existence, but rather a certain uneasiness about how he would be received, joined to an almost unconscious, unsophisticated belief that he would not be treated as a mere nobody in particular. I shall never die like this, because I have no basis to uphold me in the hour of death. My father parted with his life in absolute faith and the deep contrition of a true Christian. At the moment when he received the last sacraments he was so venerable, so purely saintly, that his image will remain with me always.

How futile, how miserable, appears to me my scepticism in presence of that immense power of faith that, stronger even than love, triumphs over death at the very moment when it extinguishes life. After having received the last sacraments, a great tenderness took possession of him. He grasped my hand strongly, almost convulsively, and did not let it go again, as if through me he wanted to hold fast to life. And yet it was neither fear nor despair that moved him, he was not in the least afraid. Presently I saw the eyes riveted upon my face grow dim and fixed, his forehead became moist, as if covered by a gentle dew; he opened his mouth several times as if to catch his breath, — sighed deeply once more, — and died.

I was not present at the embalming of the body, — I had not the strength; but after that I did not leave the dear remains for a minute, out of fear they might treat him as a thing of no consequence. How truly awful are those last rites of death, — the whole funereal paraphernalia, the candles, the misericordia, with the covered faces of the singers. It still clings to my ears, the "Anima ejus," and "Requiem æternam." There breathes from it all the gloomy, awful spirit of Death. We carried the remains to Santa Maria Maggiore, and there I looked for the last time at the dear, grand face. The Campo Santo looks already like a green isle. Spring is very early this year. The trees are in bloom and the white marble monuments bathed in sunshine. What an awful contrast, the young, nascent life, the budding trees, the birds in full song, — and a funeral. Crowds of people filled the cemetery, for my father was known for his benevolence in Rome as much as my aunt is at Warsaw. All these people so full of life, as if reflecting the joys of spring, jarred upon my feelings. Crowds, especially in Italy, consider everything as a spectacle got up for their special benefit, and even now their faces betrayed more curiosity to see a grand funeral than any sympathy. Human selfishness knows no limit, and I am convinced that even people morally and intellectually educated, when following a funeral, feel a kind of unconscious satisfaction that this has happened to somebody else, and it is not they who are to be interred.

My aunt arrived, as I had summoned her by telegram. She, from the standpoint of faith, looks upon death as a change essentially for the better; therefore received the blow with far more calmness than I. This did not prevent her from shedding bitter tears at her brother's coffin.

Afterwards she spoke to me long and tenderly, — a conversation full of exceeding goodness, I took much amiss at the time, for which I am sorry now. She did not mention Aniela's name, — spoke only of my future loneliness, and insisted upon my coming to Ploszow; where, surrounded by tender hearts, especially the one old heart which loved me beyond everything on earth, I would feel less sad. I saw in all this only her desire to continue her matchmaking; and in presence of my recent bereavement this seemed to me improper, and irritated me very much. I felt not inclined to think of the life before me, nor of love-speeches or weddings, with the shadow of death across my path. I refused peremptorily, even curtly; told my aunt I was going away, — most likely to Corfu, then would come back to Rome in order to arrange my father's affairs, and after that would come to Ploszow.

She did not insist upon having her own way. Feeling deeply for me, she was even more gentle than usual, and left Rome three days after the funeral. I did not go to

Corfu; instead of that, Mr. and Mrs. Davis carried me off to their villa at Peli, where I have been now for several days. Whether Mrs. Davis is sincere or not I do not know, and will not even enter upon that now; I know only that no sister could have shown more sympathy and solicitude. With a nature poisoned by scepticism, I am always prone to suspect and misjudge those around me; but if it should be proved that I misjudged this woman, I should feel truly guilty, — because her goodness to me is quite extraordinary.

26 March.

My windows look out upon the vast blueness of the Mediterranean, encompassed by bands of a darker blue on the far horizon. Close to the villa, the crisped waves glitter like fiery scales; in the distance, the sea is glassy and still, as if lulled to sleep in its blue veil. White lateen sails flash in the sun, and once a day a steamer from Marseilles for Genoa passes hence, dragging in her wake woolly coils of smoke that hang over the sea like a dark cloud, until it gradually dissolves and disappears. The restfulness of the place is indescribable. Thoughts dissolve like yonder black cloud between the blue sky and azure sea, and life is a blissful vegetation.

I felt very tired yesterday, but to-day I inhale with eager lungs the fresh sea-breezes, that leave a salty taste on my lips. Say what they like, the Riviera is one of the gems of God's creation. I fancy to myself how the wind whistles at Ploszow; the sudden changes from mild spring weather to wintry blasts; the darkness, sleet, and hail, with intermittent gleams of sunshine. Here the sky is transparent and serene; the soft breeze which even now caresses my face comes through the open window together with the scent of heliotropes, roses, and mignonette. It is the enchanted land, where the orange blossoms, and also an enchanted palace; because everything that millions can buy, combined with the exquisite taste of Mrs. Davis, is to be found in this villa. I am surrounded by masterworks of art, — statues, pictures, matchless specimens of ceramics, chased works by Benvenuto. Eyes feast on nature, feast on art, and do not know where to dwell longest, — unless it be on the splendid pagan, the mistress of all these splendors, and whose only religion is beauty.

But is it quite just to call her a pagan? because, I say again, whether sincere or not, she shares my sorrows and tries to soothe them. We talk for hours about my father, and I have often seen tears in her eyes. Since she found out that music acts soothingly upon my mind, she plays for hours, and often until late at night. Sometimes I sit in my room in the dark, look absently at the sea riddled by a silver network, and listen to the sounds of her music mingling with the splashing of the waves. I listen until I feel half distracted, half sleepy, — until in sleep I forget the real life, with all its sorrows.

29 March.

I do not even feel inclined to write every day. We are reading together the Divina Commedia, — or rather, its last part. There was a time when I felt more attracted by the awful plasticity of the Inferno. Now I like to plunge into the luminous mist, peopled with still more luminous spirits, of the Dantesque heaven. At times it seems as if amid all that radiance I see the dear, familiar features, and my sorrow becomes almost sweet to me. I never before understood the exceeding beauty of heaven. Never has human mind taken such a lofty flight, encompassed such greatness, or borrowed such a slice from infinity as in this sublime, immortal poem. The day before yesterday and the two days following, we read it together in the boat. We usually go out a long distance, and when the sea is quite still I furl the sail; and we read, rocked by the waves, — or rather, she reads and I listen.

Surrounded by the glories of the sunset, far from the shore, with the most beautiful woman reading to me Dante, I was under a delusion that I had been transferred to another world.

30 March.

At times the sorrow that seemed to be lulled to sleep wakes up with renewed force. I feel then as if I wanted to fly hence.

Villa Laura, 31 March.

To-day I thought a great deal about Aniela. I have a strange feeling, as if lands and seas divided us. It seems to me as if Ploszow were a Hyperborean island somewhere at the confines of the world. We have delusions of that kind when personal impression takes the place of tangible reality. It is not Aniela who is far from me, it is I who go farther and farther away from the Leon whose heart and thoughts were once so full of her. This does not mean that my feelings for her have vanished. By close analysis I find they have only changed in their active character. Some weeks ago, I loved her and wanted something; I love her still, but want nothing. My father's death has scattered the concentration of the feelings. It would be the same, for instance, had I begun some literary work, and some unfortunate accident interrupted the even flow of my thoughts. But that is not all. Not long ago, all the faculties of my mind were strung to their highest pitch; now, under the influence of a heavy sorrow, a soft atmosphere, and the gently rocking sea, they have relaxed. I live, as I said before, the life of a plant; I rest as one rests after a long fatigue, and as if immersed in a warm bath. Never did I feel less inclined to any kind of exertion; the very thought of it gives me pain. If I had to choose a watchword, it would be, "Do not wake me." What will happen when I wake up, I do not know. I am sad now, but not unhappy; therefore I do not want to wake up, and do not consider it my duty. It is even difficult to me to recall the image of the Ploszowski who fancied himself bound to Aniela. Bound, — why? by what reason? What has happened between us?

A slight, almost imperceptible kiss on the forehead, — a caress which, among near relations, can be put down to brotherly affection. These are ridiculous scruples. I have broken ties far different from these without the slightest twinge of conscience. Were she not a relation, it would be a different matter. It is true, she understood it in a different way, and so did I at the time, — but let it pass. One prick of conscience more or less, what does it matter? We do worse things continually, to which the disappointment I caused Aniela is mere childishness. Conscience that can occupy itself with such peccadilloes must have nothing else to do. There is about the same proportion of such kinds of crime to real ones as our conversations on the terrace to real life.

Upon the whole, I do foresee what will happen; but I want to be left in peace at present and not think of anything. "Do not wake me." To-day it was determined that we ought to leave Peli as soon as the hot weather sets in, — perhaps in the middle of April, — and go to Switzerland. Even that terrifies me. I fancy Mrs. Davis will have to place her husband under restraint; he shows symptoms of insanity. He says not a word for whole days, but sits staring either at the floor or at his finger-nails; he is afraid they will come off. These are with him the consequences of a wild life and narcotics.

I leave off writing as it is our time for sailing.

2 April

Yesterday there was a thunderstorm. A strong southern wind drove the clouds along as a herd of wild horses. It pulled and tore, chased and scattered them, then got them under and threw them with a mighty effort upon the sea, which darkened instantly as man in wrath, and began in its turn to send its foam aloft, — a veritable battle of two furies, which, battering each other, produce thunder and lightning flashes. But all this lasted only a short time. We did not go out to sea, as the waves were too rough. Instead of it we looked at the storm from the glazed balcony, and sometimes looked at each other. It is no use deluding myself any longer; there is something going on between us, — a subtle change in our relations to each other. Neither of us has said a word or overstepped the boundary line of friendship; neither has confessed to anything, and yet speaking to each other we feel that our words serve only to disguise our thoughts. It is the same when we are in the boat, reading together, or when I listen to her music. All our acts seem mere shadows, — an outward form that hides the real essence of things, with its face still veiled, but following us wherever we go. Neither of us has given it a name; but we both feel its presence. Manifestations like these take place probably every time man and woman begin to influence each other. I could not tell exactly when it began; but I confess it did not come upon me quite unexpectedly.

I accepted their hospitality because Mrs. Davis was my father's friend; and it was she who, after his death, showed me more sympathy than any one else in Rome. I have so much consciousness of self, am so able to divide myself, that soon after my arrival here, in spite of my heavy sorrow I had the presentiment that our mutual relation would undergo a change. I hated myself that so soon after my father's death I should harbor thoughts like these; but they were there. I find now that my presentiments were right. If I said that the changed relation has still its face veiled, I meant to say that I do not know exactly when the veil will be torn asunder, and I am under the spell of expectation. I should be unsophisticated indeed, if I supposed she were less conscious of all this than I. She is probably more so. Most likely she is guiding all these changes; and everything that is happening happens according to her wishes and cool reflection. Diana the Huntress is spreading her net for the game! But what does it matter to me? what is there for me to lose? As nearly every man, I am that kind of game which allows itself to be hunted for the purpose of turning at a given moment against the hunter. In such circumstances we all have energy enough. In a hand-to-hand fight, like this, the victory rests always with us. I know perfectly well that Mrs. Davis does not love me, any more than I love her. We simply react upon each other through our pagan nature, our sensuous and artistic instincts.

With her it is also a question of vanity, — the worse for her, as it may lead her whither love leads. I shall not go too far. In my feeling for her there is neither affection nor tenderness, — nothing but rapture at the sight of nature's masterwork, and the attraction natural in a man when that masterwork is a woman. My father said that the height of victory would be to change an angel into a woman; I maintain that it is no less a triumph to feel around one's neck the arms, palpitating with life, of a Florentine Venus.

As far as beauty goes she is the highest expression of whatever the most exalted imagination is able to conceive. She is a Phryne. It would turn most men's heads to see her in a tight-fitting riding-habit that shows the outline of her figure as beautiful as that of a statue. In the boat, reading Dante, she looked like a Sybil, and one could understand a Nero's sacrilegious passion. Hers is an almost baleful beauty. Only the joining eyebrows make her appear a woman of our times, and this makes her all the more irritating. She has a certain habit of pushing back her hair by putting both hands at the back of her head; then her shoulders are raised; the whole shape acquires a certain curve, and the breast stands firmly out, — and one feels a desire to carry her off in one's arms from everybody's eyes.

In each of us there is a hidden Satyr. As to myself, as I said already, I am highly impressionable; therefore, when I think of it, that there is something going on between me and this live statue of a Juno, that some mysterious power pushes us towards each other, — my head is in a whirl, and I ask myself what would I wish for more perfect than this.

3 April.

As much as ever woman can show kindness and sympathy to a friend in trouble, she has shown to me. And yet, strange to say, all this kindness has upon me the effect of moonlight, — radiance without warmth; she possesses perfection of form, but there is no soul; with her all is premeditation, but not nature. There speaks again the sceptic; but I shall never be so intoxicated as to lose my capacity of observation. If this divinity were kind, she would be kind to everybody. Thus, for instance, the way she treats her husband is enough to destroy any illusion as to her heart. The unfortunate Davis is such a bloodless creature that he feels chilly in the hottest sunshine, and oh! so chilly at her side. I never noticed in her the slightest sign of compassion for his misery. He simply does not exist, for her. This millionnaire, in the midst of all his wealth, is so poor that it would rouse any one's pity. He is apparently indifferent to everything; and yet the human being, with ever so little consciousness, feels kindness. The best proof of it is that Davis feels grateful to me because I speak to him now and then about his health.

Perhaps it is the instinctive attraction of the weaker towards the stronger organism. When I look at that face as white as chalk, no bigger than my fist, those feet like walking-sticks, and that shrunken figure, wrapped up in a plaid during the hottest of weathers, I am truly sorry for him. But I will not make myself out better than I am. I may pity the man; but compassion will not stand in my way. It has often struck me that, when woman is in question, man becomes pitiless; it is still a remnant of the animal instinct that fights to the uttermost for the female. In such a fight between human beings, whatever shape it takes, the weaker goes to the wall. Even honor is no curb; it is only religion that condemns it absolutely.

12 April.

I have not written for nearly ten days. The veil was rent a week ago. I always suspected the sea would help us to an understanding. Women like Laura never forget the fitting background. If they do charitable deeds because it enhances their beauty, the more they want beauty when they fall. Joined to this is their passion for anything out of the common, which does not spring from the poetical faculties of their mind, but from a desire to adorn themselves. I have not so lost my head as not to be able to judge Laura, though really I do not know whether she has not the right to be what she is, and to think the sun and stars are made on purpose for her adornment. Absolute beauty, in the nature of things, must be essentially egotistic, and subject everything to its rule. Laura is the very incarnation of beauty, and nobody has the right to ask anything else from her than to be always and everywhere beautiful; at least, I do not ask for more.

Thanks to my skill in seamanship, we can be alone on our excursions. A week ago, on a sultry day, Laura expressed a wish to go out in the boat. Like a Hecate, she exults in heat. A gentle breeze drove us a long distance from the shore, and then the wind fell. The lateen sail hung motionless from the mast. The rays of the sun, reflected from the glassy surface of the water, increased the heat, although it was late in the afternoon. Laura threw herself on the Indian matting, and resting her head against the cushions, remained motionless, all in a red glow, from the sun filtering through the awning. A strange laziness had taken possession of me, and at the same time the sight of this woman with her Greek form that showed through the clinging drapery sent a thrill of admiration through my veins. Her eyes were veiled, the lips slightly parted; her whole presence expressed powerlessness, and seemed to say, "I am weak."

We came back late to the villa, and the return will remain for a long time in my memory. After a sunset in which sky and earth seemed to be wedded in a splendor without limit and without division, there came a night of such beauty as I had never seen on the Riviera. From the vast deep rose the immense red orb of the moon, which filled the air with a mellow light, and at the same time made a broad, luminous path on the sea, on which we glided towards the shore. There was a gentle swell on the water, like a heaving sigh. From the little harbor the voices of the Ligurian fishermen, singing a chorus, came up to us. A light breeze from the shore wafted towards us the scent of orange-blossoms. Although not prone to let myself be carried away by my sensations, I was under the spell of this unutterable sweetness that floated over land and sea, and clung like dew to soul and body.

From time to time my eyes rested upon the Helen-like woman whose white draperies glistened in the moonlight, and I fancied myself living in ancient Greece, and that we were floating somewhere, maybe towards the sacred olive groves where the Eleusinian mysteries were enacted. Our rapture did not seem any more a rapture of the senses, but a cult, a mystic alliance with that night, that spring, and all nature.

15 April.

The time fixed for our departure has arrived, but we do not depart. My Hecate does not fear the sun, Mr. Davis likes it, and as far as I am concerned, whether here or in Switzerland is a matter of indifference.

A strange thought has taken hold of me; I almost shrink from it, but nevertheless will confess: It seems to me that a Christian soul, though the spring of faith be dried up therein, cannot live altogether on the mere beauty of form. This means more sorrow in store for me; if the thought proves true the whole basis of my life falls to the ground. We are beings of a different culture. Our souls are full of Gothic arches, pinnacles, twisted traceries we cannot shake off, and of which Greek minds knew nothing. Our minds shoot upward; theirs, full of repose and simplicity, rested nearer the earth. Those of us in whom the spirit of Hellas beats more powerfully consider the beautiful a necessity of life, and search after it eagerly, but instinctively demand that Aspasia should have the eyes of Dante's Beatrice. A similar longing is planted within me. When I think of it, that a beautiful human animal like Laura belongs to me and will belong as long as I wish it, a twofold joy gets hold of me, — the joy of the man and the delight of the artist; and yet there is a want and something missing. On the altar of my Greek temple there is a marble goddess; but my Gothic shrine is empty. I admit that in her I have found something bordering upon the perfect, and I defend myself from a suspicion that this perfection throws a big shadow. I thought once that Goethe's words, "You shall be like unto gods and beasts," embraced all life and were the highest expression of his wisdom; now, when I follow the commandment, I feel that he omitted the angel.

17 April.

Mr. Davis came into the room when I was sitting at Laura's feet, my head leaning against her knees. His bloodless face and dim eyes showed no feeling beyond indifferent sullenness. In his soft slippers embroidered with Indian suns, he shuffled across the room and into the library. Laura looked magnificent, her eyes flashing with unrestrained wrath. I rose and awaited what would happen. A thought crossed my mind that Mr. Davis might come back, a revolver in his hand. In such a case I should have pitched him through the window, revolver, plaid, and Indian slippers. But he did not come back; I waited a long time in vain. I do not know what he was doing there; whether he was thinking over his misery, weeping, or perfectly indifferent. We all three met again at lunch, and he was sitting there as if nothing unusual had happened. Perhaps it was my fancy that made me think that Laura looked menacingly at him, and also that his apathetic expression was even more mournful than usual. I confess that such a tame ending of the business is the most painful to me. I am not one to provoke a quarrel, but ready to answer for my deeds; finally, I would rather the man were not so defenceless, such a small, miserable creature. I have a nasty feeling, as if I had knocked down a cripple, and never yet felt so disgusted with myself.

We went out in the boat as usual. I did not want Laura to think I was afraid of Davis; but there we had our first quarrel. I confessed to her my scruples and she laughed at them. I said to her plainly, —

"The laughter does not become you; and remember, you may do most things, but not what is not becoming."

There was a deep frown on the meeting eyebrows, and she replied bitterly, —

"After what has passed between us, you may insult me even with more impunity than you could Davis."

After such a reproach there remained nothing else but

to ask her forgiveness; and presently, harmony being restored, Laura began to talk about herself. I had another instance of her cleverness. Generally the women I have known intimately showed a desire to tell me their life. I do not blame them for it; it shows that they feel the need to justify themselves in their own eyes and ours. We men do not. Yet I never met a woman either so clever as not to overstep the artistic proportions in her confession, or so sincere as not to tell lies in order to justify herself. I call to witness all men who when the occasion occurs may verify how wonderfully similar all these cases of going astray are, and consequently how tedious. Laura, too, began to talk about herself with a certain eager satisfaction, but only in this respect did she follow the beaten track of other fallen angels. In what she told me there was a certain posing for originality, but she was certainly not posing as a victim. Knowing she had to deal with a sceptic, she did not want to call forth a smile of incredulity. Her sincerity was skirting upon the bold, almost the cynical, one might say, were it not that to her it is a system of life in which æstheticism has taken the place of ethics. She prefers simply a life in the shape of an Apollo to that of humpbacked Pulcinello; that is her philosophy. She had married Davis not so much for his wealth as for the purpose of making her life as beautiful as lay in human power, — beautiful not in the common meaning of the word, but in the highest artistic sense. Besides she did not consider she had any duties toward her husband, as she had never even pretended to love him; she had for him as much pity as repugnance, and as he was indifferent to everything, he was of no more account than if he were dead. She added that she did not take account of anything that was contrary to her ideas of a purely beautiful and artistic life. Regard for society she had very little, and who thought otherwise of her would be utterly wrong. She had felt friendship for my father, not because of his social position, but because she had looked upon him as a masterwork of nature. As to myself, she had loved me for a long time. She understood perfectly that I would have prized her more had the victory been less easy, but she did not care to bargain when her happiness was at stake.

This kind of principles, announced by that perfect mouth in a soft voice full of metallic vibrations, gave me a strange sensation. While speaking to me she drew her draperies close to her as if to make room for me at her side. At times her eyes followed the motions of the sea-gulls circling above our heads, then again they rested keenly upon my face as if she wanted to read the impression her words had made upon me. I listened to her words with a certain satisfaction, as they proved to me that I had judged her pretty correctly. Yet there was something in them quite new to me. I had always rendered her justice as to her cleverness, but I thought her acts were the instinctive outcome of her nature. I had never supposed her capable of inventing a whole system in order to support and justify the impulses of her nature. This showed her in a somewhat nobler light, as it proved that where I had suspected her of more or less mean calculation, she only acted according to her own principles, — maybe bad, even terrible, but always principles. For instance, I had suspected her of wanting to marry me after Davis's death, — she proved me utterly in the wrong. She herself began to talk about it. She confessed that if I were to ask her for her hand she might not be able to refuse me, as she loved me more than I believed (here as I am a living man I saw a warm blush mounting to her neck and brow), but she knew this would never happen; sooner or later I would leave her with a light heart, — but what of that? If she dipped her hand into the water and felt the refreshing coolness, should she refuse herself this delight because the sun would suck the cool moisture?

Saying this she bent over the gunwale, which showed her figure in all its immaculate perfection, and after plunging her hands into the water, she stretched them out to me moist and pink and gleaming in the sunshine.

I took hold of the hands, and she, as if echoing my sensations, said in a caressing voice, "Come."

20 April.

I did not see Laura the whole of yesterday, as she was not well. She had caught a chill sitting out late on the balcony, and it had affected her teeth. What a nuisance! Fortunately the day before yesterday a doctor arrived who is to remain in attendance upon Mr. Davis; otherwise I should not have a soul to speak to. He is a young Italian, small of stature, very dark, with an enormous head and very sharp eyes. He seems very intelligent. It is evident that from the very first he has grasped the situation, and found it very natural, for without hesitation he addressed me as the master of the house. I could not help laughing when he came this morning and asked me whether he could see the countess so that he might prescribe for her. They have some very quaint notions in this country. Usually, when a married woman is suspected to belong to somebody else, the world is in arms to hunt and run her down, often with thoughtless cruelty. Here, on the contrary, they worship at the altar of love, and one and all take sides with and plot for the lover. I told the doctor I would see whether the countess would see him. I penetrated into Laura's sanctum. She received me unwillingly, because her face is a little swollen, and she did not wish me to see her in that state. And in truth her face reminded me of my old drawing lessons. I noticed even then that with a modern face one may commit inaccuracies, change this or that, and provided the expression, the idea of the face remain intact, the likeness will not suffer. It is quite a different thing drawing from the antique; the slightest inaccuracy, the least deviation, destroys the harmony of the face and makes it different altogether. I had an example in Laura.

The swelling was very slight, — I scarcely noticed it as she obstinately turned the sound part of her face to me; but as her eyes were a little reddened, the eyelids heavier than usual, it was not the same face, perfect in its harmony and beauty. Of course I did not let her see this, but she received my greeting half-disturbed, as if troubled with a bad conscience. Evidently according to her principles toothache is a mortal sin.

Queer principles these, anyway! I too have the soul of an ancient Greek, but beyond the Pagan there is something else in me. Laura will be sometime very unhappy with her philosophy. I can understand that one may make a religion of beauty in a general sense, but to make a religion of one's own beauty is to prepare great unhappiness for ourselves. What kind of religion is that which a simple toothache undermines, and a pimple on the nose shatters into ruin?

25 April.

We shall have to leave for Switzerland, for the heat is almost unbearable. Besides the heat, there is the Sirocco, that comes now and then like a hot breath from Africa. The sea-breezes somewhat mitigate the fierceness of this visitor from the desert, but it is none the less very disagreeable.

The Sirocco acts injuriously on Mr. Davis. The doctor watches him closely lest he should take opium, and consequently become either very irritable or else quite stupefied. I notice that in his greatest fits of anger he is afraid of Laura and myself. Who knows whether a homicidal mania is not already germinating in the half-insane brain? or maybe he is afraid we are going to kill him. Generally speaking, my relation with him is one of the darkest sides of the part I am enacting. I say one of the darkest, because I am fully aware that there is more than one. I should not be my own self if I did not perceive that my soul not only is stagnating, but is getting swiftly corrupted in the arms of that woman. I cannot even express what loathing, what bitterness and pangs of conscience, it caused me at first that I should have plunged myself into the depth of sensuous raptures so soon after the death of my father. It was not only my conscience, but also the delicacy of feelings which I undoubtedly possess, that revolted against it. I felt this so deeply that I could not write about it. I have grown more callous since. I still reproach myself from time to time, and seriously reflect, but the feeling has lost its poignancy.

As to Aniela, I try to forget her, because the memory is troublesome, or rather I cannot arrive at a clear understanding as to the whole Ploszow episode. At times I feel inclined to think that I was not worthy of her; at others, that I made an ass of myself over a girl like dozens of others. This irritates my vanity, and makes me feel angry with Aniela. One moment I feel an unsavory consciousness of guilt in regard to her, in another the offence appears to me futile and childish. Taken altogether, I do not approve of the part I played at Ploszow, nor do I approve of the part I am playing here. The division between right and wrong is becoming more and more indistinct within me, and what is more I do not care to make it clearer. This is the result of a certain apathy of mind, which again acts as a sleeping draught; for when the inward struggle tires me out I say to myself: "Suppose you are worse than you were — what of that? Why should you trouble about anything?"

Then I see another change in myself. Gradually I have got used to what at first chafed my honor, —the insulting of the crippled man. I notice that I permit myself hundreds of things I would not do if Davis, instead of being physically and mentally afflicted, were an able-bodied man capable of defending his own honor. We do not even take the trouble of going out to sea. I never even imagined that my sensitiveness could become so blunted. It is very easy to say to myself: "What does the wretched Eastern matter to you?" But verily I cannot get rid of the thought that my black-haired Juno is no Juno at all,—that her name is Circe, and her touch changes men (as one might say in correct mythological language) into nurslings of Eumæus.

And when I ask myself as to the cause, the answer shatters many of my former opinions. It is this: our love is a love of the senses, but not of the soul. The thought again comes back that we, the outcome of modern culture, cannot be satisfied with it. Laura and I were like unto gods and beasts with humanity left out. In a proper sense our feelings cannot be called love; we are desirable to each other, but not dear. If we both were different from what we are, we might be a hundred times more unhappy, but I should not have the consciousness that I am drawing near the shelter of Eumæus. I understand that love merely spiritual remains a shadow, but love without spiritualism becomes utter degradation. It is another matter that some people touched by Circe's wand may find contentment in their degradation. It seems a sad thing and very strange that I, a man of the Hellenic type, should write thus. Scepticism even here steps in, and in regard to Hellenism I begin to have my doubts whether life be possible with those worn-out forms; and as I am always sincere, I write what I think.

30 April.

Yesterday I received a letter from my aunt. It was sent after me from Rome and dated two weeks back. I cannot understand why they kept it so long at Casa Osoria. My aunt was sure I had gone to Corfu, but thought I might have returned by this, and writes thus:—

"We have been expecting to hear from you for some time, and are looking out with great longing for a letter. I, an old woman, am too deeply rooted in the soil to be easily shaken, but it tells upon Aniela. She evidently expected to hear from you, and when no letter came either from Vienna or Rome, I saw she felt uneasy. Then came your father's death. I said then, in her presence, that you could not think now of anything but your loss; by and by you would shake off your trouble and return to your old life. I saw at once that my words comforted her. But afterwards, when week passed after week and you did not send us a single line, she grew very troubled, mostly about your health, but I fancy because she thought you had forgotten her. I, too, began to feel uneasy, and wrote 'poste restante' to Corfu, as we had agreed. Not getting any reply, I am sending another letter to your house at Rome, because the thought that you may be ill makes us all very unhappy. Write, if only a few lines; and, Leon, dear, pull yourself together, shake off that apathy, and be yourself again. I will be quite open with you. In addition to Aniela's troubles, somebody has told her mother that you are known everywhere for your love affairs. Fancy my indignation! Celina was so put out that she repeated it to her daughter, and now the one has continual headaches, and the other, poor child, looks so pale and listless that it makes my heart bleed. And she is such a dear girl, and as good as gold. She tries to look cheerful so as not to grieve her mother, but I am not so easily deceived, and feel deeply for her. My dearest boy, I did not say much to you at Rome, because I respected your affliction; but a sorrow like that is sent by God, and we have to submit to His will and not allow it to spoil our life. Could you not write a few words to give us some comfort,—if not to me, at least to the poor child? I never disguised it from you that my greatest wish was to see you two happily married if it were in a year or two, as Aniela is a woman in a thousand. But if you think otherwise it would be better to let me know it in some way. You know I never exaggerate things, but I am really afraid for Aniela's health. And then there is her future to be thought of. Kromitzki calls very frequently upon the ladies, evidently with some intentions.

I wanted to dismiss him without ceremony, especially as I have my suspicions that it was he who spread those tales about you; but Celina solemnly entreated me not to do this. She is quite distracted, and does not believe in your affection for Aniela. What could I do? Suppose her motherly instinct is right, after all? Write at once, my dear Leon, and accept the love and blessing of the old woman who has only you now in the world. Aniela wanted to write to you a letter of condolence after your father's death, but Celina did not let her, and we had a quarrel over this. Celina is the best of women, but very provoking at times. Kind greetings and love from us all. Young Chwastowski is establishing a brewery on the estate. He had some money of his own, and the rest I lent him."

At first I thought the letter had not made any impression upon me; but presently, when walking up and down the room, I found that I had been mistaken. The impression increased every minute, and became very strong indeed. After an hour I said to myself with amazement: "The deuce is in it! I cannot think of anything else but that." Strange how quick my thoughts travel, chasing each other like clouds driven by the wind. What a creature of nerves I am! First, a great tenderness for Aniela woke up within me. All that I had felt for her not long ago, and that had lain dormant in odd nooks of my soul, stirred into life. To go at once, soothe her, make her happy, was the first impulse of my heart, — not clearly defined, perhaps, but very strong all the same. When I imagined to myself the tearful eyes, her hands resting within mine, the old feeling for her woke up with renewed strength. Then the idea crossed my mind to compare her to Laura, — with a fatal result for Laura. I felt sick of the life I was leading; felt the want of a purer atmosphere than I was breathing here, — of restfulness, gentleness, and above all, rectitude of feeling. At the same time a great joy filled my heart, that nothing was lost yet, everything could be made right; it depended only upon my will. Suddenly I bethought myself of Kromitzki, and of Aniela's mother, who, not trusting me, is evidently on his side. A dull anger rose within me, which, gradually increasing, smothered all other feelings. The more my reason acknowledged that Pani Celina was right in mistrusting me, the more I felt offended that she should harbor that mistrust. I worked myself up into a terrible rage against everybody, including myself. What I thought and felt can be expressed in a few words: "Very well, let it be as they wish!"

The letter came yesterday; to-day, analyzing myself more quietly, I find to my own astonishment that the offence not only rankles in my mind, but also has taken firmer root. I say to myself all that a soberly thinking man can say in mitigation thereof, and yet I cannot forgive either Aniela or her mother the Kromitzki business. Aniela could have put a stop to it with one word, and if she has not done it, she is sacrificing me to her mother's headaches. Besides, Kromitzki lowers Aniela in my eyes, stains her, and brings her down to the level of marriageable girls. I cannot even speak of it quietly.

Maybe my reasoning and feeling are those of an exasperated man; maybe that love of self is too predominant in me. I know that I am able to look at and judge myself as a stranger would; but this dualism does not help me in the least. I am more and more embittered. To write about it irritates my nerves,—therefore, enough!

1 May.

During the night I thought, "Perhaps to-morrow I shall be more composed." Nothing of the kind. I am simply in a rage with Aniela, Aniela's mother, my aunt, and myself. The wind ought to be tempered for the shorn lamb, and they forget that my wool is deucedly thin. After all, I am comfortable where I am. Laura is like a marble statue. Near her nothing troubles me very much, because there is nothing except beauty. I am tired of over-strained, tender souls. Let Kromitski comfort her.

2 May.

I carried the letter to the post-office myself. It was not a long one: "I wish Pan Kromitzki every happiness with Panna Aniela, and Panna Aniela with Pan Kromitzki. You wished for a decision, dear aunt, and I comply with your wish."

3 May.

I was thinking whether my aunt's allusion to Kromitzki was but a piece of female diplomacy in order to bring me to book. If so, she is to be congratulated upon her skill and knowledge of human nature.

10 May.

A week has passed. I have not written because I feel half suffocated, torn by doubts, sorrow, and anxiety. Aniela has never been, and is not indifferent to me. The words of Hamlet recur to me: —

"I loved Ophelia; forty thousand brothers
Could not, with all their quantity of love,
Make up my sum."

I should only have to change the outcry: —

"I loved Aniela; forty thousand Lauras could not make up my sum."

And needs must be that with my own hands I wrought the evil. There is a glimmer of comfort in the thought that to be united to a man like me might be a worse fate for her, — but it is not so. If she were mine I would be true to her. Then again it rankles in my mind that perhaps a Kromitzki is sufficient to her happiness.

When I think of this everything seethes within me, and I feel ready to send off another such letter.

It is done with! that is the only comfort for people like me, for then they can fold their hands and idle away their time as before. Perhaps it is a sign of exceptional weakness, but I find some comfort in it. Now I can think in peace.

I put to myself the question, "How is it that a man who not only boasts of a thorough knowledge of self, but also possesses it, has for some time almost blindly followed his instinctive impulses?" Of what use is self-knowledge if at the first commotion of the nerves it hides in a remote nook of the brain and remains there, a passive witness to impulsive acts? To investigate things *post factum?* I do not know of what use this can be to me, but as I have nothing else to do, let us investigate. Why did I act as I did? It must be because though I am an intelligent man, very intelligent even (the deuce take me if I intend to boast or flatter myself), I lack judgment. And chiefly it is the calm, masculine judgment that is wanting. I do not control my nerves, I am hypersensitive, and a crumpled roseleaf would irritate me. There is something feminine in my composition. Perhaps I am not an exception, and there are more of that type in my country, which is of small comfort. This kind of mind may have much understanding, but is a bad guide through life; it darts restlessly here and there, hesitates, sifts, and filters every intention, and at last loses itself among cross-roads. Consequently the capacity for acting gets impaired, and finally it degenerates into a weakness of character, an innate and not uncommon fault with us. Then I put to myself another question. Let us say my aunt had not made any allusion to Kromitzki, would the result have turned out differently? And truly I dare not say yes. It would not have come so swiftly, — that is certain; but who knows whether in the end it would have turned out more satisfactory. Weak characters want infinite accommodations; only powerful ones are spurred on by opposition. Laura, who in certain things is as subtle as musk, most likely understood this and therefore showed herself so — gracious.

Finally, what is the upshot of it? Am I a milksop? Not in the least. A man who looks straight at truth would not shrink from confessing it, — but no. I feel that I could go on an arctic expedition without a moment's hesitation, be a missionary in darkest Africa. I am possessed of a certain pluck, inherited courage, which would carry me through many bold adventures and risky enterprises. My temperament is lively; perhaps less nimble than Sniatynski, I am yet no laggard. But when it comes to solving any of life's problems my scepticism renders me powerless, my intellect loses itself in observations, reasonings, the will has nothing to rest upon, and my acts depend mainly upon external circumstances.

12 May.

I never liked Laura, though I was and am still under the spell of her physical charms. This at first sight looks like a paradox, but nevertheless is a common enough occurrence. One may love and not like the person in question. As often as I happened to meet a love full of thorns and apt to take easily offence, it was only because there was no real liking at the bottom. Now Sniatynski and his wife are not only in love, but they like each other immensely, and therefore are happy. Ah me! I feel I could have liked Aniela, and we might have been as happy! Better not think about it. As to Laura, she will meet many who may fall in love with her raven hair and statuesque beauty, but she will never inspire real liking. This singular woman attracts irresistibly, and at the same time repulses. I have said that beyond beauty there is nothing else; for even her uncommon intelligence is only the humble slave kneeling at the feet of her own beauty. Not more than a week ago I saw Laura giving money to a child whose father had been drowned recently, and I thought to myself: "She would put the child's eyes out in the same way, gracefully and sweetly, if she thought it would add to her beauty." One feels these things, and one may lose one's head over a woman like that, but it is impossible to like her. And she who understands so many things does not understand this.

Yet how beautiful she is! A few days ago, when she came down the steps leading into the garden, swaying lightly on those magnificent hips, "I thought I should drop," as the poet Slowacki says. Decidedly I am under the sway of two powers,—the one attracting, the other repelling. I want to go to Switzerland, and I want to go back to Rome. I do not know how it will end. Ribot rightly says that a desire to do a thing is only a consciousness, not an act of volition; still less is it an act of volition to have a twofold desire. I received a letter from my lawyer, who wants to see me about the affairs of the succession; these are mere formalities, and they could arrange things without me, did I feel disinclined to move. But it will serve as a pretext. For some time I have liked Laura even less than formerly. It is for no fault of hers, as she is always the same, but as it happens, I have transferred to her some of the dislike I have for myself. At the time of my inward struggles I turned to her not only for peace, but also for a kind of wilful degradation; now for that very reason I feel displeased with her. She did not even know of the storm raging in my breast; besides, what could it matter to her, as it was nothing which could serve her as an ornament? She only noticed that I was feverish and more impulsive than usual; she asked a little after the cause, but without insisting too much. Perhaps after all the attraction here will win and I shall not depart; in any case, I am going to tell her that I am obliged to go. I am curious to know how she will take it, still more curious as I can imagine it very well. I suspect that with all her love for me, which is very like my love for her, she does not really like me, — that is, if she ever takes the trouble to like or to dislike anybody. Our minds have certain points of resemblance, but thousands of contradictions.

I am terribly tired. I cannot help thinking of the sensation my letter has made at Ploszow. I think incessantly of this even when with Laura; I see before me continually Aniela and my aunt. How happy Laura is in her everlasting repose! I have such difficulty to bear with my own self.

I shall be glad of a change. Peli, though a seaside resort, is very empty. The heat is quite exceptional. The sea is calm; no waves wash against the shore; it seems exhausted and breathless from the heat. At times the wind rises, but it is a suffocating blast, that raises clouds of white dust which covers the palms, fig-trees, and myrtles, and penetrates through the blinds into the house. My eyes ache as the walls reflect a glaring sun, and in the daytime it is impossible to look at anything.

To Switzerland or to Rome, but away from here. It seems anywhere it would be better than here. We all prepare for the journey. I have not seen Mr. Davis for four or five days. I fancy his insanity will break out any day. The doctor tells me the poor man challenges him to fight. He considers this a bad sign.

ROME, CASA OSORIA, 18 May.

It was evidently solitude I wanted. I feel as I felt after my arrival at Peli, sad, but at the same tıme peaceful. I feel even more peaceful here than in my first days at Peli, because there is none of that uneasiness Laura's presence used to give me. I walk about the still, gloomy house, and find thousands of details that remind me of my father, and the memory grows fresh again in my heart. He too had vanished into the distant haze, and now I meet him again as in his former, real life. There on the table in his studio are the lenses through which he looked at his specimens, the bronze implement he used in scraping the dry soil from the pottery; colors, brushes, manuscripts, and notes about the collections are lying about. At times I have a feeling as if he had gone out and would return presently to his work, and when the illusion disappears a great sorrow seizes me, and I love not only his memory, but love him who sleeps the eternal sleep on the Campo Santo.

And I feel sad; but the feeling is so infinitely purer than those which had such absolute sway over my mind those last weeks that I feel more at ease, — a better man, or, at least, not so corrupt as I had seemed to myself. I notice also that no reasoning, nor the most desperate argumentation can deprive us of a certain feeling of satisfaction, when we come in contact with nobler elements. Whence comes that irresistible, irrepressible tendency towards the good? Spinning out this thread I go very far. Since our reason is considered a reflection of the logical principle of all life, may not our conception of good be a similar reflection from an absolute good. Were it so, one might throw at once all doubts to the wind, and shout, not only, "Eureka!" but also, "Alleluia!" Nevertheless, I am afraid lest the foundation fall to pieces, like many others, and I dare not build on it. Besides the reasoning is but vague; I shall go back to it undoubtedly, because this means the extraction of a thorn, not from the feet, but from the soul. Now I am too tired, too sad and restful at the same time.

It seems to me that of all creatures upon earth it is only the human being that can act sometimes against his volition. I wanted to leave Peli for some time, and yet day after day passed, and I remained. The day previous to my departure I was almost certain I should stop, when unexpectedly Laura herself helped me to a decision.

I told her about the lawyer's letter and my going away, only to see how she would receive the news. We were alone. I expected some exclamation from her part, some emotion, and lastly a "veto." Nothing of the kind took place.

Hearing the news, she turned to me, passing her hand gently over my hair; she brought her face close to mine, and said:—

"You will come back, will you not?"

By Jove! it is still an enigma to me what she meant. Did she suppose I was really obliged to go? or, trusting to the power of her beauty, had she no doubt whatever that I would come back? or, finally, did she grasp at the chance to get rid of me?—because after such a question there remained nothing for me but to go. The caressing touch and accompanying question are a little against the last supposition, which after all seems to me the likeliest. At odd moments I am almost certain she wanted to say by it:—

"It is not you who dismiss me; it is I who dismiss you."

I confess that, if it was a dismission, Laura's cleverness is simply amazing; all the more so, as the manner was so sweet and caressing, and left me in uncertainty whether she was mocking me or not. But why delude myself? By that simple question she had won the game. Perhaps at other times my vanity would have suffered; but now it leaves me indifferent. That same evening, instead of coolness, there was perfect harmony between us. We separated very late. I see her still, walking with me, her eyes lowered, as far as my room. She was simply so beautiful that I felt sorry I was going. The next morning she said good-by to me at the station. The bunch of tea-roses I lost only in Genoa. Strange woman! As I went further on my journey, I felt side by side a physical longing and a great relief. I went on to Rome without stopping, and now feel as a bird released from his cage.

22 May.

There is scarcely anybody I know in Rome. The heat has driven them to their villas, or up into the mountains. In the daytime there are few people in the streets except tourists, mostly Englishmen in pith-helmets, puggarees, red Baedekers, with their everlasting "Very interesting!" on their lips. At noon our Babuino is so deserted that the footstep of a solitary passer-by re-echoes on the pavement. But in the evening the street swarms with people. At that time I feel usually very depressed, nervous, and restless. I go out, and walk about until I am tired; and that gives me relief. I walk mostly on the Pincio, three or four times along that magnificent terrace. At this time lovers stroll about. Some couples walk arm in arm, their heads close together, their eyes uplifted, as if overflowing with happiness; others sit in the deep shadows of the trees. The flickering light of the lamp reveals now and then half-concealed under his plumes the profile of a Bersagliere, sometimes the light dress of a girl, or the face of a laborer or student. Whispers reach my ear; love-vows and low snatches of song. All this gives me the impression of a carnival of spring. I find a singular charm in thus losing myself among the crowd, and breathe their gayety and health. There is so much happiness and simplicity! This simplicity seems to penetrate into my whole being, and acts more soothingly upon my nerves than a sleeping draught. The evenings are clear and warm, but full of cool breezes. The moon rises beyond Trinitá dei Monti, and sails above that human beehive like a great silver bark, illuminating the tops of trees, roofs, and towers. At the foot of the terrace glimmers and surges the city, and somewhere in the distance, on a silvery background, appears the dark outline of St. Peter's, with a shining cupola like a second moon. Never did Rome seem more beautiful to me, and I discover new charms every day. I return home late, and go to bed almost happy in the thought that to-morrow I shall wake up again in Rome. And I do sleep. I do not know whether it is the exercise I take, but I sleep so heavily that it leaves a kind of dizziness when I wake up in the morning.

Part of the morning I spend with the lawyer. Sometimes I work at compiling a catalogue of the collections for my own use. My father did not leave any instructions as to his collections; consequently they are my property. I would hand them over to the city, in fulfilment of his wishes, if I were quite sure he did wish it. As he did not will them away, he, moved by my aunt's remonstrances, may have left it to me to bring them sometime or other over to Poland. That my father thought of this in later times is proved by the numerous bequests and codicils in his will. Among others there is one that touched me more deeply than I can tell: "The head of the Madonna by Sassoferrato I leave to my future daughter-in-law."

25 May.

The sculptor Lukomski began a month ago a full-length statue of my father, from a bust done by himself some years ago. I call upon him often in the middle of the day to watch the progress of the work. The studio is a barn-like building, with a huge skylight on the north side; consequently no sun comes in, and the light is cold. When I sit there I seem to be out of Rome altogether. To heighten the illusion, there is Lukomski, with his Northern features, light beard, and the dreamy blue eyes of a mystic. His two assistants are Poles, and the two dogs in the yard are called Kruk and Kurta, — in short, the place has the appearance of a northern isle in a southern sea. I like to go there for the quaintness of the thing, and I like to watch Lukomski at his work. There is in him at the same time so much power and simplicity. He is especially interesting when he stands back a short distance so as to get a better view of his work, and then suddenly goes back as to an attack. He is a very talented sculptor. The shape of my father seems to grow under his hand, and assume a wonderful likeness. It will be not only a portrait, but a work of art.

If anybody, it is he who is altogether absorbed in the beauty of form. It seems to me that he works out his thoughts by the help of Greek noses, heads, arms, and torsos, more than by help of ideas. He has lived fifteen years at Rome, and still goes to galleries and museums, as if he had arrived yesterday. This proves that worship of form may fill a man's life, and become his religion, provided he is its high priest. Lukomski has as much veneration for beauty in human shape as devotees for holy shrines. I asked him which he considered the most beautiful woman in Rome. He answered, without hesitation, "Mrs. Davis;" and there and then, with his plastic thumbs, with the expressive motion common to artists, he began to draw her outline in the air. Lukomski, as a rule, is self-contained and melancholy; but at this moment he was so animated that his eyes lost their mystic expression. "Like this, for instance," he said, drawing a new line, "or like that. She is the most beautiful woman not only in Rome, but in the whole world." He says that when she lifts her head, the neck is as the continuation of the face,—the same breadth, which is very rare; sometime on the Transtevere one might see women with similar necks; but never in that perfection. Really, who seeks to find a flaw in Laura's beauty, must seek in vain. Lukomski goes so far as to maintain that statues ought to be raised to women like her in their lifetime. Of course, I did not contradict him.

29 May.

The Italian law procedure begins to bore me. How slow they are, in spite of their vivacity! and how they talk! I am literally talked to shreds. I sent for some of the newest French novels, and read for whole days. The writers make upon me the impression of clever draughtsmen. How quickly and skilfully each character is outlined! and what character and power in those sketches! The technical part can go no farther. As to the characters thus drawn, I can only say what I said before,—their love is only skin deep. This may be the case now and then; but that in the whole of France nobody should be capable of deeper feelings, let them tell this to somebody else. I know France too well, and say that she is better than her literature. That running after glaring, realistic truth makes the novel untrue to life. It is the individual we love; and the individual is composed not only of face, voice, shape, and expression, but also of intelligence, character, a way of thinking,—in brief, of various intellectual and moral elements. My relation to Laura is the best proof that a feeling founded upon outward admiration does not deserve the name of love. Besides, Laura is an exceptional case.

31 May.

Yesterday I lunched with Lukomski; in the evening I loitered as usual on the Pincio. My imagination sometimes plays me strange tricks. I fancied that Aniela was leaning on my arm. We walked together, and talked like people who are very fond of each other. I felt so happy,—so different from what I had felt near Laura! When the illusion vanished I felt very lonely; I did not want to go home. That night I could not sleep at all.

How utterly unprofitable my life is! These continual searchings of my mind are leading me into the desert. And it might have been so different! I am surprised that the memory of Aniela should be still so fresh and green. Why is it that I never dream of walking arm-in-arm with Laura? And since I come to mention her name, I add inwardly, "Perdition upon the memory!" I often think I have been holding happiness by both wings, and let it escape.

2 June.

I never was so amazed in my life as to-day, in regard to Lukomski. We went together to the museum on the Capitol. When near the Venus, he surprised me by saying he preferred the Neapolitan Psyche by Praxiteles, as being more spiritual. A strange confession from a sculptor like him; but a greater surprise was in store for me near "The Dying Gladiator." Lukomski looked at him for nearly half an hour, then said, through clenched teeth, as he does when deeply moved, —

"I have heard it said a hundred times that he has a Slavonic face, but really the likeness is wonderful. My brother has a farm, — Koslowka, near Sierpiec. There was one of the laborers, Michna, who was drowned driving horses through the water. I tell you it is exactly the same face. I come here very often for an hour, because I feel a longing to look at it."

I could not believe my ears, and was surprised the roof of the Capitol did not come down on our heads. Sierpiec, Koslowka, Michna, here in the world of the antique, of classic forms! and from whose lips? — from those of Lukomski! I saw at once, peeping out from beneath the sculptor, the man. And that is the artist, I thought, — that the Roman, the Greek! You come here to look at the Gladiator, not so much for the sake of the form, as because he reminds you of Michna from Koslowka. I begin to understand now the taciturnity and melancholy. Lukomski evidently guessed my thoughts; for, the mystic eyes looking straight before him, he began in a broken voice to reply to my unuttered words: "Rome is well enough, — to live in, but not to die in! I am getting on fairly well, — no right to complain. I remain here because I must; but the longing for the old place tears me like all the devils. When the dogs bark at night in the garden, I fancy the sound comes from the village; and I feel as if I could scratch the walls. I should go mad if I did not go there once a year. I am going now, shortly, because I cannot breathe here any longer."

He put his hand to his throat, and screwed up his mouth as if to whistle, to hide the trembling of the lips. It was almost an explosion, — the more astounding, as it was so unexpected. A sudden emotion seized me at the thought of the vast difference between me and such men as he and Sniatynski. Even now I think of it with a certain apprehension. There are vast horizons out of my reach. What an intensity of feeling there is in those men! They may be happy or wretched with it; but how immeasurably richer they are than I! There is no danger of life becoming to them a desert and a barren wilderness. In each of them there is life enough for ten. I too feel conscious of ties to my country; but the consciousness is not so pressing, does not burn with the same steady light, and is not part of myself. My existence does not depend upon any Koslowka, Michna, or Ploszow. Where men such as Sniatynski or Lukomski find live springs from which they draw their motive vigor, I find dry sand. And yet, if they had not this basis, there remains still, for one his sculpture, for the other his literature. It seems incredible that a man possessing so many conditions of happiness should be not only so little happy, but clearly does not see the reason why he should exist at all.

It is doubtless my bringing up which has something to do with it, — those Metzes, Romes, Paris; I have always been as a tree taken from its soil and not firmly planted in another. Partly it is my own fault; because I am putting points of interrogation all along the road of life, and philosophize where others love only. The consequence is that philosophy, instead of giving me anything, has eaten my heart away.

8 June.

I note down the occurrences of a whole week. I received, among other letters, one from Sniatynski. The honest fellow is so concerned about the turn my affair with Aniela has taken that he does not even abuse me. He tells me, though, that his wife is angry past forgiveness, and does not allow my name to be mentioned in her presence, — considers me a perfect monster, who finds his only delight in gloating over fresh victims. For once I am a good Christian, and not only do not bear malice to the little woman, but feel very friendly towards her. What a warm, generous heart hers is! Sniatynski evidently thinks the question finally settled; for he refrains from advice, and only expresses sorrow.

"God grant," he writes, "you may find another like her." Strange, when I come to think of it! It seems to me that I do not want another like Aniela, or a better one either, — I want her. I say it seems to me; for it is a feeling without any definite shape. I carry within me something like an entangled skein; I weary myself, and yet am not able to reduce it to any kind of order. In spite of all my self-knowledge, I cannot quite make out what it is that makes me feel sad. Is it because I find I love her, or is it because I feel I could love her very much? Sniatynski unconsciously replies to this question in these words: "I have heard or read that gold nuggets have sometimes a large admixture of quartz, which must be crushed in order to get at the gold. I suppose your heart is thus covered with an incrustation, that only partly melted while you were staying at Ploszow. You did not remain long enough, and simply had no time to let your love grow sufficiently strong. You have, maybe, energy enough to act, but not enough to decide; but you would have found the energy if the feeling had been powerful enough. You went away, and according to your custom, began to ponder, to think it over; and it came to pass, as I was afraid it would, that you philosophized away your own happiness and that of another." What strikes me most in Sniatynski's words is that they are almost a repetition of what my father said to me. But Sniatynski penetrates deeper; for he adds almost immediately: "It is the old story, — he who inquires too deeply into his own mind ends by disagreeing with himself; and who disagrees with himself is incapable of any decision. Truly times must be out of joint, when only asses have any power of action left, and those who have a little more intelligence use it to doubt everything, and to persuade themselves that it is not worth while to attempt anything." I have read similar observations in one of the French authors; and by Jove! he is right.

I almost wish Sniatynski had given me a downright scolding, instead of larding his letter with sentences like this: "In spite of all your good qualities it will come to this, that you will always be a cause of suffering and anxiety to those who love you." He brings it home with a vengeance. I have caused suffering to Aniela, her mother, and my aunt, and to myself also. I feel inclined to laugh a little as I read further: "According to the laws of nature, there is always something growing within us; beware, lest it be a poisonous weed that will destroy your whole existence!" No, — I am not afraid of that. There is some mould sown by Laura's fair hands, but it grows only on the outward crust of which Sniatynski speaks, and has not struck any roots. There is no need of uprooting anything; it is as easily wiped off as dust. Sniatynski is more reasonable when he is himself again, and steps forth with his pet dogma that lies always close to his heart: "If you consider yourself a superior type, or even if you be such, let me tell you that the sum total of such superiority, is socially, a minus quantity."

I am far from considering myself a superior type, unless it be in comparison to such as Kromitzki; but Sniatynski is right. Men like me escape being minus quantities in society only when they are men of science or great artists, — not artists without portfolios. Often they take the part of great reformers. As to myself I could only be a reformer as regards my own person. I went about with that thought all the day.

It is surpassing strange that, knowing my own shortcomings so well, I do not make any attempt to mend matters. For instance, after debating for half a day whether to go out or not, ought I not to take myself by the collar and thrust myself into the street? I am a sceptic? — very well! Could I not act for once as if I were not a sceptic? A little more or less conviction, what does it matter? What ought I to do now? Pack up my things and go straight to Ploszow. I could do it easily enough. What the result of such a step would be, I do not know, but at any rate it would be doing something. Then Sniatynski writes: "That ape is now every day at Ploszow, keeping watch over the ladies, who, without that additional trouble, are worn to shadows."

Perhaps it is too late. Sniatynski does not say when he was last at Ploszow, perhaps a week ago or maybe two; since then things may have gone much farther. Yes, but I do not know anything for certain, and when all is said how can it be worse than it is already? I feel that anybody with a little more energy in his composition would go at once, and I should feel more respect for myself if I brought myself to do it, especially as Sniatynski, who is usually so enterprising, does not urge me. The very thought brightens me up, and in this brightness I see a beloved face which at this moment is dearer to me than anything else in the world, and — per Baccho! I shall most probably do it.

9 June.

"La nuit porte conseil." I will not go at once to Ploszow, it would be a journey in the dark; but I have written a long letter to my aunt, quite different from that I wrote at Peli. Within a week, or at the most ten days,

I shall get an answer, and according to it I shall either go or stay, — in fact, I do not know myself yet what I shall do. I might count upon a favorable answer if I had written for instance like this: "Dearest aunt, send Kromitzki about his business; I beg Aniela to forgive me. I love her, and my dearest wish is to make her my wife." Unless she were married already, — and things could not have been managed there so speedily, — such a letter could have but one result. But I did not write anything of that kind. My missive was intended to reconnoitre the position, sent in fact as a scout to find out how affairs were progressing, and partly, to learn what Aniela was thinking. To say the truth, if I did not express myself more definitely, it is because experience has taught me to mistrust myself. Ah! if Aniela, in spite of the wrong inflicted upon her by me, refused Kromitzki, how gratified I should feel towards her; and how immeasurably higher she would rise in my esteem if once removed from the ranks of marriageable girls whose only aim is to get a husband. What a pity I ever heard about Kromitzki. Once rid of the entanglement with Laura, I should have flown on wings to Aniela's side. This dear aunt has managed things with a clumsy hand in writing to me about Kromitzki and the encouragement he had from Aniela's mother. In these times of overwrought nerves, it is not only women that are like sensitive plants. A rough touch, and the soul shrinks, folds itself up, maybe forever. I know it is foolish, even wrong, but I cannot help it. To change myself I should have to order at an anatomist's a new set of nerves, and keep those I have for special occasions. No one, not even Pani Sniatynski, can judge me more severely than I judge myself. But is Kromitzki better than I? Is his low, money-making neurosis better than mine? Without any boastfulness I may say that I have more delicacy of feeling, nobler impulses, a better heart, more tenderness, and — his own mother would be obliged to own it — more intelligence. It is true I could not make millions to save my life; but then Kromitzki has not achieved it yet; instead of that, I could guarantee that my wife would spend her life in a broader and warmer atmosphere; there would be more sincerity in it and nobler aims.

It is not the first time I have compared myself to Kromitzki, and it makes me angry considering what a vast difference there is between us. We are like inhabitants of different planets, and as to our souls, if one has to climb up to reach mine, such as Aniela would have to stoop very low to reach his. But would this be such a difficult task for her? It is a horrible question; but in regard to women I have seen so monstrous things, especially in my country where the women generally speaking are superior to the men, that I am obliged to consider it. I have seen girls, angels in all but wings, full of noble impulses, sensitive to everything beautiful and uncommon, not only marry louts of narrow and mean characters, but adopt after marriage their husbands' maxims of life, vanities, narrowness, and commonplace opinions. What is more, some of them did this eagerly, as if former ideals were only fit to be thrown aside with the bridal wreath. They seemed to labor under the conviction that only thus they could prove themselves true wives. It is true that sometimes a reaction follows, but in a general sense Shakspeare's Titania is a common enough type, to be met with every day.

I am a sceptic from the crown of my head to the soles of my feet, but my scepticism springs from pain, for it hurts me to think that such may be Aniela's fate. Perhaps she too will shrug her shoulders at the memory of her girlish aspirations, and consider contracts in Turkestan better adapted to practical life. A dull wrath seizes me at the thought, all the more as it will be partly my fault, that is, if it should come to that.

On the other side these reflections and vacillations are not merely the result of a want of decision, as Sniatynski seems to think. I have such a high conception about marriage, such lofty demands, that they take away my courage. It is true that often husband and wife fit each other like two warped boards, and yet jog through life contentedly enough; but this would not be enough for me. For the very reason that I believe in happiness so little, I should like to attain it; but can I attain it? It is not so much the unhappy marriages I have met with that make me so wavering, but the few happy ones I have seen; at the remembrance of these I ask myself, "Is it possible I could be so happy?" And yet happiness is not met with in fiction only, — but how to know where to look for it!

11 June.

In the last few days I have become quite intimate with Lukomski. He is not so self-contained and melancholy as he used to be. Yesterday, towards evening, he came to see me; we went out for a walk as far as the Thermes of Caracalla; then I asked him to come back with me, and he stopped until midnight. I had a long talk with him, which I note down, as it made upon me a certain impression. Lukomski seemed a little ashamed of the exhibition of feeling he had made near "The Dying Gladiator;" but I led him on and gradually came to know the man as he really was. As we were growing very friendly I ventured to remark, —

"Excuse the question, but I cannot understand why a man so fond of domestic life has not taken to himself a companion. Neither your studio, your assistants, nor your dogs can give you the feeling of a home you are missing, as a wife would."

Lukomski smiled, and pointing to the ring on his finger, said, —

"I am going to be married shortly. We are only waiting because the young lady is in mourning for her father; I am to join her in two months."

"At Sierpiec?"

"No, she comes from Wilkomierz."

"What took you to Wilkomierz?"

"I have never been there. I met her by accident on the Corso in Rome."

"That was a fortunate accident, was it not?"

"The most fortunate in my life."

"Was it during the Carnival?"

"No. It happened in this way: I was on my way to the studio when, in the Via Condotto, I saw two fair-haired women inquiring in very bad Italian the way to the Capitol. They were saying: 'Capitolio, Capitole, Capitol,' and nobody seemed to know what they wanted, because here, as you know, they call it 'Campidolio.' I could not have been mistaken, — they were Poles, evidently mother and daughter. They were overjoyed when I addressed them in Polish; I was very glad too, and so I not only showed them the way but went there with them."

"You have no idea how this interests me; and so you went together?"

"Yes, we went together. On the way I looked at the younger lady; a figure like a young poplar, graceful, pretty, a small head, ears a perfect model, the face full of expression, and eyelashes pure gold, such as, you find only at home; there is nothing of that kind here, unless now and then at Venice. She pleased me very much too because of that thoughtfulness for her mother, who was in grief, having lost her husband; I thought she must have a good heart. For about a week I went with them everywhere, and then asked for the young lady's hand."

"After a week's acquaintance; is it possible?"

"Yes, because the ladies were going back to Florence."

"At any rate you are not one of those who take a long time to make up their minds."

"At home it would have taken much longer; but here, sir, the very thought they were my countrywomen made me long to kiss their hands."

"Yes, but marriage is such an important step."

"That is true; but three or four weeks more would not help me to a clearer view of it. I had certain scruples, I confess; I feel a little reluctant to speak of it. In our family there is hereditary deafness. My grandfather at an advanced age became quite deaf. My father was deaf at forty. One can live with that, but it is a great drawback, because deaf people as a rule are irritable. I debated within myself whether it was right for a young girl to marry a man threatened with such a defect, and who in course of time might become a burden to her."

I began to observe now that Lukomski had in the expression of his eyes, and the way he listened to what was said to him, a certain peculiarity noticed in deaf people. His hearing was still excellent, but he evidently feared that he might be losing the faculty.

I told him he had no right to let that stand in his way.

"I thought so a little myself. It is not worth while to spoil one's life for a thing that may never happen. There is the cholera that sweeps now and then over Italy; it would be foolish for Italians not to marry for fear they might leave orphans and widows. Besides I have done what I considered my duty. I told Panna Vanda that I loved her and would give my life to call her my own, but there was this impediment. And do you know what her answer was? 'When you are no longer able to hear me saying I love you, I will write it.' All this did not come off without some crying, but an hour afterwards we made merry over it. I pretended to have suddenly grown deaf, to make her write, 'I love you.'"

This conversation fixed itself in my mind. Sniatynski is wrong when he maintains that among us only asses have still a kind of will. This sculptor had a real motive to reflect, and yet a week seemed sufficient for such a weighty decision. Maybe he does not possess the same knowledge of self as I, but he is a very intelligent fellow. What a plucky woman the future Pani Lukomska is; I like her ready answer. Aniela would do the same. If, for instance, I were to lose my eyesight, Laura would care only in so far as she could show me off, a picturesque Demadoc, singing at her feast; but Aniela would take care of me even if she were not my wife.

I must acknowledge that, having such convictions, a week of indecision seems a long time; and here I have been wavering for five months, and the letter I wrote to my aunt was not very decisive either.

But I comfort myself with the thought that my aunt is a clever woman, and loving me as she does, will guess what I meant to say, and will help me in her own way; and then there is Aniela who will assist her. Nevertheless, I regret now that I did not write more openly, and I feel half inclined to send another letter, but will not yield to the impulse. Perhaps it will be as well to wait for the reply. Happy those people, like Lukomski, whose first impulse is towards action.

15 June.

Whatever name I might give to the feeling I cherish for Aniela, it is different from anything I ever felt before. Either night or day she is never out of my thought; it has grown into a kind of personal affair for which I feel responsible to myself. This never used to be the case. My other love affairs lasted a longer or shorter time, their memories were pleasant sometimes, a little sad at others, or distasteful as the case might be, but never absorbed my whole being. In the idle, aimless life we are leading, woman, perforce, occupies a large space, — she is always before us; we bestow our attentions upon her until we become so used to it that she counts only as a venial sin in our lives. To disappoint a woman causes us but little trouble of conscience, though a little more perhaps than she feels in disappointing us. With all the sensitiveness of my nature, I have a rather blunted conscience. Sometimes it happened I said to myself, "Now is the time for a pathetic lecture!" but I only shrugged my shoulders and preferred to think of something more pleasant. This time it is altogether different. For instance, I think of something that has no connection with it whatever; presently I am overcome by a feeling that something is missing, a great trouble seizes me, a fear as if I had forgotten something of great importance, not done a thing I ought to have done; and I find out that the thought of Aniela has percolated through every nook and cranny of the mind, and taken possession of it. It knocks there night and day like the death-tick in the desk of Mickiewicz's poem. When I try to lessen or to ridicule the impression, my scepticism and irony fail me, or rather help me only for a moment; then I go back to the enchanted circle. Strictly speaking, it is neither a great sorrow nor a sting of conscience; it is rather a troublesome fastening upon one subject, and a restless, feverish curiosity as to what will happen next, — as if upon that next my very life depended. If I analyzed myself less closely, I should say it was an all-absorbing love that had taken possession of me; but I notice that there is something besides Aniela that causes me anxiety. There is no doubt as to her having made a deep impression upon me; but Sniatynski is right, — if I had loved her as much as Sniatynski loved his wife, I should have desired to make her my own. But I — and this is quite a fact — do not desire her so much as I am afraid to lose her. It is not everybody perhaps who could perceive the singular and great difference. I feel quite convinced that but for Kromitzki and the fear of losing Aniela, I should not feel either anxieties or trouble. My entangled skein is gradually getting straighter, and I can see now more clearly that it is not so much love for Aniela as fear of losing her, and with her some future happiness, that moves me, and still more the utter loneliness I see before me should Aniela go out from my life.

I have noticed that the stoutest pessimists, when fate or men try to take something out of their lives, fight tooth and nail, and cry out as loud as the greatest optimists. I am exactly in the like position. I do not cry out, but a terrible fear clutches at my heart, that a few days hence I shall not know what to do with myself in this world.

16 June.

I had indirect news of Laura through my lawyer, who is also their legal adviser. Mr. Davis is already in a lunatic asylum, and Laura at Interlaken, at the foot of the Jungfrau. Perhaps she has some ideas about climbing the mountain heights, drapes herself in Alps, eternal snow, and rising sun, sails gracefully on the lake, and bends over precipices. I expressed my regret at Mr. Davis's condition, and the lady's, who at so early an age was left without protection. Thereupon the old lawyer set my mind at rest, telling me that Count Maleschi, a Neapolitan, and Laura's cousin, had gone to Switzerland. I know him. He is beautiful as an Antinous, but an inveterate gambler, and somewhat of a coward. It appears I was a little out of my reckoning when I compared Laura to the tower of Pisa.

It has happened to me literally for the first time that the memory of a woman whom I did not love, though I made her believe I did, rouses within me much ill-feeling. I am so ungrateful and ungenerous to her that it makes me feel ashamed. Plainly, what reason have I for any ill-feeling, and what has she done to me that I cannot forgive ? It is because, as I said before, from the very beginning of our relations, though not through any fault of hers, I did many things I have never done before in my life. I did not respect my sorrow, had no consideration for the weakness and helplessness of Davis, got corrupted, slothful, and finally sent off that fatal letter.

It is all my fault! But the blind man when he stumbles over a stone, curses the stone, not the blindness that made him stumble.

17 June.

To-day I paid Lukomski, gave a power of attorney to the lawyer, had my things packed, and am ready for the journey. Rome begins to pall upon me.

18 June.

I have been counting that my aunt's reply ought to have reached me by this. Putting aside all the worst suppositions, I try to guess what she is going to tell me. I regret, for I do not know how many times, that my letter was not more conclusive. Yet I wrote that I would come to Ploszow if I felt sure my presence would be acceptable to my aunt's guests, sending them my kindest regards at the same time. I also mentioned that during the last days of my stay at Peli I felt so irritable that I scarcely knew what I was doing. The letter, while I was writing it, seemed to me very clever; now it appears to me as the height of folly. It was simply that my vanity did not permit me to revoke clearly and decidedly what I had written previously. I counted upon my aunt grasping at the opportunity I gave her for settling matters, and then I meant to make my appearance as the generous prince. Human nature is very pitiful. Nothing now remains but to hold fast to the hope that my aunt would guess how it stood with me.

With my anxiety increasing every moment, I feel not only that I could have loved Aniela, but that I do love her beyond expression, and also that I might become an incomparably better man. Strictly speaking, why do I act as if beyond nerves and egoism there were nothing else in me? and if there be anything else, why does not my auto-analysis point it out to me? I have the courage to draw extreme conclusions, and do not hide the truth from myself, but I decidedly negative the notion. Why? Because I have the unshaken conviction that I am better than my actions. The cause of the latter is partly a certain incapacity of life, partly the inheritance of my race and the disease of the times in which I live, and finally that over-analysis which does not permit me to follow the first, simple impulses of nature, but criticises until it reduces the soul to utter impotence. When a child I used to amuse myself by piling up coin upon coin until the column, bending under its own weight, tumbled down into one chaotic heap. I am doing now exactly the same with my thoughts and intentions, until they collapse and roll over each other in a disorderly confusion. For this very reason it has always been easier for me to play a passive part than an active one. It appears to me that many cultured people are attacked by the same disease. Criticism of ourselves and everything else is corroding our active power; we have no stable basis, no point of issue, no faith in life. Therein lies the reason why I do not care so much to win Aniela as I am afraid of losing her. In speaking of a disease common to our time, I will not confine myself exclusively to my own case. That somebody takes to his bed when an epidemic disease is raging is a very common occurrence; nowadays criticism of everything is the epidemic spreading all over the world. The result is that various roofs that sheltered men collapse over their heads. Religion, the very name of which means "ties," is getting unloosened. Faith, even in those who still believe, is getting restive. Through the roof of what we call Fatherland social currents begin to filter. There remains only one ideal in presence of which the most hardened sceptic raises his hat, — the People. But on the base of this statue mischievous spirits are beginning already to scribble more or less ribald jokes, and, what is still more strange, the mist of unbelief is rising from the heads of those who, in the nature of things, ought to bow down reverently. Finally there will come a gifted sceptic, a second Heine, to spit and trample on the idol, as in his time did Aristophanes; he will not, however, trample on it in the name of old ideals, but in the name of freedom of thought, in the name of freedom of doubt; and what will happen then I do not know. Most likely on the huge, clean-wiped slate the devil will write sonnets. Can anything be done to prevent all this? Finally, what does it matter to me? To attempt anything is not my business; I have been trained too carefully as a child of my time. But if all that is thought, that is achieved and happening, has for its ultimate aim to increase the sum of general happiness, I permit myself a personal remark as to that happiness; by which I do not mean material comfort, but that inward spiritual peace in which I as well as anybody else may be wanting. Thus my grandfather was happier than my father, my father happier than I, and as to my son, if ever I have one, he will simply be an object of commiseration.

FLORENCE, 20 June.

The house of cards has tumbled down. I received a letter from my aunt. Aniela is engaged to Kromitzki, and the marriage will take place in a few weeks. She herself has fixed such a short date. After receiving the news I took a railway ticket, with the intention of going straight to Ploszow, conscious all the time that it was a foolish thing to do, which could lead to nothing. But the impulse was upon me, and carried me along; when, collecting the last remnants of common-sense and reflection, I stuck fast here.

FLORENCE, 22 June.

Simultaneously with my aunt's letter, I received a "faire part" addressed in a female hand. It is not Aniela's handwriting, or her mother's; neither of them would have done it. Most likely it is Pani Sniatynska's malicious device. Upon the whole, what does it matter? I got a blow with a club on the head, and feel dizzy; it has shaken me more than it has hurt. I do not know how it will be later on; they say one does not feel a bullet wound at once. But I have not sent a bullet through my head, I am not mad; I look at the Lung Arno; I could sit down to a game of patience if I knew how to play; in fact, I am quite well. It is the old story, — among sincere friends the dogs tore the hare to pieces. My aunt considered it her Christian duty to show Aniela the letter I had written from Peli.

FLORENCE, 23 June.

In the morning, when I wake up, — or rather, when opening my eyes, — I am obliged to repeat to myself that Aniela is marrying Kromitzki, — Aniela, so good, so loving, who insisted on sitting up to take care of me when I returned from Warsaw to Ploszow; who looked into my eyes, hung upon every word that came from my lips, and with every glance told me she was mine. That same Aniela will not only be Kromitzki's wife, but within a week from the wedding will not be able to conceive how she could ever hesitate in her choice between such a man as Ploszowski and a Jupiter like Kromitzki. Strange things happen in this world, — so terrible and irrevocable that it takes away the desire to live out the mean remnant of one's existence. Most likely Pani Celina together with Pani Sniatynska make a great ado about Kromitzki, and praise him at my expense. I hope they will leave Aniela in peace. It is my aunt's doing; she ought not to have allowed it, if only for Aniela's sake, as she cannot possibly be happy with him. She herself says Aniela has accepted him out of despair.

Here is that long, cursed letter: —

"I thank you for the last news,—all the more as that first letter from Peli was not only conclusive, but also very cruel. I could scarcely believe that you had not only no affection for the girl, but also neither friendship nor compassion. My dear Leon, I never asked nor advised you to become engaged to Aniela at once,—I only wanted you to write a few kindly words, not to her directly, but in a letter to me. And believe me, it would have been sufficient; for she loved you as only girls like her can love. Put yourself in my position,—what could I do after having received your letter? How could I conscientiously allow her to remain in her illusion, and at the same time in that anxiety that evidently undermined her health? Chwastowski always sends a special messenger for papers and letters, and brings them himself when he comes to breakfast. Aniela saw there was a letter from you, because the poor child was always on the lookout for Chwastowski, and took the letters from him under pretext that she wanted to put them under my napkin; and the real reason was that she might see whether there was a letter from you. I noticed how her hands trembled when she poured out the tea. Touched by a sudden foreboding, I hesitated whether to put off the reading of your letter until I had gone into my room; but I was anxious about your health, and could not wait. God knows what it cost me not to show what I felt, especially as Aniela's eyes were fixed upon my face. But I got a firm grip of myself, and even managed to say: 'Leon is still sorrowing, but, thank God! his health is all right, and he sends you kind messages.' Aniela inquired, as it were in her usual voice, 'Is he going to remain long in Italy?' I saw how much the question meant to her, and had not the heart to undeceive her then,—especially as Chwastowski and the servants were there; so I said merely: 'No, not very long; I believe he will soon come to see us.' If you had seen the flame that shot up in her face, the sudden joy that kindled her eyes, and the effort she made not to burst into tears. Poor child! I feel inclined to cry every time I think of it. What I went through in the solitude of my own room, you cannot imagine; but you wrote distinctly, 'I wish her happiness with Kromitzki;' it was duty, my conscience told me, to open her eyes. There was no need to send for her, — she came herself. I said to her, 'Aniela, dear, you are a good girl, and a girl that submits to God's will. We must be open with each other. I have seen the affection that was springing up between you and Leon. It was my dearest wish you might come to love each other; but evidently the Lord willed it otherwise. If you have still any illusions, you must try to get rid of them.' I took her into my arms; for she had grown deadly white, and I was afraid she might faint. But she did not lose consciousness, but hid her head on my knees and said over and over again: 'What message did he send me?' I did not want to tell her, but then it struck me it might be better for her if she knew the whole truth; and I told her you wished her happiness with Kromitzki. She rose, and after a moment said, in a quite changed voice: 'Thank him for me, aunty!' and then left the room. I am afraid you will not thank me for repeating to her your very words, without disguising them under any kind expressions; but since you do not want Aniela, the more plainly she is told about it the better. Convinced that you treated her badly, she may forget you all the sooner. Besides, if it give you pain, remember how much pain and anxiety you have caused us, — especially Aniela. Yet she has more control over herself than I even expected. Her eyes were quite dry the whole day, and she gave no sign of inward trouble; she is anxious to spare her mother, about whose health she is much concerned; she only clung more to her and to me, — which moved me so deeply that it made my chin tremble. Pan Sniatynski, who came to see us the same day, did not notice anything unusual in Aniela. Knowing he is in your confidence, I told him all about it; and he was dreadfully shocked, and got into such a rage with you that it made me quite angry with him. I need not repeat what he said,—you know his ways. You, who do not love Aniela, cannot understand how happy you might have been with her; but you have done wrong, Leon, in making her believe you loved her. Not only she,—we all thought the same; and that is where the sting lies. Only God knows how much she suffered; and it was this that made her accept Kromitzki,—it was done out of despair. She must have had a long talk with her mother, and then it was decided. When Kromitzki arrived the day after, she treated him differently; and a week later they were engaged. Pan Sniatynski heard about it only a few days ago, and he was tearing his hair; and as to my own feelings, I will not even try to put them into words.

"I was more angry with you than I have ever been in my life with anybody, and only your second letter has pacified me a little, though it convinced me at the same time of the futility of my dreams. I confess that after the first letter, and before Kromitzki had finally proposed, I still thought: 'Perhaps God will be good to us and change his heart; maybe he has written thus in a fit of anger!' but when afterwards you sent kind messages to Aniela without denying or contradicting what you had written in the first letter, I saw it was of no use deceiving myself any longer. Aniela's wedding is to take place on the 25th of July, and I will tell you why they have fixed upon such a short date. Celina is really very ill, thinks she will soon die, and is afraid her death might delay the marriage, and thus leave Aniela without a protector. Kromitzki is in a hurry because he has his business to attend to in the East; lastly, Aniela wishes to drain the cup with as little delay as possible. Ah! Leon, my boy, why should all this have happened, and why is that poor child made unhappy?

"I would never have allowed her to marry Kromitzki, but how could I say a word against it, feeling as I do that I am guilty in regard to Aniela. I was over-anxious to see you settled in life, and never considered what might be the consequences for her. It is my fault, and consequently I suffer not a little; I pray every day for the poor child.

"After the ceremony they will immediately leave for Volhynia. Celina remains with me for the present; she was thinking of Odessa, but I will not let her go on any account. You know, my dear boy, how happy I am when you are with me, but do not come now to Ploszow for Aniela's sake; if you wish to see me I will come to you, but we must spare Aniela now as much as we can."

Why deceive myself any longer? When I read that letter I felt as if I could ram my head against the wall, — not in rage or jealousy but in utter anguish.

23 June.

I cannot possibly fold my hands and let things take their own way. This marriage must not take place; it would be too monstrous. To-day, Thursday, I have sent a telegram to Sniatynski, entreating him by all the powers to be at Cracow by Sunday. I shall leave here to-morrow. I asked him not to mention the telegram to anybody. I will see him, talk to him, and beg him to see Aniela in my name. I count much upon his influence. Aniela respects and likes him very much. I did not apply to my aunt, because we men understand one another better. Sniatynski, as a psychologist, can make allowance for the phase of life I have been passing through lately. I can tell him, too, about Laura; if I were to mention such a thing to my aunt she would cross herself as if in presence of the Evil One. I first wanted to write to Aniela; but a letter from me would attract attention and cause a general confusion. I know Aniela's straight-forwardness; she would show the letter to her mother, who does not like me and might twist the words so as to suit her own schemes, and Kromitzki would help her. Sniatynski must see Aniela alone. His wife will help him. I hope he will undertake the mission, though I am fully aware what a delicate task it is. I have not slept for several nights. When I shut my eyes I see Aniela before me, — her face, her eyes, her smile, — I even hear her voice. I cannot go on like this.

CRACOW, 26 June.

Sniatynski has arrived. He has promised to do it, — good fellow, God bless him for it! It is four o'clock at night, but I cannot sleep, so I sit down to write, for I can do nothing else. We talked together, discussed and quarrelled till three o'clock. Now he is sleeping in the adjoining room. I could not at first persuade him to undertake the mission. "My dear fellow," he said, "what right have I, a stranger, to meddle in your family affairs, and such a delicate affair too? Pana Aniela could reduce me to silence at once by saying, 'What business is it of yours?'"

I assured him that Aniela would do nothing of that kind. I acknowledged he was right in the main, but this was an exceptional case, and general rules could not apply to it. My argument that it was for Aniela's sake seemed to convince him most; but I think he is doing it a little for my sake too; he seemed sorry, and said I looked very ill. Besides, he cannot bear Kromitzki. Sniatynski maintains that money speculations is the same as taking money out of somebody else's pocket and put it in one's own. He takes many things amiss in Kromitzki, and says of him: "If he had a higher or honester aim in view I could forgive him; but he tries to gain money for the mere sake of having it." Aniela's marriage is almost as repugnant to him as to me, and his opinion is that she is preparing a wretched life for herself. At my entreaties he promised to take the first train in the morning.

The day after both he and his wife will go to Ploszow, and if they do not find a chance of seeing Aniela alone, carry her off to Warsaw for a few hours. He is going to tell Aniela how much I suffer, and that my life is in her hands. He is able to do it. He will speak to her with a certain authority, gently and persuasively; he will convince her that a woman, however wounded her heart may be, has no right to marry the man she does not love; that doing so she acts dishonestly, and is not true to herself; that, likewise, she has no right to throw over the man she loves, because in an access of jealousy he wrote a letter he repents of now from the veriest depths of his heart.

Towards the end Sniatynski said to me:—

"I will do what you wish under one condition: you must pledge me your word that in case my mission fails, you will not go to Ploszow and make a scene which the ladies might pay for with their health; you may write to Aniela if you wish, but you will not go, unless she gives you permission."

What does he take me for? I promised unreservedly, but his words increased my anxiety. But I count upon Aniela's heart and Sniatynski's eloquence. Ah! how he can speak! He did not encourage my hopes, but I can see he is hopeful himself. As a last resource he promised to get Aniela to delay the marriage for six months. In that case the victory is ours, for Kromitzki will draw back. I shall remember this day for a long time. Sniatynski, when in presence of a real sorrow, can be as gentle as a woman, and he was anxious to spare my feelings. Yet it costs me something to lay bare even before such a friend my madness,—weak points,—and put into his hands my whole fate, instead of fighting it out by myself. But what does it all matter when Aniela is in question?

27 June.

Sniatynski left early. I went with him to the station. On the way I kept repeating various instructions as if he were an idiot. He said teasingly that if he were successful in his mission, I would begin again philosophizing. I felt a desire to shake him. He went away with such a cheerful face I could swear he feels sure not to fail.

After his departure I went straight to St. Mary's Church, and I, the sceptic, the philosopher, I who do not know, do not know, do not know, had a mass offered in the names of Leon and Aniela. I not only remained during mass in church, but put down here, black on white: Perdition upon all my scepticism, philosophy, and my "I do not know!"

28 June.

It is one o'clock in the afternoon. Sniatynski and his wife are starting for Ploszow. Aniela ought to agree at least to a postponement of her marriage. Various thoughts cross my mind. That Kromitzki is greedy for money there is not the slightest doubt; then why did he not fix his attentions on a richer girl? Aniela's estate is large, but encumbered with debts, — perhaps it was the landed property he wanted, so as to secure himself a position and a citizenship. Yet Kromitzki, with his reputation as a rich man, could have got all this, and money with his wife besides. Evidently Aniela attracted him personally and for some time. It is not to be wondered at that Aniela should captivate any one.

And to think that she was waiting, as one waits for one's happiness or salvation, for one word from me! My aunt says it, that she was lying in wait for Chwastowski, to take the letters from him. A terrible fear seizes me that all this may not be forgiven, and that I am doomed and all those that are like me.

10 o'clock in the evening.

I had a terrible neuralgia in the head; it has passed now, but what with the pain, the sleeplessness, and anxiety, I feel as if I were hypnotized. My mind, open and excited on one point, concentrated upon one thought, sees more clearly than it has ever done before how the affair will end. It seems to me that I am at Ploszow; I listen to what Aniela says to Sniatynski, and I cannot understand how I could buoy myself up with false hopes. She has no pity on me. These are not mere suppositions, they are a dead certainty. Truly, something strange is going on with me. A terrible gravity has suddenly fallen upon me, as if up to this moment I had only been a child, — and such a terrible sadness. Am I going to be ill? I made Sniatynski promise to send me a telegram. No message has as yet arrived, though, properly speaking, it will not tell me anything new.

29 June.

The telegram has come. It contains these words: "It is of no use, — pull yourself together and travel." Yes, I will do it. Oh, Aniela!

Paris, 2 April.

It is some ten months since I put down anything in my journal; it had become such a familiar friend that I missed it. But I said to myself: what is the use of it? If I put down on paper thoughts worthy of a Pascal; deeper than the ocean depth; loftier than the Alps, — it would not change the simple fact that she is married. With that fact staring at me, my hands dropped powerless. Sometimes life concentrates itself in one object, not necessarily an important one; but if that fails us we seem at a loss what to do with ourselves. It is strange, — almost laughable, — but for a long time I remained in a state of mind in which the most commonplace functions of life seemed irksome and useless, and it took me some time to remember that I used to go to clubs and theatres, shaved, dressed, and dined before I knew her. The first months I travelled a great deal, straying as far as Iceland. The sight of Swedish lakes, Norwegian fiords, and Icelandic geysers conveyed to me no direct impressions; I only tried to imagine what Aniela would have felt or said to such a view, — in short, I saw with her eyes, thought her thoughts, and felt with her heart. And when presently I remembered that she was Aniela no longer, but Pani Kromitzka, I went straight to the nearest railway station or ship to go somewhere else, as what I looked upon had ceased to interest me. It did not matter to me in the least that I played a part in one of the so commonly ridiculed dramas where thousands of fools have played the same parts before. And death is a drama; and those who are entering its gates think the world is coming to an end; and so it is, — for them.

I do not know, and will not enter into it now, whether my feeling the first few months was one of fathomless despair. Everything is relative. I know only that my whole being was absorbed by one woman, and I understood for the first time the void created by the death of a dearly loved being.

But gradually the habit — not the zest — of life recovered its vital power. This is a common enough fact. I have known people, inwardly intensely sad, without a grain of cheerfulness in their souls, yet keep up an appearance of cheerfulness because they had once been cheerful, and the habit clung to them. And time dulls the pain, and I found an antidote to the poison. I read once, in a book of travels by Farini, that the Caffres, when stung by a scorpion, cure themselves by letting the scorpion sting them in the same place. Such a scorpion, — such an antidote, — was for me, and is generally for most people, the word, "It is done; there is no help for it."

It is done, therefore I suffer; it is done, and I feel relieved. There is an anodyne in the consciousness that it cannot be helped. It reminds me of the Indian carried away by the Niagara: he struggled at first with all his strength against the current; but seeing the hopelessness of his efforts, threw away his oar, laid himself down in the bottom of the canoe, and began to sing. I am ready to sing now. The Niagara Falls have that advantage — they crush the life out of a man; there are others that throw him on a lonely barren shore without water. This has happened to me.

The evil genius bent upon wrecking my life had not taken in account one thing: a man crushed and utterly wretched cares less for himself than a happy one. In presence of that indifference fate becomes more or less powerless. I was and am still in that frame of mind that, if angry Fortuna came to me in person, and said: "Go to perdition," I should reply calmly: "Be it so," — not out of sorrow for the loss of Aniela, but from mere indifference to everything within or without me.

This is a special kind of armor which not only protects the man himself, but also makes him dangerous to others. It is clear that he who does not spare himself will not spare others. Even God's commandment does not say: "Love thy neighbor more than thyself." It does not follow that I mean to cut somebody's throat one of these days. What I said has merely a theoretical bearing upon life in general; nobody will be any the worse for it; for if indifference diminishes altruism, it also lessens egoism. If I were to sleep with my neighbor under the same cloak, I should not surrender it altogether; neither should I take it all to myself.

Dangerous, and even very dangerous, such a man as I am may become when at length he is aroused from his lethargy, drawn forth from the seclusion of his egotism, and forced into definite action. He then acquires the precision of motion, and also the merciless power, of an engine. I have gained that mechanical power. For some time I have noticed that I impress others by my way of thinking and my will more strongly than formerly, though I have not sought it in the least. The everlasting source of weakness is love of self, vanity, and coquetry in regard to others. Almost unconsciously everybody tries to please, to gain sympathy; and towards that end often sacrifices his own opinions and convictions. At present this coquetry, if not altogether gone, is greatly diminished; and the indifference as to whether I please or not gives me a kind of superiority over others. I have noticed that during my travels, and especially now at Paris. There are many here who at one time had an ascendency over me; now I have the ascendency, for the very reason that I care less for it.

In a general way I look upon myself as a man who could be energetic if he wished to exert himself; but the will acts in proportion to the passions, and mine are in the passive state.

As the habit of giving an account to myself for my thoughts and actions still remains with me, I explain in this way that in certain conditions of life we may as strongly desire not to live, as in others we should wish the contrary. Most likely my indifference springs from this dislike of life. It is this which renders it different from the apathy of such men as Davis.

It is quite certain that I have grown more independent than formerly, and might say with Hamlet that there is something dangerous in me. Fortunately nobody crosses my path. Everybody is as supremely indifferent and cool towards me as I am in regard to them. Only my aunt in far-away Ploszow loves me as of old; but I suppose even her love has lost its active character, and there will be no more match-making in my behalf.

3 April.

Alas! that indifference I compared to pure water without taste or color is only apparently colorless. Looking more closely I perceive tiny bubbles which dim its purity. They are my idiosyncrasies. Everything else has left me and they remained. I do not love anybody, have no active hatred towards any one, but am full of aversions in regard to various people. One of these is Kromitzki. I do not hate him because he has taken Aniela from me; I dislike him for his long, flat feet, his thick knees, lank figure, and that voice like a coffee-mill. He was always repulsive to me, and I mention the fact now because that aversion has such a strange vitality in me. I cannot help thinking of people who jar upon my nerves. If only Kromitzki and Pani Celina came under that category, I might think those antipathies were hatred in the disguise of aversion. But it is not so. There are others who have roused at some time or other an aversion in me that clings quite as perversely to my memory. As I cannot ascribe it to the state of my health, — I never felt better in my life, — I explain it in this way: The world has robbed me of my love, time has dried up hatred, and as the living individual must feel something, I live upon what remains to me. I must also say that he who feels and lives thus does not get a surfeit of happiness.

My former sympathies have cooled down very considerably. To Sniatynski I have taken a dislike which no reasoning on my part can overcome. Sniatynski has many grand qualities and is pleasantly conscious of them, which gives him, as painters express it, a certain mannerism. I suppose it is exceedingly rare that a man who sees that his individual characteristics impress people favorably does not fall in love with his own type, and end by exaggerating it. Sniatynski consequently has grown artificial, and for the sake of the pose sacrifices his innate delicacy; as in case of the abrupt telegram he sent to Cracow, after his mission with Aniela had failed, — his advice to travel, which I should have done without it, — and I received another letter from him at Christiania soon after Aniela's wedding, written in a friendly spirit, but very abrupt and artificial. I might give its substance as follows: "Panna Aniela is now Pani Kromitzka, — the thing is done; I am sorry for you; do not think the bottom is falling out of the universe; there are other things in the world of more importance, the deuce take it. Norway must be splendid just now. Come back soon and set to work. Good-by," and so forth. I do not repeat it word for word, but such was the gist of the letter. It impressed me unpleasantly, first because I had not asked Sniatynski to lend me his yard-measure to measure my sorrow with; secondly, I had thought him a sensible man, and supposed he understood that his "more important things" are merely empty words unless they imply feelings and inclinations that existed before. I wanted to write to him there and then and ask him to release me from his spiritual tutelage, but thinking better of it did not answer at all, — I fancy that is the easiest way of breaking off a correspondence. Entering more minutely into the matter, I find that neither his telegram nor his letter have caused my dislike. Properly speaking, I cannot forgive him that for which I ought to feel grateful,— his mediation between me and Aniela. I myself implored him to undertake it, but exactly because I implored him, entrusted him with my fate, confessed to him my weaknesses, and made him in a way my protector, and because the humiliation and sorrow which overwhelmed me passed through his hands, — this, perhaps, explains my dislike towards him. I felt angry with myself, and angry with Sniatynski as having a part in it. It is unjust, I know, but I cannot help it, and my friendship for him has burned out like a candle.

Besides, I have never been quick in forming ties of friendship. With Sniatynski my relations were closer than with anybody else, perhaps because we lived each of us in a different part of Europe. I had no other friends. I belong in general to the class of persons called singles. I remember there was a time when I considered this a sign of strength. In the animal world, for instance, the weak ones mostly cling together, and those whom nature has endowed with powerful claws and teeth go single, because they suffice unto themselves. This principle can be applied to human beings only in exceptional cases. Incapacity for friendship proves mostly dryness of heart, not strength of character. As to myself, the cause of it was a certain shyness and sensitiveness. My heart is like that plant which closes its leaves at the slightest touch. That I never formed ties of friendship with a woman is a different thing altogether. I had a desire for friendship in regard to those from whom I expected more. I feigned it sometimes, as the fox makes believe to be dead in order to secure the rooks. It does not follow that I disbelieve in friendship between man and woman. I am not a fool who measures the world according to his own standard, or a churl who is for ever suspecting evil; besides, various observations have proved to me that such a friendship is quite possible. As there exists the relation of brother and sister, the same feeling may exist between two persons who feel as brother and sister towards each other. Moreover, the capacity for that kind of friendship belongs to the choicer spirits who have a natural inclination for Platonic feasts, such as poets, artists, philosophers, and generally, people who cannot be measured by the common standard. If this be a proof that I was not made of the stuff artists, poets, and great men are made of,—the worse for me. Most likely it is so, since I am nothing but Leon Ploszowski. There was a time when I felt that if Aniela had become my wife, she would not only have been my love, but also my dearest friend. But I prefer not to think of it. Ghosts of this kind visit me far too often, and I shall never have any peace until I banish them altogether.

4 April.

I meet Mrs. Davis here pretty often, and call upon her at her house. And nothing else! There is some dislike, a little contempt under a thick layer of ashes, and for the rest, the usual social intercourse. She is still too beautiful to be classified among my idiosyncrasies. I cannot love her, and do not take the trouble to hate her. She understood that at once, and adapted herself to circumstances. All the same she cannot always conceal her irritation at my self-possession and cool independence; but for that very reason shows me greater consideration. It is very strange, that easiness with which women from closest relations pass on to mere acquaintanceship. Laura and I treat each other as if there had never been anything between us, — not only before people, but even when we are alone together. It does not seem to cost her the slightest effort; she is polite, cool, and self-possessed, affable in her way, and her manners influence me to such a degree that I should never dream of calling her by her Christian name.

The Neapolitan cousin, Maleschi, used to roll his eyes so ferociously at me that I almost considered it my duty to ask him not to injure his optics; he has now calmed down, seeing how very distant our relations to each other are, and is very friendly towards me. He has already fought a duel about Laura, and in spite of the reputation of coward he had in Italy, showed a deal of pluck. Poor Davis has passed to Nirvana some months ago, and I suppose after a decent interval of widowhood, Laura will marry Maleschi. They will make a splendid couple. The Italian has the torso and head of an Antinous; in addition to that, a complexion like pale gold, raven black hair, and eyes as blue as the Mediteranean. It may be that Laura loves him, but for some reason known only to herself, she bullies him a great deal. Several times in my presence she treated him so uncivilly that I was surprised, as I had thought her æsthetic nature incapable of such an exhibition of temper. Aspasia and Xantippe in one.

I have often noticed that women, merely beautiful, without striking qualities of the soul, who are looked upon as stars, are something more than stars; they are a whole constellation, two in fact, — a Great Bear to their surroundings, a Cross to their husbands. Laura was a Cross to poor Davis, and is now a Bear in regard to Maleschi. She would treat me a little in that way, too, if it were not that she is not familiar with the ways of Parisian society, and considers it safer to have me for an ally than an enemy. It is very strange, but she does not create here the same sensation as in Italy, or on the Mediterranean. She is simply too classical, too beautiful for Parisians, whose taste is to a certain degree morbid, as appears in their literature and art; and characteristic ugliness more strongly excites their blunted nerves than simple beauty. It is a noted fact that the most celebrated stars of the *demi-monde* are rather ugly than beautiful. In regard to Laura, there is another reason for her non-success with the Parisians. Her intelligence, though very uncommon, is upon too straight lines, wanting in that kind of dash so appreciated here. There are thinkers, and deep thinkers, too, in Paris, but in society those mostly win a reputation whose minds are nimble enough to cling to any subject, as a monkey to a branch by his tail or feet, turning head over heel. The more these jumps are sudden and unexpected, the surer the success. Laura understands this, and at the same time is conscious that to do this would be as easy for her as to dance on a rope. She considers me an adept in these kinds of gymnastics, and consequently wants me.

To increase the attraction of her salon, she has made it into a temple of music. She herself sings like a siren, and thereby attracts many people. I meet there often a pianiste, Clara Hilst, a young, good-looking German girl, very tall of figure, whom one of the painters here describes thus: "C'est beau, mais c'est deux fois grandeur naturelle." In spite of her German origin, she has met with a considerable success. As to myself, I evidently belong to the old school, for I do not understand the music of the present, which consists in a great deal of noise and confusion. Listening the last time to

Miss Hilst's playing at Laura's, I thought to myself that if the piano were a man who had seduced her sister, she could not belabor him more mercilessly. She also plays on the harmonium. Her compositions are thought of a great deal here, and considered very deep; most likely because those who could not understand them, hearing them for the tenth time, hope the eleventh time will make them more intelligible. I must confess that these remarks sound malicious, perhaps bold in one who does not profess to be a judge. Yet it seems to me that music for the understanding of which one has to be a professor of the Conservatorium, and for which people intellectually developed, let alone simple folk, do not possess the key, is not what it ought to be. I am afraid that musicians following the same track will end by creating a separate caste, like the Egyptian priests, in order to keep knowledge and art exclusively to themselves.

I say this because I notice that since Wagner's time, music, compared, for instance, to painting, has taken a quite different direction. The newer school of painting is narrowing spontaneously the limit of its proportions, tries to divest itself from philosophical and literary ideas; does not attempt speeches, sermons, historical events that require a commentary, or allegory that does not explain itself at a glance; in fact confines itself with the full consciousness of doing so to the reproduction of shape and color. Music since Wagner's time goes in the opposite direction, — tries to be, not only a harmony of sound, but at the same time the philosophy of harmony. I sometimes think a great musical genius of the future will say, as Hegel did in his time: —

"There was only one who understood me, and he understood me wrongly."

Miss Hilst belongs to the category of musical philosophers, which is all the more strange, as her mind is full of simplicity. This caryatid has the limpid, innocent eyes of a child, and is unsophisticated and sincere like one. She is surrounded by a great throng of admirers, who are attracted by her beauty, and more still by the nimbus that makes a woman touched by the hand of the Muses always a centre of attraction; nevertheless, not a breath has touched her fair fame. Even the women speak well of her, for she disarms them by her invariable good humor and sincerity. She is as gay as any street urchin, and I have seen her laughing as school-girls laugh, the tears running down her face, which would be considered bad form in anybody but an artist, who is a privileged person. Hers, from a moral point of view, is a beautiful character, though beyond her art, she is not endowed with great intellectual gifts. Laura, who, in the main, does not like her, hinted to me several times that the caryatid is in love with me. I do not believe it; she might love me, perhaps, if I tried to make her. One thing is certain, she likes me very much, and felt sympathy for me the first time we met. I return the sentiment, and do not try to disturb her peace of mind. When I meet a woman for the first time I look upon her, from old habit I suppose, as a possible conquest; it is the first instinct. A second thought is quite different. Generally speaking, women interest me in the way precious stones interest a jeweller who has retired from business. Seeing a valuable gem, I say to myself it is worth having, and then I remember that I have sold out, and go on my way.

In spite of all that, I once, half in jest, urged her to go to Warsaw, and promised to escort her as honorary *impresario.* I do not say that such a journey would be without charm. I really intend going. My aunt has given me her town house, and wants me to come over in order to take the property. Besides, I always go to Warsaw for the races. Who would believe that my aunt, a grave, serious-minded lady, devoted to the management of the estate, to prayer and benevolent schemes, had such a worldly weakness as horse-racing. It is her one passion. Maybe the knightly instincts which women inherit as well as men, find an outlet in this noble sport.

Our horses have been running for Heaven knows how many years, — and are always beaten. My aunt never fails to attend the races, and is an enthusiast about horses. While her own horses are running, she stands on the back seat of her carriage, leaning on a stick, her bonnet usually awry, and watches for the result, — then gets very angry, and for at least a month makes Chwastowski's life a burden to him. At present I hear she has reared a wonderful horse, and she bids me to come and witness the triumph of the black and orange colors. I shall go. There are other reasons too which make me inclined to go. As I have said, I am comparatively speaking calm, do not wish for anything, or expect anything, am resigned in fact to that kind of spiritual paralysis until the time comes when bodily paralysis carries me off, as it carried off my father. Nevertheless, I cannot forget altogether, therefore it is only a partial paralysis. The one being I ever loved presents herself before my mind in two shapes. The one is called Pani Kromitzka, the other Aniela. As far as Pani Kromitzka is concerned, I am indifferent and a stranger; but Aniela still haunts me and brings with her, as gifts, the consciousness of wrong, my foolishness, spiritual crookedness, pain, bitterness, disappointment, and loss. Verily a munificent spirit! I might be even now perfectly contented if somebody could take from my brain that particular part wherein memory dwells. I try to drive away the thoughts of what might have been if things had turned out differently, but cannot always manage it. My munificent, generous angel will come now and then, and from her cornucopia shower her gifts upon me. At times the idea comes into my mind that Pani Kromitzka will lay the ghost of Aniela, — and that is one reason I wish to go; to look upon her happiness, her married life, and all those changes which must have made her different from the old Aniela. Perhaps I may meet her at Ploszow, as she will want to see her mother, after so many months of separation.

I suppose that I do not delude myself, and that "ceci tuera cela." I count mostly upon my nerves, which are so easily worked upon. I remember that when I had made Aniela's acquaintance and her charm began to act upon me with such irresistible force, the very mention of Kromitzki in connection with her made her less desirable. This will be more so now, when she belongs to him body and soul. I am almost certain the remedy will prove efficacious, and that "ceci tuera cela." And if not, if it should turn out differently, what have I to lose? I do not wish to gain anything, but should not be sorry perhaps to know that the guilt was not on my side only, and that henceforth the burden would have to be divided between us two; this might give me a kind of satisfaction. I say, it *might*, because I am not sure that it would. Thoughts of revenge are very far from me. It is only on theatrical boards that disappointed lovers are thirsting for revenge; in real life they go away with distaste, that is all. Moreover, to make Pani Kromitzka believe that she had done wrong in rejecting my repentance I should have to believe firmly in it myself,—and strange to say, there are moments I am not sure of anything.

5 April.

I know for certain I shall meet Pani Kromitzka. Her husband has sold the estate, betaken himself to Baku on business speculation, and has sent his wife to join her mother at Ploszow; so my aunt tells me in her letter. I received the news if not indifferently, at least with perfect composure, but I notice that the impression gradually gained upon me. At present I cannot think of anything else, as the fact is of so great importance to the two women. After so short a space as ten months he sold the estate which over four hundred years had been in Aniela's family, and to the preservation of which Pani Celina had devoted her own life. Then comes a Pan Kromitzki and sells it with a light heart because he wants the money for his speculations. Suppose he does make millions — will that compensate the women for the loss of what they prized above money? What will they think of him now? My aunt writes that she is sitting by Pani Celina's bedside, who after receiving the news of the sale grew worse at once. I am quite certain that Aniela, when putting her signature to the deed which empowered her husband to dispose of the land, did not know what she was signing. She is even now defending her husband. My aunt quotes from Aniela's letter: "A great misfortune has happened, but it was not Charles's fault." Defend him, defend him, O loyal wife; but you cannot prevent my thinking that he has wounded you deeply, and that at the bottom of your heart you despise him. Neither kisses nor soft words will efface from your memory the one word "sold." And Pani Celina thought that after the marriage he would devote his money towards clearing off the debts and disincumbering the property! Dear ladies, I, a man who does not boast of civic virtues, would not have done it, if for no other reason than innate delicacy of feeling, affection for you, and fear to wound you. But for speculations, ready money is wanted. I hope it is not merely prejudice, but these millions I heard so much about appear to me like a great point of interrogation. Maybe he will get them; perhaps the capital realized from the sale will help him towards it; but if he had possessed the wealth he used to boast of, would he have dealt his wife and mother-in-law such a blow, and sold their ancestral seat? My aunt writes that he left immediately after the sale for Baku, and intends to go as far as Turkestan. Aniela being too young to live by herself must needs come to Ploszow, as her mother cannot leave it at present, because she is too ill to travel; and besides my aunt will not let her go, and she is afraid of crossing her in any way. I know Aniela too well to suspect her of any calculations. She is the very essence of disinterestedness. But the mother, who would grasp all the world for her only child, doubtless counts upon the chance of a legacy for Aniela. And she is not mistaken either. My aunt, who never quite believed in Kromitzki's millions, gave me to understand several times that she meant to do something for Aniela; she said it with a certain hesitation, almost humbly, as she considers everything ought to go to a Ploszowski, and that to leave anything to another would be a wrong to the family. How little she knows me! If Aniela were in want of a pair of shoes and I had to sell Ploszow and give all I possess, she should have them. I might be prompted by a less noble motive, — for instance, to appear different from a Kromitzki, — but from whatever motive, I should give it certainly. But there is no question of that now. I am thinking continually that she is living at Ploszow, and will remain there as long as Kromitzki's journeys last, which may be God only knows for how long. I shall see Pani Kromitzka every day. At the thought of this I feel a certain uneasiness, with a strong admixture of curiosity as to our future relations towards each other; and I clearly see what might happen if my disposition and feelings in regard to her were different. I never lie to myself; I repeat again that I am going there in order to cure myself, that I do not love Pani Kromitzka, and never will love her; that on the contrary, I am in hope that the sight of her will drive Aniela out of my heart far more successfully than all the fiords and geysers; but I would not be myself, the man who has lived much and thought much, if I did not see the danger which under other circumstances such a position might bring forth.

If I wanted to revenge myself, if the very name Pani Kromitzka did not excite my loathing, what could stand in my way or hinder me, — in quiet Ploszow, where would be we two only, and the elder ladies, as unsuspicious and unsophisticated in their stainless virtue as any babies? In regard to this I know my aunt and Pani Celina. In the higher spheres of society one meets sometimes women thoroughly corrupted; but there are many, especially among the older generation, who pass through life like angels, with no thought of evil ever coming near them. Neither my aunt nor Pani Celina would ever dream of any danger threatening Aniela now she is married. Aniela herself belongs to that kind. She would not have rejected my prayers had she not given her word to Kromitzki. But Polish women of this kind would rather break a heart than break their word. At the very thought of it a dull wrath seizes me. I crush down within me the desire every one has to prove the truth of his opinion. I do not want to argue at all with Pani Kromitzka, but if somebody else would do it, — point out to women like her that the laws of nature, laws of affection, cannot be broken with impunity, that they are stronger than any ethic laws, I should be glad of it. It is true I have sinned in regard to Aniela, but I wished to make amendment from the very depth of my heart, and she rejected me, — rejected me perhaps so as to be able to say to herself: "I am not a Leon Ploszowski; I have given a promise, and do not take it back." This is not virtue, it is want of heart; it is not heroism, but foolishness; not rectitude of conscience, but vanity. I cannot forget, I cannot; but Pani Kromitzka will help me. When I come to see her in her new matronly dignity, satisfied with her heroism, self-possessed, in love, or apparently so, with her husband, watching me furtively to see whether I have been punished, and punished sufficiently, full of happiness and her own virtues, the ghost of my old love will be laid, and I can go back to where the reindeer lives without Aniela's memory following me like the sea-gulls in the track of ships.

It is possible that Pani Kromitzka will put on the airs of an injured victim, and her whole manner to me may say: "It is your fault!" Very well. We have seen some of that in the world. As artificial flowers have one defect, the want of scent, artificial crowns of thorn have one advantage, they do not prick, and may be worn as a bonnet, very becoming to a pretty face. Whenever I met one of those victims who married out of despair I felt a desire to say: "It is not true! you were a victim maybe in good faith as long as the chosen one did not approach you in his slippers. From that moment you ceased to be pathetic, and are only ridiculous, and the more so if you pose as a victim."

6 April.

How beautiful and wise is the Greek word "ananke." It was fated that through a woman I should lose my peace of mind, though I had ceased to care for her. The news that her ancestral seat is sold, and she herself coming to live at Ploszow, moved me so deeply that I could not sleep. Various questions knocked at my brain, asking for admittance. I tried to solve the question whether I had any right to lead Pani Kromitzka from the path of virtue. I neither wish, nor will I endeavor to do so, because she has ceased to attract me; but would it be right? I fill my life with these questions of "to be, or not to be," because I have nothing else to do. Thoughts like mine are not reckoned among the delights of life. It is like the dog trying to catch his tail; he does not catch anything. I do not prove anything, only tire myself; but have the satisfaction that another day has passed, or another night gone by.

I observe at the same time, that with all my scepticism, I am still beset with scruples worthy of the vicar of Ploszow. The modern man is composed of so many threads that in trying to set himself right, he gets more and more entangled. It was in vain I repeated to myself, if only in theory, that I had the right. A voice, as from the parish church, seemed to say at intervals: "No! no! you have not the right!" But scruples like these ought to be kept down, as for me this is a question of keeping my mind evenly balanced. At this quiet evening time, I feel just in the humor for it. This afternoon, at a well-known painter's studio, I heard Mrs. Davis maintain, in discussion with two literary men, that a woman ought to be unapproachable all her life, if only "pour la netteté du plumage," and Maleschi repeated, "Oui, oui, — du plumaze." Oh, ye gods and fishes! I fancied all the crabs in the Mediterranean rolling on their backs in silent laughter, and raising their claws to heaven, imploring Jove for a thunderbolt! By the bye, Mrs. Davis borrowed that sentence from me, and I borrowed it from Feuillet. I kept my gravity, and did not permit myself the slightest smile, but it put me into a merry, cynical humor, the reflection of which still remains with me, and is for the moment the best weapon against scruples of conscience.

Now for the start. Would it be right for me to fall in love with Pani Kromitzka, and in case of success lead her from the path of duty? First, let us look at it from a point of honor, as people consider it who call themselves, and whom the world regards as, gentlemen. There is not a single paragraph there against it. It is one of the queerest codexes ever invented under the sun. If, for instance, I steal somebody's money, the disgrace falls upon me, and not upon the man who is robbed, according to the world's rule of honor; but if I rob him of his wife, it is not I, but the robbed man who is disgraced. What does it mean? Is it a mere aberration of the moral sense, or is it that between stealing a man's purse and stealing his wife, there is such a vast difference that the two cases cannot be even compared? I have often thought over this, and have come to the conclusion that there is a great difference. A human being can never be as absolutely a property as a thing, and the taking away somebody's wife is an act of a double will. Why should I respect the rights of a husband if his own wife does not? What is he to me? I meet a woman who wants to be mine, and I take her. Her husband does not exist for me: her vows are no affair of mine. What should hold me back? Respect for the matrimonial institution? But if I loved Pani Kromitzka, I would cry out from the very depth of my soul: "I protest against this marriage; protest against her duties towards Kromitzki. I am the worm this marriage has crushed; and they tell me, writhing in anguish, to respect it, — me, who would sting it with my last breath." Why; for what reason? What do I care for a social institution that has wrung from me the last drop of blood, deprived me of my very existence? Man lives on fish. Go tell the fish to respect the order that it be skinned alive before being put on the fire. I protest and sting, — that is my answer. Spencer's ideal of a finally developed man, in whom the individual impulses will be in perfect harmony with social laws, is nothing but an assumption. I know perfectly that such as Sniatynski would demolish my theory with one question: "You are then for free-love?" No, nothing of the sort. I am for myself. I do not wish to hear anything about your theories. If you fall in love with another woman, or your wife with somebody else, we shall see what becomes of your rules, paragraphs, and respect for social institutions. At the worst, I might be called inconsequent. I was inconsequent, too, when I, a sceptic, had a mass offered up for Leon and Aniela, and prayed like a child, and swallowed my tears like any fool. In future I will always be inconsequent when it suits me and makes me happier. There is only one logic in the world, — the logic of passions. Reason holds the reins for a time, but when the horses tear along in mad career, she sits on the box and merely watches lest the vehicle should go to pieces. The human heart cannot be rendered love-proof, and love is an element strong as tidal waves. The very gates of hell cannot overcome a woman who loves her husband, for the marriage vows are only the sealing of love's compact; but if it be mere duty, the first tide will throw her on the sands like a dead fish. I cannot bind myself not to let my hair grow, or to remain always young; and as often as I did so, the laws of nature would take their course in spite of human bonds. It is strange, but all that I am writing is pure theory. I have no schemes I need justify before myself, and yet all these reflections have stirred my soul to such an extent that I had to leave off writing. My calmness is evidently artificial. I walked up and down the room for an hour, and at last found out what disturbed me.

It is very late. From the windows of my room I see the cupola of the Invalides gleaming in the moonlight, as once I saw St. Peter's cupola, when, full of hope, I walked on the Pincio, thinking of Aniela. Unconsciously I had given myself up to those memories. Whatever there be or awaits us in the future, one thing is certain: I could have been happy, and she might be ten, nay, a hundred times happier than she is. Even now, if I had any hidden schemes, or if she were to me the greatest temptation, I would respect her unhappiness. I would not hurt her for anything. The very thought of it would take away my courage and decision, I had such an amount of tenderness for her.

But all that is in the past. The sceptic dwelling within me creeps up again with another question: Would she be really so unhappy? I have verified, not once, but several times, the fact that women are unhappy only while they struggle. The battle once over, regardless of the result, there follows a period of calm and happiness. I knew at one time a woman in Paris who resisted most persistently for three years. When at last her heart got the upper hand and she gave in, she only reproached herself for not having done so sooner.

But what is the use of putting all these questions or trying to solve problems? I know that every principle is open to argument, and every proof to scepticism. The good old times when people doubted everything except their intelligence to recognize the true from the false, have gone. At present there is nothing but labyrinths upon labyrinths. I had better not think of anything but the journey before me. And Kromitzki sold his wife's ancestral home and thus inflicted on her a cruel blow! I had to write it down black on white once more, otherwise I could not believe it.

10 April.

I went towards evening to say good-by to Mrs. Davis, and dropped in for a regular concert. Laura seems really very fond of music. Miss Hilst was playing on the harmonium. I always like to see her, but especially when she sits down to the harmonium, and playing the prelude, keeps her eyes on the keys. There is so much earnestness and intentness in her face, combined with calmness. She reminds me of Saint Cecilia, the most sympathetic of all saints, with whom I should have fallen in love had she lived in our times. A pity Clara is so tall; but one forgets it when she is playing. From time to time she lifts her eyes, as if recalling to memory a note heard somewhere in the spheres, or seeking inspiration, and she herself looks like one inspired. She rightly bears the name of Clara, for it would be difficult to find a more transparent soul. I said I liked to see her; as to her music, it is still the same; I do not understand it, or rather I follow her meaning with the greatest difficulty. Nevertheless, in spite of my satirical remarks, I think she has a remarkable talent.

When she had finished I approached her, and still half jestingly said the time had come and I was ready to escort her to Warsaw according to our agreement. I was surprised to see her take my proposition so seriously. She said that she had wanted to go there for some time, and was quite ready; it was all a question of informing an old relative who always went with her, and of taking a dumb piano, as she practised even on her journeys.

The prospect began to alarm me somewhat. If she goes, I shall have to help her in getting up a concert, and I would rather go straight on to Ploszow. As a last resource I could hand her over to Sniatynski, who would be more useful to her than I. Besides, Miss Hilst is the daughter of a rich mill-owner at Frankfurt, and it is not a question of material success with her. The eagerness with which she agreed to the journey made me thoughtful. I had half a mind to tell her that I did not object to the dumb piano so much as to the elderly relative. Men are so prone to lie in wait for women that few approach a young and pretty one without an afterthought. As to myself, though wholly absorbed by something else, the idea of the old relative travelling with us was unpleasant, the more so as my person evidently plays some part in this so quickly arranged journey. Paris presents a far wider scope for her musical talent, and she does not care for gain; why should she be so anxious to go to Warsaw? Laura, as I have said, has hinted more than once that Miss Hilst has more than a liking for me. A strange woman, Laura! Clara's innocence excites her envy, but only as it might be excited by a beautiful jewel, or by rare lace, — with her it is merely a question of adornment. Maybe for that reason she would like to push that big child into my arms. She does not care for me any longer; I am an ornament she has worn already.

That woman, though unconsciously, has wrought me such irreparable harm that I ought to hate her, but cannot, — first, because I am conscious that, had she never crossed my path, I should have probably found some other means to wreck my happiness; secondly, as Satan is a fallen angel, so hatred is degenerated love, and I never loved Laura. There is a little contempt for her, a little dislike, and she returns the feeling undoubtedly a hundredfold.

As to Clara's feelings, Laura may be right. To-day I saw it clearer than ever. If that be the case, I am grateful to her. For the first time in my life I long for the pure friendship of a woman. A soul so restless as mine will find solace and comfort in such a friendship.

We conversed together to-day, Clara and I, like old

friends. Her intelligence is not large, but clear and discerning between bad and good, ugly and what she considers beautiful; consequently her judgment is not shifty, but calm and serene. She has that kind of spiritual healthiness often met with in Germans. Coming across them now and then I observe that the type I belong to is very rare among them. The Germans and the English are generally positive and know what they want. They too are sounding the fathomless depth of doubt, but they do it methodically as scientists, not as sensitive geniuses without portfolio like me; in consequence of which their recent transcendental philosophy, their present scientific pessimism, and their poetic *Weltschmerz* have only a theoretical meaning. Their everyday practice consists in adapting themselves to the rules of life. According to Hartmann, the more humanity gains in intensity and consciousness, the more unhappy it grows. The same Hartmann, with the calmness of a German *Cultur-träger*, becomes practical when he raises his voice in favor of suppressing the Polish element as detrimental to German supremacy. But, putting aside this incident, which belongs to the category of human villanies, Germans do not take theories seriously, and therefore are always calm and capable of action. This same calmness Clara possesses. Things which rend and trouble human souls must have come near her some time or other, but if so they left no trace and were not absorbed by her; thus she never lost faith in truth and in her art. If she has any deeper feeling for me than mere friendship, the feeling is unconscious and does not ask for anything in return. If it were otherwise, it would be the beginning of her tragedy, as I could not return her love and might make her unhappy. I am not so conceited as to think that no woman could resist me, but I am of the opinion that no woman can resist the man she truly loves. It is a trite saying that "a fortress besieged is a fortress surrendered," but there is some truth in it when adapted to woman, especially when behind the entrenchment of her virtues she harbors such a traitor as her own heart. But Clara may rest tranquil. We shall travel peacefully together: she, her old relative, myself, and the dumb piano.

16 April.

I arrived at Warsaw three days ago, but have not been able to go to Ploszow as, shortly after my arrival, I got a cold in my teeth and my face is swollen. I do not wish to show myself to the ladies in that state.

I have seen Sniatynski, and my aunt, who has welcomed me as the prodigal son. Aniela arrived at Ploszow a week ago. Her mother is very ill, so ill that the doctors who advised her to try Wiesbaden now declare she could not bear the journey. She will therefore remain at Ploszow until she recovers—or dies, and Aniela with her, until Kromitzki winds up his business or thinks it proper to give her a home. From what my aunt says this may take him some months. I tried to get from my aunt as much news about Aniela as I could, which is easy enough, as she speaks about her with perfect freedom. She simply cannot understand how a married woman could excite any feeling except in the way of relationship; or rather, she has never even considered the question. She spoke openly about the sale of Aniela's home, which she considers a great shame. She got so excited over it as to break her watch-chain and let the watch roll on the floor.

"I will tell him so to his face," she said. "I would rather have lent him the money had I known anything about it. Only what would have been the use? His speculations are a gulf. I do not know whether any good will come out of it, but in the meanwhile everything is swallowed up in it. Let him only come, and I will tell him that he makes Aniela unhappy, kills her mother, and will end in ruining them and himself." I asked my aunt whether she had said anything about this to Aniela.

"To Aniela?" she replied. "I am glad you have come; it relieves my mind and makes it easier to bear. I cannot speak about it with Aniela. I tried it once when I could not contain myself any longer. I made some remark and she grew very angry, then burst out crying and said, 'He was obliged, he was obliged, and could not help it.' She does not allow anybody to say a word against him, and would like to cover all his shortcomings before the world; but she cannot deceive an old woman like me, and I know that at the bottom of her heart she must condemn him as I do."

"Do you mean she does not love him?"

My aunt looked at me in unfeigned surprise.

"Not love him? Of course she loves him. Whom should she love if not him? That's just where the sting lies; she grieves because she loves him. But one may love and yet have one's eyes open to what is wrong."

I had my own opinion on that point, but preferred not to express it, and allowed my aunt to proceed.

"What I resent most in him are his lies. He assured Celina and Aniela that in a year or two he would be able to buy the estate back. Just tell me, is this possible? and those women believe he is in earnest!"

"According to my opinion it is quite impossible. Besides, he will go on speculating."

"He knows it even better than we do, and yet he goes on lying to the women."

"Perhaps he does it to relieve their anxiety."

My aunt grew angrier still.

"Relieve their anxiety! fiddlesticks! they would not have had any anxiety if he had not sold it. Do not defend him, it is of no use. Everbody blames him. Chwastowski was wild about it. He had looked into the affairs, and says that without any ready money he could have cleared the estate himself in a few years. I would have given the money and so would you, would you not? and now it is too late."

Presently I inquired about Aniela's health, with a

strange, troubled foreboding I might hear something which, though perfectly natural and in the order of things, would give a shock to my nerves. My aunt caught the drift of my thoughts and replied with as much acerbity as before: —

"There is nothing whatever the matter with her. All he could do he did; that was to sell his wife's estate. No, there is nothing expected."

I turned the conversation to something else. I told my aunt I had arrived together with the celebrated pianist Miss Hilst, who, having considerable means of her own, wished to give a few concerts gratis. My aunt is a queer mixture of eccentricities. She began by abusing Miss Hilst for not coming in winter, when the time for concerts was more propitious; presently began considering that it was not too late yet, and wanted to go and call upon her at once. I could scarcely persuade her to put off her visit until I had told Miss Hilst about it. My aunt is a patroness of several charitable institutions, and it is with her a point of honor to get for them as much as she can at the expense of other institutions, consequently was afraid somebody else might forestall her with the artist.

When leaving me she asked, "When are you coming to stay at Ploszow?"

I replied that I was not going to stay there at all. I had thought of that during the journey and came to the conclusion that it would be better to have my headquarters at Warsaw. Ploszow is only six miles from here, and I can go there in the morning and stay as long as I like. It is indifferent to me where I live, and my living here will prevent people talking. Besides, I do not want Pani Kromitzka to think I am anxious to dwell under the same roof with her. I spoke of this to Sniatynski, and saw that he fully agreed with me; he seemed anxious to discuss Aniela with me. Sniatynski is a very intelligent man, but he does not seem to understand that changed circumstances mean changed relations, even between the best of friends. He came to me as if I were the same Leon Ploszowski who, shaking in every limb, asked for his help at Cracow; he approached me with the same abrupt sincerity, desiring to plunge his hand up to his elbow under my ribs. I pulled him up sharply, and he seemed surprised and somewhat angry. Presently he fell in with my humor, and we talked together as if the last meeting at Cracow had never taken place. I noticed, nevertheless, that he watched me furtively, and not being able to make me out tried indirect inquiry, with all the clumsiness of an author who is a deep psychologist and reader of the human mind at his desk, and as unsophisticated as any student in practical life. As Hamlet of yore, I might have handed him a pipe and said, "Do you think I am easier to be played on than a pipe? Call me what instrument you will, though you can fret me, yet you cannot play upon me."

I had been reading Hamlet the night before, as I have read it many a time, and involuntarily these words came into my mind. It seems to me surpassing strange that a man of my time, in whatever position or complicated trouble of soul, should find so much analogy to himself as I find in this drama, based upon Holinshed's sanguinary and gross legend. Hamlet is the human soul as it was, as it is, and as it will be. In conceiving this drama, Shakspeare overstepped the limit fixed even for genius. I can understand Homer and Dante, studied by the light of their epoch. I can comprehend that they could do what they did; but how an Englishman of the seventeenth century could foreknow psychosis, a science of recent growth, will be to me, in spite of my study of Hamlet, an everlasting mystery.

Having mentally handed over to Sniatynski Hamlet's pipe, I recommended to his care Miss Hilst, and then began to discuss his pet theories. Upon his wanting to know what brought me back, I said it was the longing for the country, and consciousness of unfulfilled duties towards it. I said it in a careless, off-hand way, and Sniatynski looked puzzled, not knowing whether I spoke seriously or mockingly. And again the same phenomenon of which I spoke in Paris repeated itself here. The moral ascendency he had gained over me gradually disappeared. He did not know himself what to think, but he saw the old key would not serve any longer. When he said good-by I again recommended to him Miss Hilst. He looked at me keenly.

"Do you attach much importance to her success?"

"Yes, very much. She is a person I hold in great esteem, and have much friendship for."

In this way I centred all his attention on Miss Hilst. Most likely he thought I had fallen in love with her. He went away angry, and could not disguise his feelings. He shut the door sharply; and when I accompanied him as far as the staircase, and turned back to the anteroom, I heard him descending the staircase, taking four steps at once, and whistling, — which he always does when angry. Besides, it was quite true, what I said about Miss Hilst. I wrote to-day to Clara, explaining why I had not been to see her, and received a reply at once. She is delighted with Warsaw, and especially its inhabitants. All the musical world has called upon her, and they are vying with each other in politeness and offers of help. Whether they would be quite as enthusiastic had she come to settle here, is another question; but Clara has the gift to win friends wherever she goes. She has already seen something of the town, and was much charmed with the Sazienki Park and Palace. I am glad she likes it, — the more so as the country, soon after crossing the frontier, seemed to her rather depressing. Truly, only those born on the soil can find any charm in the vast solitary plains, where the eye finds very little to rest upon. Clara, looking through the carriage window, said more than once: "Ah! I can understand Chopin now!" She is utterly mistaken, — she does not understand Chopin and his feelings, any more than she is in touch with his native land.

I, though a cosmopolitan by education, by atavism understand our nature, and am surprised myself at the spell a Polish spring casts upon me, and it seems as if I could never feel tired of it. Properly speaking, what does the view consist of? Sometimes, on purpose, I put myself into a stranger's place, — a painter's, having no preconceived ideas about it, and look at it with his eyes. The landscape then makes upon me the impression as if a child had drawn it, or a savage, who had no notion about drawing. Flat fallow-land, wet meadows, huts with their rectangular outline, the straight poplars around country-seats on the distant horizon, a broad, flat plain, finished off with a belt of woods, — that "ten miles of nothing," as the Germans call it; all this reminds me of a first attempt at drawing landscape. There is scarcely enough for a background. From the moment I cease looking upon it with a stranger's eyes, I begin to feel the simplicity of the view, incorporate myself with that immense breadth, where every outlined object melts into the far distance, as a soul in Nirvana; it has not only the artistic charm of primitiveness, but it acts soothingly upon me. I admire the Apennines; but my spirit is not in touch with them, and sooner or later they become wearisome. The human being finds a resting-place only where he is in harmony with his surroundings; and is reminded that his soul and the soul of nature are of the same organization. Homesickness springs from the isolation of the soul from its surroundings. It appears to me that the principle of psychical relationship could be applied in a still wider sense. It may seem strange that I, brought up in foreign lands, permeated by their culture, should harbor such views; but I go farther still, and say a foreign woman, even the most beautiful, appears to me more as a species of the female kind than a soul.

I remember what I wrote at one time concerning Polish women, but one statement does not contradict the other; I may perceive their faults, and yet feel myself nearer to them than to strangers. Besides, my old opinions — at least, the greater part of them — are now in tatters, like a worn-out garment.

But enough of this! I notice with a certain shame and surprise that all I have been writing has been done in order to distract my thoughts. Yes, that is true. I speak about landscapes, homesickness, and so forth, while all my thoughts are at Ploszow. I did not want to acknowledge it, even to myself. I feel restless, and something seems to weigh me down. It is very probable that my going there and the getting over the first meeting will be easier and far simpler than I imagine. Expectancy of anything is always oppressive. When a young lad, I had a duel; and on the eve of the day I felt troubled. Then, too, I tried to think of something else, and could not manage it. My thoughts are not at all tender, not even friendly, towards Pani Kromitzka; but they swarm around me like angry bees, and I cannot drive them away.

17 April.

I have been to Ploszow, and found things very different indeed from what I had pictured to myself. I left Warsaw at seven in the morning in a cab, counting I should be in Ploszow by eight. The oppressive feeling still remained with me. I had said to myself that I would not make any plans about that first meeting, or my future bearing towards her. Let chance be my guide. But I could not help speculating how it would be, — how she would greet me, what she would try to make me understand, and what our future relation to each other would be. Not having formed any plans of my own, I fancied, I do not know why, that she would want to act according to a well-defined system. Trying to fathom this, I felt almost inimical towards her. Then again, at the thought that the meeting might cause her pain, I felt something akin to pity, and seemed to see her before me as she used to be. I saw distinctly the low brow with the wealth of auburn hair, the long eyelashes, and the small, delicate face. I tried to guess how she would be dressed. Memories came back of words she had said, expressions of the face, graceful motions, dresses. With strange pertinacity, the one memory remained with me, — her coming into the room after she had tried to disguise her emotion by applying powder to her face. At last these memories became so vivid as to equal a second-sight. "There she is again," I said to myself; and in order to pull myself together, I began talking to the driver, and asked him whether he were married; whereupon he replied that without the old woman at home, there would be no go, then said something I did not hear, as I had caught sight of the Ploszow poplars in the distance. I had not paid any heed to the time we had been on the road.

At the sight of Ploszow I felt more troubled still, and my eagerness increased. I tried to pay attention to outward things, changes that had taken place during my absence, and look at the new buildings on the road. I repeated to myself mechanically that the weather was very fine, and the spring exceptionally early this year. And indeed, the weather was magnificent; the morning air was crisp and transparent; near the cottages the apple-trees, in full bloom, were scattering their petals like snowflakes on the grass; it was like a long line of pictures by the modern school of painters. Wherever the eye turned, there was that luminous *plein-air* in the midst of which moved the figures of people working in the fields or near their cottages. I saw it all, observed every detail; but, strange to say, I was not able to take it in, or give myself up to it altogether. The impressions had lost their absorbing power, and remained only on the surface of the brain, the brain itself being full of other thoughts. In this state of divided attention I approached Ploszow.

Presently the cool air of the lime avenue fanned my

face, and I saw at the other end, far off, the windows of the house. The scattered, futile thoughts hammered and knocked louder than ever at my brain. I stopped the driver from going straight to the house, and dismissed him, I do not know why, at the gate. Followed by his thanks, I went on foot straight towards the veranda. I cannot explain to myself why I felt so troubled, unless it was that within these well-known walls something unknown was awaiting me, which was in close connection with the tragic past. Crossing the courtyard, I felt such a weight upon my chest that it obstructed my breath. "What the deuce is the matter with me?" said I, inwardly. As I had dismissed the cab, nobody had heard me coming. The hall was empty; I went in to the dining-room to wait until the ladies came down.

I knew they would come soon, as the table was laid for breakfast, and the samovar, whispering and growling, was sending coils of steam aloft. Again not the slightest detail escaped my notice. I observed that the room was cool and comparatively dark, as the windows faced the north. For a moment my attention was fixed on the three luminous streaks the light from the windows made upon the polished floor. I looked at the carved sideboard I remembered since a child, and then recalled the conversation I had in this same room with Sniatynski, and we looked through the window at his wife and Aniela, in fur boots, coming from the hothouses.

At last a feeling of great solitude and sadness overcame me, and I went close to the window to get more light and make further observations in the garden. But all this did not restore my balance of mind. The only real thought my mind was full of was that I should meet her in a few minutes. There are people who out of fear are capable of the most heroic deeds. With me it is different. Fear, uncertainty of what may come next, rouses me to anger. This happened now. The difference between the old

Aniela and the present Pani Kromitzka impressed itself upon me more forcibly than ever. "If you borrowed the very moonbeams for your head-dress, if you were a hundred times more beautiful than my fancy can paint, you would be as nothing to me, — less than nothing, because an object of aversion." My anger rose still, for I fancied that she would come to me in order to point out my guilt, my wrong-doing; that she would be still desirable, but unapproachable. "We shall see," I replied inwardly, under the vivid impression that with this woman there was awaiting me a duel; a struggle in which I should lose and gain at the same time, — lose the haunting memories and regain peace. At that moment I felt the power to overcome any obstacles, repulse any attack.

Then the door opened quietly, and Aniela came in.

At the sight of her I felt my brain in a whirl, and my finger-tips grew icy cold. The being before me bore the name of Pani Kromitzka, but had the sweet, hundred times beloved features and inexpressible charm of the Aniela I had known. In the chaotic bewilderment of my brain there was only one sound I heard distinctly: "Aniela! Aniela! Aniela!" And she did not see me, or took me for somebody else as I stood against the light. But when I drew nearer, she raised her eyes and stood still as if turned into stone. I cannot even describe the expression of sudden terror, confusion, emotion, and humility which shone in her face. She had grown white to the lips, and I was afraid she might faint. When I took her hand it felt as cold as ice. I had expected anything but that. I thought she would let me know in some way or other that she was Pani Kromitzka, but there was nothing of the sort. She stood before me moved, frightened, my former little Aniela. It was I who had made her unhappy, — I who was guilty, a hundred times guilty; and at this moment she looked at me as if she herself asked to be forgiven. The old love, contrition for the past, and pity overwhelmed me to such a degree that I almost lost my head, and thought I must take her into my arms, and soothe her with endearing words, as one soothes a beloved being. I was so agitated by the unexpected meeting, not with Pani Kromitzka, but Aniela, that I could only press her hand in silence. And yet I felt obliged to say something; therefore, pulling myself together, I said, as if in somebody else's voice, —

"Did aunt not tell you I was coming?"

"Yes; she told me," said Aniela, with an evident effort.

And then we fell back into silence. I felt that I ought to ask after her mother, and about herself, but could not force myself to do so. I wished from my soul somebody would come and deliver us from this position. Presently my aunt came in with the young Doctor Chwastowski, the agent's son, who for a month past has had the care of Pani Celina. Aniela slipped away to pour out the tea, and I began to talk with my aunt. I had recovered my presence of mind entirely when we sat down to breakfast. I began now to inquire after Pani Celina's health. My aunt, telling me about her, appealed every moment to the doctor, who turned to me with that peculiar shade of superciliousness with which a newly patented scientist treats outsiders, and at the same time with the watchfulness of a democrat who is afraid of slights where none are intended. He appeared to me very conceited; and after all, I treated him with far greater politeness than he exhibited towards me. This amused me a little, and helped to keep my thoughts, which the sight of Aniela confused, under control. From time to time I looked at her across the table, and repeated to myself: "The same features, the same little face, the same low brow shaded by a wealth of hair; it is the same Aniela, almost a little girl, my love, my happiness; and now lost to me forever." There was inexpressible sweetness in the sensation, mingled with exquisite pain. Aniela, too, had recovered from her emotion, but looked still frightened. I tried to draw her into conversation, speaking about her mother. I was partly successful; she seemed a little more at ease, and said,—

"Mamma will be very glad to see you."

I permitted myself a doubt as far as her mother was concerned, but listened to her voice with half-closed eyes; it was sweeter to me than any music.

We were conversing more freely every moment. My aunt was in excellent spirits,—first, because of seeing me once more at Ploszow, and also because she had seen Clara and got from her the promise of a concert. When leaving the artist she had met two other ladies, patronesses of charitable institutions, ascending the staircase bent on the same errand. They were too late, and that had put her in a high good-humor. She asked me a great many questions about Clara, who had made an excellent impression upon her. Towards the end of breakfast, to satisfy my aunt's curiosity, I had to say something about my travels. She was amazed to hear I had been as far as Iceland, and asked what it looked like; she then remarked,—

"One must be desperate to go to such places as that."

"Yes; I did not feel very cheerful when I went."

Aniela looked at me for a moment, and there was that hunted, half-frightened expression in her eyes again. If she had put her hand upon my naked heart she could not have given it a sharper pull. The more I had prepared myself for an exhibition of triumphant coldness and satisfaction at my disappointment, the more I felt crushed now by that angelic compassion. All my calculations and foresight had been put to naught. I supposed she could not help showing herself off as a married woman. And now I had to remind myself that she was married; but in the recollection there was no loathing, nothing but inexpressible sorrow.

It is in my nature that in every moral suffering I try to reopen my wounds. I wanted to do that even now by speaking about her husband; but I could not do it. It seemed to me cruel, almost a profanation. Instead of that I said that I should like to see her mother, if she were able to receive me. Aniela went to see, and presently came back and said, —

"Mamma will be pleased to see you."

We crossed to the other side of the house, my aunt going with us. I wanted to say a kind word to Aniela so as to put her more at ease; but my aunt was in the way; presently I thought it would be even better if I said it within my aunt's hearing. Near the door, leading into Pani Celina's rooms, I stopped and, turning to Aniela, said, —

"Give me your hand, my dear little sister."

Aniela put her hand into mine; I saw her eyes lighting up with gratitude for the words "little sister," and the pressure of her hand seemed to say: —

"Oh! let us be friends! let us forgive each other!"

"I hope you two will agree together," muttered my aunt.

"We shall, we shall; he is so good!" replied Aniela.

And truly, my heart was very full of good-will at that moment.

Entering Pani Celina's room, I greeted her very cordially, but she replied with a certain constraint, and I am sure she would have received me with still greater coldness had she not feared to offend my aunt. But I was not hurt by this; her resentment is quite justifiable. Maybe, in her mind, she connects me with the loss of her estate, and thinks all this would not have happened if I had acted differently. I found her much changed. For some time she has been confined to her invalid chair, on which they wheel her on fine days into the garden. Her face, always delicate, looked as if moulded in wax. There are still traces that show how beautiful she must have been, and at the same time so unhappy.

I asked after her health, and expressed the hope that, with the return of the fine weather, she would soon recover her strength. She listened with a sad smile, and shook her head; two tears rolled silently down her face.

Then, fixing her sad eyes upon me, she said, —

"You know Gluchow has been sold?"

This evidently is the thought ever present, — her continual sorrow and gnawing trouble.

When Aniela heard the question she grew very red. It was a painful blush, because a blush of shame and sorrow.

"Yes, I have heard," I said quickly. "Perhaps it can be recovered; if so, nothing is lost; and if not, you must submit to God's will."

Aniela cast a grateful glance at me, and Pani Celina said, —

"I have lost all hope."

It was not true; she still clung to the delusion that the estate might be recovered. Her eyes looked hungrily at me, waiting for the words which might confirm her secret hopes. I resolved to gratify her wish, and said, —

"It seems to have been a case of necessity, and I do not see how any one can be blamed for it. Yet there are no obstacles which cannot be overcome where there is a will and adequate means. Sometimes it has happened that a sale has been invalidated in law from some omission of formality."

By the bye, this was not strictly true; but I saw it was balm to Pani Celina's sore heart. I had also stood up for Kromitzki, without mentioning his name, which neither of the others had done in my presence.

To say the truth it was not generosity which prompted me, but rather a desire to conciliate Aniela, and show myself before her in the light of goodness and nobility.

And Aniela was grateful; for, when we had left the room, she came out to me, and, stretching out her hand, said, —

"Thank you for being so good to mamma."

For all answer I raised her hand to my lips.

My aunt too seemed touched by my goodness. I left her and, lighting a cigar, went into the park for a quiet stroll to collect my thoughts and impressions; but I met there the young doctor who was taking his morning constitutional. As I wished to conciliate every one at Ploszow, I went up to him, and asked him, with the special regard due to science and authority, what he thought about Pani Celina's chances of regaining her health. I saw that this flattered him a little, and gradually he began to lose some of his democratic stiffness, and enlarged upon the theme of Pani Celina's illness with the ready eagerness of a young scientist who has had no time yet to doubt his powers. In speaking, he used every now and then Latin expressions, as if addressing a colleague. His strong, healthy frame, a certain power of speech and eye impressed me favorably. I saw in him a type of that new generation Sniatynski at one time had spoken of to me. Walking along the avenues, we had one of the so-called intellectual conversations, which consist a great deal in quoting names of books and authors. Chwastowski is thoroughly acquainted with certain subjects; but I have read more, and this seemed to astonish him not a little. At moments he looked almost vexed, as if he considered it an encroachment upon his own territory that I, an aristocrat, should know so much about certain books and authors. But then again I won his approbation by the liberality of my opinions. My liberality consists merely in a kind of tolerance for other people's views, and looking upon them without party feeling; and that from a man of my position and wealth was sufficient to win over the young radical. At the end of our conversation we felt towards each other as men do who have understood each other, and agreed on many points.

Most likely I shall be the exception of the rule as regards Doctor Chwastowski. As in my country every nobleman has his particular Jew in whom he believes, — though he dislikes the race in general, — so every democrat has his aristocrat for whom he feels a special weakness.

When going away I asked Doctor Chwastowski about his brothers. He said that one of them had a brewery at Ploszow, which I knew already from my aunt's letter; a second had a bookshop at Warsaw; and a third, who had been at a mercantile school, had gone as assistant with Pan Kromitzki to the East.

"It is the brewer who has the best of it just now," he said; "but we all work, and in time shall win good positions. It was lucky our father lost his fortune; otherwise every one of us would sit on his bit of land 'glebæ adscripti,' and in the end lose it as my father did."

In spite of the preoccupation of my mind I listened with a certain interest. "There are, then," I said to myself, "people that are neither over-civilized nor steeped in ignorance. There are those that can do something and thus form the intermediate, healthy link between decay and barbarism." It is possible that this social strata mostly exists in bigger towns, where it is continually recruited by the influx of the sons of bankrupt noblemen, who adapt themselves to burgher traditions of work, and bring to it strong nerves and muscles. I then recalled what Sniatynski once said when I left him: "From such as you nothing good can come; your fathers must first lose all they have, else even your grandsons will not work." And here are Chwastowski's sons who take to it, and push on in the world by help of their own strong shoulders. I, too, perhaps, had I no fortune, should have to do something, and should acquire that energy of decision in which I have been wanting all my life.

The doctor left me presently as he had another patient at Ploszow, a young cleric from the Warsaw seminary, the son of one of the Ploszow peasants. He is in the last stage of consumption. My aunt has given him a room in one of the out-buildings, where she and Aniela look after him. When I heard of this I went to pay him a visit, and instead of the dying man I expected to see, I found a young, rather thin-looking lad, but bright and full of life. The doctor says it is the last flicker of the lamp. The young cleric was nursed by his mother, who, upon seeing me, overwhelmed me with a shower of gratitude copious enough to drown myself in.

Aniela did not visit the sick man that day, but remained with her mother. I saw her only at dinner, at which also the mother was present in her invalid's chair. It is only natural that Aniela should devote her time to her mother, and yet I fancy she does it partly to avoid being alone with me. In time our mutual relations will establish themselves upon an easier footing, but I quite understand that at first it will be a little awkward. Aniela has so much intelligence of heart, so much goodness and sensibility, that she cannot look upon our present position with indifference, and has not worldly experience enough to preserve an appearance of ease. This practice comes with later years, when the live spring of feelings begins to dry up and the mind acquires a certain conventionality.

I had let Aniela see there was no resentment in my heart towards her, and I shall not allude even to the past, and for that reason did not try to see her alone. In the evening during tea we discussed general topics. My aunt questioned me about Clara, who interests her very much. I told her all I knew about her, and from that we drifted into conversation about artists generally. My aunt looks upon them as people sent into the world by kind Providence to give performances for the benefit of charitable institutions. I maintained that artists, provided their hearts were pure and not filled with vanity and love of self, might be the happiest creatures in the world, as they are always in contact with something infinite and absolutely perfect. From life comes all evil, from art only happiness. This was, indeed, my point of view, supported by observation. Aniela agreed with me, and if I took note of the conversation it is because I was struck by a remark of Aniela's, simple in itself, but to me full of meaning. When we spoke about the contentment arising from art she said: "Music is a great consoler."

I saw in this involuntary confession that she is unhappy, and is conscious of it. Besides, in regard to that, I never had any doubts. Even the face is not the face of a happy woman. If anything, it is more beautiful than before,—apparently calm, even serene; but there is none of that light which springs from inward happiness, and there is a certain preoccupation that was not there formerly. In the course of the day I noticed that her temples have a slight yellow tint like that of ivory. I looked at her with an ever renewed delight, comparing her to the Aniela of the past. I could not get enough of this exchange of memories with reality. There is something so irresistibly attractive in Aniela that had I never seen her before, if she were among thousands of beautiful women and I were told to choose, I should go straight to her and say: "This one and no other." She answers so exactly to the feminine prototype every man carries in his imagination. I fancy she must have noticed that I watched and admired her.

I left at dusk. I was so shaken by the sensations of the day, so utterly different from all my preconceived ideas, that I had lost the power of dissecting my thoughts. I expected to find Pani Kromitska, and found Aniela; I put it down once more. God only knows what will be the consequence of this for us both. When I think of it I have the sensation of a great happiness, and also a slight disappointment. And yet I was right, theoretically, in expecting those psychical changes which necessarily take place in a woman after she is married, and I might easily be led to think she would show in some way that she was glad she had not chosen me. There is not another woman who would have denied herself that satisfaction of vanity. And as I know myself, my sensitiveness and my nerves, I could take my oath on it, that if such had been the case I should have been now full of bitterness, anger, and sarcasm, — but cured. In the mean while, things have fallen out differently, — altogether differently. She is a being of such unfathomable goodness and simplicity that the measure I have for goodness is not large enough for her.

What will happen next, what will happen to me or to her, I cannot say. My life might have run on quietly towards that ocean where all life is absorbed, — now it may run like a cataract down to a precipice. Let it be so. At the worst I can only be a little more unhappy, that is all. Until now I have not been lying on a bed of roses, with that consciousness of my useless life continually before me.

I do not remember; somebody, was it my father? said that there must always be something growing within us, that such is the law of nature. It is true. Even in the desert the forces of life hidden in the depth bring forth palms in the oasis.

21 April.

I live nominally at Warsaw, but have spent four consecutive days at Ploszow. Pani Celina is better, but the cleric Latyzs died the day before yesterday. Doctor Chwastowski says it was a splendid case of pulmonary consumption, and with difficulty conceals his satisfaction that he foretold the exact course of the disease up to the last hour. We had been to see the young man twelve hours before he died. He was quite merry with us, and full of hope because the fever had left him, which was only a sign of weakness. Yesterday, when sitting with Aniela on the veranda, the cleric's mother came up to tell us about his death, in her own quaint way, in which sorrow blended with quiet submission to the inevitable. In my pity for her, there was a great deal of curiosity, for up to now I had not much occasion to see anything of the inner life of the peasants. What quaint expressions they use! I tried to remember her words in order to note them down.

She embraced my knees, then Aniela's, after which she put the outside of her hands over her eyes, and began to wail: "O little Jesus, dear — O Maria, holiest of Virgins! He is dead, my poor lamb, dead! He was eager to see the Lord face to face; more eager than to stop with his little father and mother! Nothing could hold him back, not even the ladies' cares! Wine he had in plenty, and good food, and that could not save him; O little Jesus, dear! O holiest of Virgins! O Jesus mine!"

In her voice there was certainly a mother's sorrow! but what struck me most was the modulation of the voice, as if set to some local music. I never heard before the peasants lament their dead, but I am quite sure they all do it in more or less the same way, as if according to certain rules.

Tears were trembling on Aniela's eyelashes, and with that peculiar goodness only women are capable of, she began to inquire into the details of his death, guessing that it would soothe the poor woman to speak about it.

And in fact she began at once most eagerly: —

"When the priest had left him I said thus: 'Whether you die or not is in God's hands! You are nicely prepared now, so lay ye down and go to sleep.' Says he: 'Very well, little mother,' and fell in a doze, and I too; as, not reproaching the Lord with it, I had not had a proper sleep for three nights. At the first crow my old man comes in and wakes me; thus we were both sitting there, and he still asleep. I says to the old man: 'Is he gone?' and he says, 'Happen and he is gone.' I pulled him by the hand; he opened his eyes and said: 'I feel better now.' Then he remained quite still for about five *paters* and *aves*, and smiled toward the ceiling. This made me angry, and I says: 'Oh, you good-for-nothing, how can you laugh at my misery? But he only smiled at death, not at my misery, for he began breathing very hard, and that was all he did until the sun rose."

She began moaning again, and then invited us to come and see the body, as he was dressed already, and looked as beautiful as a picture. Aniela wanted to go at once, but I held her back; besides, the woman had already forgotten all about it, and began now lamenting her poverty. Her husband, it seems, had been a well-to-do peasant proprietor, but they had spent every bit of money upon their son's education. Acre after acre had been bought by the neighbors, and at present they had nothing but the hut, — no land whatever. One thousand two hundred roubles he had cost them. They had hoped to find a shelter for their old age with him at a parsonage, and now God had taken him. The old woman declared, with all the stoicism of the peasant, that they had already made their plans, and would go a begging. She seemed not afraid of it, and spoke of it with a kind of half-concealed satisfaction. She was only afraid the community might raise difficulties about the certificate, which, for some reason unknown to me, seemed to be necessary for the new profession. Hundreds of realistic details mingled with the calling upon the Lord Jesus, the Holy Virgin, and laments over the dead son. Aniela went into the house, and returned presently with some money for the woman. I arrested her hand; another idea, I thought good at the time, had crossed my mind.

"So you spent a thousand two hundred roubles on your son?" I said to the woman.

"That's so, please the gracious Pan. We thought when he got his church we would go and live with him. The Almighty willed it otherwise; no church for us now, but the church door" (place where beggars sit).

"I will give you the thousand two hundred roubles; you can buy some land if you like, and start fresh again."

I should have given it at once, but had not enough money by me; I intended to take it from my aunt, and told the woman to come back for it in an hour. She stared at me with wide-open eyes, without saying a word, and then with a cry fell down at my feet. But I got rid of her and her gratitude very soon, as she was in a hurry to be off to tell her husband the good news.

I remained alone with Aniela, who seemed moved deeply, and who repeated:—

"How good you are! how good you are!"

"There is not much goodness in it," I said in a careless manner. "I did not do it for these people I have seen for the first time in my life. I did it because you care for them,—to please you." It was true; they did not interest me more than any other people would in the same position, but I would have given ten times as much to please Aniela. I said it on purpose, as words like these said to a woman carry a deep meaning. It is almost the same as if I told her, "I would do anything for you, because you are everything to me." And, moreover, no woman can defend herself against a tacit confession such as this, or has any right to be offended. I had disguised the meaning, treating it as the most natural thing in the world; but Aniela perceived the drift, and lowering her eyes in evident confusion, said: "I must go back now to mamma," and left me alone.

I am quite aware that in acting thus I introduce a disturbing element into Aniela's soul. I perceive, too, with surprise, that if, on the one hand, my conscience cries out against this wilful destroying of the peace of the one being for whom I would give my life, on the other hand, it causes me a savage delight, as if thereby I satisfied man's innate instinct of destruction. I have also the conviction that no consciousness of evil, or sting of conscience, will stop me. I am too headstrong to let anything stand in my way, especially in presence of that powerful, inexpressible spell she has cast upon me. I am now as that Indian who threw away his oar, and gave himself up to fate. I do not reflect now that it was my fault, that all might have been so different, and that

I had only to stretch out my hand to secure the happiness I am now yearning for in vain. But it could not be otherwise. I have come to the conclusion that generations which had lost all vital power, have made me what I am; that nothing remains but to cast away the oars and let myself drift with the current.

This morning we three — my aunt, Aniela, and I — went to the funeral of the young cleric.

It was a strange sight, this village procession headed by the priest, the coffin on a cart, followed by a crowd of peasants, men and women who were singing a tune sad and weird as if set to some Chaldean music. At the furthest end, the men and women were talking to each other in a drawling, half-sleepy way. Going along, among the rowan trees, the procession came now and then into the glare of the sun, and then the kerchiefs flashed into flames of blue, and red, and yellow, which but for the coffin and the incense of juniper berries, made the procession rather look like a wedding than a funeral. Death does not seem to make much impression upon the rustic mind; perhaps they regard it in the light of an everlasting holiday. As we stood by the open grave, I noticed their faces following the ceremony with concentrated attention and curiosity; but I saw no trace of thoughtfulness or reflection at the inexorable end, after which begins the great, terrible Unknown.

I looked at Aniela as she stooped for a handful of soil to throw upon the lowered coffin. She was paler than usual, and with the sun shining upon her I could read the transparent features as an open book. I was certain she was thinking of her own death. To me it seemed simply monstrous, a horrible improbability, that this face so full of expression, so full of life and charming individuality, should at some time be stony white and remain in eternal darkness.

And as if a sudden frost had nipped all my thoughts, I grew suddenly conscious that the first ceremony I assisted at with Aniela was a funeral. As a person in long sickness, having lost faith in medicine, turns to quack doctors and wise women, so the sick soul, doubting everything, still clings to certain superstitions.

Probably no one is so near the gulf of mysticism as the absolute sceptic. Those who have lost faith in religious and sociological ideals, those whose belief in the power of science and the human intellect is shaken, that whole mass of highly cultured people, uncertain of their way, deprived of all dogmas, hopelessly struggling in the dark, drift more and more towards mysticism. It seems to spring up everywhere, — the usual reaction of a society whose life is based upon positivism, the overthrow of ideals, empty pleasures, and soulless striving after gain. The human spirit begins to burst its shell, which is too narrow, too much like a stock exchange. One epoch draws to an end, and then appears a simultaneous evolution in all directions. It has struck me often with amazement that, for instance, the more recent great writers seem not to know how very close upon mysticism they are. Some of them are conscious of it, and confess so openly. In every book I opened lately, I found, not the human soul, will, and personal passions, but merely fatal forces with all the characteristics of terrible beings, independent of personal manifestations, living alone within themselves, like Goethe's "Mother."

As regards myself, I too come near the brink. I see it and am not afraid. The abyss attracts; personally it attracts me so much that if I could I would go to the very bottom, and will some time when I am able.

28 April.

I intoxicate myself with the life at Ploszow, the daily sight of Aniela, and forget that she belongs to somebody else. Kromitzki, who is somewhere at Baku, or further still, appears to me as something unreal, a being deprived of real existence, something bad that might come down upon us, as for instance, death, but of which one does not think continually. But yesterday something happened to bring him before my mind. It was a small and apparently most natural incident. Aniela received at breakfast two letters. My aunt asked whether they were from her husband, and she replied, "Yes." Hearing that, I felt the sensation a condemned man may feel when they rouse him from a sweet dream in order to tell him to have his hair cut for the guillotine. I saw my whole misfortune more distinctly than ever before, and the sensation remained with me the whole day, especially as my aunt, quite unconsciously, of course, was bent upon torturing me further. Aniela wanted to put off the reading of the letters, but my aunt insisted upon her opening them, and presently inquired how Kromitzki was.

"Thank you, aunty, he is very well."

"And how are his affairs going on?"

"Thank God! he writes that everything prospers beyond expectation."

"When does he think of coming back?"

"He says as soon as he can possibly manage."

And I, with my sensitiveness, had to listen to these questions and answers. If my aunt and Aniela had started unexpectedly a quite improbable cynical conversation it could not have shocked me more. The first time since my arrival at Ploszow I felt something like resentment towards Aniela. "Have a little mercy at least, and do not speak of that man in my presence; do not return thanks for being asked after him, and say 'Thank God!' because he is prosperous," I thought. In the mean time she had opened the second letter, and looking at the date, said: "It has been written at an earlier date;" then began to read. I looked at the bowed head, the parting of the hair, the drooping lashes — and it seemed to me that the reading lasted very long. I thought what a world of mutual interests and aims bound these two together, and that for some indispensable reason they must feel that they belonged to each other. I felt that I had no part in it, and that by force of circumstances I should always be outside her life even if I won her love. Up to now I had felt the depth of my misery as one sees the depth of a precipice veiled by clouds. Now the mist lifted, I looked down and comprehended its whole extent.

My nature is so constituted that under great presure it resists. Up to the present my love had not dared to ask for anything, but at this moment hatred began to clamor loudly for the abolition of merciless laws, those ties and bondages. Aniela did not read many minutes, but during that time I ran through a whole gamut of tortures, because other thoughts relating to my self-analysis and criticism were haunting me. I said to myself that the agitation, the very bitterness I felt, were nothing but the ridiculous characteristics of female ill-humor. How is it possible to live with nerves such as mine? If such a simple thing as a letter from the husband to his wife makes you lose your balance, what will happen when he himself comes to claim her?

I said to myself: "I will kill him!" and at the same time I felt the ridiculousness and folly of the answer.

Aniela having finished her letters noticed at once that something was amiss, and looked at me with troubled eyes. Hers is one of those sweet dispositions that cannot bear to see unfriendly faces, or live in an atmosphere of cold displeasure. This springs from a great tenderness of heart. I remember how uneasy she used to be when first she witnessed the disputes between my aunt and Chwastowzki. Now she was evidently ill at ease. She began to speak about the concert and Clara, but her eyes seemed to say: "What have I done, what is the matter with you?" I merely replied by a cold glance, not being able to forgive her either the letters or her conversation with my aunt. After breakfast I rose at once and said I was obliged to go back to Warsaw.

My aunt wanted me to stop to dinner; after which, according to our agreement, we were to start together for the concert. But I pleaded some business; the truth was I wanted to be alone. I gave orders for the carriage to be ready, and then my aunt remarked: —

"I should like to show some gratitude to Miss Hilst, and thought of inviting her to Ploszow for the day."

Evidently my aunt considers an invitation to Ploszow such a great reward that she doubted whether it would not be out of all proportion.

After a moment's pause she began again: —

"If I were quite sure that she is of a proper standing."

"Miss Hilst is a personal friend of the queen of Roumania," I replied, a little impatiently; "and if there be any honor, it will be altogether on our side."

"Well, well," muttered my aunt.

"You will come with us to the concert?" I said, turning to Aniela.

"I am afraid not. I shall have to remain with mamma; and besides, I have some letters to write."

"Oh! if it is a question of wifely tenderness I will not insist."

This ironical remark gave me a momentary relief. "Let her be aware that I am jealous," I thought; "she herself, her mother, and my aunt belong to those women of the angelic kind, who do not believe there can be any evil in the world. Let her understand that I love her, become familiar with the thought, troubled by it, and fight it. To bring into her soul a strange, decomposing element, a ferment like this, is half the battle. We shall see what will happen afterwards."

It was a momentary but great relief, and very much like a wicked delight. But presently, when alone in the carriage, I felt angry with myself and disgusted, — disgusted because I became conscious of the littleness of all I had thought and felt, based as it was upon overstrung and fanciful nerves worthy an hysterical woman, not a man. It was a heavy journey, far heavier than the one when after my return from abroad I went the first time to Ploszow. I was reflecting upon that terrible incapacity for life which casts its shadow upon my existence and the existence of those like me, and came to the conclusion that its main source is the feminine element which predominates in our character. I do not mean by this that we are physically effeminate or wanting in manly courage. No! it is something quite different. Courage and daring we are not deficient in; but as regards psychical elements, every one of us is a she, not a he. There is in us a lack of the synthetic faculty which distinguishes things that are important from those that are not. The least matter discourages, hurts, and repulses us; in consequence of which we sacrifice very great things for small ones. My past is a proof thereof. I sacrificed inexpressible happiness, my future and the future of the beloved woman, because I had read in my aunt's letter that Kromitzki wished to marry her. My nerves took the bit between their teeth, and carried me where I did not wish to go. This was nothing but a disease of the will. But it is a feminine disease, not a masculine one. Is it to be wondered at that I act as an hysterical woman? It is a misfortune I brought with me into the world, to which whole generations have contributed their share, as also the conditions of life in which we exist.

The shaking myself thus free from all responsibility did not give me any relief. When I arrived at Warsaw I intended to call upon Clara, but was prevented by a severe headache; which got better towards evening before my aunt came up.

She found me already dressed, and we drove together to the concert, which was a great success. Clara's fame had attracted the whole musical and intelligent world, and the charitable purpose the aristocratic circles. I saw many people there I knew, among them Sniatynski and his wife. The concert room was crowded. But I was out of humor, and everything irritated me. I do not know why, but I felt afraid Clara's performance would be a failure. When she appeared on the platform a programme clung to the folds of her dress; I thought it would make her appear ridiculous. She herself in full evening dress seemed to me more like a stranger than a friend. I involuntarily asked myself whether it was the same Clara I was so intimate with. When the hearty applause had ceased she sat down to the piano, and I acknowledged to myself that she had a noble and artistic presence, full of simplicity and quite free of any affectation. On all faces there was the concentrated attention of people who have no understanding of art, but like to pass for connoisseurs and judges. She played Mendelssohn's concerto, which I know by heart, — but whether it was the thought that much was expected from her, or that the unusually enthusiastic reception had moved her, she played worse than I had ever heard her. I was sorry for it and looked at her with astonishment; our eyes met for a moment. The expression of my face put the final touch to her confusion, and I heard a few dim notes without force or expression. I was quite sure now she would fail. Never had the piano, with its lack of continuity, its sound smothered by the acoustic properties of the room, seemed to me a more miserable instrument. At times it seemed as if I heard the sharp, staccato sounds of a harp. Presently Clara recovered her self-possession, but upon the whole I thought she had played but indifferently. I was very much surprised indeed when after she had finished there rose such a storm of applause as I had not heard even in Paris, where Clara was received with exceptional enthusiasm. During the short pause, amateurs and professionals began discussing the music, and in their animated faces I read perfect satisfaction. The cheering lasted until Clara reappeared on the platform. She stepped forth with downcast eyes, and I who could read her face saw what she wanted to express: "You are very kind, and I thank you for it; but it was not good and I feel inclined to cry." I too had applauded with the rest, for which I received a passing glance full of reproach. Clara loves her art too much to be gratified by undeserved applause.

I felt sorry for her, and should have liked to say a few encouraging words, but the continued cheering did not permit her to leave the platform. She sat down again and played Beethoven's Sonata in cis-moll, which was not on the programme. There is, I believe, no composition in the whole world that shows with the same distinctness the soul torn by tragic conflict; especially in the third part of the Sonata, the *Presto-agitato.* The music evidently responded to the tune of Clara's soul, and certainly harmonized with my own disposition, for never had I heard Beethoven interpreted and understood like this before. I am not a musician, but I suppose even musicians do not know how much there is in that Sonata. I cannot find another word than "oppressiveness" to describe the sensation wrought upon the audience. One had a feeling as if mystical rites were being performed; there rose before me a vast desert, not of this world, weird and unutterably sad, without shape, half lit up by a ghostly moon, in the midst of which hopeless despair waited and sobbed and tore its hair. It was terrible and impressive because so unearthly; and yet irresistibly attractive, — never had my spirit come in such close proximity to the infinite. It was almost an hallucination. I imagined that in the shapeless desert, in the dusk of a world of shadows, I was searching for somebody dearer to me than the whole world, one without whom I could not and would not live, and I searched with the conviction that I should have to search forever and never find what I was looking for. My heart was so oppressed that at times I could scarcely breathe. I paid no attention to the mechanical part of the execution, which no doubt was as perfect as the expression.

All in the room seemed under the same spell, not excepting Clara herself.

When she left off playing she remained for a moment with uplifted head and eyes, lips slightly parted, and face very pale. And it was not a mere concert effect, it was real inspiration and forgetfulness of self.

There was a great hush in that crowd, as if they expected something, or were benumbed by sorrow, or tried to catch the last echo of sobbing despair, carried away by a wind from the other world.

Presently there happened what probably never happened in a concert room before. A great tumult arose, and such an outcry as if a catastrophe were threatening the whole audience. Several musicians and reporters approached the platform. I saw their heads bowed over Clara's hands, she had tears on her eyelashes, her face looked still inspired, but calm and serene. I went with the others to press her hands.

From the first moment of our acquaintance Clara had always addressed me in French; now for the first time, returning the pressure of my hand, she said in German:

"Haben Sie mich verstanden?"

"Ja," I replied, "und ich war sehr unglucklich!" And it was true.

The continuation of the concert was one great triumph. After the performance Sniatynski and his wife carried Clara off to their house. I had no wish to go there. When I reached home, I felt so tired that without undressing I threw myself upon the sofa, and remained there an hour without moving, yet not asleep.

After a long time I became conscious that I had been thinking about the young cleric's funeral, Aniela, and death. I rung for lights, and then began to write.

29 April.

Kromitzki's letters have stirred me to such a degree that I cannot get over the impression. My unreasonable resentment towards Aniela is passing, and the more I feel how undeserved was my harshness, the more contrite I become, and the more tenderly I think of her. Yet more clearly than ever I see how these two are bound by the power of a simple fact. Since yesterday I have been in the clutches of these thoughts, and that is the reason I did not go to Ploszow. There I am obliged to keep watch upon myself and to put on an appearance of calmness, and at present I could not do it. Everything within me — thoughts, feelings, nerves — has risen up in revolt against what has been done. I do not know whether there can be a more desperate state of mind than when we do not agree with something, protest with every fibre of heart and brain, and at the same time feel powerless in presence of an accomplished fact. I understand that this is only a foretaste of what is awaiting me in the future. There is nothing to be done, — nothing. She is married, is Pani Kromitzka; she belongs to him, will always belong to him; and I who cannot consent, for to do so would mean losing my own self, am obliged to consent. I might as well protest against the earth turning round as against that other law which bids a woman stand by her husband. Does this mean that I ought to respect that law? How can I submit when my whole being cries out against it? At moments I feel inclined to go away, but I understand perfectly that beyond this woman the world has for me as much meaning as death, — that is, nothingness; moreover, I know beforehand that I shall not go, because I could not muster strength enough to do so. Sometimes I have thought that human misery goes far beyond human imagination, — imagination has its limits, and misery, like the vast seas, appears to be without end. It seems to me that I am floating on those seas. But no, — there is still something for me to do.

I read once, in Amiel's memoirs, that the deed is only the crystallized matter of thought. But thoughts may remain in the abstract, — not so feelings. Theoretically I was conscious of it before; it is only now I have come to prove it actually on myself. From the time of my arrival at Ploszow until now, I have never clearly and distinctly said to myself that I wanted to win Aniela's love, but it was merely a question of words. In reality I know that I wanted her, and want her still. Every look of mine, every word, and all my actions are tending that way. Affection which does not include desire and action is a mere shadow. Let it be understood, — I want her. I want to be for Aniela the most beloved being, as she is to me. I want to win her love, all her thoughts, her soul; and I do not intend to put any limit to my desires. I shall do everything my heart dictates, and use all means my intelligence sees most efficient to win her. I shall take from Kromitzki as much of Aniela as I can; I shall take her from him altogether if she be willing. In this way I shall have an aim in life; shall know why I wake up in the morning, take nourishment during the day, and recuperate myself in sleep. I shall not be happy; for I could be happy only if she were exclusively my own, and I could crush the man who had her before me. But I shall have something at least to live for. It will be my salvation. And this is not a resolution taken upon the spur of the moment; it is only a translation into words of all the forces that work within me, — the will and the desires which belong to the feeling and make an indivisible part of it.

I throw all my scruples to the winds. Even the fear that Aniela might be unhappy loving me must give way before the great truth, great as the universe, that the presence of Love fills the life, gives sustenance to it, and is a hundred thousand times worth more than emptiness and nothingness of existence.

Thousands of years ago it was known to the world that virtue and righteousness alone give power to life; that emptiness and nothingness dwell in the realm of evil. The moment when that dear head rests on my breast, when the beloved lips meet mine, truth and goodness will be with us. In the midst of doubts which crowd my brain, that one truth shines clearly, — of this I can say I believe in it. At last I have found something certain in life. I know perfectly what a gulf there is between my belief and the small conventional moralities created for every-day use. I know that to

Aniela it will be a strange, fearsome world; but I will take her by the hand and lead her there, because I can tell her with sincere conviction that there are truth and goodness.

I find great solace in these thoughts. The greater part of the day passed miserably enough, because of the consciousness of my impotency to overcome the obstacles that stand in our, mine and Aniela's, way. The thought crossed my mind: "Suppose, after all, she loves her husband?"

Fortunately for me, a visit from Doctor Chwastowski interrupted my train of thoughts. He had come from Ploszow to consult with one of the physicians who at some time had attended Pani Celina. Before going back he had come to see me. He said Pani Celina was still neither better nor worse, but Pani Kromitzka was confined to her room with a severe headache. Then he began to speak about Aniela, and I listened with pleasure, as it seemed in some way to make up for the loss of seeing her. He spoke intelligently enough, for a young man of so little experience. He said he had made it a rule to look mistrustingly upon mankind in general, not because he thought it the right point of view, but because it was the safest. As to Pani Kromitzka, he was quite sure hers was a nature of exceptional goodness and nobility. He spoke of her with a scarcely disguised enthusiasm, and I had some suspicion he felt more than admiration for her. But this did not trouble me in the least; there is too great a distance between her and this young medical student. On the contrary, I felt pleased that he appreciated her, and asked him to stop as long as he could; his presence did me good, as it kept me from thinking.

In the course of our conversation I asked about his plans for the future. He replied that first he must save some money in order to go abroad and see something of foreign hospitals; afterwards he intended to settle at Warsaw.

"What do you understand by settling at Warsaw?"

"Work at some of the hospitals, and a possible practice."

"And then you will get married, I suppose?"

"I suppose so; but there is plenty of time for that."

"Unless you meet somebody that subjugates your will; as a doctor you know that love is a physiological necessity."

Young Chwastowski wants to show himself off as a sober-minded man above human weaknesses; so he only shrugged his broad shoulders, smoothed his short-cropped head, and said: "I acknowledge the necessity; but do not intend to allow it to occupy too large a space in my life."

He looked very knowing, but I replied gravely: "Considering somewhat deeper the question of feeling, who knows whether it be worth while to live for anything else?"

Chwastowski pondered over this a little while.

"No," he said, "I do not agree with you. There are many other objects in life, — for instance, science, or even social duties. I do not say anything against matrimony; a man ought to marry for himself as well as to have children. But matrimony is one thing, and continual love-making another."

"What is the difference between them?"

"The difference is obvious, sir. We are like ants constructing an ant-hill. We have our work to do, and not much time to spare for love and women. That is all very well for those who cannot work, or who do not want to do anything."

Saying this he looked like a man who speaks in the name of all that is strongest in the country, and expresses himself well. I looked with a certain satisfaction at this healthy specimen of mankind, and acknowledged that, except for a certain touch of youthful arrogance, he spoke very sensibly.

It is quite true that woman and love do not occupy a large space in the life of those who work, and those who have before them great undertakings and serious aims. The peasant marries because such is the custom, and he wants a housekeeper. There is very little sentiment in him, although poets and novelists want us to believe the contrary. The man of science, the statesman, the leader, the politician devote only a small part of their life to woman. Artists are exceptional. Their profession brings them in touch with love, for art exists through love and woman. Generally, it is only in rich communities that woman reigns supreme and fills the life of those who have no serious work in hand. She encompasses all their thoughts, becomes the leading motive of their actions, and the exclusive aim of their exertions. And it cannot be otherwise. There is myself for instance. The community to which I belong is not as rich as others, but personally I am rich. These riches prevented me from doing anything, and I have no fixed aim in life. It might be different had I been born an Englishman or a German, and not been handicapped by that *improductivité Slave.* No one of the compound active principles of civilization attracts me or fills up the void, for the simple reason that civilization is faint and permeated with scepticism. If it feels its end is drawing near and doubts itself, why should I believe in it and devote to it my life? Generally speaking, I live as if in mid air, with no firm hold upon the earth. If my disposition were cold and dry, if I were dull of mind or merely sensuous, I could have limited my life to mere vegetation or animal enjoyment. But it happened otherwise. I brought with me into the world a bright intellect, a luxuriant organism, and vital powers of no mean degree. These forces had to find an outlet, and they could find it only in the love for a woman. There remained nothing else for me. My whole misfortune is that, as a child of a diseased civilization, I grew up crooked; therefore love. too. came to me crooked.

Simplicity of mind would have given me happiness, but what is the use to speak of it? The hunchback, too, would be glad to get rid of his hump, but he cannot, because hump-backed he came from his mother's womb. My hump was caused by the abnormal state of civilization that brought me into the world. But straight or crooked, I must love, and I will.

4 May.

My reason is now altogether subservient to feeling, and is, in truth, like the driver who passively clings to his box, and can do nothing but watch whether the vehicle will go to pieces. I went back to Ploszow a few days ago, and all I say and all I do are only the tactics of love. He is a clever doctor — is Chwastowski — to prescribe for Aniela exercise in the park. I found her there this morning. There are moments when the feeling in my heart — though I am always conscious of it — manifests itself with such extraordinary power that it almost frightens me by its magnitude. Such a moment I had to-day, when at a sudden turn of the road I met Aniela. Never had she appeared to me more beautiful, more desirable, and more as if she were my own. This is exactly the only woman in the world who by virtue of certain natural forces, scarcely known by name, was to attract me, as the magnet attracts iron, to reign over me, to attach me to her, and become the aim and completion of my life. Her voice, her shape, her glances intoxicate me. To-day, when I thus unexpectedly met her, I thought it was not only her personal charm she carried with her, but the charm of that early morning, that spring and serene weather, the joy of all the birds and plants, — in fact, she seemed to be more an incarnation of beauty and nature than a woman. And it struck me then that, if nature had created her thus that she should react upon me more than upon any other man, nature had meant her to be mine, and that my right had been trodden under foot by this marriage. Who knows whether all the crookedness of the world does not spring from the non-fulfilment of certain laws, and whether that be not the cause of the imperfectness of life?

They are wrong who say that love is blind. On the contrary, nothing — not the smallest detail — escapes its eyes; it sees everything in the beloved being, notices everything; but melts it all in one flame in the great and simple "I love." When I came close to Aniela, I noticed that her eyes were brilliant as if from recent slumber; that on her face and the light print dress fell the golden rays of the morning sun filtering through the young leaves; her hair was tied in a loose knot, and the flowing morning dress showed the outline of her shoulders and supple waist, and in its very carelessness had a certain freshness, which enhanced a thousandfold her charm. It did not escape my notice how much smaller than usual she looked among the tall elm trees of the avenue, — almost a child; in brief, nothing escaped me, but all my observations changed into the rapture of one who loves deliriously. She returned my morning greeting with some confusion. For the last few days she seems afraid of me, for I hypnotize her with every glance and word. Her peace of thought is already disturbed, and the ferment has entered her soul. She cannot help seeing I love her, but does not own it, not even to herself. Sometimes I have a sensation as if I were holding a bird in my hand, and heard its heart palpitating under my fingers. We walked together in embarrassed silence, which I did not care to interrupt. I know this uneasiness is oppressive to her; but it renders her my accomplice, and brings me nearer to the end. In the silence which surrounded us not a sound was audible but the crunching of the gravel under our feet, and the whistling of the golden orioles, which are plentiful in the park. I started at last a conversation. I directed it to suit my plans, for however much my mind is closed against influences that have no bearing upon my feeling, within their sphere I have a well-nigh redoubled presence of mind, — an acuteness of perception, as have those plunged into a hypnotic trance, and in a given direction see more clearly than people in their normal state. We passed speedily on to personal topics. I spoke about myself in the confidential tone in which one speaks to those nearest, who alone have the right to know everything. There sprung up between us a whole world of mutual understanding and thoughts, common to us both. Since such a bond ought to exist by virtue of marriage, — between her and her husband, — I was leading her towards spiritual faithlessness by such gradual steps that she scarcely could be aware of it.

Nevertheless, the subtle nature perceived the drift. But I had taken her by the hand, and led her; yet while leading, I felt a moral resistance. I was fully aware the resistance would grow stronger if I pushed much farther, and she perceived the danger. But I saw too that I was gaining ground, and that step by step I could lead her where I wanted.

In the meantime I spoke on purpose about the past.

"Do you remember," I said, "how in the days gone by — those happier days — you asked me why I did not remain in the country, and turn my abilities to some use. It was when I came home late, and you were sitting up for me. I cannot tell you even what power you had over me. I could not then begin to work, I had to go away; then came my father's death. But I never forgot those words. I have come back now to live and to work at home, and if I ever achieve anything it will be owing to you, — your influence will be the source of my achievement."

There ensued a momentary silence between us, broken only by the whistling of the orioles. Aniela was evidently searching for a reply, and at last said, —

"I cannot believe that a man like you should not be able to find a more weighty inducement. You know very well it is your duty, and what is past is past, and now everything is changed."

"I am not so sure of that," I replied. "Perhaps, when once I start, I shall find in the work itself some pleasure and encouragement. But a man like me, who, in spite of what you are saying about duty, has never been fully conscious of it, must have some personal reason for changing the whole tenor of his life; and the more he is unhappy, the more he wants that personal inducement. Why should I tell you what is not true? I am not happy. The consciousness of duty is a beautiful thing, no doubt; but unfortunately I do not have it. You, who are so much better, nobler than I, could have taught it me; but it was fated otherwise. But even now, if only for the sake of those times when you wanted me to do something, I can do it still if you will help me."

Aniela hastened her steps, as if she wanted to return home, and said almost in a whisper, —

"Do not say that, Leon; please do not. You know I cannot do it."

"Why can you not? Do not understand me wrongly. You are and always will be a very dear sister to me. It is only this I wanted you to know."

Aniela almost feverishly gave me her hand, which I raised reverently to my lips.

"Yes, I will be that, — always that," she replied quickly.

And I saw what a heavy weight I had lifted from her mind; how that one word "sister" had calmed and moved her. This made me recover all my self-possession; for, when I had touched her hand with my lips, it almost grew dark before my eyes, and I wanted to take her in my arms, and tell her the whole truth. In the mean time Aniela's face had grown brighter and more cheerful. As we came nearer the house, her trouble seemed to slip off from her, and seeing how much I had gained by taking this way with her, I continued in the same strain of friendly conversation.

"You see, little sister, there is such a void around me. My father is no more; my aunt is a saintly woman; but she does not understand new times and new people. Her ideas are different from mine. I shall never marry, — think only what a lonely man I am. I have nobody near me, — nobody to share my thoughts, my plans, or my sorrows; nothing but loneliness around me. Is it not natural that I look for sympathy where I might expect to find it? I am like the crippled beggar, who stands waiting at the gate until they give him a small coin. At this moment the beggar is very poor indeed, and he stands under your window, and begs for a little friendliness, sympathy, and pity. A very small coin will satisfy him, — you will not refuse him that, Aniela, will you?"

"I will not, Leon; I will not, since you are so unhappy —"

Her voice broke, and she began to tremble. Again I had to make a great effort to restrain myself; and as I looked at her, something like unshed tears took me by the throat.

"Aniela! little Aniela!" I exclaimed, not knowing what to say.

But she waved her hands, as if to ward me off, and said, her eyes full of tears, —

"Let me go — I shall be better presently. I can not go back like this; let me go."

And she went swiftly away.

"Aniela, forgive me!" I called after her.

My first impulse was to follow her, but I thought it would be better to leave her to herself, and I only followed her with my eyes. She went quickly back into the avenue we had crossed together, and then turned into a side path. Sometimes the foliage hid her from my eyes, then again the light dress lit up by the sun appeared between the trees. From the distance I saw how she shut and opened her sunshade, as if trying by physical exertion to overcome her emotion. During all that time I inwardly called her the most endearing names that love could invent. I could not go away without looking once more into her eyes; but I had a long time to wait. She came at last, but passed quickly by, as if afraid of another shock; she only smiled at me in passing, with angelic sweetness, and said, "I am all right again."

On her face, pink with exercise, there was no trace of tears. I remained alone, and a mad, indescribable joy got hold of me, hope filled my heart, and there was one thought dominating everything: "She loves me, she fights against it, does not yield, deludes herself — but loves." At times, the most self-possessed of men, in the superabundance of some emotion, comes near the brink of madness. I was so near it then that I felt a wild desire to hide myself in the deepest recess of the woods, tear the grass, and shout at the top of my voice, "She loves me!" At present, when I am able to think more calmly of this joy, I find it was composed of various active forces. There was the joy of the artist who sees that a masterpiece he has begun is progressing satisfactorily; maybe also the satisfaction of the spider when the fly comes near the web; but there was also kindness, pity, great tenderness, and all that over which angels rejoice, as the poet has it. I felt sorry the defenceless little thing should fall into my hands; and that pity increased the love, and the desire to conquer Aniela. I felt also a sting of conscience that I had deceived her, and yet I had the consciousness that I had spoken the truth when I asked for her sympathy and friendship. I want it as I want my health. But I did not confess to all my desires, because the time for it has not yet come. I did not tell her the whole truth, so as not to frighten the timid soul. I shall come to it by and by, and the road which leads towards it in the straightest line is the best.

10 May.

The weather is still serene, and everything is serene between us. Aniela is calm and happy. She thoroughly believes in what I said, and, as I did not ask for anything but sisterly affection, and her conscience approves, she allows her heart to follow its dictates. I alone know that it is a loyal way of deceiving herself and her husband; for under cover of sisterly affection there is another feeling, the growth of which I am watching daily. Of course I do not intend to undeceive her until the feeling grows too strong for her. By and by she will be enveloped in a flame which neither will, nor consciousness of duty, nor the modesty of the woman white as a swan, will be able to keep under control. Constantly the thought dwells with me that since I love her most, mine is the higher right. What can there be more logical or more true? The unwritten code of ethics of all people, of whatever faith, says that the mutual belonging of man and woman to each other is based upon love.

But to-day I am so restful and happy that I prefer to feel rather than to reason. There is now between us a great cordiality, ease, and intimacy. How we were made for each other, cling to each other, and how the dear little thing delights in the warmth, delusive warmth of brotherly affection. Never since my return have I seen her so cheerful. Formerly when I looked at her she reminded me of Shakspeare's "Poor Tom." A nature like hers wants love, as her body wants air to breathe. Kromitzki, occupied with speculations, does not love her enough, perhaps does not know what love means. She might rightly say with Shakspeare, "Poor Tom 's acold." When I think of this my heart is stirred, and I make a silent vow that she shall never feel cold as long as I live.

If our love were wrong there could not be within us such peace. That Aniela does not call it by its proper name means nothing; it is there all the same. The whole day passed for us like an idyl. Formerly I disliked Sundays; now I find that a Sunday, from morning until night, may be like a poem, especially in the country. Soon after breakfast, we went to church in time for the early mass. My aunt followed in our rear; even Pani Celina, profiting by the fine weather, was wheeled thither in her Bath chair. There were not many people in church, as most of them go later for high mass. Sitting on the bench by Aniela's side, I had the blissful illusion that I was sitting with my affianced wife. From time to time I looked at the sweet, dear profile, at the hands which were resting on the desk before her, and the concentration in her face and bearing gradually infected me. My senses went to sleep, my thoughts became purer, and I loved her at that moment with an ideal love, because I felt more than ever how different she was from any other woman, how infinitely better and purer.

For a long time I had not felt anything like what I felt in this quiet village church. Added to Aniela's presence there was the impressive dignity of the church itself, the soft, flickering light of the candles in the dim recess of the altar, shafts of colored light coming through the windows, the chirping sparrows, and the still mass. All this, with the dreaminess of an early morning, had something unutterably soothing. My thoughts began to flow as evenly as the incense at the altar. Nobler feelings stirred within me, and a desire to sacrifice my own self. An inward voice began to remonstrate: —

"Do not disturb that transparent water; respect its purity."

When the mass came to an end, and we left the church, I saw, to my greatest amazement, both the Latyszes crouching near the church gate, with wooden plates in their hands, asking for alms. My aunt, who knew about my gift, grew very angry upon seeing them there, and began to abuse them roundly. But the old woman, still holding out her wooden plate, and not at all abashed, said quietly: —

"His lordship's generosity is one thing, and God's will is another. We must not go against the Lord's will. When the little Lord Jesus told us to sit here, we must, now and forever and ever, Amen."

There was nothing to say against this kind of reasoning; especially that "forever and ever, Amen," imposed upon me, to such an extent that I gave them some money for the oddity of the thing. These people at the bottom of their hearts believe in fate, which they dress up in Christian forms, and submit to it blindly. These Latyszes, to whom I gave a thousand two hundred roubles, are now better off than they ever were in their lives, and yet they went to sit at the church gates because such was their fate, — which the old woman translated into the "will of God."

When we were wending our way homewards, the bells were ringing for high mass. On the road appeared groups of men and women. From the more distant hamlets one could see them going Indian file along the narrow paths amid the corn, which, though still green, had shot up to a considerable height, owing to the early spring. As far as the eye could reach, in the pure translucid atmosphere, the bright colored kerchiefs of the girls appeared above the wheat-fields like so many poppy flowers. By the bye, there is nowhere in Europe such a breadth of atmosphere as in Poland. What struck me most of all was the distinctly Sunday character of the day, not in the people alone, but also in nature. It is true the weather was splendid, but it seemed as if the wind were hushed because it was Sunday; even the corn did not rock, not a leaf shook on the poplars, the stillness was perfect; yet there was the cheerfulness of the Sunday in the festive garments, and in the dancing sunbeams.

I explained to Aniela how, from an artistic point of view, those bright spots harmonized with the landscape and melted in the distance into a blue haze. Then we began to talk about the peasants. I confessed that I did not see anything but a crowd of more or less picturesque models; but Aniela looks at them from a quite different point of view. She began telling me many characteristic traits, some sad, and some amusing, and while talking grew very animated, and at the same time as lovely as a summer's dream.

The conversation again drifted towards the old couple we had left sitting under the church gate, and especially the old woman, whose reasoning had amused us so much. I began comparing her position to my own. As my aunt remained with Pani Celina, whom the servant wheeled along at a certain distance behind, I could with freedom allude to our last conversation in the park.

"Not long ago," I said, "I asked you for alms, and you bestowed them on me. I see now that this does not bind me to anything, and I may again hold out my wooden platter at the church gate."

"Eh! to ask other charitable souls for the same," replied Aniela. "Aunty is going to invite one charitable soul to Ploszow, I understand."

"If it is Miss Hilst you mean, she is too big to find room in a single heart; it wants three at least to hold her," but Aniela did not leave off teasing, and shaking her little finger at me, said: —

"It is a suspicious case, very suspicious."

"At present there is no ground for suspicion," I replied. "My heart is a repository of brotherly feelings, and there reigns supreme the spiteful little being who is tormenting me at present."

Aniela ceased laughing and jesting, slackened her pace, and presently we joined the elder ladies. The remainder of the day passed without a cloud, and so pleasantly that at times I fancied myself again a schoolboy. My eyes still spoke to her of love; but my desires slept. My aunt went to Warsaw after lunch, and I remained in Pani Celina's room, reading to her Montalembert's letters, with whom my father at one time had a regular correspondence. These letters would have seemed very tedious to me but for Aniela's presence. Raising my eyes now and then, I met her glance, which filled me with inexpressible joy. Unless I have lost all power of judgment, she looks at me as would look a pure, innocent woman, unconsciously loving with all her soul. What a good day it has been!

My aunt came back towards evening, and announced visitors. To-morrow both the Sniatynskis are coming, and Clara Hilst.

It is very late, but I do not want to sleep, for I am loathe to part with the memories of the day. Sleep cannot be more beautiful. The park is literally alive with the song of the nightingales, and there is still in me a great deal of the old romanticist. The night is clear and limpid, and the sky full of stars. Thinking of Aniela, I say a hundred times good-night to her. I see that side by side with the *improductivité Slave,* there is in me a great deal of purely Polish sentimentality. I had not known myself in that capacity before. But what does it matter? I love her very much.

13 May.

Clara and the Sniatynskis have not arrived. Instead of this, there came a letter, informing us they would come to-morrow, the weather permitting. To-day we had a thunder-storm, the like of which they have not experienced here for a long time. About ten o'clock in the morning a hot wind rose, which smothered everything in clouds of dust. The wind fell at times, and then rose again with such fury that it seemed to lay the trees flat. Our beautiful park was filled with the sound of crashing branches, and clouds of dust mingled with torn-off leaves and twigs. The great lime-tree close to the pavilion, where young Latysz died, was split in two. It was fearfully close, there was no air, and the wind seemed to come straight from a heated furnace, and carried with it a breath of carbon. I, used to the Italian *scirocco,* did not mind it so much, but Pani Celina suffered greatly, and indirectly, Aniela. My aunt was in a bad temper about the damage done to the park, and as usual, vented it on Chwastowski. The peppery old gentleman, who probably was caned often enough over his Homer, had evidently not forgotten the Odyssey, nor his ready speech either, for he replied to my aunt that if he were Æolus he would not serve her as agent, and bear with her unjust tantrums. My aunt gave way this time, merely because of the redoubled threats from the skies. It had grown very still all at once, but from the south, banks of cloud, black as a funereal pall, overcast with a sickly red sheen, came rolling up. In a moment it grew as dark as night, and Pani Celina rung for lights. Shortly afterwards the darkness yielded to an ominous reddish light. Chwastowski rushed off in a hurry to give orders for the cattle to be driven home, but the cow-herds had started without waiting for orders, for presently we heard distinctly the mournful lowing of the cattle. Then my aunt fetched the bell of Our Lady of Loreto, and went around the house ringing energetically. I did not even try to explain to her that ringing a bell in that motionless atmosphere might rather attract than avert a thunderbolt, and in spite of the consciousness that in case of danger I could not be of the slightest help, I was ashamed to let her risk the danger alone. The old lady was simply magnificent when, with her head thrown back, she seemed to defy the black and copper-colored banks of clouds, and shook at them her Loreto bell. I did not regret having gone with her, if only to see a symbolic picture. At a moment when everything trembles before the approaching horror, crouches in terror almost stupefied, faith alone has no fear ; it defies, and rings a bell. This is, from whatever side we look at it, an element of incalculable power in the human soul.

We returned when the first thunder began to growl all around the horizon. A few minutes later the roar became incessant. I had a sensation as if the thunder rolled on the lower stratum of the clouds, and the whole mass would burst at any moment and come with a deafening crash upon the earth. A thunderbolt fell into the pond at the other end of the park, followed by another so close by that the house shook on its foundations. My ladies began to say the Litany; I felt uncertain what to do; if I joined them it would be hypocrisy on my part, and if I did not it would look as if I were showing myself off as an ill-bred wiseacre, who cannot make allowance for country customs and female terrors. But I was wrong; they were not afraid; their faces were calm, even serene. It was evident that the familiar Litany was to them a sufficient armor against all dangers, and that there was no fear in their hearts. The thought crossed my mind what a stranger in spirit I was in presence of these Polish women, of whom each knows ten times less than I, and according to human measure, is worth ten times as much as I. They are like books of comparatively few pages, each page containing clear and simple rules, whereas I, with all those volumes of which I am composed, do not possess a single undoubted truth.

It was but a passing thought, as presently the storm that broke upon us with terrific force engaged all my attention. The wind rose again, crashing among the trees. It fell at moments, and then the rain came down in streams; no drops were visible, but long spouts that seemed to join sky and earth. The avenues in the park were like foaming brooks. Sometimes a strong gust of wind whipped the water into a fine spray that hung between earth and sky and obscured the whole view. The deafening roar of thunder went on incessantly. The air was saturated with electricity. My pulses were beating loudly; in the rooms an irritating smell of sulphur made itself felt. The raging elements without seemed to influence me in a strange way, and I began to lose control over myself.

"Do you want to see the storm?" I asked Aniela.

"Very well. Where from?"

"Come into the next room, there is a larger window."

We went and stood at the window. It was very dark

then, and every moment white and red forks of lightning tore across the clouds, opening the skies and at the same time illuminating our faces and the dark world without. Aniela was calm, but seemed every moment more desirable.

"Are you afraid?" I whispered.

"No."

"Give me your hand."

She looked at me wonderingly. Another moment and I should have folded her in my arms and pressed my lips against hers, and then let Ploszow be razed to the ground, by the tempest. But she was terrified, not by the storm, but by the expression of my face and that whisper; she drew back from the window and returned to the room where the elder ladies were sitting.

I remained alone, — with a feeling of anger and humiliation. That I should have taken advantage of Aniela's confidence is quite certain, and yet I felt offended by her want of trust, and resolved to pay her out in some way. I stood for an hour at the window looking absently at the lightning flashes. Then it grew lighter and lighter outside; at last the clouds parted, and the sun shone forth fresh and bright and as if wondering at the devastation the tempest had wrought.

It was very considerable; the avenues were still flooded with yellow, foaming water, above which floated broken branches. Here and there big trees were lying about, snapped across or torn out by the roots; the bark was partly stripped from the trunks of pine trees, leaving what looked like gaping wounds. Everywhere the eye could reach there was ruin and devastation, as if after a battle.

When the water had drained off a little I went out toward the ponds to ascertain the extent of the damage. Suddenly the whole park became alive with people, who, with an almost savage energy, began to tear off the broken branches and chop at the fallen trunks. It appears they were peasant-lodgers who had no right in the woods. In the main, I did not care whether they gathered the sticks, but as they had come through the broken fence without permission, and in such a savage manner, I, being out of humor, began to drive them away, my anger rising at their stubborn resistance. At last I threatened them with the village authorities, when suddenly, close by, the sweetest voice in the world said in French: —

"Is there any harm in their clearing the park, Leon?"

I turned round and saw Aniela, her head covered with a kerchief tied under her chin. With both hands she was holding up her dress, showing up to the ankles her little feet encased in high boots; bending slightly forward she looked at me entreatingly.

At her sight my anger vanished at once. I forgot the unpleasant sensations that had troubled me a little while before, and looked at her as if I could never fill myself enough with the sight.

"Is it your wish?" I asked.

Then, turning to the people, I said: —

"Take the wood, and thank the lady for the permission."

This time they obeyed with alacrity. Some of them, evidently strangers to Ploszow, addressed her as "gracious Panienka" (Miss), which caused me unspeakable delight. If Ploszow were mine they might cut down every tree at her wish. In half an hour every broken branch and fallen tree was cleared away, and the park looked really all the better for it. Walking with Aniela along the paths I found a great many swallows and other birds, either killed by the storm or half dead and drenched with rain. I picked them up, and handing them one by one to Aniela, I touched her hands, looked into her eyes, and again felt happy. The idyl of the day before repeated itself for us both, and brought with it ease and cheerfulness. My heart was full of joy, for I saw what Aniela could not see, — that in our brotherly relation there was twice as much tenderness as would be or ought to be between the most loving brother and sister. I was quite sure now that, unconsciously, she loved me as much as I loved her. In this way one half of my hopes and schemes are realized already; there remains only to bring it home to her and make her own to the feeling. When I think of that I remember, with a heart beating fast with happiness, what I wrote down some time ago: that "no woman in the world can resist the man she truly loves."

15 May.

Our visitors did not come yesterday but to-day, which was very sensible, as all traces of the storm have disappeared and the weather is very fine. This fifteenth of May will be one of the best remembered days in my life. It is now past midnight; I am wide awake, as if I never wanted to sleep again, and intend to write until morning. I am collecting my thoughts so as not to begin at the end, and put it all down in proper order. Force of habit is a great help in this.

My aunt sent the carriage for the Sniatynskis and Clara very early, in consequence of which they arrived before noon. The ladies were bright, cheerful, and chirping like sparrows, glad of the fine weather and their excursion. What toilets, and what quaint hats! Clara looked very well in a light, striped dress that made her seem less tall than usual. I observed that Aniela, after the first greeting, looked at her searchingly and seemed struck by her beauty, of which I had scarcely said anything to her. I had not refrained out of calculation, but had been so occupied with Aniela that I had not thought of it. For instance, though I had met Pani Sniatynska several times I had never noticed she wore her hair short, which suits her style of beauty. The light, curly hair falling over her brow gives her the expression of a resolute, rosy-faced boy. We are excellent friends again. There was a time she would have liked to kill me, so angry was she about Aniela. Evidently her husband had told her what I suffered, and women have a special weakness for those who suffer for love's sake; she has forgiven me and reinstalled me in her favor. The presence of such a bright, vivacious, easy-going woman was a great help in bringing Clara and Aniela into closer relation. I saw that my aunt met Clara with great heartiness; but Aniela, in spite of her sweet disposition, seemed shy, and kept aloof from her. At lunch, amid a cheerful conversation, she thawed a little. Clara seemed struck by Aniela's beauty, and as she always says what she thinks, she expressed her admiration with so much grace and enthusiasm that Aniela had to yield.

Pani Celina, who now perhaps for the first time found herself in company with an artist, looked gratified, and turning to her said that "though Aniela's mother, she must say that as a child she was very pretty, — promising far greater beauty." Both Sniatynskis joined in the conversation. He began to discuss with Clara various female types, then spoke of Aniela's type and its æsthetic perfection in a highly amusing objective manner, as if she were a portrait hanging on the wall, rather than a living presence. She, listening to this, blushed and lowered her eyes, truly like a little girl, which made her look more charming than ever.

I was silent, but inwardly compared these three female faces, treating them also objectively, that is, putting aside the fact that one of them was the loved one, and as such occupied an exceptional position; even then everything spoke in her favor. Pani Sniatynska's, especially in her short curly hair, is a charming head, yet nothing but what may be found in any English Keepsake. Clara's beauty rests mainly upon her calm expression, the blue eyes, and that transparent complexion so often met with in German women; but for her art, which surrounds her as with a nimbus, she could only be called a handsome woman. Aniela is not only an artistic production of an exceedingly noble style as regards her features, but there is something individual in her that cannot be measured by any standard. Maybe her individuality rests upon the fact that, being neither dark nor fair, she gives the physical impression of a brunette and the spiritual one of a blonde. The cause of this is perhaps the great abundance of hair on a comparatively small head; enough that she is unique in her kind. She excels even Mrs. Davis in this regard, whose beauty was without a flaw, but it was the beauty of a statue. Mrs. Davis only excited the admiration of my senses, while Aniela rouses in me the idealist, who goes in rapture over the poetry of her expression.

But I will not even compare these two so utterly different beings. I yielded to these reflections during lunch, because the topic in question had brought me on that track; besides, the analysis of Aniela's beauty always gives me a keen delight. My aunt interrupted the discussion, deeming it proper, as lady of the house, to say something about Clara's last concert. She spoke much and very well; I never supposed she had such knowledge of music; she paid her some graceful compliments with the air of a *grande dame*, in that flowing, winning style only people of the older generation are capable of. In short, I observed that my downright, outspoken aunt was still able to recall the times of powder and patches. Clara seemed quite charmed, and did not remain behindhand in graceful acknowledgment.

"I shall always be able to play well at Warsaw," she said, "because I am in touch with my audience, but I play best in small circles of friends where I feel in sympathy with everybody, — and if you will permit, I will give you a proof of it after lunch."

My aunt, who was very anxious that Pani Celina should hear her, yet had misgivings whether it would be right to ask her to play, was much pleased by the proposal. I began to speak of Clara's performances at Paris and her triumphs at Erard's concerts; Sniatynski gave an account of what was said at Warsaw; and so the time passed until we rose from lunch. Clara herself got hold of Pani Celina's invalid chair and would not allow anybody to help, declaring laughingly that she was by far the strongest among us, and was not afraid to tire her hands. Presently she sat down to the piano, and as evidently Mozart suited her disposition, she gave us Don Juan. The first notes sounded, she was a different Clara; not the merry, lively child any longer, but an incarnate Saint Cecilia. There shone in her the close relationship of outward form with the spirit of harmony, which surrounded her with a dignity above common womanhood. I made another observation, namely: that a man in love can find food for his feelings even in what tells against the loved woman. When I thought how far my Aniela was from being a Sybil, saw her sitting in a corner of the drawing-room so small and still, as if crushed down by some weight, I loved her all the more, and it made her if possible dearer to me than ever. It also occurred to me that a woman is not in reality what she appears to people in general, but such as the man who loves sees her; therefore her absolute excellence is in proportion to the power of love she inspires. I had no time to follow out this idea, but it pleased me because I saw dimly before me the conclusion that in the name of this excellence the woman ought to give her heart to him who loves her most.

Clara played superbly. I watched the sensation on the others' faces, when presently I noticed that Aniela was looking at me for the same reason. Was it mere curiosity, or an involuntary uneasiness of heart which could not say what it feared and yet was afraid? I said to myself: "If the last supposition were true it would be a proof that she loves me." The thought filled me with joy, and I resolved to find an answer to it in the course of the day. Thenceforth I bestowed all my attention upon Clara, and was more attentive to her than I had ever been before. In the woods whither we had driven, I walked with her, glancing furtively now and then at Aniela, who remained with the Sniatynskis. Clara was in rapture with the woods, which are indeed at their best now, the fresh green of the leafy trees forming a perfect canopy over the more sombre looking pines.

The sun filtering across the branches converted the earth, carpeted with ferns and tender mosses, into a delicate golden embroidery. There were the cheerful voices of spring around us, the cuckoo's call and the woodpecker's knock-knock at the trees. When we joined the others I asked Clara to translate into music the voices of spring. She said there was already a *Frühlingslied* singing within her, and she would try to give it expression. Truly she looked as if the song was there, — besides she is like a great harp that speaks only in sounds.

Her face was bright with burning blushes; Aniela instead looked fagged, though she evidently tried to keep up with the Sniatynskis, who were as lively as a couple of school-children on their holiday. They began finally to race with each other, and Clara joined in the sport, which she ought not to have done, considering her size, as the quick motion was anything but graceful, — nay, almost ridiculous.

When they were thus running after each other I remained alone with Aniela. According to my plan of operations I was anxious to bring her mind to full consciousness through the uneasiness with which she seemed to be oppressed.

"There is something troubling you, Aniela; what is it?" I asked.

"No, nothing whatever."

"It seemed to me as if you were dissatisfied with something; is it that you do not like Clara?"

"No; I like her very much, and do not wonder she is so much admired."

Further conversation was made impossible by the return of the truants. It was also time to go back. On the way, Sniatynski asked Clara whether she felt really satisfied with her stay at Warsaw.

"The best proof I can give you of this is that I do not think of going away yet," she replied gayly.

"We must try to keep you with us always," I interpolated.

Clara, in spite of the simplicity with which she accepts all that is said to her, looked questioningly at me, then grew a little confused, and replied, —

"They are all very kind to me here."

I was conscious that my words were in a way dishonorable, as they might mislead Clara; but all I cared for was the impression they would make upon Aniela. Unfortunately, I could not see her face, as she was buttoning her gloves, with her head bent so low that her hat concealed it from me. This sudden movement seemed to me a good sign.

The elder ladies were awaiting us with the dinner, which lasted until nine o'clock; and then Clara improvised her *Frühlingslied.* I am almost certain that since Ploszow existed there had never been heard such music within its walls, but I paid very little attention to it. I sat near her in the dusk, as she did not want the lamps lit. Sniatynski waved his arm as if it were a bâton; which evidently annoyed his wife, as she pulled his sleeve several times. Aniela sat quite motionless; maybe she, too, was absorbed in her own thoughts, and did not listen to the *Frühlingslied.* I was almost certain she was thinking about me and Clara, and especially about the meaning of the words I had said to Clara. It was easy enough to guess that even if she did not love me, or had the slightest consciousness that my love was any other but brotherly affection, she would feel sore and disappointed if that were about to be taken away from her. A woman who is not happy in her married life clings round any other feeling, if it be only friendship, as the ivy clings to the tree. I had no doubt whatever that if at this moment I knelt down at her feet and told her it was she, and she alone, that I loved, she would feel a sudden joy, as one feels upon recovering something very precious. And if so, I debated within me, why not hasten the solution, if only a way could be found, — frightening her as little as possible, or making her forget all terror in her joy. I began at once to devise ways and means, as I understood it must be done in such a way as to make it forever impossible for her to cast me off. My mind worked very hard at it, as the problem was not an easy one. Gradually a great emotion stole over me; and strange to say, it was more on Aniela's account than on my own that I felt moved, — for I realized suddenly what a great wrench it would be, and I was afraid for her.

In the mean time it had grown lighter in the drawing-room; the moon had risen above the trees, and cast luminous shafts across the floor. The melodies of the *Frühlingslied* still filled the air, and the nightingales responded to it through the open French window. It was a glorious evening, warm and balmy, and full of harmony and love. I thought involuntarily that, if life does not give us happiness, it presents us with a ready frame for it.

In the luminous dusk my eyes searched for Aniela; but she looked at Clara, who at this moment seemed more a vision than a substantial being. The moonlight, advancing more and more into the room, rested now upon her; and in the light dress she looked like the silvery spirit of music. But the vision did not last long. Clara finished her song; whereupon Pani Sniatynska rose, and saying it was late, gave the signal for departure. As the evening was so warm, I proposed we should see our visitors off as far as the high-road, about half a mile from our house. I did this on purpose, so as to walk home with Aniela. I knew she could not well refuse such a mere act of politeness, and I was also sure my aunt would not go with us.

I gave orders for the carriage to drive on and wait on the road, and we went on foot through the lime avenue. I offered my arm to Clara, but we walked all abreast, accompanied by the croaking of the frogs in the Ploszow mere.

Clara stopped a moment to listen to that chorus, which ceased now and then, to start afresh with redoubled vigor, and said, —

"This is the finale of my Song of Spring."

"What an exquisite evening!" remarked Sniatynski, and then began to quote the beautiful lines from the "Merchant of Venice": —

"How sweet the moonlight sleeps upon this bank!
Here will we sit and let the sounds of music
Creep in our ears: soft stillness and the night
Become the touches of sweet harmony."

He did not remember the rest, but I did, and took up the strain: —

"Sit, Jessica. Look how the floor of heaven
Is thick inlaid with patines of bright gold:
There 's not the smallest orb which thou behold'st
But in his motion like an angel sings,
Still quiring to the young-eyed cherubins;
Such harmony is in immortal souls;
But whilst this muddy vesture of decay
Doth grossly close it in, we cannot hear it."

Then I repeated to Clara, who does not understand Polish, the lines in French, improvising the translation. She listened to it, then raised her eyes heavenward, and said simply, —

"I was always certain there is music in the spheres."

It appeared that Pani Sniatynska was equally certain of it, and reminded her husband that she had discussed it with him not long before, but he was not quite sure he remembered; whereupon a slight matrimonial dispute took place, at which Clara and I laughed. Aniela had not joined the conversation at all; did she feel hurt that I had offered my arm to Clara, and paid her some attention? The very supposition made me feel happy. Yet I tried not to lose my head, and said to myself, "Do not run away with the idea that she knows what jealousy means;

she is only a little sad and feels lonely, that is all." I would have given at this moment a whole host of artists such as Clara for a few words with Aniela, — to tell her that I belong to her, and only to her. Then Sniatynski began a discussion about astronomy, of which I heard now and then a few words, though this science attracts me more than I can tell, — for in its very nature there is no limit, either in itself or for the human mind; it is infinite.

We reached at last the end, where our guests mounted into the carriage. Presently the wheels rattled on the road, the last good-bys reached our ears, and I was alone with Aniela. We turned homewards, and for some time walked side by side in silence. The croaking of the frogs has ceased, and from the distance came the sound of the watchman's whistle and the loud baying of the dogs. I did not speak to Aniela, because the silence seemed fraught with deep meaning, — both our minds being full of the same subject. When about half-way I said to Aniela, —

"What a pleasant day it has been, has it not?"

"Yes. I never heard such beautiful music before."

"And yet you seemed not in your usual spirits, and though you will not tell me the cause, I notice every passing cloud on your face."

"You were obliged to look after your guests. You are very kind to trouble about me, but there is nothing the matter with me."

"To-day as any other day I was occupied with you only, and as a proof of it let me tell you of what you were thinking to-day." And without waiting for permission, I went on at once: "You thought I resembled somewhat the Latysz couple; you thought I had deceived you in speaking of the void around me; lastly, you thought that I had no need to ask for your friendship while I was seeking friendship elsewhere. Was it not so? Tell me the truth."

Aniela replied with evident effort: "If you insist

upon knowing — yes, perhaps it is so. But I ought to be only glad of it."

"What ought you be glad of?"

"Of your mutual friendship with Clara."

"As to our friendship, — I wish her well, that is all. But Clara, like all other women, is indifferent to me. Do you know why?"

I began to tremble a little, because I perceived that the moment had come. I waited a moment to see whether Aniela would take up my question, and then, in a voice I tried to render steady, I said, —

"Surely you must see and understand that my whole being belongs to you; that I loved you and love you still madly."

Aniela stood still as if turned to stone. By the icy coldness of my face I felt that I was growing pale; and if the world seemed to totter under that poor child's feet, it was my life, too, which was at stake. Knowing with whom I had to deal, I did not give her time to repulse me. I began to speak very quickly: —

"Do not answer me, for I do not want anything from you. I desire nothing, — nothing whatever, understand that well. I wanted to tell you that you have taken my life, and it is henceforth yours, to do with it what you like. But you have seen yourself that such is the case, and it matters nothing whether I speak of it or not. I repeat that I desire nothing, nor do I expect anything. You cannot repulse me, because I repulse myself. I only tell you as I might tell a friend, a sister. I come and complain to you, because I have nowhere else to go, that I love a woman that belongs to somebody else, — love her to distraction, — oh, Aniela! — and without limit!"

We were near the gate, but still in the deep shadow of the trees. For a moment I had the delusion that she was leaning towards me like a broken flower, that I might snatch her into my arms; but I was mistaken.

Aniela, recovering from the sudden shock, began suddenly to say, with a kind of nervous energy I had not suspected in her, —

"I will not listen to this, Leon. I will not; I will not; I will not!"

And she ran into the moonlit courtyard. Yes; she ran away from my words, — my confession. Presently she disappeared within the portico, and I remained alone with a feeling of unrest, fear, and great pity for her, and triumph at the same time that the words which should be the beginning of a new life for us both had been spoken. For, to say the truth, I could not expect anything else from her at first; but the seed from which something must spring up was sown.

When I came into the house there was no Aniela visible. I found only my aunt, walking up and down the room muttering her rosary and soliloquizing between the prayers. I said good-night, and went at once to my room thinking that it would calm me if I put down the day's impressions; but it only tired me more. I intend to go away to-morrow, or rather to-day, for I see the daylight coming through the window. I want to confirm Aniela in the conviction that I expect nothing from her, — want her to calm down and get familiar with what I told her. But to confess the whole truth, I go away also because I am afraid to meet her so soon, and would fain put it off. There are moments when it seems to me a monstrous deed to have introduced an element of corruption in this pure atmosphere. But does not the principal evil lie in her marrying a man she cannot love? What is more immoral, my love which is a manifestation of nature's great law, or the belonging of Aniela to that man, which is a shameful breaking of the same law? And I, who understand this so clearly, am yet so weak that a horror seizes me when I kick against that corrupt morality. But all these scruples melt like snow at the words, "I love." If even now my heart feels sore at the thought that at this very moment she may be awake, weeping perhaps, or torn by doubts, it is only another proof how I love her. It hurts me, and at the same time I do not see how otherwise we can arrive at happiness.

19 May.

The first night after my arrival I slept profoundly. At Ploszow I grudged every moment that kept me from Aniela, and during the night I was writing; consequently I felt deadly tired. And now I feel still heavy, but am able to think. I am somewhat ashamed that I ran away and left Aniela alone to bear the burden of my confession; but when the beloved woman is in question, a little cowardice is not dishonorable. Besides, I should not have fled had it not been necessary for the future weal of my love. Now, every day when she rises and says her prayers, walks in the park or attends her sick mother, she must, if ever so unwillingly, say to herself, "He loves me," and the thought will gradually become familiar, less terrifying to her. Human nature gets accustomed to everything, and a woman soon becomes reconciled to the thought that she is loved, especially when she returns that love. This question, "Does she love me?" I put to myself the first time when I knew I loved her still; and again I turn it over in my mind, try to weigh all the circumstances as if somebody else's fate were at stake, and I arrive at the conviction that it cannot be otherwise. When she married she loved me, not Kromitzki; she only yielded to him her hand driven by despair. If she had married a superior man who dazzled her by his fame, his thoughts, or exceptional character, she might have forgotten me. But how could a Kromitzki, with his money-grubbing neurosis, get hold of her affection? Besides, he left her soon after they were married; he sold Gluchow, which was as the very apple of the eye to these two women. Judging Kromitzki quite impartially, there was nothing in him which could win a being full of ideal impulses and feelings. Then I came back,—I, whom she had loved. I touched the chords of her heart with memories of the past, by every word and glance. I drew her towards me, not only with that skill an experience of life gives, but also with that magnetic force true love bestows on man. Adding to this the fact that she knew how much I suffered when I sent Sniatynski to her, she must have pitied me, and that pity cannot have vanished altogether. I play for my life, but the cards are in my favor. I cannot lose the game.

I am as much in my right as anybody who is defending his life. I do not say this upon the impulse of the moment, but after calm reasoning. I have no convictions, no beliefs, no principles, no stable ground under my feet, for the ground has been undermined by criticism and reflection. I have only those forces of life born with us, and they are all concentrated on one woman. Therefore I clutch my love as a drowning man clutches a plank; if this gives way there will be nothing left to live for. If common-sense asks, "Why did you not marry Aniela?" I say what I have said before: I did not marry her simply for the reason that I am not straight, but crooked, — partly because born so, partly because so reared by those two nurses, Reflection and Criticism. Why this woman and no other should be my plank of salvation, I do not know. Most likely because it was she and not another. It did not depend upon me.

If she were free to-day, I would stretch my hands out for her without hesitation; if she had never been married, who knows? — I am ashamed of the thought, and yet it may be that she would not be so desirable. Most likely, judging by the past, I should have gone on watching her, watching my own feelings, until somebody else carried her off; but I prefer not to think of it, because it makes me inclined to swear.

20 May.

I considered to-day what would happen if I gained Aniela's love, or rather brought her to confess it. I see happiness before me but no way of reaching it. I know that if in presence of these women I uttered the word "divorce," they would think the roof was crashing down over our heads. There cannot be even a question as to that, because my aunt's and Pani Celina's ideas upon that point are such that neither of them would survive the shock. I have no illusions as to Aniela; her ideas are the same. And yet the moment she owns her love, I will say the word, and she must accustom herself to it; but we shall have to wait until my aunt's and Pani Celina's death. There is nothing else for it. Kromitzki will either agree willingly or he will not. In the latter case I shall carry Aniela off, if I have to go as far as the Indies, and the divorce, or rather invalidation of the marriage, I shall conduct myself, in spite of his wishes. Fortunately, there is no want of means. As regards myself, I am ready for everything, and the inward conviction that I am right justifies me in my own eyes. This time it is not a mere love intrigue, but a feeling that absorbs my whole being. Its sincerity and strength make all my stratagems lawful. I know that I deceive her in saying that all I wish to gain is a sister's love. I deceive her when I say I do not desire anything; all this would be wrong and a lie if my love were in itself a lie. In presence of a great truth, they are mere diplomatic stratagems of love. It all belongs to the course of love. It is a known fact that even affianced lovers have recourse to stratagems, in order to make each other confess their love. As to myself, I am sincere even when I say what is not true.

21 May.

I told Aniela that I intended to work, and I will do so, if only for the reason that I said so to her. I will have the collections brought over from Rome, and found a museum. This will be Aniela's merit, and the first useful deed that springs from our love. I suppose the Italian government will raise difficulties, as there is a law that prohibits the exportation of antiquities and precious works of art. But my lawyer will arrange that for me. And that reminds me of the Madonna by Sassoferrato, which my father bequeathed to his future daughter-in-law. I will have it sent over at once, because I want it.

22 May.

Human nature is ever malicious. I have a grim satisfaction in thinking how ridiculous a man like Kromitzki must seem, who is turning summersaults in the East in his effort to make money, while somebody whispers love vows into his wife's ears; and sooner or later Aniela must see it in this light. The whole Kromitzki can be summed up in the one fact: he sold Gluchow and left the women without a home. He thought perhaps they would live in Odessa or Kieff; in the mean while Pani Celina's illness brought Aniela to Ploszow.

Yet he knew how precarious the lady's health was; he ought to have foreseen that she might fall ill, and that Aniela would remain alone with the burden of sorrow and trouble. If his business requires his presence in the East, why did he marry at all?

To-morrow I go back to Ploszow. I feel very lonely here, and besides I feel the longing to look once more into Aniela's eyes, and at times feel guilty, as if I had been shirking a duty by running away. It was necessary at the time, but I must go back now. Who knows? greater happiness than I suppose may be waiting for me, — perhaps she too is longing for me.

I called upon the Sniatynskis, and Clara, whom I did not find at home. I paid also a visit to the celebrated beauty, Pani Korytzka. The latter carries her historical name like a jockey cap, and her wit as a riding-whip; she hits people with it between the eyes. I came off unscathed; she even tried a little coquetry on me. I made a dozen or so calls and left cards. I wish people to think that I am settled at Warsaw.

As the bringing over of my father's collections is only a matter of will and ready money, I am seeking what else there is for me to do. Men of my position are usually occupied with the administration of their fortune; and very badly they administer it on the whole, far worse than I. Very few take any part in public life. I mentioned before that here they still amuse themselves with aristocracy and democracy; there are even some whose whole aim in life consists in backing up social hierarchy, and stemming the tide of democratic currents. It is a sport as good as any other, but since I am no sportsman, I take no interest in that amusement. Even if it were no mere play, if there were some sense at the bottom of it, I am too much of a sceptic in regard to both parties to belong to either. Democracy, by which I mean patented democrats, not people of humble extraction, acts upon my nerves. As to aristocracy, methinks that if their *raison d'être* is based upon services rendered to the country by their ancestors, those services have often been such that the sooner their descendants don the hair-shirt and cover their heads with ashes the better. Besides, these two parties, with the exception of a few foolish individuals, do not really believe in themselves. Some feign sincerity in order to serve their own ends, and as I never feign anything, it is clear that to take part in such struggles is not the work for me. Then there are those of the Sniatynski order who stand above both parties, but are always ready to drown both in their synthesis. They are, as a rule, strong men; but even if I could agree with them I should have to do something, — mere consciousness of duty is not work. Sniatynski writes plays. Truly, when I look things straight in the face, I find that I am outside the parenthesis, and do not see my way to get inside. It is strange that a man who has considerable means, culture, certain capacities, and a wish for something to do, should find nothing he can put his hands to. Again I feel inclined to swear, as it is all owing to that intellectual splitting of hairs. They ought to make a diagnosis upon me, as to the disease of Time's old age, which in me has reached the acute stage. He who is a sceptic in regard to faith, in regard to science, conservatism, progress, and so on, has indeed difficulty in finding anything to do.

In addition to all that, my aspirations are far greater than the possibility of satisfying them. Life rests upon work; and therefore, here people work at something or other. But it is the work of a dray-horse, carting grain to the granary. I could not do it even if I wished. I am a high-stepper, fit only for a carriage, and of no use on sandy, rutty roads, where common horses do the work better and more steadily. At the building of a house I could not carry the bricks, but might do something in the ornamental line, but where it is a question of four simple walls and a sound roof, artisans such as I are not wanted. If at least I had a mighty impulse towards work, I still might be able to force myself to do something. But in the main, it is only a question of appearances. I wish to work in order to please the woman I love. Aniela in regard to that has exalted notions, and it would certainly please her. Moreover, for that very reason my vanity and also my calculations urge me to bid for a prominent position, which would raise my value in her eyes. I will see what can be done, and in the meanwhile my purse will do the work for me. I shall have the collection sent over, support various institutions, and give money where it is wanted.

What a strange power there is in woman! She comes in contact with a genius without portfolio, an exceptionally useless implement like me, and then, without any preaching on her part, he feels himself in duty bound to do all sorts of things he never dreamed of doing before.

The deuce take me if I ever thought of bringing my

collections to Paris or Vienna for the sake of a Parisian or Viennese. I am going back to Ploszow; I long to be near my good spirit.

23 May.

When I went away from Ploszow for some time, it was to bring Aniela to some kind of decision. At Warsaw and on the way back to Ploszow, I tried to guess what she had resolved upon. I knew she could not write to her husband: "Come and take me away, for Ploszowski is making love to me;" she would not have done so even if she hated me. There is too much delicacy of feeling in her to do that. Putting aside that an encounter between me and Kromitzki might be the consequence of such a step, Aniela would have to leave her sick mother, who cannot go away from Ploszow.

Aniela's position is indeed a difficult one, and I counted upon that before I made my confession. The thought crossed my mind that she might take it into her head to avoid me altogether, and shut herself up in her mother's rooms. But I dismissed the thought. In the country and under the same roof it would be quite impracticable, or at any rate so conspicuous as to rouse the elder ladies' attention and consequently act injuriously upon her mother's health. In truth I take the utmost advantage of her position, but who that is in love does not do the same? I foresaw that Aniela, even if she returns my love, will not allow meain the future to repeat my avowel, — she will resist more than any other married woman; for what with her principles and her modesty, the slightest sign of yielding would appear to her an incredible crime. But how can she prevent me from telling her my love? There is only one way, — by getting from me a voluntary promise; I guessed she would speak to me about it, and I was right.

When I arrived at Ploszow she seemed pale, and a little worn, but looked at me with a resolute face. It was evident the dear child had laid by a whole store of arguments to convince me with, and believed that after displaying them there would be nothing for me but to remain silent forever. Angelic delusion; to think there is only one truth in the world. No! do not enter into any arguments with me, my Aniela, for if I believe in any truth, it is the truth and right of love; besides, I am too wily, and each argument will be turned inside out like a glove and made into a weapon against yourself. Neither argument nor reasoning, not even my pity will save you; for the whiter, the more perfect and angelic you prove yourself, the more I shall love you, and the more I love, the more desirable you will be to me. I have nothing but crocodile tears for you, which will only sharpen my rapacity. Such is the mazy circle of love. At the sight of Aniela I felt myself drawn into that circle. In the afternoon, that same day, when Pani Celina had fallen asleep on the veranda, Aniela motioned me to follow her into the park. From the earnest expression of her face, I guessed that the time had come for those arguments, and I followed her eagerly. As we went farther from the veranda, I noticed that Aniela's animation began to flag; she had grown paler and seemed frightened at her own temerity; but she could not draw back now, and began in an unsteady voice: —

"If you only knew how unhappy I have been these last days — "

"Do you think I have been much happier?" I replied.

"I know you have not, and because of that I have a request to make. You understand everything, and are so good and generous you will not refusedwhat I ask you."

"Tell me, what do you want me to do?"

"Leon, you must leave there, go abroad again, and do not come back until mamma and I are able to leave Ploszow."

I was sure she would ask me that. I remained silent for a while as if searching for an answer.

"You can do with me what you like," I said; "but tell me, why do you send me into exile?"

"I do not send you into exile; but you know why —"

"I know," I replied, with unfeigned sadness and resignation; "it is because I am ready to give the last drop of my blood for you, because I would shield you with my body from any danger, because I love you more than my life, — these are heavy sins indeed!"

"No," she interrupted, with feverish energy, "but because I am the wife of a man I love and respect, — and I will not listen to such words."

Impatience and anger seized me; I knew she did not speak the truth. All married women shield themselves with love and respect for the husband when they arrive at a turning-point of their life, though there may not be a shadow of that feeling in their hearts; nevertheless, Aniela's words sent a shock through my nerves, and I could scarcely repress the exclamation: "You say what is not true! you are perjuring yourself, for you neither love nor respect the man;" but the thought that her energy would not hold out long made me refrain, and I replied, almost humbly: —

"Do not be angry with me, Aniela; I will go."

I saw that my humility disarmed her, and that she felt sorry for me. Suddenly she pulled a leaf from a low-hanging branch, and began to tear it nervously to pieces. She made superhuman efforts not to burst into tears, but I saw her breast heaving with agitation.

I, too, was moved to the very depth of my soul, and continued with difficulty: —

"Do not wonder that I hesitate to comply with your wish, for it is very heavy upon me. I have told you that I do not wish for anything but to breathe the same air with you, to look at you, and God knows it is not too much I ask for; yet such as it is, it is my all. And you take it away from me. Think only; everybody else is allowed to come here, to speak to you, look at you — but me. Why am I shut out? Because you are dearer to me than to anybody else! What a refined cruelty of fate! Only put yourself in my place. It is difficult for you, who have never known what loneliness means; you love your husband, or think you do, which comes to the same; put yourself for a moment into my position, and you will understand that such a sentence is worse than death. You ought to feel at least a little pity. Driving me from here, you take everything from me. I told you I had come home to do some useful work, in which I might find peace, forgetfulness, and redeem my former sins; only recently I resolved to bring over my father's collections; and you want me to renounce all that, bid me go away and begin again a wandering, aimless, life. But have your wish; I will go if you tell me the same three days hence, for I fancy you did not quite understand what all this meant for me. Now you know, I only ask for three days' respite, nothing more."

Aniela covered her eyes with her hands and moaned: "Oh, my God! my God!"

There was something inexpressibly touching in the low cry, like the wail of a child at its own powerlessness. There was a moment I felt tempted to promise everything she asked. But in that wail I saw the promise of a future victory, and I would not lose its fruits.

"Listen to me," I said, "I will go at once, this very moment, and put seas between us, if you tell me that it is necessary for your own peace of mind. I speak to you now as a friend, a brother! I know from my aunt that you loved me; if that love be still alive I will go at your bidding."

Sincere pain on my part dictated these words; but it was a terrible trap for Aniela, which might wring a confession from her. If that had happened — I do not know — maybe I should have kept my word, but as the heavens are above us, I would have taken her into my arms. But she only shuddered as if I had touched an open wound; then her face flamed up in anger and indignation. "No!" she exclaimed with desperate passion, "it is not true! not true! You may do as you like, go away or stay, but it is not true!" The very passion with which these words were uttered showed me that it might be true. I felt inclined to tell her so with frank brutality, but I saw my aunt coming towards us. Aniela was not able to conceal her emotion, and my aunt looking at her asked at once: —

"What is troubling you, child? what have you two been talking about?"

"Aniela was telling me how grieved her mother was about the sale of Gluchow — and I do not wonder she took it so much to heart."

Whether Aniela's strength was exhausted, or the untruth I made her take a silent part in filled the cup of bitterness to overflowing, she burst into incontrollable sobs that shook her like a reed; my aunt folded her into her arms and hushed her as if she were a little child.

"Aniela, my darling, there is no help for it; let us submit to God's will. The hail has ruined five of my farms, and I did not even say a word about it to Chwastowski."

The mention of the five farms appeared to me so inappropriate, selfish, and futile in presence of Aniela's tears that it made me quite angry with my aunt.

"Never mind the farms," I said brusquely, "she is grieved about her mother;" and I went away in sorrow, for I felt I was torturing the woman I loved beyond anything. I had conquered along the whole line, yet I felt profoundly sad, as if the future were full of unknown terrors.

25 May.

To-day is the third day since our conversation, and as Aniela has not referred to it again, I remain. She does not say much to me, nor does she avoid me altogether, fearing to attract notice. I try to be good, friendly, and attentive, but do not thrust myself in her way. I want her to think I keep my feeling under control, but she cannot help seeing it is there, and increasing every moment. At any rate we have a little world to ourselves, where only we two dwell; we have our mutual secret from the others. When we speak about indifferent topics we both know that at the bottom of our hearts there is something we both think about but do not put into words. This forms a tie; time and patience will do the rest. From my love I weave a thousand threads around her, which will bind us more and more. This would be all in vain if she loved her husband; it would make her hate me. But the past speaks in my favor, and the present does not not belong to Kromitzki. I still think it over with the greatest impartiality, and I come to the same conclusion, that she cannot love him. Aniela's resistance is the inward struggle of an exceptionally pure soul, that does not allow a breath of faithlessness to come near it. But she is without help in that struggle. I know the resistance will be long, and difficult to overcome; I must always be on the watch, give a clear account to myself of every trifle, and weave around her strong and invisible threads. Even if I should commit any mistakes they will be only the result of my love, and as such will be rather a help than a hindrance.

26 May.

I told Sniatynski about my intention to have my Roman collections conveyed to Warsaw, — calculating that it would reach the press, which could not fail to laud me up to the sky as a public benefactor. Aniela involuntarily must compare me to Kromitzki, which will count in my favor. I sent also a telegram to Rome, asking for the Sassoferrato.

During breakfast I told Aniela, in presence of the others, that my father had left the picture to her in his will; which confused her, and she guessed at once that he had looked upon her as his future daughter. It is true there was no name mentioned in the will, and for that very reason I want Aniela to have it. The mention of this bequest reawoke in us both a host of memories. I had done this on purpose to turn Aniela's thoughts to the past, when she loved me and could love me in peace. I know the remembrance must be mingled with some bitter thoughts, even some resentment; it cannot be otherwise; but it would be worse without the message I sent her through Sniatynski. This message is the only extenuating circumstance in the whole guilty affair. Aniela knows that I wanted to undo the wrong, that I loved her then, suffered, and repented,—am repenting still, and that if we are unhappy she too helped to bring that unhappiness on both. She is bound to absolve me in her heart, regret the past and dream what the future might have been but for my misdeeds and her severity. Even then I was reading in her face that she felt frightened at her own thoughts and visions, and tried to drive them away by a conversation upon indifferent subjects. My aunt is so full of the approaching races and the expected victory of Naughty Boy, who is put down for the government stakes, that she cannot think of anything else. Aniela thereupon began to talk about the races, and made some random remarks and asked a few questions, until my aunt got scandalized and said:—

"My dear child, I see you have not the slightest notion about races."

I said to her with my eyes: "I know you want to stifle your feelings;" and she understood me as if I had said it in so many words. And indeed, I am quite certain that she is as much absorbed in our mutual relation as I am. The thought of love independent of matrimony is already planted in her soul; it is there, and does not leave her for a moment. She must live with it, and get reconciled to it. In such a case a woman, even if she had loved her husband, would turn from him. A drop of water will hollow out a stone. If Aniela loves me ever so little, if she only loves the past, she will be mine.

I cannot think of it calmly, because the foretaste of happiness is almost choking me.

There are here and there quicksands on the seashore, and the unwary traveller who wanders there is lost. At times it seems to me that my love is like one of those quicksands, and that I am dragging Aniela into it; I myself am sinking, sinking — Let it be so — but together!

28 May.

My aunt is spending six to eight hours out of the twenty-four at Burzany, one of her farms, a mile from Ploszow, where she passes her time in contemplation of Naughty Boy, and in looking after Webb, the English trainer. I was there above an hour yesterday. Naughty Boy is a fine animal, — let us hope he will not be naughty when the great day arrives. But what does it matter to me? Various business is taking me to town, but I am loath to leave Ploszow. Pani Celina has been worse the last few days, but young Chwast, as my aunt calls him, says it is merely a passing symptom; he considers it necessary that somebody should always be with the sick lady, to distract her from the thoughts which dwell upon the loss of the dear ancestral home, and consequently weaken her nerves. I try to show her almost a son's attention, because in this way I earn Aniela's gratitude, and she gets used to consider me as belonging to them. I have now not the slightest ill-feeling towards the old lady, — she is too unhappy herself; and besides, I begin to love everything and everybody that belongs to Aniela, — with one exception.

Yesterday I spent several hours with the invalid, together with Aniela and Chwast. We were reading and talking. Pani Celina does not sleep at night, and as the doctor does not approve of sleeping-draughts, she dozes off in the daytime after any lengthy conversation, and strange to say, only a sudden silence wakes her up. For this reason we keep up the conversation or the reading.

It was the same to-day. But for the doctor's presence I could speak to Aniela with the greatest freedom.

Just at this time the daily papers are fully occupied with the divorce of the beautiful Pani Korytzka. Everybody talks about it, and my aunt, who is related to the husband, is greatly shocked. I resolved to make the most of my opportunity, and plant ideas in Aniela's mind that had not been there before.

"You are quite wrong, dear aunt, to blame Pani Korytzka. To me it seems that she acts as a true and honest woman should. Where love begins, human will ends, — even you must acknowledge that. If Pani Korytzka loves somebody else, nothing remains for her but to leave her husband. I know what you are going to say, and also what Aniela thinks, — that duty still remains; is it not so?"

"I think you too must be of the same opinion," replied Aniela.

"Most certainly. The question is which way lies Pani Korytzka's duty."

I do not know why, but the young doctor stipulated that he did not recognize any free will, but afterwards listened attentively, evidently pleased with the boldness of my views.

But seeing astonishment on Aniela's face, I went on quickly: —

"What can there be more barbarous or unnatural than to ask a woman to sacrifice the man she loves to the man she does not love? Religious beliefs may be in contradiction with one another, but they all agree upon the same ethics, that marriage is based upon love. What then is matrimony? It is either something inviolable and essentially holy when resting upon such a basis, or if otherwise, only a contract in contradiction to religion and morality, and as such ought to be dissolved. Otherwise speaking, a woman's duties spring from her feelings, and not from a number of more or less solemn ceremonies, which in themselves are only so many forms. I say this because I am a man who puts truth above mere forms. I know the word 'faithlessness' sounds very terrible. But do not delude yourselves with the notion that a woman is faithless at the moment she leaves her husband. She is faithless the very moment she feels that her love for him is gone. What follows after is only a question of her capacity to bring things to a logical conclusion, of her courage and her heart that knows, or does not know, the meaning of love. Pani Korytzka loved the man for whom she divorces her husband before she was married; the marriage was contracted in a moment of misunderstanding, she mistaking an exhibition of jealousy for indifference. This was her only mistake; which she wants to correct now that she understands that it was not right to sacrifice the man she loved to the man she looked upon with indifference; nobody but those who will not see can call her bad or a hypocrite."

There was as much fiction as truth in what I was saying. I knew my aunt would never agree to the theory that the will ends when love steps in; but I said it to impress Aniela with the idea that there was no doubt about it. That first lover was also an invention of my own, to make the story more to the point. But I was perfectly sincere when speaking about the rights and duties springing from feeling. It is quite another thing that I might not stand up for this theory if it did not suit me just then; but man is always subjective, especially the man who has doubted all objective truths.

I stood up for myself, and should have been foolish to speak against my own interest. I counted that this kind of reasoning would hasten the evolution of her soul, encourage her, and finally justify her in her own eyes. Considering her great sensitiveness, I thought some of it would take root She understood me perfectly, and I could see that every word thrilled her nerves; her color came and went; she put her hands to her burning face to cool it. At last, when I had ceased speaking, she replied: —

"Everything may be proved in some way or other; but when we do wrong our conscience tells us, 'It is wrong, wrong!' and nothing can convince it to the contrary."

Young Chwastowski must have thought Aniela wanting in philosophical development, and as to myself I had a sensation like that, for instance, when a weapon comes into contact with a stone wall. Aniela's reply, in its simplicity and dogmatism, brought to naught all my arguments. For if the principle that the will ends where love steps in might be open to doubt, there is no doubt whatever that where dogma begins reasoning ceases. Women generally, and Polish women especially, agree with logic as long as it does not bring them into danger. At the approach of danger they shelter themselves behind the fortifications of simple faith and catechismal truth, which strong feeling might force to surrender, but reasoning, never. It is their weakness, and at the same time their strength. In consequence of this their power of reasoning is weaker than man's, but their saintliness in certain conditions becomes unassailable. The devil can lead a woman astray only when he inspires her with love; by way of reasoning he can do nothing, even if for once he has the right on his side.

In presence of these reflections I feel disheartened. I am thinking that any structure, however cleverly and artfully raised by me, will be pulled down by the simple words: "It is wrong; conscience does not permit it."

In presence of that I am powerless. I must be very careful so as not to estrange or frighten her by the boldness of ideas I try to acclimatize in her mind. And yet I cannot give up all endeavors of this kind. Though they do not occupy the first place in the plan of subduing her, they may hasten the solution. They would be of no use whatever if it were true that she did not love me. If I had made a mistake,—but even then there would be some kind of solution.

29 May.

To-day I found Aniela standing on a chair before the old Dantzic clock which had gone wrong. At the moment she raised herself on tip-toe to reach the hands, the chair gave way. I had only time to cry out, "Take care! you are falling!" I caught her in my arms, and put her on the floor. For the twinkling of an eye I held the dear girl in my arms, her hair touched my face, her breath fanned my cheek. I felt so dizzy that I had to steady myself by grasping the back of a chair, — and she saw it. She knows I love her madly. I cannot write any more.

30 May.

My whole day was poisoned, for Aniela has received another letter from Kromitzki. I heard her telling my aunt that he does not know himself when he will be able to return, — may be shortly, or it may be two months hence. I cannot even imagine how I shall be able to bear his presence near Aniela. At times it seems that I simply could not bear it. I count upon some lucky chance that will prevent his coming back. Chwastowski says Pani Celina ought to go to Gastein as soon as she can bear the journey. Gastein is such a distance from Baku that it may be too far for Kromitzki to go. I shall go there as sure as there is a heaven above us. It is a happy thought of Chwastowski's; the baths will do us all much good. I too feel fagged and in want of bracing mountain air, and still more in want of being near Aniela. To-morrow I shall go to Warsaw, and send a telegram to the manager of the bathing establishment to secure rooms for the ladies. If no rooms are to be had, I am ready to buy a villa. When Pani Celina spoke of the trouble and difficulties it would give Aniela were she to go there, I only said: "Leave it all to me;" and then, in a lower voice, to Aniela: "I will take care of her as if she were my own mother." I saw that Pani Celina, who believes less and less in Kromitzki's millions, was afraid I might arrange things on too expensive a scale; but I have already settled it in my mind to show her a fictitious agreement, and take the greater part of the expenses upon myself. Of course, I never mentioned that I intended going there myself. I will arrange it so that the proposal shall come from my aunt. I am quite sure that, as soon as I unfold my plans of going somewhere in the hills to recruit my health, the good soul will fall into the trap, and say. "Why not go with them? it will be more comfortable for all of you." I know it will frighten Aniela, and in the most secret recess of her heart please her a little. Maybe it will remind her of the poet's line, "You are everywhere: above me, around me, and within me." Then truly, my love will surround her as with an enchanted circle, enter her heart in the guise of thoughtfulness towards the mother, — in the guise of little services she cannot refuse without exciting her mother's suspicions; all this will gradually sink into her heart, in the guise of gratitude and pity for my sufferings, will thrust itself upon her with all the force of old memories.

She hears my praises sung by everybody: by my aunt, who loves me blindly as she always did; by young Chwastowski, who, to show the impartiality people of his opinions are capable of, maintains I am an exception in the "rotten sphere." I have even won over Pani Celina by my attentions; she likes me now, and involuntarily, I dare say, regrets that I am not Aniela's husband. All around Aniela there is one great suggestion of love.

And you, dearest, are you going to resist all these powers? When will you come and tell me: "I cannot hold out any longer; take me, — I love you"?

WARSAW, 31 May.

Pani L., the patroness of a charitable institution, asked Clara to give another concert for the benefit of the destitute. Clara refused on the plea that she is busy upon a great musical work that engages all her attention. The letter, — a very pattern of polite refusal, — was accompanied by exactly the same sum of money the first concert had brought in. It is easy to imagine what a sensation this act of generosity made in Warsaw. The papers were full of it, raising the musician and her generosity to the sky. Naturally, her private means, which are considerable, gained in dimensions. I do not know how society came to couple our names; perhaps, our acquaintance, dating from a long time, our intimacy, and the exaggerated news of her wealth gave rise to the rumor. I was at first a little angry on hearing this; but upon maturer reflection, resolved not to give any direct denial, because this puts my attentions towards Aniela beyond all suspicion.

When I went to Clara's morning reception, Pani Korytzka came up to me, and, with that witty, aggressive air of hers, asked me in presence of some dozen people from the musical world and Warsaw society, in an audible voice, —

"Tell me, cousin, who was that mythological person that could not resist the Siren?"

"Nobody resisted, *ma cousine*, except Ulysses; and he only because he was tied to the mast."

"And why have you not taken these precautions?"

I saw some covert smiles lurking in the faces of those who witnessed the attack, and I retorted, —

"Sometimes even that is of no use. You know that love sunders the strongest ties."

In spite of all her self-possession, Pani Korytzka grew confused, and I gained one of those tiny victories which are comprised in the proverb, "The scythe hit upon a stone," or in plain English, "The biter bit."

Whether people repeat to each other that I am going to marry Clara or not, does not trouble me in the least; in fact, for the above stated reason I do not mind it at all; but I did not expect that this visit would turn out so unpleasant, and Clara herself be the cause of it. When all the people had left, and only Sniatynski and I remained, she sat down to the piano, and played her new concerto, — played it so magnificently that we could not find words to express our admiration; repeating at our request the finale, she said, suddenly, —

"This is my farewell, because everything comes to a finale."

"Surely you are not thinking of leaving us?" asked Sniatynski.

"Yes, in ten days at the furthest I must be at Frankfurt," replied Clara.

Thereupon Sniatynski turned to me, —

"And what do you say to that, — you who at Ploszow gave us to understand, made us hope, Miss Hilst would remain with us always?"

"Yes; and I say the same now: her memory will always remain with us."

"Yes; I understood it so," replied Clara, with naïve resignation.

Inwardly I was furious, — with myself, Sniatynski, and Clara. I am neither so vain, foolish, nor mean that every conquest of that kind should rejoice me; therefore felt annoyed at the thought that Clara might love me, and nourish some baseless hopes. I knew she had some kind of undefined feeling, which, given time and occasion, might develop into something more lasting; but I had no idea this vague feeling dared to wish or expect something. It suddenly struck me that the announcement of her departure was prompted by a desire to find out how I would receive the news. I received it very coolly. A love like mine for Aniela ought to teach compassion; yet Clara's sadness and the mention of her departure, not only did not move me, but seemed to me an audacious flight of fancy and an insult to me.

Why? Not from any aristocratic notions; that is certain. I could not account at once for the strange phenomenon; but now explain it thus, — the feeling of belonging to Aniela is so strong and exclusive that it seems to me that any other woman wanting but one pulsation of my heart endeavors to steal something that is Aniela's property. This explanation is sufficient for me. No doubt, by and by I shall bid Clara good-by, and feel as friendly as ever towards her; but the sudden announcement of her departure gave me a distaste for her. It is only Aniela who may with impunity trample on my nerves. Never did I look at Clara so critically and resentfully; for the first time I became fully aware of the amplitude of her figure, the bright complexion, the dark hair, and blue, somewhat protruding eyes, the lips like ripe cherries, — in brief, her whole beauty reminded me of the cheap chromo-lithographs of harem beauties in second-class hotels. I left her in the worst of humors, and went straight to a book-shop to select some books for Aniela.

For a week I had been thinking what to choose for her reading. I did not wish to neglect anything, though I did not attach undue weight to this, as it acts very slowly. Besides, I have noticed that to our women, though their imagination is more developed than their temperament, a book is always something unreal. If it falls even into the hands of an exceptionally susceptible person, it creates in her at the most an abstract world, that has no connection with real life whatever. To almost none of them it occurs that ideas taken from books can be applied to any practical purpose. I am convinced that if a great writer tried to prove, for instance, that purity of thought and mind were not only superfluous in a woman, but even blameworthy from a moral point of view, — Aniela would opine that the principle might apply to the whole world with the exception of herself. The utmost I can hope for is that the reading of appropriate books will render her familiar with a certain kind of broad views and thoughts. That is all I wish for. Loving her from my whole soul, I want her to respond to that love, and do not neglect any means towards that end. I, who never deceive myself, confess openly that I want Aniela to sacrifice for me her husband, but I do not want to corrupt her or to soil her purity. Let nobody tell me that this is a sophism, and that the one includes the other. The tormenting devil that is always within me raising difficulties says: "You create new theories; the way of faithlessness *is* the way of corruption." How these conflicting thoughts tear me to pieces! I reply to the familiar spirit: "I might doubt opposite theories quite as much; I contrive what I can in defence of my love, — it is my natural law." And there is a greater law still, the law of love. Some feelings are mean and commonplace, others lofty and full of nobility. A woman that follows the call of lofty feeling does not lose the nobility of her soul. Such a great, exceptional love I try to awake in Aniela, and therefore I may say conscientiously that I do not want to corrupt her.

Besides, these inward arguments do not lead to anything. Even if I had not the slightest doubt that I am doing wrong, if I were unable to give any conclusive answer to the tormenting spirit, I would not cease loving; and always following where a greater power leads me, I should go according to my feeling, and not according to abstract reasoning.

But the true misfortune of those analytic and hyper-analytic modern people is that, though not believing in the result of their analysis, they have the invincible habit of inquiring into everything that goes on within themselves. It is the same with me. For some time I have been questioning myself how it is possible that a man absorbed by a great feeling should be able to be so watchful, so calculating about ways and means, and to account for everything as if somebody else did it for him. I could reply to it in this way: The man of the period reserves above everything part of himself to observe the other part. Besides, the whole activity of a mind full of forethought, of reflections apparently cool, stands eventually in proportion to the temperature of the feeling. The hotter this grows, the more cool reason is forced into service. I repeat, it is a mistake to represent love with bandaged eyes. Love does not suppress reason, as it does not suppress the breathing, or the beating of the heart, — it only subjugates it. Reason thereupon becomes the first adviser, the implement of war, — in other words, it plays the part of an Agrippa to a Cæsar Augustus. It is holding all the forces in readiness, leads them into war, gains victories, and places the monarch on the triumphal car; it erects finally, — not a Pantheon, like the historical Agrippa, — but a Monotheon, where it serves its only divinity. In the microcosm called man, the part reason plays is a still greater one than that of chief commander, — for it reflects into infinite parts the consciousness of everything and of self, — as a collection of properly arranged mirrors reflect a given object infinitely.

1 June.

Yesterday I received news from Gastein. The rooms for Pani Celina and Aniela are ready. I sent them the particulars, together with a parcel of books by Balzac and George Sand. To-day is Sunday, and the first day of the races. My aunt has arrived from Ploszow and taken up her abode with me. That she went to the races is a matter of course, she is altogether absorbed in them. But our horses, Naughty Boy and Aurora, which arrived here two days ago with the trainer Webb and Jack Goose, the jockey, are on the list for Thursday; therefore my aunt's attendance at the Sunday races was merely a platonic affair. The goings on here are past all description. The stables have been converted into a kind of fortress. My aunt fancies the jockeys of other racing studkeepers shake in their shoes at the very mention of Naughty Boy, and are ready to use every means to prevent his running; consequently in every orange boy or organ grinder that comes into the yard, she sees an enemy in disguise, bent upon some evil practice. The Swiss porter and the servants have strict orders to keep an eye upon everybody that comes in. In the stables, the precautions taken are still stricter. The trainer Webb, being an Englishman, remains impassive, but the unfortunate Jack Goose, a native of Burzany, and whose name is a literal translation from the Polish Kuba Gonsior, fairly loses his head; my aunt scolds him and the grooms, natives also of Burzany, whenever she fancies things are going wrong. She was so much at the stables that I did not see much of her, and only when departing she told me that Aniela was to come for the races. I suppose Pani Celina consented to this in order to please my aunt; besides, she can very well remain alone for one day, with the doctor and the maids to look after her. Aniela, who is walled up at Ploszow day after day, really wants a little change. For me this is joyful news indeed. The very thought that she will be under my roof has a singular charm for me. Here I began to love her and maybe her heart kept beating a little faster after that entertainment my aunt gave here in her honor. Everything here will remind her of the past.

2 June.

It is fortunate I did not have the rooms altered to suit a museum. I have an idea to give a dinner-party after the races. In this way I shall be able to keep her here a few hours longer, — and besides, she will understand that it is all for her.

3 June.

I ordered a cartload of plants and flowers to put along the staircase and in the rooms. Aniela's room remains exactly as it was when she occupied it. I suppose the ladies will arrive in the morning and Aniela will want to change her dress. I had a large mirror put there, and every requisite for a lady's toilet. Aniela will meet everywhere proofs of thoughtfulness, memory, and faithful love. Only now, while writing, it strikes me how much easier I feel when occupied with something, when outward activity takes me out of the enchanted circle of reflection and pondering over myself. Even driving nails into the wall for the pictures of the future museum would be better than twisting one idea around another. Why cannot I be a simple-minded man? If I had been that in times gone by I should be now the happiest man in the world.

4 June.

I went to-day to invite the Sniatynskis and several other people to dinner. Sniatynski has spread the news of my founding a museum for the public, and I am at present the hero of the day. All the papers write about it, improving the occasion as usual by pitching into those that waste their substance abroad instead of doing good to the country. I know their style so well, and it amuses me. There are the usual phrases about a citizen's duties and "noblesse oblige," but it suits my purpose. I gathered the whole packet to show my aunt and Aniela.

5 June.

The races have been fixed a day sooner because of to-morrow's holiday. Aniela and my aunt arrived this morning with a maid and sundry boxes containing their racing toilets. The first glance at Aniela filled me with terror. She does not look well at all; her face is wan and has lost its former warm color; it seems smaller too, and there is something misty about her that reminds me of Puvis de Chawannes' figures. My aunt and her mother do not notice it, because they see her every day; but to me, after the absence of a few days, the change is very remarkable. I am seized with contrition and sincere pity. It is evident that the inward struggle is telling upon her. If she would only end it, and follow the dictates of a heart that is mine, — a hundred times mine and pleads for me, — all her troubles would cease and happiness begin. I am getting deeper and deeper into the quicksands. It seemed to me that I knew her so well; every detail and every feature stands out before my eyes when I do not see her, and yet when I meet her, after a few days' absence, I discover a new charm, and find something new I like in her. How she satisfies my every taste, and I am deeply conscious that she is my type, — my only affinity. This consciousness gives me a belief, half mystic, half approaching the natural hypothesis, that she was meant for me. When hearing the sound of wheels, I ran down to meet her, and again had the sensation one might call falling under the spell; again the reality seemed to me more perfect than the picture I carry in my heart. She was dressed in a dust-cloak of Chinese silk; a long gray veil was twisted round her hat and tied under her chin, and from amid that frame the dear face, always more like a girl's than a married woman's, smiled at me. Her greeting was more cheerful and more frank than usual; it was evident the morning drive and the prospect of a little pleasure had brightened her spirits; this filled me with delight. I thought, "She is glad to see me again, and Ploszow appears to her dull and empty without me." I offered one arm to my aunt and the other to Aniela, as the staircase is wide enough for three persons, and led them upstairs. At the sight of all the plants and flowers she uttered a little cry of wonder.

"It is my surprise," I said.

I pressed her arm slightly, so slightly that it might have passed for an accidental movement, and then turning to my aunt, said: —

"I am giving a dinner in honor of the Ploszowski success."

My aunt was deeply gratified with my belief in that event. Ah! if she knew how little I care for Naughty Boy, and all the races the Ploszow horses might win on all the race-courses of Europe. Aniela evidently guessed something of this, but she was in such spirits that she only cast a passing glance at me, and bit her lips to hide a smile.

I well-nigh lost my head. In the covert smile I saw a shade of coquetry I had never noticed there before. It is impossible, I thought, that she should have no vanity whatever, and not feel flattered in the least, on perceiving that all I am doing is done through her and for her sake.

My aunt divested herself of her travelling-wraps, and without delay went to inspect Naughty Boy and Aurora, and I showed Aniela the list of the invited guests.

"I tried to bring together people you like; but if there is anybody else you would like to have, I will go myself, or send an invitation."

"Show it to aunty;" replied Aniela, "let her decide."

"No; aunty will sit at the head of the table, and we shall go to her with our congratulations or condolences, as the case may be; but the part of lady of the house I have assigned to you."

Aniela blushed a little, and, trying to change the conversation, said: —

"Leon, I do hope Naughty Boy will win; aunty has set her heart upon it, and will be so vexed if it should turn out otherwise."

"I have won already, because I have as guest under my roof a certain small person who is sitting opposite me."

"You are making fun; but I am really anxious about it."

"My aunt," I replied, more seriously, "will have some compensation if she loses. My collections will be in

Warsaw in a few weeks, and this has been the dearest wish of her life. She always tried to make my father give them to the town. All the papers are full of it, and praise me to an extent you have no idea of."

The dear face lit up with pleasure.

"Show me; read it to me," she said eagerly.

I had a desire to kiss her hands for that glimpse of brightness. It was a new proof. If I were indifferent to her, would she rejoice so much when I am praised?

"Not now," I replied. "I will read it when my aunt comes back, or rather she must read it, and I will hide my blushes behind you; you, at least, shall not see how foolish I look."

"Why should you look foolish?"

"Because the thing is not worth all the fuss, and if there be any merit in it, it is yours, not mine. They ought to praise you. I would give a good deal if I could tell those journalists: 'If you think well of it, go *en masse* and kneel at certain little feet and pour out your gratitude there!'"

"Leon! Leon!" interrupted Aniela.

"Now do not say a word, lest I should feel tempted to divulge the great secret."

Aniela did not know what to say. The words were those of a man in love; but the tone was so playful and jesting that she could not possibly receive them in a tragic spirit.

I was glad I had discovered a way by which I could convey a deeper meaning without absolutely frightening her. But I did not take too much advantage of it, and presently, in a more serious tone, began telling her about the projected changes in the house.

"The whole story is to be given up to the collections, with the exception of the room in which you lived last winter. This remains as it was. I have only permitted myself to adorn it a little for your reception."

Saying this I led her to the door. Standing on the threshold she exclaimed with astonishment: —

"Oh, what lovely flowers!"

I said in a low voice: —

"And you the most lovely among them!"

Then added, earnestly: —

"You believe me, Aniela, if I tell you that it is in this room I wish to die some day!"

Oh, how much sincerity there was in these words. Aniela's face grew misty; all the radiance had gone. I saw that my words had touched a chord, as all words do that come from the depth of the soul. For a moment her whole body swayed as if some inward power pushed her towards me. But she resisted still. She stood before me, her eyes veiled by the long lashes, and said, with mournful dignity: —

"Let me be at ease with you, Leon; do not sadden me."

"Very well, Aniela; I will not say anything more; here is my hand upon it."

I gave her my hand, and she pressed it warmly, as if by that pressure she wanted to say all she forbade her lips to utter. It indemnified me for all I had suffered, and almost made me stagger on my feet. For the first time I felt distinctly that I was taking for my own this being, — body and soul. It was a sensation of such immeasurable happiness as to cause me almost pain. New, unknown worlds began to open for me. From this moment I grew quite convinced that her resistance was only a question of time.

My aunt returned from the stables in excellent humor; no attempt had been made upon Naughty Boy's precious health. The trainer, Webb, to all inquiries, had the same answer, — "All right." Jack Goose was animated by the boldest spirit. We went to the window to see the future conquerors come from the stables; for it was time they went to the Mokotoff Field, there to pace around until their turn arrived. A few minutes later we saw the grooms leading them into the yard, encased from top to bottom as in a pillow-slip. Only the soft eyes were visible through the slit; and from below, the shapely feet that seemed wrought in steel. They were followed by Webb and our little home-bred Englishman, Jack Goose, in a new overcoat, which concealed his silks and jockey-boots. I called out to him through the open window:—

"Mind, and don't get beaten, Kuba!"

He raised his cap, and pointing with it at Naughty Boy, replied in the purest, not London, but Bursany, dialect:—

"Bedom prosz jasnie hrabiego widzieli, ale ino jego-zad." (They will see him, my lord, but only his hind-quarters.)

We sat down to a hurried lunch; nevertheless my aunt had time to read what the papers had to say about the future museum. It is strange how sensitive women are to public applause for their nearest mankind. My aunt fairly beamed at me through her spectacles, and was incomparable when she now and then, interrupting the reading, glanced keenly at Aniela, and then said in her most dogmatic tone:—

"They do not exaggerate the least bit. He was always like that."

Praise heaven there was not another sceptic mind present, otherwise I should have looked foolish indeed.

It was time for the ladies to dress. Before leaving the room my aunt turned to me and said with the most innocent expression of face:—

"We must be quick, for I promised to call for Panna Zawilowski; she was going with her father, but as he is suffering from an attack of gout I shall have to chaperon her."

With this she went to her room. We looked at each other, Aniela and I; the corners of her mouth twitched with merriment. "Aniela, it is a new matrimonial scheme, what shall I do?" She put a finger to her lips in warning that I spoke too loud, and disappeared within her room, presently the lovely head peeped out through the half-open door.

"I just remembered you have not asked Miss Hilst," she said.

"No, I have not asked her."

"Why?"

"Because I love her on the sly," I retorted, laughing.

"Seriously, why did you not invite her?"

"If you wish I will invite her now."

"It is as you wish," she replied, and disappeared again.

But I preferred not to invite Miss Hilst.

An hour later we were driving in the Belvederski Avenue. Aniela wore a cream-colored dress trimmed with lace. I have such a knack of saying with my eyes what my lips must not utter, that Aniela read in them my rapture. I recognized it in her face, that looked half-pleased, half-vexed. We stopped on the way before the Zawilowski villa, and before I had time to ring, the door opened, and Panna Zawilowska herself came out. She stood before me a vision in silver gray, rather a cold vision, as she barely nodded to me before going to my aunt. She is rather plain than pretty, — a blond with steely blue eyes and studied manners. She is considered a very pattern of distinction, and with good reason; that is, if distinction means the same as stiffness. Her treatment of me is as cold as her eyes, too cold even to be quite natural. If this is a method adopted on purpose to chafe my vanity, it is very foolish, for it only bores me, and does not provoke me in the least. I am rather glad of it, as it permits me to pay her only such attentions as simple politeness exacts.

To-day I paid her a little more attention; she served me in fact as a screen to avert any suspicion from Aniela. Presently we drove on again, but very slowly, as in front and in rear as far as the eye could reach, all sorts of vehicles were moving in the same direction. Before us and behind, there was a perfect stream of sunshades; the various colors of which shone in the sun and created a warmly tinted shadow from beneath which peeped forth women's heads with delicate and refined features. There was the average number of pretty faces, but they expressed a want of temperament. I did not even see it in the financial world, which, besides many other things, puts on temperament rather than possesses it in reality. Among the carriages not a few displayed considerable taste, and the bright toilets changing and gleaming in the sun on a background of green trees, the crowds of fine people and fine horses gave the whole show a highly civilized appearance, not lacking either in picturesqueness. I was glad to see Aniela pleased with the motion and turmoil. Replying to my casual remarks she looked at me with gratitude as if it were I that had arranged it all for her pleasure. Sitting opposite, I could look at her without constraint, but I turned oftener towards Panna Zawilowska, from whom blew a cold air, as from a decanter of iced water, which began to amuse me; her words and manner seemed to imply that she agreed to my society, because politeness did not permit her to do otherwise. I treated her with a certain good-humored courtesy that seemed to iritate her not a little.

We arrived at last on the Mokotoffskie Pola. There was a reserved place near the grand stand for my aunt's carriage, and presently various acquaintances with tickets stuck on their hats came up and congratulated her upon the promising appearance of Naughty Boy. One of the greatest horsebreeders said to her that the horse was a splendid animal, though not sufficiently trained; but as the turf was soft from yesterday's rain, a strong animal like Naughty Boy stood a fair chance of coming in a winner.

It seemed to me that he spoke a little ironically, which made me feel uneasy. Naughty Boy's defeat would spoil the day for my aunt, and indirectly for me, too, as her bad humor would damp our pleasure. In the mean while I looked around me at the field, and searched for known faces. The race course was thronged with people. The grand stand looked like a dark, compact mass, relieved by bright female toilets. The course was surrounded by rows after rows of spectators; even the town walls were alive with them. On either side of the grand stand stood a long line of carriages; each separately looked like a flower-basket. Not very far from where I stood I became suddenly aware of a pink face and agressive little nose that could not belong to anybody but Pani Sniatynska. I went up to her and she told me her husband had just left her to look for Miss Hilst; and then, almost in one breath, asked me how my aunt was, whether Aniela was at the races, how the ladies would manage their journey to Gastein since Pani Celina could not walk, whether I thought Naughty Boy would win the race, and what we would do if he lost, and how many people had I invited to dinner. While standing near her carriage I noticed what a sweet expression her face has, and the pretty foot that peeped forth from the carriage; but as to answering all the questions, I should have to borrow Gargantua's mouth, as Shakspeare says. Replying to one or two of the questions and saying I hoped to see her after the races, I followed Sniatynski's track in search of Clara. I found her carriage not far from my aunt's. Clara looked like a hill covered with heliotrope blossoms. I found her surrounded by a host of admirers and artists, conversing gayly with them. Her face clouded when she saw me, and my reception was of the coolest. A friendly word from me would have changed all that, but I remained cold; after a quarter of an hour's polite and ceremonious conversation, I went farther, exchanging here and there a few words with people I knew, and then turned toward our own carriage. The first two races had taken place, and Naughty Boy's turn came at last.

I looked at my aunt; the expression of her face was very solemn; she evidently tried her best to keep cool. On the contrary, Aniela's face showed evident uneasiness. We had to wait some time before the horses came out, because the weighing lasted unusually long. Suddenly

Sniatynski came running up, gesticulating with both hands, and showing some bits of paper.

"I have put a pot of money on Naughty Boy," he exclaimed; "if he betrays me, I shall have to throw myself upon your well-known charity."

"I trust —" began my aunt, with all her dignity.

But she did not finish her sentence, as at this moment from amid the dark mass of people there rose the varicolored caps and silks of the jockeys. The horses were slowly trotting along. Some of them, finding themselves in the open, quickened their pace; others followed more leisurely. At the start they passed us in a group and not very fast, so as to save their horses' strength, the race being a double one. But at the second turn they were drawn out in a line. It looked as if the wind had scattered the petals of some flowers along the road. The first was a jockey in white, closely followed by another in pale blue and red, then two together, one in red, the other in red and yellow; our Kuba in orange and black was last but one, followed by a jockey in white and blue. This order did not last long. When the horses had reached the other side of the course, there arose some commotion in the carriages. The more excited ladies climbed up on the seats so as not to lose the least part of the race; their example was followed by my aunt, who evidently could not sit still any longer.

Aniela offered her place to Panna Zawilowska, who, after some ceremonious protests, accepted it; and I helped Aniela to the back seat, and, as she had nothing to hold on by, offered her my hand. I confess that I did not think of the race so much as of the dear little hand that rested so trustingly in mine.

My aunt's back obscured the view a little; but raising myself on tiptoe, I swept the whole field with my eyes, and saw the jockeys drawing near the curve of the other side. Seen from this distance, they looked like bright-colored beetles flying through the air; the motion appeared slow, and the throwing out of the horses' fore and hind legs almost mechanical. But in spite of the apparent slowness, they cleared the ground very swiftly.

The order of the riders was changed again. The white was still leading, followed by the red; but our Kuba was third now. The others remained behind, and the distance between them grew wider every moment. Naughty Boy was evidently not the worst among them. For a moment I lost sight of him, and presently saw him again as they passed us. The red was close upon the white, and Kuba gaining ground. I now observed for the first time that the white would have no chance, as the horse's flanks shone with moisture, as if water had been poured over him. It was clear the race would lie between the red and orange and black. At the worst, Naughty Boy would be second, and the defeat not so complete. What inspired me with confidence was the horse's pace; he threw out his legs so evenly, as if he performed a daily task. The spectators' excitement became greater every moment.

"Has Naughty Boy lost?" asked Aniela, in a low, excited voice, seeing the order in which the horses came past the stand.

"No, dear; they have still another round," I replied, pressing her hand slightly. She did not withdraw her hand; it is true that her whole attention was absorbed in the race. When the horses came to the other side, Kuba was second, the white was so exhausted that he had to fall back, and the three following riders came up to him. It was now a race between the two, and there were only five or six lengths between them. Suddenly a loud murmur from the stand told us that something unusual had happened; Kuba was coming up to his adversary. The murmurs on the stand grew into a tumult. Aniela was so carried away by excitement that she squeezed my hand nervously, and asked every moment, "What are they doing now?" The riders were on the left side of the field. The red, by the help of his whip, had gained a little; but presently Naughty Boy almost touched him with his nose. In this furious pace they came both on a line with the stand, where we lost sight of them again. The struggle would be over now in a few seconds. On the stand there was a momentary silence, which suddenly changed into loud, prolonged cheering. Many people were running along the lines which hide the road, and at this moment we saw the red nostrils; the horse's head, stretched out like a cord, orange and black, was carried along as if by a hurricane. The bell rang on the grand stand,—the victory was ours.

The red had lost by a dozen lengths.

I must say for my aunt that she never lost her self-possession. Nobody but me noticed the few drops of perspiration which stood on her forehead; she fanned with her pocket-handkerchief. Aniela was excited, amused, and happy. We both congratulated our aunt; even Panna Zawilowska said a few French sentences, stiff and proper, as if taken from a copy-book. Presently a crowd of acquaintances thronged around our carriage, and my aunt's triumph was complete.

I was also intoxicated, but by something quite different; namely, the pressure of Aniela's hand. In vain I said to myself that it was nothing but the excitement of the moment; because it occurred to me that a woman's resistance often passes a crisis in such moments of exaltation, when carried beside herself by some amusement, beautiful view, or other circumstance different from the even tenor of every-day life. Then a certain relaxation of the nerves takes place, in presence of which a loss of the usual balance is easily explained. Taking into account this special state of Aniela's mind, I arrived at the conclusion that she did not fight against her feeling any longer; and I resolved to put an end to it.

I suppose at Ploszow there will be no difficulty about a chance. We go back to-morrow. To-day's entertainment, the dinner, the conversation, and the excitement are so many drops of narcotic. She does not even suppose what happiness there is in store for us; but she must surrender her soul to me, wholly and unconditionally.

Though my aunt had notified Pani Celina that we might remain at Warsaw until the next day, we really intended going back after dinner, — when something occurred that prevented our starting. Dinner and tea afterwards lasted until ten o'clock. When the last of our guests had departed somebody came to tell my aunt that Naughty Boy had been taken ill. There was a great confusion. The vet was sent for in a hurry, but it was midnight before he arrived. My aunt would not think of going so late as that.

Aniela wanted to go very much, but knew I would have to go with her; and she is still afraid of me. My aunt told her she would only rouse the whole house, disturbing thereby her mother, and wound up by saying: —

"Leon does not mind my looking at his house as my own; consequently you are my guest. It would be the same if I gave up Ploszow to him; I should live there, and you with me, — at least, so long as Celina has not recovered her health."

And finally Aniela had to remain.

It is now three o'clock in the morning. It is already growing light; but lanterns are still flitting across the yard near the stables, where they are busy with Naughty Boy.

My aunt, when wishing us good-night, announced that she intended to remain a day longer at Warsaw; whereupon I said that I had left some papers at Ploszow, and would go and fetch them, and see Aniela home at the same time. We shall be alone, and I will hesitate no longer. The blood rushes to my heart at the thought that I shall travel, though only a short distance, with the dear love close to my heart, and listen to her confession that she loves me as much as I love her.

The sky is clouded, and it has begun to rain. A few hours only divide me from the moment when a new life is to begin for me. Of course I do not sleep; I could not sleep now for anything in the world. There is no heaviness on my eyelids, — I write, and recall memories. I still seem to feel the pressure of her hand on mine. I made that soul, educated, developed it, and prepared it for love. I am like the head of an army, who has foreseen all chances, arranged and calculated everything, and does not sleep on the eve of the day that will decide his fate. But Aniela sleeps peacefully on the other side of the house; and even her dreams plead for me, for my love. When I think of this, all my nerves are vibrating.

In that ocean of trouble, evil, foolishness, uncertainties, and doubts we call life, there is one thing worth living for, as certain and as strong as — nay, stronger than — death; and that is love. Beyond it there is nothingness.

6 June.

I went with Aniela, and am even now asking myself, "Have I gone mad?" I did not hold her close to my heart, did not hear an avowal of love. I was spurned without a moment's hesitation; all her modesty risen in arms, she reduced me to a mere nothing. What is it? Am I a fool without brains, or has she no heart? What am I fighting against? What are the obstacles in my way? Why does she spurn me? My head is in such a chaotic state that I can neither think, write, nor reason. I only repeat to myself, over and over again, "What is it that bars my way?"

7 June.

I have made an enormous mistake somewhere; there is something in Aniela I have not observed or taken into account. For two days I have tried to understand what has happened to me, but my head was in such a whirl that I could not think. Now I am collecting my thoughts, pulling myself together to look the situation in the face. It would be clear enough if Aniela were guarded by a strong love for her husband. I could understand then the offended modesty and indignation with which a being, so meek and sweet-tempered usually, spurned me from her feet. But I cannot even suppose such a thing. I have still enough brains left to know that it is a mistake to see things too black, as it is a mistake to see them too rose-colored. Where should her love for Kromitzki have come from? She married him without love. In the short time they lived together, he deceived her and sold the land so dear to both of those women, and injured her mother's health. They have no child; besides, a child does not teach a woman to love her husband; it only teaches her to take him into account; it makes her safer, — that is to say, it strengthens the union of hands, not of hearts. Aniela besides does not belong to that kind of women to whom love comes suddenly, as a revelation after marriage; women like that pine more after their husbands, or more readily take a lover. I speak of all this in such a matter of fact way that it hurts me; but why should I spare myself? Finally, I am convinced she has no feeling even approaching to love for Kromitzki, — what is more, does not even respect him; she does not permit herself to despise him, that is all. I consider that as proved, otherwise I should be blind.

Then if her heart at the moment of my return was a *tabula rasa* I must have contrived to write something on it, I who managed this in other conditions, and was more bent on it than I ever was on anything in my life, who worked upon her feelings of friendship, touched the chords of pity and memories of the past, not neglecting anything, considering every trifle, and moreover am possessed of the power a strong, earnest feeling gives. I take myself by the shoulders: "Man, whatever you may be, you are not a provincial lion, that considers himself irresistible to any woman chance throws in his way;

have you not deluded yourself into the belief that she loves you?"

What speaks in favor of its being a delusion?

At the first glance, her resistance.

But I never supposed for a moment that she would not resist. I fancy to myself any other married woman, desperately in love with another man; can one suppose she would not resist and struggle against it and the loved one, until her strength gave way? Resistance is not the outcome of love, but since those two forces can exist side by side like two birds in a nest, one does not exclude the other.

I write this diary not only because it has become my second nature, my passion, not only because it gives an outlet for my pent-up feelings, but still more because it gives me a clear view and keeps account of all that is passing. I read over again the pages where I have written down my and Aniela's history from the time of my arrival at Ploszow. I have taken note of well-nigh every glance, every smile and tear, caught every tremor of her heart; and no! I do not deceive myself, the analysis is not wrong! Hers were the tears, the words, the glances and smiles of a woman — maybe unhappy — but not indifferent. I must have influenced her, made an impression upon her. I am not blind; it tears my heart day after day to see how her face is getting smaller, the hands more transparent — and it makes my hair stand on end to think she is paying out her life in this struggle. But all these are invincible proofs. Her heart, her thoughts belong to me. For that very reason she is unhappy — perhaps even more unhappy than I.

I read over what I wrote a moment ago, — that I did not even suppose she would not resist. I thought so soon after my return to Ploszow, but lately and when she was at Warsaw I fancied that I saw signs of yielding. I was wrong. She did not give way in the least, showed no sign of pity; my words to which she would not even listen seemed blasphemy to her. I saw in her eyes sparks of anger and resentment; she tore away her hands I covered with kisses, and the words: "You insult me!" were continually on her lips. Her energy daunted me the more as I had least expected such an explosion of wrath. Ah me! She threatened to leave the carriage and go on foot in the pelting rain to Ploszow. The word "divorce" acted upon her as a red-hot iron. I obtained nothing, nothing, nothing with all my eloquence and audacity; neither my entreaties nor my love moved her; she took everything as an insult to her womanhood, spurned my love and trampled on it. To-day when I see her so meek and sweet-tempered it seems like a horrid dream, and I can scarcely believe that it is the same woman. I cannot hide it from myself; I have met with a defeat so complete and decisive that if I had the strength, or anything else to live for I ought to go away at once.

Supposing she does love me, what good can it be to me if that feeling is to remain for ever imprisoned within her own heart, and never show itself — either in word or deed? I might as well be loved by Greek Helen, Cleopatra, Beatrice, or Mary Stuart. Such must be the feeling which does not desire anything, exact anything, and is sufficient unto itself. Maybe her heart belongs to me, but it is a faint heart, incapable of any action.

Possibly she poses before herself as a lofty soul, sacrificing her love upon the altar of duty — and pleases herself in that pose. It is a satisfaction worth doing something for. Be it so! Sacrifice me; but if you think you sacrifice much in immolating your feeling, and feed your duty upon it, you are mistaken. I cannot, I cannot either think or write calmly.

8 June.

A coquette is like a usurer, giving very little and exacting upon it a high percentage. To-day, as I am growing more composed and can think again, I must render

Aniela justice; she never encouraged me or exacted anything. What I mistook for a touch of coquetry at Warsaw was mere joyfulness of a youthful spirit that had shaken itself momentarily free from all trouble. All that has happened was brought on by me. I made mistake after mistake, and it is all my fault.

To know something, and to make it a matter of calculation are two different things. We account to ourselves for unknown factors which act upon the soul of a given individual, but in dealing with the same we generally take ourselves as a point of issue. This happened to me. I knew, or at least was conscious of the fact, that Aniela and I are as different from each other as if we were the inhabitants of two separate planets, but I did not always remember it. Involuntarily I counted upon her acting in a certain position as I should have acted.

In spite of the consciousness that we two are the most dissimilar beings under the sun, as opposite as the poles, I note it down with a certain surprise, and seem not able to get used to the thought. And yet it is true. I am a thousand times more like Laura Davis than Aniela.

And now I begin to understand why I failed.

The rock I split against is the want of that which has vanished within me, thereby freeing my thoughts, but bringing instead of it the mortal disease that has become my tragedy; it is the catechismal simplicity of the soul.

Now I can account for it clearly, perhaps not quite satisfactorily, for I am of so complex a disposition as to have lost the very instinct of simplicity. "I hear thy voice, but I see thee not." My spiritual sight suffers from Daltonian disease and cannot distinguish colors.

I cannot even understand how any one can accept a principle, however hallowed by ages, without looking at it from both sides, pulling it to pieces, into shreds and atoms, until it crumbles into dust and cannot be put together any more.

Aniela cannot understand that a principle once considered good, hallowed by religion, as well as by public opinion, could be considered otherwise than as a sacred duty.

It does not matter to me whether she is conscious of it, or it is instinctive impulse reasoned out by her intelligence, or merely acquired; it is enough that it has entered her very nature.

I had a glimpse of it the other day when I spoke about Pani Korytzka's divorce suit: "You can prove everything, and yet when one does wrong conscience tells us: 'It is wrong, it is wrong!'" I did not then attach the importance to these words that belonged to them. In Aniela there is no wavering, no doubt whatever. Her soul winnows the chaff from the grain with such precision that there can be no question about its purity. She does not try to find her own norma, but takes it ready-made from religion, general moral principles, and clings to them so strongly that they become her very own, for they permeate her system. The simpler the differential quality of good and evil, the more absolute and merciless it grows. In this ethical code there are no extenuating circumstances. As according to it the wife belongs to her husband, she who gives herself to another does wrong. There are no discussions, no considerations, or reflections, — there is the right hand for the righteous, the left for the sinners, God's mercy above all, — but nothing between, no intermediate place.

It is the code of the honest villager, so simple that people like me do not understand it. It seems to us that human life and human souls are too complex to find room in it. Unfortunately we have not found anything to replace it, and consequently we flutter here and there like stray birds, in loneliness and alarm.

The greater part of our women still hold fast to that code. Even those who occasionally stray from it do not permit themselves a momentary doubt as to its truth and sacredness. Where it begins, reasoning leaves off.

The poets erroneously represent woman as an enigma, a living Sphinx. Man is a hundred times more of an enigma and a Sphinx. A healthy woman that is not hysterical may be either good or bad, strong or weak, but she has more spiritual simplicity than man. Forever and all times the Ten Commandments are enough for her, whether she live according to their tenets, or through human frailty set them aside.

The female soul is so dogmatic that I have known a woman whose very atheism took the form of religion.

It is strange that this code of the honest villager does not exclude in women either keen intelligence, a subtle mind, or loftiness of ideas. Their soul seems to have something of the humming-bird which flits in and out the thickest shrubs, without getting entangled in their branches, or touching a single leaf.

This may be said especially in regard to Aniela. The greatest subtility of feeling and thought goes hand in hand with the utmost simplicity of moral ideas. Her Ten Commandments are the same as the village girls', with the exception that those of the latter are wrought on coarse linen, and hers on a web as fine as lace. Why do I discuss this question? Simply because it is a question of my happiness, almost my life; for I feel that with all my complex and intricate philosophy of love, I cannot get over the Ten Commandments. And how can I conquer them, since I do not even believe in that philosophy, while Aniela's faith in her principles is calm and unshaken?

Only the lips that have been drinking at the fountain of doubt opine that a forbidden kiss is not a sin. A religious woman may be carried away, as a tree is swept away by a hurricane, by forbidden love, but she will never acknowledge it.

Shall I ever be able to carry off Aniela? It is possible that my present state of despondency and discouragement is only a passing one, and to-morrow I shall feel more hopeful, — to-day all seems impossible.

I wrote once in this same diary that in certain families they inoculate their children with modesty as they inoculate for small-pox. The rule which says the wife shall belong to the husband, and in which Aniela believes so firmly, is strengthened by that modesty, so knitted into her being, so worked into the system, that I could sooner fancy Aniela cold and lifeless than baring her bosom in my presence.

And I can still delude myself with the idea that I may expect anything from her! It is simple idiocy!

What am I to do then? Go away?

No; I shall not go away. I will not, and cannot.

I will remain, and since my love is idiotic, I will do as idiots do. Enough of systems, calculations, forethought! Let things take their own way. My former ways did not lead to anything.

9 June.

She is not a bit happier than I am. What I saw to-day confirmed my suspicion that she is fighting a heavy battle, with nothing to help her except the truth of her own faith and convictions.

After the departure of Pan Zawilowski and his daughter, who had paid us a visit, my aunt, evidently with a certain purpose, began to enlarge upon the good qualities of Panna Zawilowska. I burst out into a sudden rage; I was tired, my nerves over-wrought by sleeplessness and irritated beyond measure. I exclaimed: "Have your way then! If it be a question of marriage only, and not of happiness, I will propose to-morrow to Panna Zawilowska. She or somebody else; what does it matter?"

Anybody might have seen it was merely irritation, not conviction, that dictated words I should never have acted upon. But Aniela had grown very white. She rose and without apparent reason began to unfasten the cords of the blind with trembling hands. Fortunately my aunt was so taken aback by the suddenness of my outburst that she did not notice her. She said something, I did not hear what, as all my attention was concentrated upon

Aniela. It is true that by reasoning I had come to the conclusion that something must be going on in her heart, but to reason out a thing and to see it, are two different things. As long as I live I shall never forget that white face and those trembling hands. I had now a tangible proof, which, however I might explain it by the suddenness of my announcement, is still proof enough. Sudden news either of the death or marriage of anybody that is indifferent to us does not pale our cheeks.

I thought a few days ago: "Of what use is it to me that she loves me, if that love is to remain forever hidden in her breast?" and yet when I came to read, as I did now, the confirmation of it, my hope rose at once and all doubts vanished. Again a vision of possible victory flashed before my eyes, — alas! to be dissolved almost at once into nothing. My aunt, saying something, went out of the room, maybe to wipe away a furtive tear at my hardness, and I went up to Aniela.

"Aniela dear! I would not marry that girl for anything in the world, but you ought to enter a little in my position. I have troubles enough to bear, and even here they will not leave me in peace. You know best that I could never dream of such a step."

"On the contrary, I should be glad if that happened," she said, with evident effort.

"It is not true! I have seen you changing color, — I have seen it."

"Permit me to go away."

"Aniela mine! you love me! do not lie to me and to yourself; you love me!"

She grew white to her lips.

"No," she replied quickly; "but I am afraid I might learn to hate you."

And with that she left the room. I know that to a woman who fights with herself, a bitter and forbidden love often seems akin to hatred; and yet Aniela's words staggered me and extinguished the newborn hope, as one blows out a candle. There are many quite natural things in this world which we are strong enough to bear but for our nerves. I am struck by a truth not recognized by me formerly, not recognized generally, — that love for another man's wife, if only a pastime is the greatest vileness, and if real, the greatest misfortune that can happen to any man; the more worthy the woman the greater the misfortune. I have a burning curiosity within me, very bitter at the same time, as to what Aniela would do if I said to her: "Either put your arms round my neck and own that you love me, or I will blow out my brains here before your eyes!" I know it would be the meanest thing in the world, and I should never force her hand in that way; no! whatever I may be, I am not bad enough for that! But I cannot help thinking, "What would she do?" I am almost certain she would not survive the shock and the scorn of herself, but she would not yield. When I think of this I curse her and worship her at the same time; I hate her and love her more than ever. The worst is I do not see how I shall ever get out of this enchanted circle. Added to the passion of the senses this woman wakes in me, I have for her a dog-like affection. I envelop her with my eyes and thoughts, can never satiate myself with the sight of her, and at the same time she is the most desirable of women, and the very crown of my head. No other woman ever attached me to her so absolutely and in that twofold manner.

At times this influence of hers over me seems well-nigh incredible; then again I explain it, and as usual take the worst view of it. I have lived too quickly, passed already the zenith, and am going down hill, where it is dark and cold. I feel that in her I could recover my lost youth, vitality, and the desire for life. If she be lost to me, then truly nothing remains but to vegetate, and gloominess unutterable as the foretaste of decay. Therefore I love Aniela with the instinct of self-preservation, — not with my senses only, not with my soul, but also from the fear of annihilation.

Aniela does not know all this; but I suppose she pities me, just as I torture her, who would give my life to make her happy. And therefore I say again that the love for another man's wife is the greatest misfortune, since it leads the man to make her unhappy whose happiness he would ensure at the cost of his own. The result of this is that we are both unhappy. But you, Aniela, have at least your dogma to support you, whereas I am verily like a boat drifting without helm and oar.

I am not well in health either. I sleep very badly, or rather scarcely at all. I should like to fall ill and lie unconscious for a month without memories, without trouble — and rest. It would be a kind of holiday. Chwastowski examined me yesterday, and said I had the nerves of a decaying race, but had inherited a fair supply of muscular strength. I believe he is right; but for that I should have succumbed ere this to my nerves. Maybe to my very strength I may ascribe this present concentration of feeling; it had to find an outlet somewhere, and as it did not find it either in science or other useful work, it all got absorbed into love for a woman. But owing to my nervous system it is turbid, stormy, and crooked, — above all, crooked.

What sensations I pass through every day! Towards evening the dear old aunt came to me and began to apologize for praising Panna Zawilowska to me. I kissed both her hands, and in my turn asked her to forgive my momentary show of temper. She then said, —

"I promise never to mention her again. It is true, my dear Leon, I wish from all my heart to see you married, for you are the last of our race; but the Lord knows what is best. But believe me, dearest boy, it is not family pride, but your happiness I am thinking of."

I soothed her agitation as well as I could, and then said: —

"You must not mind me, dearest aunt; I am like a woman, — a nervous woman!"

"You a woman?" she said, indignantly. "Everybody is liable to make mistakes. I only wish everybody had as much intelligence and character as you; the world would then be quite a different place!"

Ah, me! how can I dispel these illusions? Sometimes I grow quite desperate as I say to myself: "What business have I in this house, among these women who have taken a monopoly for saintliness? For me it is too late to convert myself to their faith; but how many troubles, disappointments, misfortunes may I not bring upon them?"

10 June.

To-day I received two letters, — one from my lawyer in Rome, the other from Sniatynski. The lawyer informs me that the difficulties the Italian government usually raises at the exportation of art treasures can be got over, my father's collections being private property and as such not under government control, and that they could be transported simply as furniture.

I shall have to see to the arrangement of the house, which I do unwillingly, as my heart is not any more in the scheme. What does it matter to me now, and what is the use of it? If I do not give it up altogether, it is only because I spread the news about it myself, and cannot possibly draw back. I have fallen back into that state of mind which possessed me during my wanderings after Aniela's marriage. Again I understand nothing, cannot act or look upon anything that has no direct bearing upon Aniela. The thoughts in which I do not see her image at the bottom are meaningless to me. It is a proof how far a man may sink his own self. I read this morning a lecture by Bunge called "Vitality and Mechanism," and I perused it with exceptional interest. He demonstrates scientifically that which has been in my mind more as a dim, shapeless idea than a definite conviction. Here science confesses scepticism in regard to itself, and, moreover, not only confirms its own impotence, but clearly points to the existence of another world which is something more than matter and motion, which cannot be explained either physically or chemically. It does not concern me in the least whether that world be above matter or subject to it. It is a mere play of words! I am not a scientist; I am not bound to be careful in my deductions; therefore I throw myself headforemost into that open door, and let science prate and say a hundred times over that all is dark there. I feel it will be lighter than here. I read with almost feverish eagerness and great relief. Only fools do not acknowledge how materialism wearies and oppresses us, what secret fear lurks in the mind lest their science should prove true, what a dreary waiting for new scientific evolutions, and joy of the prisoners when they see a small door ajar through which they may escape into the open air. The worst of it is that the spirit is already so oppressed that it dares not breathe freely or believe in its own happiness. But I dared, and had a sensation as if I had escaped from a stifling cellar.

Perhaps this is only a momentary relief, for I understand well that Neo-Vitalism does not form an epoch in science; maybe to-morrow I shall go back to prison, — I do not know. In the meantime the breath of air did me good. I said to myself over and over again: "If it be possible that by way of scepticism one can arrive at the undoubted certainty of another world, mocking at mechanical explanation, being absolutely beyond all physico-chemical elucidation, then everything is possible, — every creed, every dogma, every mysticism! It is permissible then to think that, as there is infinite Space, there is also infinite Reason, infinite Good, enfolding the whole universe as in a vast cloak, under which we may find rest and shelter and protection. And if so, all is well! I shall know at least why I live and why I suffer. What an immense relief!"

I repeat once more that I am not obliged to be timid and wary in my deductions, and, as I said before, no one is so near mysticism as the sceptic. I realized it once more in myself when I began spreading my wings, like the bird which has been caged and delights in its new freedom. I saw before me endless space covered with new life. I did not know whether it was on another planet or farther still, beyond the planetary sphere, — enough that the space was different from ours, the light brighter and softer, the air cool and full of sweetness; the difference consisted mainly in the closer union of the individual spirit with the spirit of the universe; it was so close that it was difficult to understand where the individual ceased and the universe began. I felt at the same time it was upon that very dimness of the boundary that the happiness of this other life rested, as the being did not live in opposition or exclusion but in harmony with his surroundings, and thus lived with the whole power of universal life.

I do not say it was a vision; it was only a crossing of the narrow boundary beyond which reasoning leaves off and conscious feeling begins, — a feeling which as yet is only a conclusion of former premises, but carried so far as to be difficult to grasp, as a golden thread spun out to its utmost length. Moreover, I did not know how to incorporate myself with that new life and new space, — how to melt in it my own self. I had kept to a certain extent my own individuality, and there was something wanting near me, — something I searched for. Suddenly I became aware it was Aniela I was searching for. Of course, only her and always her. What could another life matter to me without her? I found her at last, and we roamed about together like the shadow of Paolo with the shadow of Francesca di Rimini. I write this down because I see in it an almost terrifying proof how far my whole being has been absorbed by this love.

What connection is there between Bunge's Neo-Vitalism and Aniela? Nevertheless, even when thinking of things far removed, it all brings me back to her. Science, art, nature, life, — all are carried back to the same denominator. It is the axis around which turns my world.

This is of great importance to me, for, in presence of all this, is it possible that I should ever listen to the advice of reason and that inward monitor that bids me to go away?

I know it all will end in ruin. But how can I go away; how summon strength and will and energy when all these have been taken from me? Tell a man deprived of his legs to go and walk about. On what? And from myself I add: "Why? whereto? My life is here."

Sometimes I feel tempted to let Aniela read this diary, but do not intend to do so. Her pity for me might be increased, but not her love. If Aniela be ever mine, she will want to look up to me for support, peace, and immovable faith for both; that is how it ought to be where happiness is at stake. Here she would find nothing but doubts. Supposing even she could understand all that has been and is going on in my mind, there are many things she could not sympathize with. We are too different from each other. For instance, when I plunge into mysticism, when I say to myself that everything is possible, even a future life, I do not shape it according to generally admitted ideas, and if those general ideas may be called a normal point of view, mine must needs be an abnormal one. Why? If everything is possible, then why not a hell, a purgatory, a heaven, or my subplanetary spaces, — and Dante's vision, which is far greater and more magnificent than mine? Then why? For a twofold reason. First, because my scepticism, which poisons itself by its own doubts, as the scorpion poisons itself with its own venom, is nevertheless strong enough to exclude the most simple and generally accepted ideas; secondly, I cannot fancy myself in the Dantean divisions with Aniela, — I do not desire such a life.

It is only part of myself that writes and thinks, the greater part is always with Aniela. At this moment I see a streak of light from her window resting on the barberry bushes. My poor love has sleepless nights too. I saw her dozing over her needle-work to-day. Seated in a deep armchair she looked to me so small, and she drew such a long breath as if from weariness. I had a feeling for her as if she were my child.

11 June

They have sent me at last the Madonna by Sassoferrato. I handed it to Aniela in presence of the elder ladies, as a thing left to her in my father's will, and so she could not refuse it. Afterwards I hung it up myself in her little sitting-room, and it looks very pretty there. I am not fond of Madonnas by Sassoferrato, but this one is so simple and so serene in its clear shades. I like to think that as often as she looks at it she will remember that it was I who gave her that relic, gave it her because I love her. In this way the love she considers sinful must in her thought be united to holy things. It is a childish comfort, but he who has no other must be satisfied even with that.

I had another crumb of comfort to-day. When the picture had been hung in its place, Aniela came to thank me. As the armchair in which Pani Celina sits was at the other end of the room, I held for a moment the hand Aniela was about to withdraw, and asked in a low voice: —

"Is it true, Aniela, that you hate me?"

She only shook her little head, as if in sadness.

"Oh, no!" she replied quickly.

This one word expressed so much. It was a way of saying that if the feeling of the loved woman were always to remain hidden in her breast, it would be the same as not to be loved at all. No! it is not the same. Let me have it, if only that. I would not give it up for anything in the world. If this were taken from me, I should have nothing to live for any more.

12 June.

I am at Warsaw in consequence of the letter from Sniatynski, received the day before yesterday, in which he asked me to take part in a farewell dinner in honor of Clara Hilst. I did not go to the dinner, which took place yesterday, but said good-by to Clara at the station. I have just returned thence. The good soul was going away, most likely disappointed, and with some resentment against me in her heart, but upon seeing me, forgave me everything, and we parted the best of friends. I felt too that I should miss her, and that the loneliness around me would be greater still. On my mystic fields there will be no farewells. This one was truly sad, — in addition to it the sky was overcast, and there was a drizzling rain that looked as if it would last for days. In spite of that a great many people had come to see the last of the celebrated artist. Her sleeping-car was filled with bouquets and wreaths like a hearse; she will have to discard them unless she lets herself be suffocated. Clara, at the moment of departure, without taking into account what people might think or say, devoted herself to me as much as the bustle of the place would permit. I went into her carriage, and we conversed together like two old friends, not paying any attention to the old and always silent relative, or to the other people, who at last retired discreetly into the corridor. I held both Clara's hands, and she looked at me with those honest blue eyes of hers, and said in a moved voice: —

"It is only to you I say it openly, that I never was so sorry to go away from anywhere as from here. There is no time to say much, with all these people around us, but believe me, I am sorry to go. At Frankfurt I meet many people, great artists, scientists; only there is a difference, — you are like one of the more delicate instruments. As regards yourself, I will not say anything."

"You will let me write to you?"

"I will write too. I wanted to ask you that. I have my music, but it is not always sufficient now. I think you too will want to hear from me now and then; though you may have many friends, you have none more sincere and devoted than I. I am very foolish; anything upsets me, and it is time to go."

"We are both wanderers on the earth, you as an artist, I as a Bohemian; therefore it will not be farewell, but au revoir."

"Yes, au revoir, and that speedily. You too are an artist. You may not play or paint, but you are an artist all the same. I saw it the first moment I met you,— and also that you may seem happy, but are very sad at heart. Remember there is a German girl who will be always as a sister to you."

I raised her hand to my lip, and she, thinking I was going, said quickly: —

"There is still time, they have only rung the second bell!"

But I really wished to leave. Oh, those wretched nerves of mine! Clara's companion wore a stiff mackintosh which rustled at her every motion; and that rustle, or rather swish of the india-rubber, set my very teeth on edge. Besides, we had only a few minutes left. I stepped aside to make place for Pani Sniatynska, who came rushing up.

"Hilst, Frankfurt," Clara called out after me; "at home they will forward my letters wherever I go!"

Presently I found myself on the platform under the window of her carriage, among all those who had come to see her off. Their farewells and good-bys mingled with the labored breathing of the locomotive and the shouts of the railway men. The window of the carriage was lowered, and I saw the friendly, honest face once more.

"Where are you going to spend the summer?" she asked.

"I don't know, I will write to you," I replied.

The panting of the locomotive grew quick, then came the last shrill whistle, and the train began to move. We gave Clara a loud cheer, she waved her hands to us, and then disappeared in the distance and the dusk.

"You will feel very lonely," said suddenly close to me Pani Sniatynska's voice.

"Yes, very," I said, and lifting my hat to her, I went home. And truly I had the feeling as if somebody had left, who in case of need would have given me a helping hand. I felt very despondent. Possibly the gloomy evening, the mist and drizzling rain, in the midst of which the street lamps looked like miniature rainbow arches, had something to do with it. The last spark of hope seemed to have died out. There was darkness not only within me, but it seemed to encompass the whole world, and weigh upon it as the atmosphere weighs upon us and permeates all nature.

I carried home with me a heaviness of feeling and great restlessness and a fear as if something unknown was threatening me. There woke up within me a sudden longing for the sun and brighter skies, for countries where there is no mist, no rain, and no darkness. It seemed to me that if I went where there was sun and brightness, it would shield me from some unknown danger.

Oh, to go away! The entire capacity of my thoughts was filled with that eager desire. Then suddenly another fear clutched at my heart: if I went away, Aniela would be exposed to that same impalpable danger from which I wanted to fly. I knew it was only a delusion of my brain, and that really my departure would be the best thing for her. Yet I could not get rid of the sensation that to desert her would be cowardice and meanness. All my reasoning cannot get over this. Besides, the going away is only an empty word; I may say it to myself a hundred times, but if I were to try to change it into fact I should find it altogether beyond my power. I have put so much of my life in that one feeling that it would be easier to cut me into pieces than to part me from it.

I possess so much control over my thoughts, such a consciousness of self that it seems to me impossible that I could ever lose my reason. I cannot even imagine it; but at moments I feel as if my nerves could not bear the strain any longer.

I am sorry Clara is gone. I have seen but little of her lately; but I liked to know that she was not far off; now Aniela will absorb me altogether, because I give to her that power which rules our likings, and makes us conscious of friendship.

When I returned home, I found there young Chwastowski, who had come to town in order to consult with his brother, the bookseller. They have some scheme in hand about selling elementary books. They are always scheming something, always busy, and that fills their life. I have come to such a pass that I rejoiced to see him as a child that is afraid of ghosts is glad to see somebody coming into the room. His spiritual healthiness seems to brace me. He said that Pani Celina was so much better that within a week she would be able to bear the journey to Gastein. Oh yes! yes! Anything for a change! I shall push that plan with all my powers. I will persuade my aunt to go too. She will do it for my sake, and in that case nobody will be astonished at my going. There is at least something I desire, and desire very much. I shall have so many chances of taking care of Aniela, and shall be nearer to her than at Ploszow. I feel somewhat relieved; but it has been a terrible day, and nothing oppresses me so much as dark, rainy weather. I still hear the drops falling from the waterspouts; but there is a rift in the clouds, and a few stars are visible.

12 June.

Kromitzki arrived to-day.

GASTEIN, 23 June.

We arrived at Gastein a week ago, — the whole family: Aniela, my aunt, Pani Celina, Kromitzki, and myself. I interrupted my diary for some time, not because I had lost the zest for it, nor because I did not feel the necessity for writing, but simply because I was in a state of mind which words cannot express. As long as a man tries to resist his fate, and wages war against the forces that crush him, he has neither brains nor time for anything else. I was like the prisoner in Sansson's memoirs, who when they tore his flesh and poured molten lead into the wounds shouted in nervous ecstasy, "Encore! encore!" until he fainted. I have fainted too, which means that I am exhausted and resigned.

A great hand seems to weigh upon me, as immense as the mountains that loom up before me. What can I do against it? Nothing but submit and remain passive while it crushes me. I did not know that one could find, if not comfort, at least some kind of peace in this consciousness of impotence and the looking straight at one's misery.

If only I could keep from struggling against it, and not disturb this state of quiescence. I could write then about things that happen to me as if they had happened to somebody else. But I know from experience that one day does not resemble another, and I am afraid of what the morrow will bring forth.

24 June.

Towards the end of my sojourn at Warsaw I put down these words: "Love for another man's wife, if only a pastime, is a great villany, and if real, is one of the greatest misfortunes that can happen to a man." Writing this before Kromitzki's arrival, I had not taken into account all the items which make up the sum of this misfortune. I also thought it nobler than it really is.

Now I begin to see that besides great suffering, it includes a quantity of small humiliations, the consciousness of villany, ridicule, the necessity of falsehood, the doing of mean things, and the need of precautions unworthy of a man. What a bouquet! Truly the scent of it is enough to overpower any man.

God knows with what delight I would take such a Kromitzki by the throat, press him to the wall, and tell him straight in his face, "I love your wife!" Instead of that I must be careful lest the thought should enter his mind that she pleases me. What a noble part to play in her presence! What must she think of me? That too is one of the flowers in the bouquet.

As long as I live I shall not forget the day of Kromitzki's arrival. He had gone straight to my house. Coming home late at night, I found somebody's luggage in the anteroom. I do not know why it did not occur to me that it might be Kromitzki's. Suddenly he himself looked out from the adjacent room, and dropping his eyeglass rushed up with open arms to salute his new relative. I saw as in a dream that dry skull, so like a death's-head, the glittering eyes, and the crop of black hair. Kromitzki's arrival was the most natural thing in the world, and yet I felt as if I had looked into the face of death. It seemed to me like a nightmare, and the words, "How do you do, Leon?" the most fantastic and most improbable words I could have heard anywhere. Presently such a rage, such a loathing combined with fear, seized me that it took all my self-control to prevent me from throwing him down and dashing out his brains. I have sometimes felt such paroxysms of rage and loathing, but never combined with fear; it was not so much fear of a living man as horror of the dead. For some time I could not find a word to say. Fortunately he might suppose I had not recognized him at first, or was astonished that a man I scarcely knew should treat me so familiarly. It still irritates me when I think of it.

I tried to recover myself; he in the mean while readjusted his eyeglass, and shaking my hand once more, said: —

"Well, and how are you? How are Aniela and her mother? Old lady always ill, I suppose. And our aunt, how is she?"

I was seized with amazement and anger that this man should mention those nearest and dearest to me as if they belonged to him. A man of the world bears most things and hides his emotions, because he is trained from his earliest years to keep himself under control; nevertheless I felt that I could not bear it any longer, and in order to pull myself together and occupy my thoughts with something else, I called for the servant and told him to get tea ready.

Kromitzki appeared uneasy that I did not reply at once to his questions; the eyeglass dropped again, and he said, hurriedly: —

"There is nothing wrong, is there? Why don't you speak?"

"They are all well," I replied.

It suddenly struck me that my emotion might give the hateful man an advantage over me, and the thought restored all my self-possession at once. I led him into the dining-room, asked him to sit down, and then said: —

"How is it going with you? Have you come to make a long stay?"

"I do not know," he replied. "I was longing for Aniela; and I fancy she too must have been anxious to have me back again. We have only been a few months together, and for a newly married couple that is not much, is it?" and he burst out into one of his wooden laughs. "Besides," he added, "I have some business here to look after. Always business, you see."

Then he began a long-winded harangue about his affairs; of which I did not hear much, except the often repeated words "combined forces," observing meanwhile the motion of the eyeglass. It is a strange thing how in presence of some great calamity small things will thrust themselves into evidence. I do not know whether this be so with everybody, but in the present instance the reiterated words "combined forces" and the shifting of the eyeglass irritated me beyond endurance. In the earlier moments of the interview I was almost unconscious, and yet I could count how often that eyeglass dropped and was put up again. It always used to be thus with me, and it was so now.

After tea I conducted Kromitzki to the room he was to occupy for the night. He did not cease talking, but went on in the same strain while with the help of the servant he unpacked his portmanteau. Sometimes he interrupted his flow of words in order to show me some specimens brought from the East. He undid his travelling straps, unfolded two small Eastern rugs, and said: —

"I bought these at Batoum. Pretty things, are they not? They will do to put before our bed."

He got tired at last, and after the servant had gone he sat down in the armchair, and still continued to talk about his affairs, while I thought of something else. When we are not able to defend ourselves from a great misfortune, there is one safety-valve, — we may be able to grapple with some of its details. I was now mainly busy with the thought whether Kromitzki would go with us to Gastein or not. Therefore after some time I remarked: —

"I did not know you formerly; but I begin to think that you are the kind of man to make your fortune. You are not in the least flighty, and would never sacrifice important affairs for mere sentimentality."

He pressed my hand warmly. "You have no idea," he said, "how much I wish you to trust me."

At the moment I did not attach any special meaning to his words. I was too much occupied with my own thoughts, and especially with the reflection that in regard to Kromitzki I had already been guilty of a lie and a meanness, — a lie, because I did not believe in his business capacities at all; a meanness, because I flattered the man I should have liked to kill with a glance. But I was only anxious to induce him not to go to Gastein; therefore I went deeper and deeper into the quagmire.

"I see this journey does not suit you in the least," I said.

Thereupon, egoist that he is, feeling things only in so far as they concern himself, he began to grumble at his mother-in-law.

"Of course it does not suit me," he said; "and between ourselves I do not see the necessity of it. There is a limit to everything, even to a daughter's affection for her mother. Once married, a woman ought to understand that her first duty is toward her husband. Besides, a mother-in-law who is always there, either in the same room or in the next, is a nuisance, and prevents a young married couple from drawing near to each other, and living exclusively for themselves. I do not say but that love for one's parents is a good thing, if not carried too far and made an impediment in one's life."

Once embarked upon that theme he gave expression to very commonplace and mean sentiments, which irritated me all the more that from his point of view there was certainly some truth in what he said.

"There is no help for it," he concluded; "I made a bargain, and must stick to it."

"Then you mean to go with them to Gastein?"

"Yes; I have some personal interest in the journey. I want to enter into closer relation with my wife's family and gain your confidence. We will speak of that later on. I am free for a month or six weeks. I left Lucian Chwastowski in charge of the business, and he is, as the English say, a 'solid' man. Besides, when one has a wife like Aniela one wants to stop with her a little while, — you understand, eh?"

Saying this he laughed, showing his yellow, decayed teeth, and clapped me on the knee. A cold shiver penetrated to my very brain. I felt myself growing pale.

I rose and turned away from the light to hide my face, then made a powerful effort to collect myself and asked: "When do you intend going to Ploszow?"

"To-morrow, to-morrow."

"Good-night."

"Good-night," he replied, his eyeglass dropping once more. He put out both hands, adding: "I am tremendously glad to have the opportunity to get more acquainted with you. I always liked you, and I am sure we shall understand each other."

We understand each other! How intensely stupid the man is! But the more stupid he is, the more horrible to me is the thought that Aniela belongs to him, is simply a thing of his! I did not even try to undress that night. I never had seen so clearly that there may be situations where words come to an end, the power of reasoning ceases, even the power of feeling one's calamity, — to which there seems to be no limit. A truly magnificent life which is given unto us! It is enough to say that those former occasions when Aniela trampled upon my feelings, and when I thought I had reached the height of misery, appear now to me as times of great happiness. If then, if even now, the Evil One promised me in exchange for my soul that everything should remain as it was, Aniela forever to reject my love, but Kromitzki not to come near her, — I would sign the agreement without hesitation. Because in the man rejected by a woman there grows involuntarily a conviction that she is like a Gothic tower far out of his reach, to which he scarcely dares to lift his eyes. Thus I always thought of Aniela. And then comes a Pan Kromitzki, with two rugs from Batoum, and drags her from the height, that inexorable priestess, down to a level with those rugs. What a terrible thing it is, that imagination can bring it all so clear before us! And how repulsively mean he is, and how ridiculous withal!

Where are all my theories, my reasonings, that love is far above matrimonial bonds, — that I have a right to love

Aniela? I still have my theories, while Kromitzki has Aniela. As the wind is tempered to the shorn lamb I thought the human being capable of carrying only a certain weight, and that if more were put upon his back he must needs break down. In my misery without bounds, and in my equally great foolishness and degradation, I felt that from the time of Kromitzki's arrival I was beginning to despise Aniela. Why? I could not justify it upon any common grounds. "One wife, one husband." This law I know by heart, like any other fool; but in relation to my own feelings it is a degradation for Aniela. What does it matter that it does not stand to reason? I know that I despise her, and it is more than I can bear. I felt that existence under these conditions would become simply impossible, and that necessarily there must be some change and the past be buried. What change? If my scorn could throttle my love, as a wolf throttles a lamb, it would be well. But I had a foreboding that something else would take place. If I did not love Aniela I could not despise her now; therefore my scorn is only another link in the chain. I understand perfectly that beyond Pani Kromitzka, beyond Pan Kromitzki and their relation to each other, nothing interests me, — nothing whatever; neither light nor darkness, war nor peace, nor any other thing. She, Aniela, or rather both she and her husband, and my part in their life, are my reason for existence. If for this same reason I cannot bear my existence any longer, what will happen then? Suddenly it came upon me, as a surprise, that I had not thought of the most simple solution of the problem, — death.

What a tremendous power there is in human hands, — the power of cutting the thread. Now I am ready. Evil genius of my life, do thy worst; pile weight upon weight, — but only up to a certain time, as long as I consent. If I find it too much I throw off the burden! "E poi eterna silenza," Nirvana, the "fourth dimension" of Zöllner — what do I know? The thought that it all depended upon me gave me an immense relief.

I remained thus an hour, stretched out on the couch, thinking how and when I would do it; and that very abstraction of my thoughts from Kromitzki seemed to calm me. Such a thing as the taking of one's life wants some preparation, and this also forced my thoughts into another groove. I remembered at once that my travelling revolver was of too small a calibre. I got up to look at it and resolved to buy a new one. I began to calculate ways and means to make it appear an accident. All this of course as a mere theory. Nothing was settled into a fixed purpose. I might call it rather a contemplating the possibility of suicide than a purpose. On the contrary, I was now certain it would not come to that soon. Now that I knew the door by which I could escape I thought I might wait a little to see how far my evils would extend, and what new tortures fate had in store for me. I was consumed by a burning and painful curiosity as to what would happen next, how those two would meet, and how Aniela would face me? I became very tired, and dressed as I was I fell into a troubled sleep, full of Kromitzkis, eyeglasses, revolvers, and all sorts of confused combinations of things and people.

I woke up late. The servant told me that Pan Kromitzki had gone to Ploszow. My first impulse was to follow and see them together. But when seated in the carriage I suddenly felt I could not bear it, that it would be too great a trial, and might hasten my escape through the open door into the unknown; and I gave orders to drive somewhere else.

The greatest pessimist instinctively avoids pain, and fights against it with all his might. He clutches at every hope and expects relief through every change. There awoke within me such a desire to make them go to Gastein as if my very life depended upon it. To make them leave Ploszow! The thought did not give me rest, and took such possession of me that I gave my whole mind to its realization. This did not present great difficulties. The ladies were almost ready to start. Kromitzki had come unexpectedly, evidently intending to give his wife a surprise. A few days later he would not have found us at Ploszow. I went to the railway office and secured places in a sleeping-car for Vienna, then sent a messenger with a letter to my aunt telling her I had bought tickets for the following day, as all the carriages were engaged for the following week, and we should have to go to-morrow.

26 June.

I still linger over the last moments spent at Warsaw. These memories impressed themselves so strongly on my mind that I cannot pass them over in silence. The day following Kromitzki's arrival I had a strange sensation. It seemed to me that I did not love Aniela any longer, and yet could not live without her. It was the first time I felt this — I might call it psychical dualism. Formerly my love went through its regular course. I said to myself, "I love her, therefore I desire her," — with the same logic as Descartes employs in the statement, "I think, therefore I exist." Now the formula is changed into, "I do not love her, but desire her still;" and both elements exist in me as if they were engraved on two separate stones. For some time I did not realize that the "I do not love her" was merely a delusion. I love her as before, but in such a sorrowing manner, with so much bitterness and venom, that the love has nothing in common with happiness.

Sometimes I fancy that even if Aniela were to confess to me her love, if she were divorced or a widow, I should not be happy any more. I would buy such an hour at the price of my life, but truly I do not know whether I should be able to convert it into real happiness. Who knows whether the nerves that feel happiness be not paralyzed in me? Such a thing might happen. Really, what is life worth under such conditions?

The day before our departure, I went to a gunsmith's shop. It was a quaint old man who sold me the revolver. If he were not a gunsmith he might become a professor of psychology. I told him I wanted a revolver, no matter whose make, Colt's or Smith's, provided it were good and of a large calibre. The old man picked out the weapon, which I accepted at once.

"You will want cartridges, sir?"

"Yes, I was going to ask you for them."

"And a case, sir?" he said, looking at me keenly.

"Of course, a case."

"That's all right, sir; then I will give you cartridges of the same number as the revolver."

It was now my turn to look attentively at him. He understood the inquiring look, and said: —

"I have been in the trade over forty years, sir, and learned something about my customers. It often happens that people buy revolvers to blow out their brains. Would you believe it never happens that such a one buys a case? It is always this way: 'Please give me a revolver.' 'With the case?' 'No, never mind the case.' It is a strange thing that a man about to throw away his life should grudge a rouble for the case. But such is human nature. Everybody says to himself, 'What the devil do I want with a case?' And that's how I always find out whether a man means mischief or not."

"That is very curious indeed," I replied; and it seemed to me a very characteristic sign.

The gunsmith, with a slight twinkle in his eye, went on: "Therefore as soon as I perceive his drift I make a point of giving him cartridges a size too large. It is not a small thing, the taking away one's life; it requires a deal of courage and determination. I fancy many a man breaks into a cold perspiration as he finally says: 'Now for the revolver! Ah, the cartridges do not fit; the gunsmith made a mistake;' and he has to put it off until the following day. And do you think, sir, it is an easy thing to do it twice over? Many a man who has faced death once cannot do it again. There were some who came the next day to buy a case. I laughed in my sleeve and said: 'There's your case, and may it last you a long time.'"

I note down this conversation because everything relating to suicide has become of interest to me, and the old gunsmith's words appeared to contain a bit of philosophy worth preserving.

27 June.

Now and then I remind myself that Aniela loved me, that I could have married her, that my life might have been made bright and happy, that it merely depended upon me, and that I wasted all that through my incapacity for action. Then I put to myself the question: "Is there any sign of insanity in me, and is it indeed true that I could have had Aniela forever?" It must be true, for how could I otherwise recall all the incidents from the time I met her first up to the present moment? And to think that she might have been mine, and as faithful and loyal to me as she is to that other one! — a hundred times more faithful, because she would love me from her whole soul. Innate incapacity? — yes, that is it. But even if it justifies me in my own eyes, what matters it to me, since it does not give me any comfort? The only thought that gives me comfort is that the descendants of decayed as well as of the most buoyant races have to go the same way, — to dust and ashes. This makes the difference between the weak and the strong a great deal less. The whole misfortune of beings like me is their isolation. What erroneous ideas have our novelists, and for the matter of that even our physiologists, about the decaying races. They fancy that inward incapacity must invariably correspond with physical deterioration, small build, weak muscles, anæmic brain, and weak intelligence. This may be the case now and then, but to regard it as a general principle is a mistake and a pedantic repetition of the same thing over and over again. The descendants of worn-out races have no lack of vital powers, but they lack harmony among these powers. I myself am physically a powerful man, and never was a fool. I knew people of my sphere built like Greek statues, clever, gifted, and yet they did not know how to fit themselves into life, and ended badly, exactly through that want of even balance in their otherwise luxuriant vital powers. They exist among us as in a badly organized society where nobody knows where the rights of the one begin and those of another cease. We live in anarchy, and it is a known fact that in anarchy society cannot exist. Each of the powers drags its own way, often pulling all the others with it; and this produces a tragic exclusiveness. I am now suffering from this exclusiveness, by reason of which nothing interests me beyond Aniela, nothing matters to me, and there is nothing else to which I can attach my life. But people do not understand that such a want of even balance, such anarchy of the vital powers, is a far greater disease than physical or moral anæmia. This is the solution of the problem.

Formerly the conditions of life and a differently constituted community summoned us, and in a way forced us, into action. Now, in these antihygienic times, when we have nothing to do with public life, and are poisoned by philosophy and doubts, our disease has grown more acute. We have come to this at last, that we are not capable of sustained action, that our vitality shows itself only in sudden leaps and bounds, and consequently the most gifted among us always end in some kind of madness. Of all that constitutes life there is only woman left for us; and we either fritter and squander ourselves away in licentiousness or cling to one love as to a branch that overhangs a precipice. As it is mostly an unlawful love we cling to, it carries within itself the elements of a tragedy. I know that my love for Aniela must end badly;

and therefore I do not even try to defend myself from it. Besides, whether I resist or submit, it means ruin either way.

28 June.

The baths and especially the cool, bracing air are improving Pani Celina's health, and she is growing stronger day by day. I surround her with every care and think of her comforts as if she were my own mother. She is grateful for it, and seems to be growing very fond of me. Aniela notices it, and cannot help feeling a certain regret at this vision of happiness that might have been ours if things had turned out differently. I am quite certain now that she does not love Kromitzki. She is and will be faithful to him; but when I see them together I notice in her face a certain constraint and humiliation. I see it every time when he, whether really in love or only showing himself off as a doting husband, fondles her hands, smoothes her hair or kisses her brow. She would rather hide herself in the very earth than be forced to submit to these endearments in my and other people's presence. Nevertheless she submits, with a forced smile. I smile too, but as a diversion I mentally plunge my hands into my vitals and tear them to pieces. At times the thought crosses my mind that this priestess of Diana is more at ease and less reticent when alone with her husband. But I do not often indulge in thoughts like these, for I feel that one drop more and I shall lose my self-control altogether.

My relation to Aniela is terrible for me as well as for her. My love shows itself in the guise of hatred, scorn, and irony. It frightens Aniela and hurts her. She looks at me now and then, and her pleading eyes say, "Is it my fault?" And I repeat to myself, "It is not her fault;" but I cannot, God help me, I cannot be different to her. The more I see her oppressed and hurt, the fiercer becomes my resentment towards her, towards Kromitzki, myself, and the whole world. And yet I pity her from my whole heart, for she is as unhappy as I am. But as water, instead of subduing a conflagration, makes it rage all the fiercer, so my feelings are rendered fiercer by despair. I treat the dearest being with scorn, anger, and irony, and thereby hurt myself far more than I hurt her; for she is capable of forgiveness, but I shall never be able to forgive myself.

29 June.

That man notices there is some ill-feeling between me and his wife, and he explains it in a manner worthy of him. It seems to him that I hate her because she preferred him to me. He fancies that my resentment is nothing but offended vanity. Truly only a husband can look upon it in this light. Consequently he tries to make it up to her by his caresses, and treats me with the kind indulgence of a generous victor.

How vanity blinds some people! What a strange creature he is! He goes every day to the Straubinger hotel, watches the couples promenading on the Wandelbahn, and with a certain delight puts the worst construction upon their mutual relations. He laughs at the husbands who, according to his views, are deceived by their wives; every new discovery puts him into better humor, and his eyeglass is continually dropping out and put back again. And yet the same man who considers conjugal faithlessness such an excellent opportunity for making silly jokes, would consider it the most awful tragedy if it happened to himself. Since it is only a question of other people it is a farce; touching his own happiness it would cry out to heaven for vengeance. Why, you fool! — go to the looking glass, see yourself as you are, your Mongolian eyes, that hair like a black Astrachan cap, that eyeglass, those long shanks; enter into yourself and see the meanness of your intellect, the vulgarity of your character,— and tell me whether a woman like Aniela ought to remain true to you for an hour! How did you manage to get her, you spiritual and physical upstart? Is it not an unnatural monstrosity that you are her husband? Dante's Beatrice, marrying a common Florentine cad, would have been better matched.

I had to interrupt my writing because I felt I was losing my balance; and yet I fancied myself resigned! May Kromitzki rest easy; I do not feel that I am any better than he. Even if I supposed I was made of finer stuff than he, it would be small comfort, since my deeds are worse than his. He has no need of hiding anything, and I am obliged to play the hypocrite, take him always into account, conceal my real feelings, deceive and circumvent him. Can there be anything meaner than pursuing such a course of action, instead of taking him by the throat? I abuse him in my diary. Such underhand satisfaction even a slave may permit himself towards his master. Kromitzki never could have felt so small as I did in my own eyes when I committed a multitude of littlenesses, devised cunning plans to make him take separate lodgings and not stop in the same house with Aniela. And after all, I gained nothing. With the simple sentence, "I wish to be near my wife" he demolished all my plans. It is simply unbearable, especially as Aniela understands every movement of mine, every word and scheme. I fancy she must often blush for me. All this taken together makes up my daily food. I do not think I shall be able to bear it much longer, as I cannot be equal to the situation, — which simply means: I am not villain enough for the conditions in which I live.

30 June.

I overheard from the veranda the end of a conversation carried on in an audible voice between Kromitzki and Aniela.

"I will speak to him myself," said Kromitzki; "but you must tell your aunt the position I am in."

"I will never do it," replied Aniela.

"Not if such is my wish?" he said sharply.

Not desirous of playing the part of eavesdropper, I went into the room. I saw on Aniela's face an expression of pain, which she tried to hide upon seeing me. Kromitzki was white with anger, but greeted me with a smile. For a moment an unreasonable fear got hold of me that she had confessed something to her husband. I am not afraid of Kromitzki; my only fear is that he may take away Aniela and thus part me from my sorrows, my humiliations, and torments. I live by them; without them I should be famished. Anything rather than part from Aniela. In vain I racked my brain to guess what could have taken place between them. At moments I thought it probable that she had told him something; but then his manner towards me would have changed, and it was if anything even more polite than usual.

Generally speaking, but for my aversion to the man, I have no fault to find with him in so far as I am concerned. He is very polite and friendly, gives way to me in everything as if he were dealing with a nervous woman. He tries all means to gain my confidence. It does not discourage him in the least that I meet his advances at times brusquely or sarcastically, and without much consideration for his feelings show up his ignorance and want of refined nerves. I do not miss any opportunity to expose before Aniela how commonplace he is in heart and intellect. But he is wonderfully patient. Maybe he is so only with me. To-day I saw him for the first time angry with Aniela, and his complexion was of the greenish hue of people who are angry in cold blood and nurse their wrath long afterwards. Aniela is probably afraid of him, but she is afraid of everybody, — even of me. It is sometimes difficult to understand how this woman with the temper of a dove can at a given moment summon so much energy. There was a time when I thought her too passive to be able to resist me long. What a disappointment! Her resistance is all the stronger, the more unexpected it is. I do not know what was the question between her and Kromitzki, but if she says that she is not going to do what he asks her, she will shake with fear but will not yield. If she were mine, I would love her as the dog loves its mistress; I would carry her on my hands, and not allow the dust to touch her feet; I would love her until death.

1 July.

My jealousy would be a miserable thing if it were not at the same time the pain of the true believer who sees his divinity dragged in the dust. I would abstain even from touching her hand if I could place her on some inapproachable height where nobody could come near her.

2 July.

I deluded myself as to my state of quiescence. It was only a temporary torpidity of the nerves, which I mistook for calmness. Besides, I knew it could not last.

3 July.

Yes, something has passed between them. They hide some mutual offence, but I see it. For some days I have noticed that he does not take her hands, as he used to and kiss them in turn; he does not stroke her hair or kiss her forehead. I had a moment of real joy, but Aniela herself poisoned it. I see that she tries to conciliate and humor him as if wishing to restore their former relations. At the sight of this a great rage possessed me, and showed itself in my behavior to Aniela. Never had I been so pitiless to her and myself.

4 July.

To-day, returning from the Wandelbahn, I met Aniela on the bridge opposite the Cascades. She stopped suddenly and said something, but the roar of the water drowned her voice. This irritated me, for at present everything irritates me. Whereupon, leading her across the bridge towards our villa, I said impatiently: "I could not hear what you were saying."

"I wanted to ask you," she said, with emotion, "why you are so different to me now? Why have you no pity upon me?"

All my blood rushed to my heart at these words.

"Can you not see," I said quickly, "that I love you more than words can tell? and you treat it as if it were a mere nothing. Listen! I do not want anything from you. Only tell me that you love me, surrender your heart to me, and I will bear anything, suffer anything, and will give my whole life to you and serve you to the last breath. Aniela, you love me! Tell me, is it not true? You will save me by that one word; say it!"

Aniela had grown as pale as the foam on the cascade. It seemed as if she had turned to ice. For a moment she could not utter a word; then making a great effort, she replied: —

"You must not speak to me in that way."

"Then you will never say it?"

"Never!"

"Then you have not the least —" I broke off. It suddenly whirled across my brain that if Kromitzki asked her, she would not refuse him; and at this thought rage and despair deprived me of all consciousness. I heard the rushing of waters in my ear, and everything grew dark before my eyes. I only remember that I hurled a few horrible, cynical words at her, such as no man should use against a defenceless woman, and which I dare not put down in this diary. I remember as in a dream that she looked at me with dilated eyes, took me by the sleeve, then shook my shoulder, and said, anxiously: —

"Leon, what is the matter with you, — what ails you?"

What ailed me was that I was losing my senses. I

tore my hand away and rushed off in the opposite direction. After a moment I retraced my steps; but she was gone. Then I understood only one thing: the time had come to put an end to life. The thought seemed to me like a rift in the dark clouds that weighed upon me. It was a strange state of consciousness, in one direction. For the moment all thoughts about myself, about Aniela, were wiped from my memory; but I contemplated the thought of death with the greatest self-possession I knew, for instance, perfectly well that if I threw myself from the rocks it would be considered an accident, and if I shot myself in my own room my aunt would not survive the shock. It was still stranger that, in spite of this consciousness, I did not feel called upon to make any choice, as if the connection between my reasoning and my will and its consequent action had been severed. With a perfectly clear understanding that it would be better to throw myself from the rocks, I yet went back to the villa for my revolver. Why? I cannot explain it. I only remember that I ran faster and faster, at last went up the stairs into my room, and began to search for the key of my portmanteau, where the revolver was. Presently I heard steps approaching my door. This roused me, and the thought flashed through my mind that it was Aniela, that she had guessed my intention, and came to prevent it. The door was flung open, and there was my aunt, who called out in a breathless voice: —

"Leon, go quick for the doctor! Aniela has been taken ill."

Hearing that, I forgot all else, and without hat I rushed forth, and in a quarter of an hour brought a doctor from the Straubinger hotel. The doctor went to see Aniela, and I remained with my aunt on the veranda. I asked her what had happened to Aniela.

"Half an hour ago," said my aunt, "Aniela came back with such a feverishly burning face that both Celina and I asked whether anything had happened to her. She replied, 'Nothing, nothing,' almost impatiently; and when Celina insisted upon knowing what was the matter with her, Aniela, for the first time since I have known her, lost her temper and cried out, 'Why are you all bent upon tormenting me?' Then she became quite hysterical, and laughed and cried. We were terribly frightened, and then I came and asked you to fetch the doctor. Thank God, she is calmer now. How she wept, poor child, and asked us to forgive her for having spoken unkindly to us."

I remained silent; my heart was too full for words.

My aunt paced up and down the veranda, and presently, her arms akimbo, stopped before me and said, —

"Do you know, my boy, what I am thinking? It is this: We somehow do not like Kromitzki, — even Celina is not fond of him; and Aniela sees it, and it hurts her feelings. It is a strange thing; he does his best to make himself pleasant, and yet he always seems like an outsider. It is not right, and it grieves Aniela."

"Do you think, aunty, that she loves him so very much?"

"I did not say very much. He is her husband, and so she loves him, and feels hurt that we treat him badly."

"But who treats him badly? I think she is not happy with him, — that is all."

"God forbid that you should be right. I do not say but she might have done better; but after all there is nothing to be said against him. He evidently loves her very much. Celina cannot quite forgive him the sale of Gluchow; but as to Aniela, she defends him, and does not allow anybody to say a word against him."

"Perhaps against her own conviction?"

"It proves all the more that she loves him. As to his affairs, the worst is that nobody knows how he stands; and this is a great source of trouble to Celina. But after all, wealth is not everything; besides, as I told you before, I will not forget to provide for Aniela, and you agree with me, do you not? We both owe her a kind of duty, not to mention that she is a dear, affectionate creature, and deserves everything we can do for her."

"With all my heart, dear aunt; she will be always as a sister to me, and shall not be in want of anything as long as I live."

"I count upon my dear boy, and can die in peace."

Thereupon she embraced me. The doctor, coming towards us, interrupted our conversation. In a few words he set our minds at rest, —

"A little nervous agitation; it often appears after the first baths. Leave off bathing for a few days, plenty of air and exercise, — that is all that is wanted. The constitution is sound; strengthen the system, and all will be well."

I paid him so liberally that he bowed, and did not put on his hat till he was beyond the railings of the villa. I would have given anything if I could have gone immediately to Aniela, kissed her feet, and begged her forgiveness for all the wrong I had done her. I vowed to myself that I would be different, more patient, with Kromitzki, — not revolt any more, nor grumble. Contrition, contrition deep and sincere, permeated my whole being. How unspeakably I love her!

Close upon noon I met Kromitzki coming back from a long walk on the Kaiserweg. I put my good resolutions at once to the test, and was more friendly with him. He thought it was sympathy because of his wife's illness, and as such accepted it in a grateful spirit. He and Pani Celina spent the remainder of the day with Aniela. She had expressed a wish to dress and go out; but they did not let her. I did not permit myself even to chafe at that. I do not remember that I ever subdued myself to the same extent. "It is all for you, dearest," I said inwardly. I was very stupid all the day, and felt an irresistible desire to cry like a child. Even now tears fill my eyes. If I have sinned greatly, I bear a heavy punishment.

5 July.

After yesterday's commotion a calm has set in. The clouds have discharged their electricity, and the storm is over. I feel exhausted morally and physically. Aniela is better. This morning we met alone on the veranda. I put her on a rocking-chair, wrapped a shawl around her shoulders, as the morning was rather chilly, and said: —

"Aniela dear, I beg your pardon from my whole heart for what I said yesterday. Forgive and forget if you can, though I shall never forgive myself."

She put out her hand at once, and I clung to it with my lips. I could have groaned aloud; there is such a gulf between my love and my misery. Aniela seemed to feel it too, for she did not withdraw her hand at once. She too tried to control her emotion, and the feeling which urged her towards me. Her neck and breast heaved as if she were strangling the sobs that rose to her throat. She feels that I love her beyond everything; that a love like mine is not to be met with every day; and that it might have been a treasure of happiness to last our whole life. Presently she grew more composed and her face became serene. There was nothing but resignation there, and angelic goodness.

"There is peace between us, is there not?" she asked.

"Yes," I replied.

"And forever?"

"How can I tell, dearest? You know best how things stand with me."

Her eyes again grew misty, and again she recovered herself.

"All will be well," she said, "you are so good."

"I, good?" I exclaimed with real indignation; "do you not know that if you had not fallen ill yesterday I should —"

I did not finish. I suddenly remembered that it would be mean and cowardly to use such a weapon against her.

I felt all the more ashamed of my rashness as I saw the troubled eyes looking anxiously into mine.

"What did you want to say?"

"I was going to say words unworthy of myself; besides, they have no meaning now."

"Leon! I must know what you meant, else I shall have no peace."

Suddenly a breath of wind blew a lock of her hair into her eyes. I rose, and with the light, tender touch of a mother, put it back into its place.

"Dear Aniela, do not force me to tell what I ought to forget. If it be a question of your peace of mind I pledge you my word that you need not have any fear for the future."

"You promise this?" she asked, still looking intently at me.

"Yes, most solemnly and emphatically; will that satisfy you, and drive out any foolish notions from the little head?"

The postman coming in with a parcel of letters interrupted our conversation. There was the usual budget from the East for Kromitzki; only one letter for Aniela, from Sniatynski (I recognized his handwriting on the envelope), and one for me from Clara. The latter does not say much about herself, but inquires most minutely what I am doing. I told Aniela who it was that had written, and she, to show me that all ill-feeling and constraint had gone, began to tease me. I paid her back in the same coin, and pointing to Sniatynski's letter said there was another poor man who had succumbed to little Aniela's wiles. We laughed and bandied jests for a little time.

The human soul, like the bee, extracts sweetness even from bitter herbs. The most unhappy wretch still tries to squeeze out a little happiness from his woes, and the merest shadow and pretext will serve his turn. Sometimes I think that this intense longing for happiness is one proof more that happiness is awaiting us in another world. I am convinced also that pessimism was invented as a comfort to satisfy a want, sum up all human misery, and put it into a philosophic formula. It satisfies our thirst for truth and knowledge, and happiness itself is nothing but satisfied craving. Perhaps love in itself is such a source of happiness that even a clouded love like ours is interwoven with golden rays. Such a ray fell on our path to-day. I had not expected it, as I had not expected that a man whose desires are without limits could be satisfied with so little.

We had scarcely read our letters when Pani Celina, who is now able to walk without help, came towards us with a footstool for Aniela.

"Oh mamma!" cried out Aniela, in a shocked voice; "You ought not to do that."

"And did you not yourself nurse me night and day when I was ill?"

I took the footstool from Pani Celina's hands, and kneeling down before Aniela, I waited until she had put her little feet upon it; and kneeling thus before her for a second filled me with happiness for the whole day. It is a fact. A very poor man lives upon crumbs, and smiles gratefully — through tears.

6 July.

I have a crippled heart, but it is capable of love. It is only now I fully understand what Sniatynski meant. If I were not a man out of joint, without an even-balanced mind, poisoned by scepticism, criticism of myself, and criticism of criticism, if my love were in harmony with law and principles, I should have found in Aniela the dogma of my life, and other dogmas, other beliefs, would have come to me in course of time. Yet I do not know; perhaps I could not love otherwise than crookedly; and in this lies my incapacity for life. In short, that which ought to have been my health and salvation has become my disease and damnation. Strange to say, there was no lack of warnings. It almost seems as if people had foreseen what would befall me. I remember constantly the words Sniatynski wrote to me when I was with the Davises at Pelı: "Something must always be growing within us; beware lest something should grow in you which would cause your unhappiness, and the unhappiness of those near and dear to you." I laughed then at the words, yet how true they were. My father, too, spoke several times as if he had pierced the veil that hides the future. To-day the remembrance is too late. I know it is useless to rake up the ashes of the past, but I cannot help it. I am sorry for myself, but more sorry still for Aniela. She would have been a hundred times happier with me than with Kromitzki. Supposing even I should have subjected her at first to analysis, and discovered various faults, I should have loved her all the same. She would have been mine, and as such she would have become part of me and entered into the sphere of my egoism. Her faults would have been my weaknesses, and we are always ready to make allowance for ourselves, and though we criticise self we do not cease to care for its well-being. Thus she would have been dear to me; and as she is infinitely better than I, in time she would have become my pride, the noblest part of my soul; I should have found out that criticism, as far as she was concerned, was out of place; gradually she would have won me over to her pure faith and wrought my salvation. All that has been wasted, spoiled, and transmuted into a tragedy for her, — into evil and a tragedy for me.

7 July.

I have been reading what I wrote yesterday, and am struck by what I said at the end, namely: that the love which might have been my salvation has become a source of evil. I cannot quite agree with the thought. How can love for a pure woman like Aniela bring forth evil? One word explains it, — it is a crooked love. I must own the truth. If two years ago somebody had told me that I, a civilized man, a man with æsthetic nerves, and living in peace with the penal code, should meditate for nights and days how to put out of the world, even by murder, a man who would be in my way, I should have taken that somebody for an escaped lunatic. Yet it is true; I have come to that. Kromitzki shuts out from me the world; he takes from me the earth, water, and air. I cannot live because he lives; and for that reason I incessantly think of his death. What a simple and complete solution of all the difficulties and entanglements his death would be. I thought more than once that since the hypnotizer can send his medium to sleep, a more concentrated power would be able to put him to sleep forever. I have sent for all the newest books about hypnotism. In the mean while with every glance I say to Kromitzki, "Die!" and if such a suggestion were sufficient, he would have been dead some time ago. But the whole result of it is that he is as well as ever, is Aniela's husband, and I remain with the consciousness that my intention is equally criminal and foolish, ridiculous, and unworthy of an active man; and it makes me lose my self-respect more and more. Yet it does not prevent my trying to hypnotize Kromitzki.

It is the old story again of the intelligent man who, given up by the doctors, goes for advice to quacks and wise women. I want to kill my enemy by hypnotism; and as it only shows my own worthlessness, it is I who suffer by it. I must also confess that as often as I am alone, I begin to think of all possible means in human power to put the hateful man out of the way. For some time I nursed the thought of killing him in a duel; but this would not lead to anything. Aniela would never marry the man who had killed her husband; then, like a common criminal, I began to think of other ways. And what is the strangest thing of all, I discovered ways which human justice would not be able to detect. Foolishness! vain thoughts! pure theory!

Kromitzki need have no fear for his life; thoughts like these will never be acted upon. I should not kill him if I could do it without more responsibility than is incurred in crushing a spider; should not kill him if we two were alone together on a desert island. If one could divide the human brain as one cuts in two an apple, and lay bare its thoughts, it would be found that mine is honeycombed with murderous thoughts. What is more, I am well aware that if I refrain from killing Kromitzki it is not by reason of any moral principle contained in the law "Thou shalt do no murder." This law I have already violated morally. I refrain from killing him because some remnants of chivalric tradition bar my way; because my refined nerves would not permit me to commit a brutal deed; in short, I am too far removed from primitive man to be physically competent to the task, though morally I slay him every day. And now I ask myself whether, in presence of a higher judgment, I should be held responsible, as if I had committed the deed.

It may be that if one could lay open the human brain, as I said before, in the most virtuous individual thoughts would be found to make our hair stand on end. I remember that, when a little boy, there came upon me a period of such religious fervor that I prayed from morning until night; and at the same time, in the midst of my pious transports, there came into my mind blasphemous thoughts, as if an evil wind had blown them thither, or a demon whispered them into my ear. In the same way I had irreverent thoughts about persons whom I loved with all my heart and for whom I would have given my life without a moment's hesitation. I remember that this, which I might call a tragedy of childhood, cost me a great deal of anguish. But I will not dwell upon that now. Going back to blasphemous or criminal thoughts, I do not think we are responsible for them, as they come from the knowledge of evil, not from an evil growing within the organism itself; and for the very reason that it is outward to ourselves we fancy an evil spirit suggesting the thoughts. Man listens to it, and being averse to evil, spurns it; and there may be some merit in this. But with me it is different. The thought of getting rid of Kromitzki does not come from the outside, but springs from me and exists within me. I have come down to that morally, and if I do not commit the deed it is a mere matter of nerves. The part of my inward Mephistopheles is confined to mocking and whispering into my ear that the deed would only prove my energy, and not be much of a crime.

These are the crossways on which I never dreamed of finding myself. I look into the depths of my own self with amazement. I do not know whether my exceptional troubles will partly atone for my errors, but one thing I know, namely: that he whose life cannot find room in the simple code Aniela and others like her cling to, if his soul is brimming over and breaks its bounds it must mix with dust and be polluted in the mud.

9 July.

To-day in the reading-room Kromitzki pointed out to me an Englishman accompanied by a very beautiful woman, and told me their story. The beauty is a Roumanian by birth and married a Wallachian bankrupt Boyar, from whom the Englishman simply bought her at Ostend. I have heard of similar transactions at least a dozen times. Kromitzki even mentioned the sum the Englishman had given for her. The story made a strange impression upon me. I thought to myself, "This is one way, however disgraceful for the seller and buyer; it is a simple method of obtaining a desired result. The woman concerned in it need not know anything about the transaction, and the agreement could be concealed under decent appearances. Involuntarily I began to apply the idea to our own situation. Suppose it answered. The whole thing presented itself to me under two aspects: in regard to Aniela as a horrible profanation; in regard to Kromitzki, not only as feasible, but at the same time gratifying my scorn and hatred for him. If he agreed to it, he would prove himself a villain, and show what kind of man he is, and what a monstrous thing has been done in giving Aniela to him. I should then be quite justified in all my endeavors to take her from him. But would he agree? I said to myself: "You hate him, and consequently believe him capable of any evil." But thinking of him objectively, I remembered that the man had sold his wife's property, had deceived her and Pani Celina, and also that the ruling passion of his life was greed for gain. It was not I alone who considered him as one wholly possessed by the gold fever. Sniatynski thought the same, and so do my aunt and Pani Celina. This kind of moral disease always leads into pitfalls. I understand that much will depend upon the state of his affairs. How they stand nobody seems to know, unless it be his agent Chwastowski. It suddenly struck me that I might get some information from this same Chwastowski, but that would take some time. Perhaps I will run over to Vienna and see his brother the doctor, who is working in the Vienna hospitals; the brothers are sure to correspond with each other. My aunt thinks that he is not doing as well as he wants us to believe, and I imagine that he has sunk all his money in some speculation from which he expects a great profit. Will he succeed? — that is the question. He himself does not know; hence his restlessness, and the multitude of letters he sends to young Chwastowski. In the mean while I will sound him cautiously, lest I should rouse his suspicions, as to what he thinks of the Boyar who sold his wife to the Englishman. I do not suppose for a moment that he will be quite sincere, but I will help him and guess the rest. The whole sum and substance of this is, that it has put a little more life into me. There is nothing more horrible than to suffer passively; and anything that rouses me from my apathy is acceptable. I repeat to myself, "At least to-morrow and the day after, you will have something to do to further your plans;" and that promises a transition from utter passiveness to a feverish activity. I must be doing something; it is a question of not losing control over my senses. I pledged my word to Aniela not to attempt my life, and I cannot go on living as I do. If the road I am taking be ignominious, the ignominy will be for Kromitzki more than for me. I must and will separate them, not only for my own sake but also for Aniela's sake. I am really feverish. Everybody seems to derive some benefit from the bathing except me.

10 July.

There are some hot days even in Gastein. What heat! Aniela is dressed in white soft flannel, such as English girls wear for lawn-tennis. We have our breakfast in the open air. She comes from her bath as bright and fresh as the snow at sunrise. The supple figure shows to great advantage in the graceful dress. The morning light falls upon her and shows distinctly every hair on the eyebrows, lashes, and the delicate down on either side of her face. The hair is glistening with moisture and looks fairer in this light, and the eyelids are almost transparent. How young she is, and how intoxicating her appearance! In her, then, is my life, in her everything I want. I will not go away, I cannot. Looking at her I seem to lose my senses from intoxication, and at the same time from pain; for close by her side sits he who is her husband. It cannot continue thus; let her belong to no one provided she be not his. She understands to a certain extent what I suffer, but not altogether. She does not love her husband, but considers it her duty to live with him. I gnash my teeth at the very thought, for in admitting his rights she degrades herself; and that is not allowed, even to her. Far better she were dead. Then she will be mine; because the lawful husband will remain behind, but not I. By this token I am more lawfully hers than he is.

There is something very strange going on within me at times. For instance, when I am very tired or when my mind is concentrated upon one point I seem to look into the future, into far-away space which remains invisible to me in a normal state. Then there comes to me such a conviction that Aniela belongs to me — that in some way she is or will be mine — that when I wake up I have to remind myself that there exists such a man as Kromitzki. Maybe in moments like those I cross the boundary which separates the living from the dead, and have a vision of things more perfect, such as the ideals we dream about, as they might shape themselves in outward form. Why is it these two worlds are not more in touch with each other? As often as I try to solve this problem I lose myself; I cannot understand this want of harmony, but feel dimly that therein lie our imperfection and our misery. The thought comforts me, for in the ideal world Aniela could not belong to a man like Kromitzki.

11 July.

Another disappointment, another plan shattered, but I have still hope that all is not lost. I spoke to-day with Kromitzki about the Boyar who sold his wife, and invented a whole story in order to discover his real feelings. We met the Englishman with his purchased wife near the Cascades. I began by praising her beauty, and then remarked: —

"The doctor here told me something about the transaction, and I think you are a little hard upon the Boyar."

"Hard upon him? not a bit; he amuses me intensely," he replied.

"There are extenuating circumstances in the case. He is not only a Boyar, but the owner of extensive tannery works. Suddenly, because of the infection, the importation of skins from Roumania was forbidden. The man recognized that unless he could tide over the time until the law was repealed he would be ruined, and with him hundreds of families to whom he gave employment. My dear fellow, he looked at it from a business point of view; perhaps business morality is a little different from general morality, and as he had once entered into that — "

"He had a right to sell his wife? To fulfil one part of his duties he had no right to trample upon another and perhaps more binding duty."

Kromitzki could not have disappointed me more thoroughly than by thus showing some decent feeling. But I did not give up my hope at once. I know that even the meanest person has still at his disposition high-sounding words wherewith to mask his real character. Therefore I went on: —

"You do not take into account one thing, namely, that the man would have dragged his wife with him into poverty. Confess it is a singular idea of duty that it should lead us to deprive those dependent on us of their daily bread."

"Do you know, I had no idea you were so deucedly sober-minded."

"You fool!" I thought to myself; "don't you understand that these are not my views, but views I want you to adopt?" Aloud I said: —

"I only try to put myself into the place of this business man. Besides, you do not consider that the woman probably did not love her husband, and that the other man was aware of it."

"In such a case they were worthy of each other."

"That is another question altogether. Looking a little deeper into the affair, and supposing that being in love with the Englishman, she nevertheless remained faithful to her husband, she may be worthier than you think.

As to the Boyar, he may be a villain for anything I know, but what can he do, I ask you, in case somebody comes to him and says: 'You are a bankrupt twice over; you have debts you cannot pay, and a wife that does not love you. Divorce that woman, and I will take care of her future, and will also take upon me all your liabilities.' It is a way of speaking, to say the man 'sold' his wife; but can a transaction like this be called a sale? Consider that the merchant who agreed to this proposition by one stroke saved his wife from poverty, — and possibly this is the right way to look upon duty,— and saved all those who depended upon him!"

Kromitzki thought a little, then dropped his eyeglass and said: —

"My dear fellow, as to business I flatter myself that I know a great deal more about it than you; but as to arguments, I confess that you would soon drive me into a corner. If you had not inherited millions from your father, you would be able to amass a fortune as a barrister. You have put the whole thing in such a light that I do not know what to think of that Roumanian chap. All I know about it is that some kind of transaction about his wife had occurred, and that, put it in whatever light you will, is always a disreputable thing. Besides, as I am somewhat of a merchant myself, I will tell you another thing: a bankrupt can always find a way out of his difficulties: he either makes another fortune and then pays his debts, or he blows out his brains and pays with his life; and at the same time, if he is married, he sets his wife free and gives her another chance."

I fumed and raged inwardly, and would have given anything if I could have shouted out to him: "You are a bankrupt already in one thing, for your wife does not love you. You see the Cascades; jump in, set her free, and give her the chance of some happiness." But I remained silent, chewing the bitter cud of my reflections. Kromitzki, however commonplace he might be, though capable of selling Gluchow and taking advantage of his wife's trust in him, was not the villain I took him for. It was a disappointment and destroyed the plan to which for the moment I had clung as to a plank of safety. Again I felt powerless, and saw looming up before me the vast solitude. Nevertheless, I held fast to that purpose because I understood that unless I could do something, I should go mad. "It will at least prepare the ground for anything that may turn up, and accustom Kromitzki to the thought of parting with Aniela," I said to myself. As I said before, nobody knows in what state Kromitzki's affairs are, but I suppose that a man who speculates is liable to losses as well as to gains. I said to him: —

"I do not know whether your principles are, strictly speaking, business principles, but at any rate they are the sentiments of an honorable man, and I respect you for them. You said, if I understood you, that a man has no right to drag his wife with him into poverty."

"No, I did not say that; I only said that to sell one's wife is a villany; the wife ought to share her husband's fate. I think but little of a fair-weather wife, who wants to break her marriage vows because her husband cannot give her the comforts of life."

"Suppose she did not agree, he might set her free against her will. Besides, if she knew that by submitting to a divorce, she could save her husband, duty well understood would bid her to yield."

"It is unpleasant even to talk about such things."

"Why? are you sorry for the Boyar?"

"Not I; I shall always hold him for a blackguard."

"Because you do not look at things from an objective point of view. But that is not astonishing. A man like you, with whom everything is prospering, cannot enter into the psychology of a bankrupt unless he be a philosopher; and philosophy has nothing to do with making millions."

I did not wish to prolong the conversation, so utterly disgusted was I with my own perversity. I had sown the seed, — a very small and pitiable seed to produce anything; and yet I clung to it tenaciously. One thing revived my hope. At the moment when I tried to make him believe that a ruined man ought to set his wife free, there was a certain constraint and trouble in his expression. I also noticed that when I spoke about his millions a slight sigh escaped him. To infer from this that he is on the brink of ruin, would be jumping at conclusions; but I may fairly conjecture that his affairs are in a precarious state. I resolved to get at the truth as quickly as possible.

In the mean while my own self seemed to be divided in two parts. The one said: "If you waver ever so little, I will push you downward if it should cost me my whole fortune. I will work your ruin, and when I come to deal with a broken man, it remains to be seen whether for certain transactions you do not find a gentler word than 'villany.'" Yet I was conscious at the same time that these were not my thoughts nor my ways of dealing; that they had been suggested to me by somebody else, and that but for my desperate position they would never have found room in me, as they are averse to my nature and repulsive to me. Money never played any part in my life, either as means or as aim. I consider myself incapable of using such a weapon, and I felt what a degradation it would be for me and Aniela to introduce that element into our relations to each other. The thought of it was so repulsive to me that I said to myself: "Will you not spare yourself? Must you even drink from such a bowl? See how you are degenerating step by step. Formerly thoughts like these would never have crossed your mind; and what is more, schemes like these are utterly useless, and will only lower you in your own eyes."

In fact, formerly, when my aunt spoke of Kromitzki's affairs in a doubting spirit, it had always caused me some uneasiness. The prospect that at some time or other he might want me to assist him or take a share in his transactions had made me consider what I should do in such a case; and I always vowed that I would decline and have nothing to do with any of his affairs; so repugnant to me was the thought of mingling money matters with my relations to Aniela. I remember that I saw in this another proof of the nobility and refinement of my feelings. To-day I grasp that weapon as if I were a banker and had lived by money transactions all my life.

I perceive with absolute certainty that my thoughts and deeds are worse than myself, and I ask myself how that can be. Most probably because I cannot find the way out of the labyrinth. I love a noble woman; my love is very great; and yet, putting the two together, the net result is crookedness, and enchanted circles where my character loses itself and even my nerves grow less sensitive. When, in former times, I erred and strayed from the right path there still remained something, some æsthetic feeling, by the help of which I still distinguished good from evil. At present I have none of that feeling, or if it still exists it is powerless. If I had only at the same time lost the consciousness of what is ugly and offensive! But no; I have it still, only it does not serve me as a curb, and is of no effect except to aggravate my troubles. Beside my love for Aniela there is no room for anything; but consciousness does not require space. I absorb love, hatred, and sorrow as a cancer breeds in a diseased organism.

He who has never been in a position similar to mine cannot understand it. I knew that from love's entanglements spring various sufferings, but I did not appreciate those sufferings. I did not believe they were so real and so difficult to bear. Only now I understand the difference between "knowing" and "believing," and the meaning of the French thinker's words: "We know we must die, but we do not believe it."

12 July.

To-day my pulses are beating wildly, and there is a singing in my ears; for something has occurred the memory of which thrills every nerve as in a fever. The day was very beautiful, the evening more lovely still, and there was a full moon. We resolved to make an excursion to Hofgastein, — all but Pani Celina, who preferred to remain at home. My aunt, Kromitzki, and I went down together to the villa gate, whence Kromitzki sped towards Straubinger's to order a carriage, my aunt and I waiting for Aniela, who lingered behind. As she did not come I went back and saw her descending the winding staircase leading from the second floor into the garden.

As the moon was on the other side, this part of the house was wrapped in darkness, and Aniela came down very slowly. There was a moment when my head was on a level with Aniela's feet. The temptation was too great; I put my hands gently around them and pressed my lips to them. I knew I should have to pay a heavy penalty for this minute of happiness, but I could not forego it. God knows with what reverence I touched her feet, and for how much pain this moment compensated me. But for Aniela's resistance I should have put her foot upon my head in token that I was her servant and her slave. She drew back and went upstairs again · but I ran down calling out loudly, so that my aunt could hear me: —

"Aniela is coming, coming."

Nothing remained for her now but to come down again, which she could do safely, as I had remained near the gate. At the same moment Kromitzki arrived with the carriage. Aniela coming up to us said: —

"I came to ask you, aunty, to let me stop at home. I would rather not leave mamma alone. You can go, and I will wait for you with the tea."

"But Celina is quite well," replied my aunt, with a shade of annoyance in her voice, "it was she who proposed the excursion, mainly for your sake."

"Yes, but —" began Aniela.

Kromitzki came up, and hearing what was the matter, said sharply: "Please do not raise any difficulties." And Aniela, without saying a word, took her seat in the carriage.

In spite of my emotion I was struck by Kromitzki's tone of voice and Aniela's silent obedience,— all the more as I had already noticed that his manners towards her during the day had been those of a man who is displeased. There was evidently the same reason, of which I knew nothing, at the bottom of this, and of the estrangement some time ago. But there was no room now for these reflections; the fresh memory of the kiss I had imprinted on her feet still overpowered my senses. I felt a great delight and joy, not unmixed with fear. I could account for the delight because I felt it every time I only touched her hand. But why the joy? Because I saw that the immaculate Aniela could not escape from me altogether, and must needs confess to herself: "I am on the downward path too, and cannot look people in the face; he was at my feet a moment ago, the man who loves me, and I am obliged to be his accomplice and cannot go to my husband and tell him to take me hence." I knew she could not do this without creating a commotion; and if she could, she would not do it, for fear of an encounter between me and Kromitzki, — "And who knows for whom she is most afraid?" something within me whispered.

Aniela's position is indeed a difficult one, and I, knowing this, take advantage of it without more scruples than are admitted by a general in time of war who attacks the enemy at his weakest point. I asked myself whether I would do the same if Kromitzki would make me personally responsible; and as I could conscientiously say "Yes," I thought there was no need for any further consideration. Kromitzki inspires me with fear only in so far as he has power to remove Aniela and put her out of my reach altogether. The very thought makes me desperate. But at this moment, in the carriage, I only feared Aniela. What will happen to-morrow? How will she take it? As a liberty, or as a mere impulse of respect and worship?

I felt as a dog may feel that has done wrong and is afraid of being whipped. Sitting opposite Aniela, I tried at moments when the moon shone on her face to read there what was to be my sentence. I looked at her so humbly and was so meek that I pitied myself, and thought she too ought to pity me a little. But she did not look at me at all, and listened or seemed to listen attentively to what Kromitzki was telling my aunt he would do if Gastein belonged to him. My aunt only nodded, and he repeated every moment: "Now, really, don't you think I am right?" It is evident that he wants to impress my aunt with his enterprising spirit, and to convince her that he is capable of making a shilling out of every penny.

The road to Hofgastein, hewn out of the rocks, skirting the precipices, winds and twists around the mountain slopes. The light of the moon shone alternately on our faces and those of the ladies opposite, according to the varying directions of the road. In Aniela's face I saw nothing but a sweet sadness, and I took courage from the fact that it was neither stern nor forbidding. I did not obtain a single glance, but I comforted myself by the thought that when concealed in the shadow, she would perhaps look at me and say to herself: "Nobody loves me as he does, and nobody can be at the same time more unhappy than he," — which is true. We were both silent. Only Kromitzki kept on talking; his voice mingled with the rush of the waters below the rocks and the creaking of the brake, which the driver often applied. This creaking irritated my nerves very much, but the warm, transparent night lulled them into restfulness again. It was, as I said before, full moon; the bright orb had risen above the mountains, and sailing through space illumined the tops of Bocksteinkogl, the Tischlkar glaciers, and the precipitous slopes of the Graukogl. The snow on the heights shone with a pale-green, metallic lustre, and as the mountain sides below were shrouded in darkness, the snowy sheen seemed to float in mid air, as if not belonging to the earth. There was such a charm, such peace and restfulness in these sleeping mountains, that involuntarily the words of the poet came into mind:—

> "At such a moment, alas! two hearts are grieving.
> What there is to forgive, they are forgiving;
> What was to be forgot, they dismiss to oblivion."

And yet what is there to forgive? That I kissed her feet? If she were a sacred statue she could not be offended by such an act of reverence. I thought if it came to an explanation between us I would tell her that.

I often think that Aniela does me a great wrong, not to say that she calls things by wrong names. She considers my love a mere earthly feeling, an infatuation of the senses. I do not deny that it is composed of various threads, but there are among them some as purely ideal as if spun of poetry. Very often my senses are lulled to sleep, and I love her as one loves only in early youth. Then the second self within me mocks, and says derisively: "I had no idea you could love like a schoolboy or a romanticist!" Yet such is the fact. I may be ridiculous, but I love her thus, and it is not an artificial feeling. It is this which makes my love so complete, and at the same time so sad; for Aniela misconstrues it and cannot enter into its spirit. Even now I inwardly spoke to her thus: "Do you think there are no ideal chords in my soul? At this moment I love you in such a way that you may accept my love without fear. It would be a pity to spurn so much feeling; it would cost you nothing, and it would be my salvation. I could then say to myself: 'This is my whole world; within its boundaries I am allowed to live. It would be something at least. I would try to change my nature, try to believe in what you believe, and hold fast to it all my life.'"

It seemed to me that she ought to agree to such a proposition, after which there would be everlasting peace between us. I promised myself to put it before her, and once we know that our souls belong to each other we may even part. There awoke within me a certain hope that she will agree to this, for she must understand that without it both our lives will remain miserable.

It was nine o'clock when we arrived at Hofgastein. It was very quiet and still in the village. Only the Gasthaus was lighted, and before Meger's some excellent voices were singing mountain airs. I thought of asking the serenaders to sing before our window, but I found they were not villagers; they were Viennese mountaineers, to whom one could not offer money. I bought two bunches of edelweiss and other Alpine flowers, and giving one to Aniela I accidentally, as it were, unloosened the other and the flowers fell under her feet.

"Let them lie there," I said, seeing she was stooping to pick them up. I went in search of some more flowers for my aunt. When I came back I heard Kromitzki say:—

"Even here at Hofgastein, by erecting another branch establishment, one could easily make a hundred per cent."

"You are still hammering at the same subject," I said quietly. I said this on purpose; it was the same as to say to Aniela: "See, while my whole being is occupied with you he thinks of nothing but how to make money. Compare our feelings; compare us with each other." I am almost certain she understood my meaning.

On the return journey I made several attempts to draw Aniela into general conversation, but did not succeed. When we arrived at the gate of the villa Kromitzki went upstairs with the ladies, and I remained behind to pay for the carriage. When I went up I did not find Aniela at tea. My aunt said she had gone to bed and seemed very tired. A great uneasiness got hold of me, and I reproached myself for tormenting her. There is nothing more crushing for the man who loves truly than the consciousness that he is bringing unhappiness on her he loves. We took our tea in silence, for my aunt was drowsy, Kromitzki seemed depressed, and I tormented myself more and more with anxious thoughts. "She must have taken it very much to heart," I thought, "and as usual has put upon it the worst construction." I expected she would avoid me the next day and consider our treaty of peace broken by that rash act of mine. This filled me with fear, and I resolved to go, or rather to escape, the next day to Vienna; firstly, because I dreaded meeting Aniela, secondly, because I wanted to see Doctor Chwastowski; and finally, I thought, — and God knows how bitter is the thought, — to relieve her of my presence for a few days and give her rest.

15 July.

A whole budget of events. I do not know where to begin, as the last sensations are the uppermost. Never yet had I such convincing proofs that she cares for me. It will cost me no small effort to put everything down in proper order. I am now almost sure Aniela will agree to the conditions I am going to propose to her. My head is still in a whirl; but I will try to start from the beginning.

I have been in Vienna and brought some news I am going to discuss with my aunt. I have seen Chwastowski. What a fine fellow he is! — works at the hospitals, is busy upon a series of hygienic articles his brother is to publish in three-penny booklets for the people, belongs to several medical and non-medical associations, and still finds time for various gay entertainments on the Kaerthner Strasse. I do not know when he finds time to sleep. And the fellow looks like a giant from a fair. What an exuberance of life! — he seems literally brimming over with life. I told him without any preliminaries what had brought me to Vienna.

"I do not know," I said, "whether you are aware that my aunt and I possess considerable capital. We are not obliged to speculate, but if we could invest our money in some enterprise where it would bring profit, the profit would be so much gain for the country. I suppose if at the same time we could render a service to Pan Kromitzki it would be a two-fold gain. Between ourselves, he is personally indifferent to us, but he is by his marriage connected with our family. We should be glad to help him provided we can do so without running any risk."

"And you would like to know how he stands in his affairs, sir?"

"Yes, I should. He seems very sanguine in his hopes, and no doubt believes himself to be right. The question is whether he does not delude himself. Therefore if your brother has written you anything without binding you to secrecy I should like to know what he says. You might also ask him to give me an exact statement as to their business transactions. My aunt relies upon you, considering that the relations which connect us with your family are of a much older standing than those connecting her with Kromitzki."

"All right; I will let my brother know about it. He mentioned something in one of his letters, but as it does not interest me very much I did not take notice of it at the time."

Saying this, he began to search in his desk among his papers, where he found it easily and then read aloud:

"'I am heartly tired of the place. No women here worth talking about, and not a pretty one in the whole lot.'" He laughed. "No, that's not what I wanted. He would like to be in Vienna." Turning over a page he handed it to me, but I found only these few lines: —

"As to Kromitzki, his speculation in oil has turned out a failure. With the Rothschilds a struggle is impossible, and he went against them. We had to get out of it as well as we could, but lost a deal of money. We have got a monopoly in the contract business; there are immense profits to be made, but there is also a considerable risk. It all depends upon the honesty of the people we deal with. We treat them fairly and trust to luck. But money is wanted, because the government pays us at stated terms, and we have to pay money down, and besides that, often receive bad material. I have to look at present after everything myself."

"We will furnish the money," I said, when I had finished reading.

On the way back to Gastein I thought it over and my better instincts prevailed. "Let the future take care of itself," I thought; and in the mean while would it not be more simple and more honest to help Kromitzki instead of ruining him? Aniela would appreciate such an act, and my disinterestedness would win her approval; and as to the future, let Providence decide about that.

But would it be an act of disinterestedness on my part? Reflecting upon it, I found that my own selfish views had a great deal to do with it. Thus I foresaw that Kromitzki, getting hold of the money, would leave Gastein immediately and release me from the torments his presence near Aniela gives me. Aniela would remain alone, surrounded by my devotion, with gratitude in her heart for me, resentment or even indignation towards Kromitzki because he had availed himself of my offer. I seemed to see new horizons opening before me. But above all, and at whatever cost, I wanted to get free of Kromitzki's presence.

I thought so much of my future relation to Aniela that I arrived at Lend-Gastein before I was aware of it. At Lend I found a great commotion. A railway accident had happened on the branch line of Zell am See, and the place was full of wounded people; but scarcely had I taken my seat in the carriage when the impression the killed and wounded had made upon me gave way to the thoughts that occupied me so exclusively. I saw clearly that some change must take place in our relation, that the present state could not be prolonged indefinitely without doing mischief to both of us and bringing us both to such a pass that it would be better for me to roll down the precipice there and then and make an end of it at once.

Aniela, though she does not yield in the least, must needs be distracted in her mind by the continual presence of that forbidden love. It is true she does not give me any encouragement, but now and then I kiss her hands, her feet; she is compelled to listen to words of love, obliged to have secrets from her husband and her mother, and always control herself and me lest I might overstep the boundary. Life under such conditions becomes unbearable to us both. It must undergo some change. At last I had found, I thought, a solution of the problem. Let Aniela frankly admit that she loves me, and say to me: "I am yours heart and soul, and will be yours forever; but let that satisfy you. If you agree to that our souls henceforth will be as one and belong to each other forever." And I bound myself to her. I fancied I was taking her hand and saying: "I take you thus and promise not to seek for anything more, promise that our relations will remain purely spiritual, but as binding as those of husband and wife."

Is such an agreement feasible, and will it put an end to our sorrow? For me it is a renunciation of all my hopes and desires, but it creates for me a new world in which Aniela will be mine. Besides that, it will make our love a legitimate right; and I would give my very health if Aniela would agree to it. I see in this another proof of the earnestness of my love, and how I wish her to be mine; I am ready to pay any price, accept any restrictions, provided she acknowledges her love.

I began to think intently whether she would agree.

And it seemed to me she would. I heard myself speaking to her in a persuasive, irrefutable manner: —

"Since you really love me, what difference can it make to you if you tell me so with your own lips? What can there be nobler, holier than the love I ask you for? I have surrendered to you my whole life, because I could not do otherwise. Ask your own conscience, and it will tell you that you ought to do this much for me. It is the same relation as Beatrice's to Dante. Angels love each other in that way. You will be near me, as near as one soul can be to another, and yet as distant as if you dwelt on the highest of heights. That it is a love above all earthly loves is all the more a reason for your not rejecting it; carried on the wings of such a love your soul will remain pure; it will save me and bring peace and happiness to both of us."

I felt within me a boundless wealth of this almost mystic love, and a belief that this earthly chrysalis would come forth in another world a butterfly, which, detached from all earthly conditions would soar from planet to planet, till it became united to the spirit of All-Life. For the first time the thought crossed my mind that Aniela and I may pass away as bodies, but our love will survive and even be our immortality. "Who knows," I thought, "whether this be not the only existing form of immortality?" — because I felt distinctly that there is something everlasting in my feeling, quite distinct from the ever changing phenomena of life. A man must love very deeply to be capable of such feelings and visions; he must be very unhappy, and perhaps close on the brink of insanity. I am not yet on that brink, but I am close upon mysticism, and never so happy as when I thus lose myself and scatter my own self, so that I have some difficulty in finding it again. I fully understand why this is the case. My dualism, my inward criticism shattered all the foundations of my life, together with the happiness these foundations would have given me. In those lands where, instead of syllogisms, visions and dim consciousness reign paramount, criticism finds no room; and this solution gives me rest and relief.

Thus I rested when I drew near Gastein. I saw myself and Aniela wedded spiritually and at peace. I had the proud consciousness that I had found a way out of the enchanted circle and into happiness. I was certain Aniela would give me her hand, and thus together we would begin a new life.

Suddenly I started as if waking from a dream, and saw that my hand was covered with blood. It appeared that the same vehicle I was travelling in had been used to transport some of the injured victims of the railway disaster. There was a deal of blood at one side of the seat, which the driver had not noticed or had forgotten to wipe off. My mysticism does not go so far as to create belief in the intervention of mysterious powers through omens, signs, or predictions. Yet, though not superstitious myself, I am able to enter the train of thought of a superstitious man, and consequently observe the singular coincidence of this fact. It seemed to me strange that in the carriage where I dreamed about the beginning of a new life some other life had perhaps breathed its last; also that with bloodstained hands I had been thinking of peace and happiness.

Coincidences like these more or less influence nervous persons, not by filling them with presentiments, but rather by throwing a dark shadow upon all their thoughts. Undoubtedly mine would have travelled in that direction had I not been close upon Wildbad. Slowly crawling up the hill I saw another carriage coming down at an unusual speed. "There will be another collision," I thought, as on the steep road it is very difficult for two carriages to pass each other. But at the same moment the driver of the vehicle put on the brake with all his strength, and the horses went at a slow pace. Suddenly, to my great astonishment, I recognized in the inmates of the carriage my aunt and Aniela. They, too, had caught sight of me; and Aniela cried out: —

"It is he! Leon! Leon!"

In an instant I was at their side. My aunt fell upon my neck, and repeated, "God has been good to us!" and breathed as rapidly as if she had been running all the way from Wildbad. Aniela had clutched my hand and held it fast; then all at once a terrible fear shone in her face, and she cried out: —

"You are wounded?"

I understood at once what was the matter, and said, —

"Not in the least. I was not at the accident at all. I got the blood on my hand from the carriage, which had been used for the wounded."

"Is it true, quite true?"

"Quite true."

"What train was it that was wrecked?" asked my aunt.

"The train coming from Zell am See."

"Oh, good God! A telegram came to say it was the Vienna train. It almost killed me. Oh, God, what happiness! Praise be to God!"

My aunt began wiping the perspiration from her face. Aniela was as white as a sheet. She released my hand, and turned her head aside to hide her tears and twitching mouth.

"We were alone in the house," continued my aunt. "Kromitzki had gone with some Belgians to Nassfeld. The landlord came and told us about the accident on the line, and you can well imagine what state I was in, knowing you were coming by that same line. I sent the landlord at once for a carriage, and this dear child would not let me go alone. What a terrible time it has been for us! Thank God, we escaped with a mere fright. Did you see the wounded?"

I kissed my aunt's and Aniela's hands, and told them what I had seen at Lend-Gastein. It appeared that the telegram sent to the Kurhaus was thus expressed: "Railway accident at Lend-Gastein; many killed and wounded." From which everybody concluded that the calamity had happened on the Vienna-Salzburg line.

I gave them a few fragmentary details of what I had seen. I did not think much of what I was saying, as my head was full of the one joyful thought: "Aniela could not wait for news at home, and preferred to come with my aunt and meet me!" Did she do this for my aunt's sake? Most assuredly not. I saw the trouble in her face, the sudden terror when she noticed the blood on my hand, and the lighting up of her whole countenance when she heard I had not been near the place at the time of the accident. I saw she was still so deeply moved as to be inclined to weep from sheer happiness. She would have burst into tears if at that moment I had taken her hands and told her how I loved her, and would not have snatched them away. And as all this was as clear as the day, it seemed to me that my torments were about to end, and that from that moment the dawn of another life had begun. From time to time I looked at her with eyes in which I concentrated all my power of love, and she smiled at me. I noticed that she was without gloves or mantle. She had evidently forgotten them in her haste and perturbation. As it had grown rather chilly, I wanted to wrap her in my overcoat. She resisted a little, but my aunt made her accept it.

When we arrived at the villa Pani Celina met me with as much overflowing tenderness and delight as if Aniela in case of my death had not been the next of kin, and heiress to the Ploszow estate. Such noble, disinterested women are not often met with in this world. I would not guarantee that Kromitzki when he comes to hear about it may not utter a discreet sigh, and think that the world would go on quite as well if there were no Ploszowskis.

Kromitzki returned very tired and cross. The Belgians he had met, and with whom he had gone to Nassfeld, were capitalists from Antwerp. He spoke of them as idiots who were satisfied to get three per cent for their capital. He said when parting for the night that he wished to talk with me in the morning about some important matter. Formerly I should have disliked the idea of this, for I suppose he will make some financial proposition. Now I almost wished to get it over at once; but I wanted to be alone with my thoughts, with my happiness, and with Aniela in my heart and soul. I pressed her hand at good-night as a lover might, and she returned a warm pressure.

"Are you really and truly mine?" I said inwardly.

16 July.

I had scarcely finished dressing in the morning when my aunt came into my room, and after wishing me good-morning said, without any preface, —

"While you were away Kromitzki made me a proposal to enter into partnership with him."

"And what answer did you give him?"

"I refused point-blank. I said to him: 'My dear cousin, thank God, I have as much as I want; and after my death Leon will be one of the wealthiest men in the country. Why should we rush into adventures and tempt Providence? If you make millions in your enterprises, it will be a good thing for you; if you lose your money, why should we lose ours with you? I do not know anything about these things, and am not in the habit of undertaking what I know nothing about.' Was I right?"

"Very much so."

"That is just what I wanted to talk over with you, and I am glad you look at it from the same point of view. You see, he was a little offended that I called his enterprises adventures; he explained everything to me, nevertheless, and told me what prospects he had for the future. Then I asked him, straight out, why he wanted a partner, since everything was going on so well. He replied that the more money was put into the concern the greater would be the profit; that out there everything was done on a great scale, and he would rather the family shared the profits than strangers. I thanked him for his family sympathies, but repeated my refusal. I saw that he was greatly disappointed. He began to grumble that nobody in the country had any brains for business; all they were capable of was to spend what they had got. He said in plain words that it was a social crime not to use one's capital to a better purpose. Thereupon I became very angry. 'My good friend,' I said, 'I have managed my estate I dare say in woman fashion, but I have not lost any money; rather I have increased my property; and as to social crimes, if anybody has the right to speak of that, it is certainly not you, who sold Gluchow. If you wanted to hear the truth, you hear it now. If you had not sold Gluchow, I should have trusted you more. As to your enterprises, it is not only I that know nothing about them, but others too are equally in the dark; one thing is quite clear to me, and that is that if your prospects were as brilliant as you make them out, you would not be in search of partners or feel hurt at my refusal. You want a partner because you cannot do without; you have not dealt openly with me, and that I dislike more than anything else.' "

"What did he say to that?"

"He said that he could not understand why he should be held responsible for the sale of Gluchow. It was not he who had let the estate slip through his fingers; it had been slipping gradually through the hands of those that had administered it badly, and it was their thoughtlessness and lavishness that had made the sale indispensable. Aniela when she married him had nothing but debts. He had saved out of the wreck more than anybody else could have done, and now instead of gratitude he met with reproaches and — wait a bit, what word did he use? — yes, and 'pathetic declamations.' "

"It is not true," I said; "Gluchow could have been saved."

"I said the same to him, and also that upon Gluchow I would have lent him the money. 'You might have sent me word through Aniela,' I said to him, 'about the sale, or told her to talk it over with me, and God knows, I would have made any sacrifice to save the property. But such is your method, — not to let anybody know what you are doing. We all believed in your millions, and that is the reason I never dreamed of offering you any pecuniary help.' He laughed ironically. 'Aniela,' he said, 'is too great a lady and far too lofty to stoop to interest herself in the details of her husband's business. I asked her twice to speak to you about the partnership, and both times she refused most decidedly. It is very easy to speak about saving Gluchow when the opportunity is gone. Judging by the reception I have met with to-day, I am entitled to believe that it would have been the same about Gluchow.'"

I had begun to listen with the greatest interest, for now I saw clearly what had led to the estrangement between Kromitzki and Aniela. My aunt continued: —

"When I heard that I said: 'Now you see how little sincerity there is in what you told me. At first you said that you proposed the partnership in order that the family might derive the benefit of it, in preference to strangers, and now it turns out that you want it for your own sake.' He is not wanting in cleverness, and therefore replied at once that in this kind of affairs the gain was on both sides, and that naturally it was a matter of concern to him to have as much capital at his disposition as he could get; for in this kind of business the larger the basis it rested upon, the more certain the profit. 'Besides that,' he said, 'taking Aniela without any money I thought I might count upon the support of the family, at least in a case like this, when the help would turn out a clear gain to the family.' He was very cross, especially when I told him he had not taken Aniela without anything, as it had always been my intention to give her the life interest of a certain sum."

"You told him that?"

"Yes. I told him all that was uppermost in my mind. 'I love Aniela,' I said, 'as if she were my own child; and for that very reason, to make her safe, I will not leave her the principal, but a life interest. The principal might be swallowed up in your speculations, which may turn out God knows how; and an annual income will give Aniela the means of a decent establishment. The principal,' I said, 'will go to your children, if you have any, after Aniela's death; and that is all I intend to do, — which of course does not exclude any smaller services I may be able to render you.'"

"And that ended the conversation?"

"Almost. I saw he was very much upset. I fancy he was especially angry because I promised a life interest to Aniela instead of a round sum down, as it shows how little I trust him. When going away he said that for the future he would look for partners among strangers, as he could not meet with less good-will, and might find a better understanding of business matters. I meekly accepted this reproach. Yesterday he went for an excursion with the Belgians and came back discontented, I suppose he tried it on with them and met with a disappointment. Do you know what I think, Leon? His business is shaky, since he is so anxious to get partners. And I may tell you that the thought troubles me; for if such be the case common-sense tells us not to have anything to do with his affairs; and yet the simplest family duty bids us to help him, if only for Aniela's sake. That is one reason why I was so anxious to talk it over with you."

"His affairs are not in such a desperate state as you think, aunty." And I told her what I had heard from Chwastowski, and guessed long ago from Kromitzki's manner, namely, that he was in want and looking about for capital. I added that it was mainly to inquire about the state of his affairs that I had gone to Vienna.

My aunt was delighted with my tactics and perspicacity; and walking up and down the room according to her habit she muttered to herself, "He is a genius in everything." She finally decided to leave everything in my hands, and to act as I thought best. Upon this, she went below, and I, after perusing yesterday's papers for half an hour, followed her.

I found the whole company gathered round the breakfast table, and one glance was sufficient to tell me that something unusual had taken place. Aniela looked frightened, Pani Celina troubled, and my aunt was flushed with anger. Only Kromitzki was quietly reading the paper, but he looked cross, and his face was as yellow as if he had been ill.

"Do you know," said my aunt, pointing at Aniela, "what news she has brought me as a morning's greeting?"

"No, what is it?" I said, sitting down at the table.

"Nothing more nor less than that in two weeks, Celina's health permitting, they are both going to Odessa or somewhere farther still."

If a thunderbolt had fallen in the middle of the table, I could not have been more startled. My heart sank within me. I looked at Aniela, who had grown very red, as if caught in the act of committing a wrong deed, and at last asked, "Where are they going? why?"

"They give me a deal of trouble at Ploszow, you know," said my aunt, imitating Aniela's voice. "They do not want to be a burden to me, the charitable souls. They evidently think I yearn after solitude; and in case you went away too, it would be ever so much better, more cheerful for me, to be by myself in that big house. They have discussed this all the night, instead of sleeping like other respectable people."

My aunt waxed angrier still, and turning upon Kromitzki asked: "Did you preside at that debate?"

"Not at all," he replied; "I was never even consulted. But if my wife has resolved to go, I suppose it is in order to be nearer me, for which I ought to feel grateful."

"There is nothing settled yet," remarked Aniela.

I, forgetting all precautions, looked steadily at her, but she did not lift her eyes; which convinced me all the more that I was the cause of this sudden resolve. I cannot find words to express what I felt at that moment, and what deadly bitterness suffused my heart. Aniela knows perfectly that I live for her only, exist through her; that all my thoughts belong to her, my actions have only her in view; that she is to me an issue of life and death; and in spite of all that she calmly decides to go away. Whether I should perish or beat my head against the wall, she never so much as considered. She will be more at ease when she ceases to see me writhing like a beetle stuck on a pin; she will be no longer afraid of my kissing her feet furtively, or startling that virtuous conscience. How can she hesitate when such excellent peace can be got, at so small a price as cutting somebody's throat! Thoughts like these spun across my brain by thousands. I felt a bitter taste in my mouth. "You are virtuous," I said inwardly to Aniela, "because you have no heart. If a dog attached himself to you as I am attached, something would be due to him. You have never shown me any indulgence, or any spark of pity; you have never confessed to me any tender feeling, and you have taken from me what you could. If you were able, you would deprive me of your presence altogether, — although you had the certainty that if I could not see you my eyes would perish forever. But I begin to understand you now, begin to see that your inflexibility is so great because your heart is so small. You are cold and unfeeling, and your virtue is nothing but an enormous egoism, that wants above everything to be left undisturbed, and for that peace is capable of sacrificing all else."

During the whole time of breakfast I did not say a word. When alone in my own room I held my head with both hands and with a weary, over-wrought brain, began to think again of what had happened. My thoughts were still very bitter. Women of narrow hearts often remain unyielding through a certain philistinism of virtue. The first thing with them is to keep their accounts in order, like any tradesman. They fear love, as the grocer fears street-risings, war, riots, exalted ideas, and audacious flights of fancy. Peace at any price, because peace is good for business. Everything that rises above the rational and commonplace standard of life is bad, and deserves the contempt of reasonable beings. Virtue has its heights and precipices, but also its level plains.

I now struggled with the exceedingly painful question whether Aniela did not belong to that kind of commonplace virtuous women, who want to keep their accounts in order, and reject love because it reaches above the ordinary standard of their hearts and minds. I searched in the past for proofs. "Who knows," I said to myself, "whether her simple ethical code is not resting upon such a foundation?" I had believed her to be one of those exceptional natures, different from all other women, inaccessible as the snowy heights of the Alps that without any slope soar straight heavenward. And now this lofty nature considers it the most proper thing that a husband in slippers should trample on those snows. What does it all mean? Whenever thoughts like these crowd my brain I feel as if I were on the brink of madness; such a rage seizes me that if I could I would throw down, trample, and spit upon the forces of life, reduce the whole world to chaos and obliterate its existence. On my journey back from Vienna I was searching for some unearthly abode where I might love Aniela even as Dante loved Beatrice. I built it of the sufferings from which as from fire my love had risen purified, of my renunciations and sacrifices, and thought that in a superhuman, simply angelic way she would be mine, and feel that she belonged to me. And now it came into my thoughts that it was not worth while to speak about it, as she would not understand me; not worth while leading her on to those heights, as she would not be able to breathe there. She might agree, in her soul, that I should go on loving her, go on suffering, since that flatters her vanity; but no compact, no union the most spiritual, no mutual belonging even in the Dantesque meaning, — to none of these will she agree, because she understands only one belonging and one right, which is expressed in a man's dressing-gown, and her soul cannot rise above the narrow, mean, matrimonial, book-keeping spirit.

I felt an overwhelming regret that I had not been in the wrecked train. The regret was as much the result of physical exhaustion as of Aniela's cruelty. I was tired, as one who has watched night after night at the sick bed of a very dear friend, and to whom death appears as a desired rest. And then I thought that if they had brought my mangled remains to Gastein something would perhaps have stirred in her. Thinking of this I suddenly remembered yesterday's Aniela, who went with my aunt in search of me. I recalled to my mind the sudden terror and the joy close upon it, those eyes full of tears, the disordered hair; and love immeasurable, love a hundred times more real than all my thoughts and reasonings took possession of me. It was like a great convulsive motion of the heart, which almost at once got buried in a wave of doubts. All I had noticed that day might be explained upon quite different grounds. Who knows whether it was I or my aunt who played the principal part in this emotion? Besides impressionable women have always a store of sympathy at command, even for the merest stranger. What more natural than that she should exhibit some feeling when he who was threatened by some danger was a relative? She would naturally be horrified at the thought of my death, and rejoice at seeing me alive. If, instead of her, Pani Sniatynska had been staying with my aunt, she too would have been terror-stricken, and I should have seen her without her gloves, and her hair in disorder. No, in regard to that I cannot delude myself any longer. Aniela knew very well that her departure would be to me a more dangerous catastrophe than a wound on my head or the loss of an arm or leg; and yet she did not hesitate a moment. I was perfectly aware that it was all her doing. She wanted to be near her husband, and what would become of me was not taken into account.

Again I felt myself growing pale with anger, hatred, and indignation, and only one step removed from madness. "Stop a little," I said to myself, pressing both hands against my temples; "perhaps she is seeking safety in flight because she loves you, and feels she cannot resist any longer." Ah me! and these thoughts sprung up, but they did not find any congenial soil and perished like the seed sown on a rock; they only roused a bitter, despairing irony. "Yes," something said within me, "hers is a love resembling the compassion which makes people remove the pillow from under the dying man's head, to shorten his agony. I shall not suffer much longer, and Zromitzki will be able to see her often and bring her such comfort as a wife expects from her husband."

Aniela at that moment was hateful to me. For the first time in my life I wished she really loved Kromitzki; she would have been less repugnant to me. Anger and resentment almost deprived me of my senses, and I saw clearly that if I did not do something, revenge myself upon her in some way, something terrible would happen to me. I jumped up, and under the influence of that thought, as if touched by a red-hot iron, I took my hat and went forth in search of Kromitzki. I did not find him either in the house or in the garden. I went to the Wandelbahn, then to the reading-rooms; he was in neither of the two places. I stopped for a moment on the bridge near the Cascades, thinking what to do next. The wind coming from that direction blew a cloud of spray into my face. This caused me a pleasant sensation and relieved the tension of my nerves. I bared my head and exposed it to the spray until my hair was quite wet. I felt a purely animal delight in the coolness. I had regained all my self-possession. There remained now only the distinct and decided wish to thwart Aniela. I said to her, "You shall not be allowed to go away, and henceforth I will treat you as a man who has paid for you with his money." I saw the way clear before me, and was not afraid of making any mistakes in dealing with Kromitzki. I found him outside Straubinger's hotel reading the paper. When he saw me he dropped his eyeglass and said:—

"I was just thinking of going to look for you."

"Let us go on the Kaiserweg."

And we went. Not waiting for him to begin, I plunged at once into the subject.

"My aunt told me about your conversation with her yesterday," I said.

"I am very sorry it took place at all," replied Kromitzki.

"As far as I can judge, you were both not as calm as one ought to be in treating affairs of that kind. My dear fellow, I will be open with you, and tell you at once that you do not know my aunt. She is the dearest woman in the world, but she has one weakness. Possessed of a great deal of common-sense and shrewdness, she likes to assert them; therefore any new scheme or proposition is met by her with a certain almost exaggerated suspicion. For that reason she invariably refuses at first to have anything to do with it. Chwastowski, her manager, might tell you something about that. In dealing with her it is always best to suggest a thing and leave her time to digest it; and besides, you rubbed her the wrong way, and that makes her always more determined; a pity you could not have avoided that."

"But how could I have irritated her? If anybody it is I who should be able to discuss matters of this kind."

"You made a mistake in saying that you had married

Aniela without a dowry; she is still very angry about that."

"I said it when she threw the sale of Gluchow in my teeth. Besides I only spoke the truth; Gluchow was so encumbered that next to nothing really belonged to Aniela."

"Plainly speaking, what induced you to sell that unfortunate estate?"

"Because by doing so I was able to do a good turn to somebody upon whom my future career depends to a great extent; besides, he paid more than I could have got from anybody else."

"Well, let that pass. My aunt felt all the more hurt as she has some intentions in regard to Aniela."

"Yes, I know. She is going to leave her a yearly income."

"Between ourselves, I tell you that she thinks of no such thing. I know she spoke to you about a life interest, because she was angry and wanted to let you feel that she mistrusted your business capacities. I as her heir ought to know something about her intentions, especially as she does nothing without consulting me."

Kromitzki looked at me keenly. "Anything she is doing for Aniela," he said, "would be against your interest as the heir."

"Yes, that is so; but I do not spend even my income, consequently I can speak about it quite calmly. If you cannot explain it any other way, consider it as a whim of mine. There are such people in the world. I may tell you that I do not intend to put any limit to my aunt's generosity, and also that she intends to give Aniela, not the life interest she spoke about, but the capital. Of course my influence might turn the scale either way, but I do not intend to exert it against you."

Kromitzki squeezed my hand with effusion, and his shoulders moved exactly like those of a wooden manikin. How repulsive the man is to me! I suppose he considered me more of a fool than an oddity; but he believed me, and that was all I wanted. He is quite right as to that, for I was decided that Aniela should have the capital instead of only a life interest. I saw that he was consumed with curiosity to know how much and when; but he understood that it would not do to show his hand so openly, and therefore remained silent as if from emotion. I continued: —

"You must remember one thing, my aunt wants careful handling I know for certain that she means to provide for Aniela; but it all depends on her will, and even her humor. In the mean while, what is it you both are doing? Yesterday you made her angry, and to-day Aniela vexed her still more. As the future heir I ought to rejoice at your blunders, and not warn you, and yet you see I am doing the opposite. My aunt was deeply hurt by Aniela's plan, and in her anger turned upon you, hoping, I fancy, that you would take her side; but you, on the contrary, supported them!"

"My dear fellow," said Kromitzki, squeezing my hand again, "I will tell you openly that I agreed to their plan because I was vexed with your aunt, and that is the top and bottom of it. There is no sense in it at all. I cannot stand exaltation, and both these women are full of it. They always seem to think they ought not to take advantage of your aunt's hospitality, that they cannot always remain at Ploszow, and so on, *ad infinitum*. I am heartily sick of it. In the mean while it is this way: I cannot take them with me to Turkestan, and when I am there it is all the same to me whether they are at Odessa or at Warsaw. When I wind up my affairs, with a more than considerable fortune, I hope I shall give them, of course, an adequate home. That will take place in a year at the latest. The sale of the business itself will bring in a considerable sum. If they were not at Ploszow, I should have to look out for some other place; but since your aunt offers her house and is pleased to have them, it would be folly not to accept the offer. My mother-in-law has only just recovered from her illness. Who knows what might happen in the future? and if things went wrong, Aniela, young and inexperienced as she is, would be alone with all these troubles. I simply cannot remain with them; even now I am in a fever to be off, and only delayed my departure in the hope that I might persuade you or your aunt into a partnership. Now I have told you all that is in my mind; and it is your turn to tell me whether I may count upon your good-will."

I breathed again. Aniela's scheme was reduced to nothing. I was delighted because I had got what I wanted. Although my love for Aniela was akin to deep hatred, it was all I had to live for, and it wanted food; and this it would get only from Aniela's presence. From Kromitzki's words I concluded that by one stroke I could gain the most wished for end, — Kromitzki's departure for an almost unlimited time. I remained impassive, and thought it more advisable to show myself a little reluctant.

"I cannot," I said, "give you any promise beforehand. Tell me first exactly how you stand."

He began to talk, and talked with great volubility, showing that once embarked upon this theme, he felt himself in his proper element. Now and then he paused to buttonhole me or press me against the rocks. When he had said something he though very convincing, he swiftly screwed his eyeglass into his eye and scrutinized my face to see what impression he had made upon me. This, added to his voice, which was like the sound of creaking hinges, and the reiteration of his "what, what," was very trying to my nerves, but I must render him justice; he did not try to deceive me. He told me substantially the same things that I had heard from Chwastowski. The affair stood thus. Great capital had already been invested in material, the purveying of which was solely in Kromitzki's hands. The danger of the business consisted in the fact that the capital already sunk came back to him only after passing through various official forms, therefore very slowly; and also in the fact that Kromitzki had to deal with purveyors whose interest it was to supply him with the very worst materials, for which he was held responsible. This last point put him more or less at the mercy of the agency, which besides had the most complete right to accept only good material. Who knows what complications might arise from that? After having listened to his statement, which lasted an hour, I replied: —

"My good fellow, considering all you have told me, neither my aunt nor I can have anything to do with the partnership."

His countenance fell, and he turned very yellow. "Tell me why," he said.

"If you, in spite of cautiousness and care, are in danger of lawsuits, we will not be mixed up in your affairs."

"Looking at things in that way, nobody would embark in any business at all."

"There is no necessity for us to do so. But supposing we entered into any partnership, how much would you want us to put into the business?"

"It is of no use to speak of that now; but if you could have come into it, let us say with seventy-five thousand roubles —"

"No, we will not put anything into the business; we do not think it advisable to do so. But as you are connected with our family, we will help you in another way. In brief, I will lend you the sum you mentioned upon a note of hand."

Kromitzki stopped, looked at me, and blinked as one who is not fully awake. But this lasted only a moment. He evidently thought it would not be wise to show too great a delight, — a mercantile caution not at all necessary, and ridiculous under present circumstances. He only pressed my hand and said: "Thank you, — at what rate of interest?"

"We will talk of that later on. I must go back now and talk with my aunt."

I said good-by at once. On the way I reflected whether Kromitzki would not think my acting thus a little curious and open to suspicion. But it was a vain fear. Husbands are proverbially blind, not because they love and trust their wives, but because they love themselves. Besides, Kromitzki, looking at us from his business point of view, considers me and my aunt as two fantastic beings, who, with little knowledge of practical matters, stick to antiquated notions about family ties and duties. He is, indeed, in many respects of such an altogether different type from us, that we cannot help looking upon him as an intruder.

When I came back to the villa I saw Aniela at the gate buying wild strawberries from a peasant woman. Passing close by, I said roughly, "You will not go away, because I do not wish it," and then went up into my room.

During dinner the conversation again turned upon the departure of the ladies. This time Kromitzki spoke up and treated the whole thing as a childish whim, to be laughed at by sensible people. He was not very considerate either to his wife or his mother-in-law, but then his nature is not a refined one. I did not say anything, —as if the question of their going or staying mattered very little to me. But I noticed that Aniela was conscious that her husband acted as a mere puppet in my hands, and she felt ashamed for him and deeply humiliated; but such was the resentment I had towards her that the sight of it did me good.

For in truth I was deeply wounded, and I cannot forgive Aniela. If, on the way from Vienna, I had not thought so much of that new compact, if I had not made a wholesale sacrifice of all my desires, passions, and senses, in fact of my whole nature, I should not have felt the disappointment so acutely. But it fell out so cruelly that, when, out of love for her, I was ready to change my whole being, when I climbed to a height I had never reached before, only to be near her, she, without any consideration or pity for me, wished to push me into the very depth of despair and without considering for a moment what would become of me! These thoughts poison even the pleasure afforded by Kromitzki's departure.

The future will bring some kind of solution, but I am too tired to speculate upon it. The simplest solution would be inflammation of the brain. It will come to that. I torment myself all the day, do not sleep at night, smoke endless cigars to stupefy myself, and sit up till daylight.

30 July.

I have not written in my diary for two weeks. I went with Kromitzki to Vienna to conclude his business; after which he remained three days and then left for the East. I had such violent headaches that I could not write. Pani Celina's cure is completed, but we still remain at Gastein because of the great heat.

Kromitzki's departure was a great relief to me, to Pani Celina,—whom he irritates to such a degree that if he were not her son-in-law she could not stand him at all,—and perhaps also to Aniela. The latter cannot forgive him that he involved me in his affairs. He, not supposing there could be anything between me and his wife except social relations, made no secret of the loan. She opposed it energetically, but could not tell him the reason,—perhaps from a secret fear that after an explanation he might compel her to remain where she is, and thus destroy the last shred of respect she has for him. I am almost sure that since the sale of Gluchow, both she and her mother distrust him, and in the secrecy of their hearts consider him worse than he really is. In my opinion he is a spiritual upstart, with a dry and wooden disposition, and incapable of any fine feeling or subtle thought. There is no generosity in him; his mind is neither deep, noble, nor sensitive; but in the general acceptance of the word he is a decent member of society. A certain natural pedantry aids him in this, which harmonizes with his money-making neurosis, — a degenerated imaginativeness seeking expression in financial adventure. Taking him all in all, he is so intensely repulsive to me — with his eyeglass, oblique eyes, long legs, and sallow, hairless face — that I doubt if I am capable of judging him objectively. Nevertheless I am quite sure that unless he loses his own money I shall not lose mine. But I put it down, in all sincerity, that I would rather he lost the money, his senses, his life, and went altogether to perdition.

I am ill. I have seen very little of Aniela lately, — partly by reason of my headaches, that kept me confined to my room, and partly because I wished to let her feel how deeply she had injured and grieved me. Not to see her cost me great self-denial, for my eyes want her as they want the light. I have already mentioned that with all her inflexibility, she has a certain weakness: she cannot bear that anybody should be angry with her; it frightens her, and she tries her best to conciliate those that are angry. She is then meek, sweet tempered, and looks into one's eyes with the pleading expression of a child who is afraid to be punished. This always moved me deeply and was my delight, as it kept up the delusion that I had only to open my arms and she would fall upon my neck, if only to soften my resentment. I cannot get rid altogether of this delusion, although convinced of its futility; and even now I cherish some hope in a corner of my heart that when we come to make it up, something will happen between us, — she will make a kind of submission and will draw closer to me. On the other hand I see in this mutual irritation a tacit acknowledgment on the part of Aniela that I have the right to love her; for if she admits the resentment springing from love, she must admit the love itself. It is a shadowy right, dim and vague as a dream, without shape or substance; yet

I cling to it, for it saves me from utter apathy and hopelessness.

2 August.

I have received another letter from Clara Hilst. She must have divined something; there is much pity and sympathy in her words, as if she knew how wretched I am. I do not know and do not want to know, whether she loves me as a sister or otherwise, I only feel that she loves me. I answered her letter in the same hearty spirit, grateful for her friendliness. She is going to Berlin now, and promises her appearance in Warsaw for the winter. She wants me to come to Berlin, if only for a few days. I will not go to Berlin, will not part from my troubles, but shall be glad to see her again at Warsaw. With Aniela I speak only of indifferent subjects, so as not to draw the attention of the elder ladies to the state of things between us. When alone we are both silent. I noticed several times that she was about to say something, but seemed afraid; as regards myself I could only say, "I love you;" and even that seems inadequate to express my feelings.

There is now resentment in my love. The thought is troubling my mind that she has a narrow heart, and that in this lies the secret of her unyieldingness. To-day, when I come to think it over more calmly, I go back to the conviction that she has some feeling for me, composed of gratitude, pity, and memories of the past; but it has no active power, cannot rise above prejudice,— even to the avowal of its existence. It does not respect itself, hides, is ashamed of itself, and in comparison with mine is as the mustard-seed to those Alps which surround us. From Aniela one may expect that she will restrict it rather than let it grow. It is of no use to hope or watch for anything from her; that conviction makes me very wretched.

4 August.

Some time ago I had a faint hope that under the influence of indignation against her husband, Aniela might come to me and say: "Since you have paid for me, I am yours." Another of my delusions. Any other woman, with exalted notions fed upon French novels, might have acted thus; or one who wanted only a pretext to throw herself into a lover's arms. No; Aniela will never do that, and if such a thought came into my mind at all it is because I too have been fed upon those pseudo-dramas of the feminine soul, which at bottom illustrate only the desire to cast virtue adrift. There is but one thing which would push Aniela into my arms, and that is her heart; but no artificial scenes, no phrases or false pathos. There is not the slightest possibility of her yielding to these.

If it be a great misfortune to love another man's wife, be she ever so commonplace, it is an infinitely greater misfortune to love a virtuous woman. There is something in my relations to Aniela of which I never heard or read; there is no getting out of it, no end. A solution, whether it be a calamity or the fulfilment of desire, is something, but this is only an enchanted circle. If she remain immovable and I do not cease loving her, it will be an everlasting torment, and nothing else. And I have the despairing conviction that neither of us will give way.

If she has a narrow heart it will not trouble her very much. As to myself I desire nothing more ardently than to get free from bondage; but I cannot get free. I say to myself, over and over again, that it must be done; and I put forth all my strength, as the drowning man does to save himself. At times I fancy that I have achieved some kind of victory, when lo! I see her passing under my window, my eyes rest upon her, and I experience a shock in my heart; the whole depth of my feeling is revealed, as the flash of lightning tears asunder the clouds and shows the depth of the sky. Ah me! what torture to have to deal with virtue, cold and merciless as the letter of the law! Even if Aniela had no heart I should still love her, as a mother would love a child though it were deformed. Pity then grows all the stronger,—and so does pain.

5 August.

What an inadequate, mean standard is human intellect when it comes to measure anything great, awesome, or very lofty. Reason, which serves well enough in the everyday conditions of life, becomes a drivelling fool, like Polonius, in exceptional cases. It seems to me that the usual ethical code cannot be considered a standard by which to measure great passions. To see in an immense feeling like mine only the infringement of this or that law, not to see anything else, not to see that it is an element and part of those higher forces that mock at empty rules, a godlike, immeasurable, creative power on which rests the All-Life, is a kind of blindness and littleness. Alas, Aniela thus looks upon my love! I suppose she often thinks I must respect her for her conduct; while I—God knows, I do not say it because it concerns my own fate, but judging her quite impartially—despise her, or at least try not to despise her for it, and say to her inwardly: "I should respect you and worship you a thousandfold if you could look upon the matter differently, not as regards our relations, but as regards love in general."

6 August.

There is something in Gastein very health-giving. To-day I noticed that Aniela has gained quite a brown color from the mountain air, and looks very well; which is all the more noteworthy, as she has had many troubles and anxieties. One of her troubles was the difference arising between her and her husband, the humiliation of his accepting a loan from me, and my love, which distracts her mind and troubles her peace. Notwithstanding all this, the delicate face is glowing with health. There is more color in it than before we came here. I recall the time when she seemed almost to fade away in my eyes. I remember how horrified I was at the thought that her life might be in danger. To-day that fear at least has ceased to haunt me. If I knew that in the future there would be even less pity for me, that my feelings for her would count for nothing, but that she would be happy and full of health, I should say: "Let her be pitiless, let her slight my feelings, provided she be well." In the composition of true feeling, there is the desire for personal happiness, but there is also tender thoughtfulness and affection.

Yesterday Aniela had donned one of her old dresses. I noticed it at once, and the whole past stood before me. God only knows what a turmoil there was within me.

7 August.

My aunt has forgiven Aniela long ago. She loves her so much that if I died she would still have somebody to cling to, provided Aniela remained. To-day the dear old aunt was lamenting that Aniela had no amusements, was sitting too much in the house and had seen nothing of the beautiful scenery around except the road to Hofgastein. "If I were only stronger on my feet I would go with you everywhere; your husband ought to have shown you something of the country, and he was continually tramping about by himself."

Aniela assured her that she was quite satisfied, and did not want more exercise.

"I have nothing to do," said I, in the most careless manner, "and walk a great deal. I can accompany Aniela wherever she wants to go, and show her all that is worth seeing, — at least in the nearest neighborhood." Then I added, in a still more indifferent voice: "It is considered quite the proper thing. In a place like this mere acquaintances walk out together, not to say anything about near relations."

Aniela did not say anything, but both the elder ladies were unanimous in their opinion that I was right. Tomorrow we are to go to the Schreckbrucke.

8 August.

We have entered into our compact, and henceforth a new life is to begin for us both. It is not quite the same as I had shaped it, but my future life must adapt itself to it. From now, everything will be clear and definite between us. There will be nothing new, nothing to be expected or looked out for, but at any rate I shall not be any longer like a man who has no roof to shelter him.

9 August.

Yesterday towards evening we went to the Schreckbrucke. The elder ladies accompanied us as far as the Cascades; there they sat down on the first bench they found, and we two went on alone. We both seemed to feel that some serious conversation would take place. At first I wanted to point out to her various places and tell her the names, but had scarcely mentioned Schareck when it struck me as so incongruous with the thoughts nearest our hearts that I grew silent. We could talk only about our two selves, or else remain silent. And we walked on in silence for a long time; this silence besides was necessary for me, and gave me time to conquer that restlessness which seizes us when we approach a great crisis. I got myself so far under control that I resolved to speak of my love, with calmness and naturally, as if it were a known and established fact. Experience had taught me that women can be attuned to any disposition. Nothing influences the feminine mind so much as the tone of conversation; and if the man in making a proposal does it with the air of one who expects the earth to swallow him as soon as he has uttered the words, that is, in terror and the consciousness that he is doing something quite unheard of, that terror and that consciousness communicate themselves very quickly to the woman. Acting in the opposite way, the proposal loses much of its impressiveness, but it goes smoother and creates less opposition. Besides, I had already told her of my love; all I wanted now was to prevent Aniela from going off at a tangent at the first tender word; in that case conversation would become impossible. It was necessary to introduce the subject in order to establish our future relations on a proper basis. Considering all this, I said in a very quiet voice: —

"You cannot have the slightest idea how deeply you hurt me by that project of your departure. I know very well that the reasons you gave were only ostensible, and that I was the cause of that sudden resolution. In making your plans you forgot only one thing, and that is what would become of me. That did not enter into your calculation at all. Believe me, it was not your departure which would have hurt me, so much as the thought that I count for nothing in your life. You might say that you meant it for the best and wanted me to forget you. Do not try that, for the remedy would be worse than you suppose."

Aniela's face in an instant was covered with burning blushes. It was evident that my words had touched her to the quick. I do not know what she would have said, on the spur of the moment, had not an accident diverted her attention. Close to the road, there suddenly appeared one of those cretins so common about Gastein. He was not a pleasant sight, with that big head, immense goître, and bestial expression of face. He had risen so suddenly from amid the tall grasses that Aniela screamed with terror. While she recovered herself and searched for some money — I had forgotten my purse — several minutes elapsed. During that time the impression my words had made upon her had grown less vivid, and as we resumed our walk she said, in a sad voice, full of inexpressible sweetness: —

"You have often been unjust to me, but never more so than now. You think that it costs me nothing, that I have no heart; and yet I am not a whit happier than you."

Her voice seemed to fail, and my pulses began to beat wildly. It seemed to me that one more effort and I should force from her a confession.

"Aniela!" I exclaimed, "for God's sake tell me what you mean!"

"I mean that since I am unhappy, you must allow me to remain honest. Dear Leon, I beg you to have pity upon me. You do not know how unhappy I am! I would sacrifice everything except my honesty. Do not ask me to give up that last plank of salvation, — because it is not right, one is not allowed to sacrifice that! Oh, Leon, Leon!"

She folded her hands and looked at me with eyes veiled by tears, and her body trembling like an aspen leaf. I do not know, if I had taken her into my arms she might have died afterwards from shame and sorrow, but probably she would not have found the strength to resist. But at that moment I forgot about my own self and saw only her. I threw at her feet my senses, my passions, and my egoism. What did it all matter where she was concerned? The beloved woman that defends herself with tears, tears that do not flow for the sake of keeping up appearances but from the depth of her sorrow, is invincible. I took both her hands, kissed them with reverent love, and said: —

"It will be as you wish; I swear it upon the love I bear you."

We both could not speak for some time. To confess the truth, I felt at this moment a better and nobler man than I had ever been before. I was like one who has passed the crisis in a severe illness, is still very weak and exhausted, but glad of the dawning life before him. Presently I began to talk to her, quietly and gently, not only as a lover but as the nearest friend, whose main object is the happiness of the being that belongs to him.

"You do not want to stray from the right path," I said; "and I will not lead you astray. You have changed me, and all the sorrows and sufferings I endure have made a different man of me. Through you I have come to understand the difference between love and passion. I cannot promise that I shall cease to love you, for I cannot; I should lie to you and to myself if I should promise that. I do not say it in temporary exaltation, but as a man who has looked into his inmost self and knows what is delusion and what truth. I will love you as if you were dead, — I will love your soul. Do you agree to that, Aniela dear? It is a sad love, but angelic. You can accept and return it. I make my vow of faithfulness this moment, and it is as binding as if it had been uttered before the altar. I shall never marry another woman; I shall live for you only, and my soul will be yours. You too will love me as if I had died. I do not ask for anything else; and you will not refuse, because there is no sin. You have read Dante? Remember, he too was married, and he loved Beatrice with the same love I ask from you; he openly acknowledged the feeling, and the Church holds his poem as almost a sacred thing. If you have that feeling for me in your heart, give me your hand, and after that nothing will be able to come between us or to mar our peace."

Aniela, after a momentary silence, gave me her hand. "I always had that friendship for you," she said, "and I promise you from my heart and soul."

I winced at the word "friendship," which is too small for me, and does not express our feelings. But I did not say anything. "The word 'love' still frightens her," I said to myself; "she will get accustomed to it by and by;" and since the thing is essentially the same, it was not worth while to disturb the peace at which we had arrived through stormy seas of misunderstandings, troubles, and sorrows. We are both so tired that the rest is welcome and is worth making some little sacrifices for.

Besides, it was a mere shadow, that disappeared in the joyful light of the thought that the dear being belongs to me and is spiritually my faithful wife. I would have given anything if to a question "Are you really mine?" she had answered in the affirmative. I would have asked the question a hundred times a day and never tired of the answer; but at this moment I did not want to frighten her. I, who can make allowance for so many things, understand that there are certain words which, however expressive of the existing state of things they may be, come with difficulty from a woman's lips, — especially from those of such a woman as Aniela. Yet every word she said was a confession that she loves me; and did she not consent that our souls should belong to each other? What more could I wish for?

When we had gone as far as the Schreckbrucke, we turned back. On the way we tried to look at our new position, as people look around a new house and try to make themselves at home in it. This did not come easy to either of us at first. Even this pleased me, for it seemed to me that thus bride and bridegroom would feel a few hours after they were joined in wedlock, while yet they had not had time to grow accustomed to each other. Nevertheless I spoke a great deal about us both. I explained to her the holiness and purity of such a union as ours. I tried to inspire her with trust and confidence. She listened to me with a bright, serene countenance, and now and then turned her beautiful eyes towards me. The serenity of the weather corresponded with the serenity of our souls. The sun had gone down behind the mountains; and they shone now in their evening dress of purple. I offered my arm to Aniela, which she accepted, and so we went together in the soothing stillness of the evening. Suddenly I noticed that her step had grown uncertain, as if she were afraid of something, and her face became very white. It lasted only a minute, but her disturbance was so evident that I got frightened for her, and began to ask what had frightened her.

At first she did not want to tell me, but when I insisted she confessed reluctantly that the unfortunate cretin had come into her mind, and that for an instant she had felt afraid he might suddenly jump up from the roadside.

"I do not know," she said, "why he should have made such a horrible impression on me, and feel ashamed to have such silly nerves, but I would not meet him again for anything in the world."

I soothed and comforted her, saying that nothing could happen to her while I was by. She still kept looking uneasily at the roadside, but presently our conversation dispersed the unpleasant impression.

It was dusk when we arrived at the Cascades, but the evening was exceptionally warm. On the square before Straubinger's a great many people were listening to some strolling harpists. I do not know why this solitary mountain pass should have reminded me so strongly of Italy. It recalled to my memory the evenings on the Pincio, when I thought how happy I could be had I Aniela at my side. I now felt her arm resting upon mine, and still more felt her soul close to my own. And thus, full of sweet peacefulness, we returned home.

10 August.

I thought to-day much about what Aniela had said to me on the way to the Schreckbrucke. I was particularly struck by the exclamation which burst from her lips: "You do not know how unhappy I am!" There was such deep sorrow, such a wail in these words, and an involuntary confession that she does not love her husband, cannot love him; and also that her heart, in spite of all her efforts, belongs to me. If so she has been as unhappy as I. I say "has been," because at present she is not. Now she can say to herself: "I can remain true and keep my faith; and for the rest, I trust to God."

11 August.

It came into my mind that I had no right to expect Aniela to sacrifice everything for me. It is not true that one sacrifices everything to love. If, for instance, I had an encounter with Kromitzki and she adjured me in the name of our love to ask his pardon on my bended knees, I would not do it. It is a fantastic, senseless supposition, yet at the very thought the blood mounts to my head. No, Aniela dear, you are right; there are things we may not sacrifice even to love.

12 August.

We went in the morning on the Windischgratzhohe. It is about three quarters of an hour on foot, but I got a horse for Aniela, which I led by the bridle. Walking at her side, I rested my hand on the horse's neck and at the same time touched her dress. Mounting on the horse's back, she held on to me for a moment and the old Adam woke up very strong in me. To kill him, I should have to annihilate my body and become a spirit. I bound myself to keep my senses and impulses under control, and I am doing so; but I did not bind myself not to have them. I might as well have bound myself not to breathe. If the touch of Aniela's hand made no more impression upon me than if it were a piece of wood it would prove that I did not love her any longer, and then all pledges would be unnecessary. Saying to Aniela that my whole nature had changed in contact with her, I did not intend to deceive her, but had not exactly defined the change. The truth is I only keep myself in check. I renounced complete happiness in order to secure a part of it. I preferred to have Aniela in this way to not having her at all, and I think that every one who knows the meaning of true love will understand me easily. If the passions are dogs, as the poets say, I have chained them up, will starve them into submission, but I cannot prevent their straining at the chain or emitting an occasional howl.

I know to what I have pledged myself, and shall keep to it; there is nothing else to do. In the face of Aniela's firmness of purpose there is no room for any agreeing or disagreeing. The fear that she may take back what she has given is enough curb for me. I rather exaggerate my caution and wariness, so as not to frighten away the bird which I call "spiritual love," and she calls "friendship." That word, which in the first moment was merely a prick, enough to make me wince, is gradually growing into a sore. At the time it seemed to me not expressive enough, and now it appears to me too cautious, too full of conditions. How strange that characteristic of feminine nature, not to call things by their name. Yet I explained distinctly to Aniela what I was asking for, and she understood me fully; and nevertheless she called the feeling "friendship," as if she wanted to veil herself with it before me, before herself and God.

Looking at it from another point, it is true that a feeling devoid of all earthly substance may be called by any name. There is sadness and bitterness in the thought. This caution, common to very pure-minded women, is undoubtedly the outcome of their modesty, but it does not permit them to be generous. I might go straight to Aniela and say to her: "I have sacrificed to you one half of my existence, and you grudgingly dole me out your words; is it right?" And I tell her so inwardly with reproachful eyes. It is difficult to imagine love without generosity, without a desire to make some sacrifices.

To-day on Windischgratzhohe we conversed together like two beings closely connected by the ties of love and friendship, but there was nothing in our speech that brother and sister might not have said to each other. If we had made such an excursion before we had entered into our compact, I should undoubtedly have taken some advantage of it, kissed her hands or feet or even tried, if only for a moment, to take her in my arms; to-day I walked quietly at her side, like one who is afraid of the slightest frown. Partly I restrained myself on purpose, thinking that in this way I should win her confidence and favor. By this silence I meant to say: "You will not be disappointed in me; I will take rather less than I have a right to, — so as not to break our compact."

But one feels hurt all the same, when the sacrifice is accepted promptly and cheerfully as soon as it is offered. Involuntarily one says inwardly to the beloved woman: "Do not let yourself be outdone in generosity." And I said so, — but in vain.

What is the result? A certain disappointment for myself. I used to think if such a compact existed between us, I should have perfect liberty within its boundaries; should be able to say, "I love you" as often as I liked, and hear the same from her lips; and that this would compensate me for all my torments, for the whole time of my suffering, — in short that I should be king in that restricted kingdom; but now it appears that my horizon gets narrower than ever, and doubts arise within me that might be compressed in the query: "What have you gained?" I try to chase the thoughts away. I have gained something. I have gained the sight of a bright and happy face; I have gained the smile; I have gained the delight of seeing her limpid eyes look fearlessly into mine. If I feel cramped and not quite at home in the new house, the reason is that I have not got used to it. Besides, formerly I was without a roof to shelter me; and if I cannot always see clearly what I have gained, I know perfectly well that I have lost nothing. I shall never forget that.

14 August.

My aunt begins to talk about going home. She is pining after her beloved Ploszow. I asked Aniela if she would like to go. She said she would; therefore I too am anxious to return. Formerly I attached some vague, undefined hope to a change of place. Now I expect nothing; but at Ploszow there are so many pleasant memories that I shall be glad to see the place again.

16 August.

The days flow now very evenly. I think much and I rest. My thoughts are often sad, at times not without bitterness, but my soul was so weary that I find this restfulness very soothing. It makes me feel conscious how much better off I am than I used to be. I am mostly with Aniela; we read together, and then discuss what we have read. Everything I say to her is only a definition, a development of love; everything tends in that direction; but strange to say I notice that now I never speak of it directly, as if that feminine objection to calling things by their proper names had also infected me. I do not know why this is so, but it is a fact. And it grieves me,—sometimes grieves me very much; and it pleases me, because I see that Aniela is pleased, and what is more, loves me for it. In order to cement the union of our souls, I have begun to speak much about myself so as not to have any secrets from her. I am reticent only about such things as might offend her delicacy of feeling or the purity of her thoughts. I tried to initiate her into the workings of a spirit undermined by scepticism and the want of a basis in life. I told her openly that I had nothing to live for except her; told her also what was going on within me after her marriage, what shocks had passed through my heart and brain since my return to Ploszow; I spoke of this all the more eagerly, as it was like a series of confessions, as it all meant: "I loved you then, as I love you now, beyond expression." She was deceived as to the meaning of these confidences and listened to them as if there had been no question about her, with emotion, sympathy, and possibly unconscious delight. I saw tears gathering in her eyes, her breast heaved as if her whole spiritual being went out to me with open arms saying: "Come to me; you have suffered enough and deserve some happiness." And I reply with my eyes: "I do not ask, do not remind you of anything; I am altogether at your mercy."

I made those confidences also for another reason, namely, to introduce the habit of mutual confidence between us, and make her tell me what was going on in her mind at the same time. But I could not manage it. I tried to ask, but the words seemed to come from her with such difficulty, there was such evident constraint and uneasiness, that I left off asking. To be quite open with me, she would have to reveal all she felt for me and what was her relation to her husband. I wanted her to come to that; but her modesty and her loyalty for the absent husband would not permit her to speak.

I understood all perfectly, but I could not help feeling very sore, and my pessimism says: "It is you who pay the score; you give everything, without getting anything in return; you are deceived in thinking her soul belongs to you; even that soul remains a blank to you; then what do you possess?"

I admit the truthfulness of the utterance, but still I count upon the future.

17 August.

I am often reminded of the poet Mickiewicz's words, "Alas! it was only a half-salvation!" But even if I did not see in that half-salvation all that is wanting, I could not arrive at perfect peace. This would be achieved only by not desiring anything more, in other words by ceasing to love. There come upon me, more and more, moments of despondency when I say to myself that this is only another enchanted circle. I found some relief from torments I could bear no longer, that is true; but relief is not the same as the removal of the pain. When the famished Arab sucks pebbles instead of drinking water, he does not satisfy his thirst; he only deceives it. Query: Do I deceive my self? There are again two persons within me: the spectator and the actor; and the one criticises and mocks the other. The sceptic Ploszowski, the Ploszowski who has no settled and unshakable belief in the existence of a soul, in love with a soul, appears simply ridiculous to that critical number two. What is, after all, my relation with Aniela? Sometimes I see in it merely the product of a diseased imagination. I am now indeed like the bird that drags one wing on the earth. I have doomed to paralysis one half of my being, live only half a life, and love with half a love. It is a vain enterprise. To separate desire from love is as impossible as to separate thought from existence. Even religious feelings, the most ideal of all feelings, manifest themselves by words, by songs, by kneeling, and kissing of sacred objects; and I would deprive the love for a woman of all embodiment, sever all connection with the earth, and make it live upon earth in a transmundane shape! Love is a natural tendency and desire. What did I take away from it? The tendency and the desire. I might as well have gone to Aniela, and said to her, "Since I love you above everything, I pledge myself to love you no longer."

There is some terrible mistake in this. I had truly lost my way in the desert; no wonder that I saw a Fata Morgana.

18 August.

Yesterday I felt oppressed and troubled by various thoughts. I could not sleep. I left off plunging into the depths of pessimism, and instead of that began to think of Aniela and call her image before my eyes. This always soothes me. My imagination strained to the utmost point brings her before me so lifelike that I fancy I could speak to her. I recalled to memory the time I had met her first as a grown-up girl. I saw the white, gauzy draperies studded with bunches of violets, the bare shoulders, and the face a little too small but fresh like a spring morning, and so original in the bold outline of the eyebrows, the long lashes, and that soft down on either side of the face. It seems to me as if I still heard her voice saying, "Do you not recognize me, Leon?" I wrote at the time that her face appeared to me like music translated into human features. There was in her at the same time the charm of the maiden and the attraction of the woman. No other woman ever fascinated me so strongly, and there must needs cross my way a Circe-like Laura to lure me away from the one woman I could love, almost my bride.

Nobody feels more than I that the words, "The spell thou hast cast upon me lasts forever," are not a mere poetic fancy, but bitter reality. Besides love and desire, I have for her an immense liking, the tenderness of affection, and am drawn to her with the irresistible force of the magnet to iron. And it cannot be otherwise, for she is still the same Aniela, and is not changed in the least. It is the same face of a little girl, with the charm of a woman, the same look, the same eyelashes, brows, shoulders, and supple waist. She has now one more charm, — that of the lost Paradise.

What a tremendous gulf between our relations in the past and those in the present. When I think of the Aniela who was waiting, as for her salvation, to hear from me the words, "Will you be mine?" I can scarcely believe it to have been true. Reflecting upon that, I feel like the ruined magnate who at one time scattered his wealth about, dazzling the world by his splendor, and in later years lived upon charity.

That night, when I thought about Aniela and evoked her image before my eyes, it suddenly occurred to me that we had no portrait of her, and a strong desire seized me to have her likeness. I grasped at the idea with enthusiasm, and it made me feel so happy that it finally drove all sleep from my eyes. "I shall have you," I said; "I shall be able to look at you at any time, kiss your hands, your eyes, your lips; and you will not be able to prevent it." I began at once to think how it might be done. I could not go and say to Aniela, "Have your portrait painted, and I will defray the expenses;" but with my aunt I could always do what I liked, and a hint will be enough to make her wish for Aniela's portrait. At Ploszow she has a whole collection of family portraits, which are her pride, and my desperation, as some of them are truly hideous; but my aunt will not have them removed out of sight. Considering her deep attachment to Aniela, I was sure she would be delighted with the idea of adding her picture to the collection. As far as she is concerned I consider the thing done; but now came the question whom to intrust with the execution of the portrait. I thought it would be impossible to induce the ladies to take Paris on their way; there I should have the choice between the accuracy and objectivism of Bonnat, the bold breadth of Carolus Duran, and the inimitable sweetness of Chaplin. Shutting my eyes, I imagined how each of them would acquit himself of the task, and I was pleased with the fancy. But I saw it was impracticable; I foresaw that my aunt would insist upon a Polish painter. I should have no objection to that, for I remembered seeing at the Warsaw and Cracow exhibition portraits as excellent as from the brush of any foreign painter. I was only afraid of the delay. As regards fancies, and also in many other things, there is something eminently feminine in my composition. When I plan a thing I want to get it done at once. As we were in Germany, not very far from Munich and Vienna, I began to choose among the German painters. I fixed upon two names: Lembach and Angeli. I had seen some fine portraits by Lembach, but only men's; besides, I did not like his self-assurance and sketchiness, which, as I am fond of French painting, I can endure only from a Frenchman. Angeli's faces did not altogether satisfy me, but I had to admit his delicacy of touch; and that is just the thing wanted for Aniela's face. Besides, in order to get Lembach we should have to go out of our way, and Angeli is on the way, — a circumstance one is ashamed to confess, not wanting to be regarded as a Philistine. But in this case I wanted to save time. "The dead ride quick," as the poet says; but lovers ride quicker still. Besides I should have chosen Angeli in any case, and finally decided that he should paint Aniela's portrait. As a rule, I do not approve of portraits in ball-dress, but I resolved to have Aniela in a white dress with violets. I want to have the delusion in looking at her that she is the Aniela of the never-to-be-forgotten times. I do not want anything to remind me that she is Pani Kromitzka. And besides, the dress is dear to me as a memory.

I thought the night would never end, so impatient was I to speak about it to my aunt. I changed my plan though, for if my aunt had the portrait painted, she would insist upon a Polish painter. I decided instead to offer Aniela's likeness to my aunt on her name's-day, which is towards the end of October. Put in this way, Aniela cannot refuse. Of course I shall have a copy for myself.

I scarcely slept at all, but look upon it as a satisfactory night, as all the hours were occupied with these plans. I dozed a little towards five, but was up and dressed at the stroke of eight. I went to Straubinger's and sent a telegram to the Vienna Kunstlerhaus inquiring whether Angeli was at home, then returned to the villa and found the ladies at the breakfast-table. I opened fire at once. "Aniela," I said, "I have come to confess my guilt in regard to you. Last night instead of sleeping I have disposed of your person, and it now remains to be seen whether you will consent."

She looked at me with half-frightened eyes. Perhaps she fancied I was going mad, or that in a fit of despair I had made up my mind to blurt out the truth before the elder ladies; but seeing my calmness she asked: —

"How have you disposed of me?"

"I wanted it to be a surprise for you, dear aunt, but I do not see how it could be done in secret, and so I must tell you what present I intend to give you for your name's-day;" and I told them what I had in my mind. My aunt, who has an excellent portrait of me, painted some years ago, was greatly delighted, and thanked me warmly. I saw that Aniela was not less pleased, and that was enough for me. There and then a lively discussion sprung up as to when and by whom the portrait was to be painted, and the question of dress, so dear to the feminine heart, had to be gone into with all details. I had a ready answer for all questions and saw my chance of getting something else besides the picture.

"It will not take much time," I said. "I have sent a telegram to Angeli, and I do not think it will delay our journey much. Aniela will give Angeli five or six sittings, and as you would have to stop at Vienna in any case to see Notnagel, there is no loss of time. The dress can be painted from a model, and the face will be finished in five sittings. But we must send at once Aniela's photograph and a lock of her hair. The hair I must have at once. Then Angeli will be able to make the rough sketch, and later on put in the finishing touches." I counted upon the fact that none of the ladies knew much about portrait-painting. I wanted the hair for myself, not for Angeli, to whom it would have been of use only if he painted Aniela's portrait from a photograph, to which he would not have consented. But I spoke as if the whole portrait depended on that lock of hair. Two hours after breakfast I received an answer to my telegram. Angeli is in Vienna, where he is just finishing the portrait of the Princess M. I wrote to him at once and sent him Aniela's photograph; then went out to Aniela, who was walking in the garden.

"And your hair?" I said; "I want to send the letter by the two-o'clock post."

She went at once into her room, and shortly afterwards returned with a lock of hair. My hand shook a little as I took it from her, but my eyes looked straight into hers and said in that glance: —

"Do you not guess that I want it for myself, that it will be for me the most precious treasure?"

Aniela did not say anything, but blushed like a girl who listens for the first time to words of love. She had guessed it. I thought that for one touch of those lips it would be worth while giving one's life. My love for her becomes so strong at times that it is akin to pain.

I have now a small part of her physical being. I got it by cunning. I the man of the world, the sceptic, I who enter into myself and analyze every thought, have come to practise little tricks and devices, like Goethe's Siebel. But I say to myself, "At the worst I am only sentimental and ridiculous." Who knows whether the second self that reduces everything to consciousness with cold criticism is not more foolish and more ridiculous? Analysis is like the pulling to pieces of a flower. It spoils the beauty of life, therefore its happiness, — the only sensible thing in life.

22 August.

After the completion of Pani Celina's cure we waited for weeks till the heat in the plains should have grown less intense, and at last the weather broke and again delayed our journey. There has been an almost Egyptian darkness for three days. The clouds which have been gathering on the summits, breeding snow and rain, have descended from the heights and enveloped Gastein as in a wet blanket. There is such a mist that in the middle of the day I have to pick my way carefully from Straubinger's to our villa. Everything is wrapped in a thick veil, — the houses, the trees, the mountains, and cascades. The shapes of things dissolve and disappear in the moist clouds that weigh upon everything, and also upon the human mind. We light the lamps at two o'clock in the afternoon. The ladies have finished packing, and we should have gone in spite of the mist, but the road is torn up by the mountain torrents beyond Hofgastein. Pani Celina again suffers from headaches, and my aunt, after receiving a letter from Chwastowski about the harvest, walks with heavy steps about the room, talking to herself and scolding Chwastowski. Aniela looked pale and out of sorts in the morning. She had a bad night and dreamed about the cretin she had seen near the Schreckbrucke. She woke up, and could not go to sleep again; she spent the rest of the night in nervous terror. It is very strange what an impression the wretched cripple has made upon her. I tried by cheerful conversation to make her forget about the incident, in which I succeeded. Since our compact on the Schreckbrucke she is without comparison brighter, more cheerful, and happier.

As regards myself, seeing Aniela thus contented, I cannot find it in my heart to complain, though it often occurs to me that our relation is mainly based upon there being no relation at all. When I entered into the compact I knew what I was doing and what shape our feeling would take; but now that shape seems to be getting more intangible and undefined, and wrapped up in a mist like that which enfolds Gastein. I have a presentiment that Aniela will not grant me what is due to me, and I dare not remind her about anything. I dare not, because a struggle is too exhausting, especially a struggle for the woman we love. I have been engaged in this struggle half a year and not gained anything; and I feel so weary that I prefer the truce, such as it is, to a renewal of my former warfare. There is also another reason. If this state of things does not exactly answer to my expectations, it pleases and conciliates Aniela. She fancies I love her in a nobler way, therefore she appreciates, I dare not say loves, me more and more. In spite of the absence of all outward signs, I see it and it gives me courage; I say to myself, "If her feeling increases, only persevere, and a time may come when it will be stronger than her power of resistance."

People generally, and women especially, fancy that the so-called Platonic love is a peculiar species of love, very rare and very noble. It is simply a confusion of ideas. There may be such a thing as Platonic relations, but Platonic love is as much nonsense as dark light. Even love for the dead consists of a longing after their bodily presence as well as their souls. Among the living this feeling is called resignation.

I did not want to say an untruth when I told Aniela I would love her as if she were dead; but resignation does not exclude all hope. In spite of all my disappointments, in spite of the consciousness that my hopes are vain, I still nourish in a corner of my heart the hope that the present state of affairs is only a halting-place on the way to love. I may repeat to myself over and over again, "Delusion! delusion!" but I cannot get rid of it until I get rid of my desire. They are inseparable. I agreed to the compact because I could not help myself, because I preferred this to nothing at all; but I consider it, almost unconsciously, as a diplomatic move which aims at complete, not half happiness. What makes me nevertheless thoughtful, surprises, and grieves me, and what I simply cannot understand, is that on this line even I am defeated. My victories lie in the dim, far-off future; but in the present, in spite of all my cunning, experience of life, strong feelings, and diplomacy, I am defeated by a being infinitely more simple than I, less skilled in life's tactics, less cautious and calculating in the course she takes. It is a defeat; there is no other word for it. What is our present relation? Nothing more than the relation of brother and sister, which she wished for and which I did not wish. Formerly I fought with the storm and often came to grief, but I steered my own bark. Now Aniela steers for us both; we go more smoothly and more evenly, but I feel I am going where I did not wish to go. I now understand why she put out her hand at once, when I mentioned Dante's love for Beatrice. She wanted to lead me. Has she calculated everything beforehand more carefully and profoundly than I? No; I do not know anybody less capable of any calculation, therefore I cannot admit the idea; yet I cannot get rid of the consciousness, bordering upon the mystical, that some one has calculated it for her.

It is all very strange, and the strangest thing of all is that I forged the fetters which bind me; I myself contrived to bring about a relation so foreign to my nature, my views, and my most ardent desires. If somebody had foretold to me, before I knew Aniela, that I should hit upon such devices, it would have made me laugh at the prophet and at myself. I, and Platonic relations! Even now I feel sometimes inclined to laugh and jeer at myself. But I cannot; it is sheer misery that has brought me to that pass.

23 August.

We leave here to-morrow. The sky is clearing up and there is a westerly breeze that promises fine weather. The mist has gathered into long, whitish billows, that hang on the mountain sides, and like huge leviathans are slowly rolling down. I went with Aniela on the Kaiserweg. This morning the question arose in my mind what would happen if the existing state of things ceased to satisfy Aniela. I have no right to overstep the boundary, and I am afraid to do so; suppose she too thought the same? Her innate modesty and shyness in themselves would prove an almost insurmountable barrier; and if, added to that, she thought the mutual agreement as binding for her as for me, we should never come to an understanding; we should suffer in vain.

Reflecting upon this, I understood the futility of such fears. She, to whom even that Platonic relation appears too broad, who consciously or unconsciously restricts, and does not even grant me what is due to me within these limits, should be the first to acknowledge any greater rights. And yet the human soul, even if in hell, will never lose hope altogether. In spite of the self-evident impossibility, I resolved to make myself safe by giving Aniela to understand that if I considered the agreement as binding, it was not the same with her.

I wanted to say many other things, especially that she was doing me a great wrong, and that my soul yearned to hear a word of love from her lips, not once but many times, and that only thus I should be able to remain on those lofty heights whereon she condemned me to dwell. But that morning she was so gay, so cheerful and kind to me, that I had not the heart to disturb her peace. Yesterday I could not understand how a being so full of simplicity had got me under her power and conquered me even on those fields I thought my exclusive domain. To-day it seems clearer to me; and I have a ready and very sad hypothesis, — she loves me less than I love her.

I knew a man who had the trick of repeating in all his sentences, "Never mind me." It would not be strange if I began to do the same. For when I feel, as I do sometimes, a desire to get rid of some words that almost burn my tongue, the sudden thought that I might mar her cheerfulness, drive away the smile, and change her good disposition, renders me mute. Ah me! how often this does happen!

The thought that I love Aniela more than she loves me has crossed my mind a hundred times; one day I think of it in one way, the next in another. I am straying among my thoughts and look at the matter in a different light every day. At one time it seems to me that she does not care for me very much, in fact is incapable of any strong feeling; and again, I not only think but am conscious that she has one of the deepest and most loving hearts I ever met in the world. I have always plenty of proofs either way. Thus I say to myself: "If her love increases, three, four, ten times as much, will there not come a time when it will grow stronger than her resistance?" Yes. Then it is only a question of how great her feeling is? No. For if the feeling were small she would not have suffered so much, and I have seen her suffer almost as much as I did myself. Against all reasoning I have one answer: "I have seen."

To-day a sentence escaped her which I shall remember, for it is an answer to my doubts. She would not have said this had I spoken about us and our love. But I spoke in a general way, as I now always do. I argued that it lay in the nature of feeling to be connected with action; that love produces acts of will. When I had finished she said quietly:—

"Not always. One may suffer."

Of course one may suffer. With these few words she had crushed my arguments and filled my heart with reverence for her. In moments like these I am happy and unhappy, as again it seems to me that she loves me as I love her, but will remain pure before God, and men, and herself. And I shall not be able to shake that temple. When all is said and done this analysis of her heart and feelings does not lead to any certainty. I am always walking in the dark. To my philosophical and social "I do not know" there is now added a personal consideration, far more serious; for this "I do not know" threatens my very life.

I forged myself the chain which binds me to Aniela, and there is no hope whatever that it ever will be broken. I love her despairingly, and it is a question whether my love be not a disease. If I were younger, less shattered in mind and nerves,—in short, of a more normal disposition, — I might, seeing the hopelessness, try to break that chain. As it is, I do not make even an effort. I love as a man with diseased nerves, a man who is close upon mania; love as old men do, clinging to love with all their might, as it is for them a question of life. Thus one may cling to a branch overhanging a precipice.

This one thing has blossomed in my life, consequently its growth is so out of all proportion. A phenomenon like this is easy to understand and will repeat itself the oftener, the more people there are like me; that is, hyper-analytical sceptics inclined to hysteria, with a great nothingness in their souls, and a strong neurosis in their veins. This modern product of our epoch, drawing to its end, may not love at all, or may look upon love as mere licentiousness; but if it happen that all the forces of one's life centre in one feeling, and come under the sway of his neurosis, the predilection will become as ineradicable as any other chronic disease. Physiologists have not fully understood this, still less novelists, who occupy themselves with the analysis of the modern human soul.

VIENNA, 25 August.

We arrived to-day at Vienna. On the way I listened to a conversation between my aunt and Pani Celina, of which I took note, as it seemed to make an extraordinary impression upon Aniela. We four were alone in the railway carriage; we were discussing the portrait, and especially the question whether the white dress would not have to be abandoned, as the making of it would take up too much time. Suddenly Pani Celina, whose mind is full of reminiscences and dates, which she quotes in and out of season, turned to Aniela and said: —

"It is just two months to-day since your husband arrived at Ploszow, is it not?"

"I believe so," replied Aniela.

At the same instant she grew very red and tried to hide her confusion by taking down one of her bags from the rack. The blush had not gone from her face when she turned round again, and there was in her face an expression of acute pain. The ladies did not notice it, for they were deep in a discussion as to the exact date of Kromitzki's arrival; but I had noticed it and it grated upon my nerves, for it reminded me that that very day she had to submit to his caresses. I was furious, and at the same time ashamed for that blush of hers. In my love there are many great thorns, but there are also a multitude of small, hideous ones. Before that unlucky remark of Pani Celina's I felt almost happy because I had the illusion that I was travelling with Aniela as my affianced wife. Now in one moment the good disposition fled. I felt resentment towards Aniela, and I showed it in my manners. She noticed it at once, and when we arrived at Vienna and were left alone for a moment, she asked: —

"Are you angry with me about something?"

"No, but I love you," I said curtly.

Her face grew sad. She thought, perhaps, that I had grown tired of the peaceful current of our life, and the old Leon had come back again. I felt angry with her, but angrier still with myself, that all my philosophy and consciousness did not serve to give me the mastery over the slightest sensations.

I went at once to Angeli, but when I arrived at his studio it was six o'clock and the studio was closed. Aniela will be rested, and to-morrow I will go with her. I have changed my idea. I do not want her in a ball-dress, showing her arms and shoulders; I will have her as she is every day, and as I love her most.

In the evening Doctor Chwastowski came to see us. He looks very well, and as strong as a giant.

26 August.

I had a very nasty dream. I begin with it the description of the day. I am not one to attach any meaning to dreams, and I am convinced that a healthy brain could not produce such stuff. Sleeplessness has troubled me now for some time, but yesterday I had scarcely closed my eyes when I fell into a heavy sleep. I do not know at what time I had that dream; it must have been towards morning, for when I awoke it was broad daylight, and I could not have dreamed long. I saw a great quantity of cockchafers and black beetles crawl from under the mattress and along the sides of the bed. They were as big as matchboxes. Presently I saw them crawling up the wall. Strange how realistic dreams can be; I distinctly heard the rustling of their feet on the paper. Raising my eyes I noticed big clusters of beetles hanging from the ceiling; but they were of a different kind, much larger, with black and white spots. On some of them I could distinguish the white belly, with two rows of feet on either side which looked like ribs. In my dream they seemed quite in their place, and yet horrible. They filled me with loathing, but I was neither astonished nor afraid. Only after I had awoke the loathing became unbearable and changed into a kind of fear, — fear of death. It was the first time I had that sensation, and that fear of death took such a form. "Who knows," I thought, "what hideous shapes are awaiting me in the darkness, on the other side of life?" Later on I remembered that I had seen some similar beetles in an entomological collection, but at the time they seemed to me something unnatural, belonging to an intangible after-life. I jumped up and raised the blind, and the sight of daylight calmed me at once. The streets were already alive with the traffic of the early morning, — vegetable carts drawn by dogs, servants going to market, and laborers to their work. The sight of the normal human life is the best remedy against phantasms like these. I feel now an immense necessity for light and life. The final conclusion of all this is that I am not well. My tragedy undermines me like a cancer. I see white threads in my hair; this might have come in the course of nature; but my face, especially in the morning, has a waxen hue, and my hands are getting transparent. I am not getting thin, it is rather the opposite, but I am conscious of anæmia as I am conscious of my psychical state, and I feel that my vital powers are passing through a crisis, and that some calamity is threatening me.

I shall never go mad. I cannot even imagine how I could ever lose control over myself. Besides, a celebrated physician, and what is more an intelligent man, told me that at a certain point of developed consciousness this was quite impossible. I think he has written a book about it. But without going mad I may be on the eve of some portentous nervous disease; and as I know a little what that means, I say sincerely that any other would be preferable.

I have not much faith in doctors, especially in those that trust to physic, but I may take some advice if only to please my aunt. I know one remedy, which would be infallible; if Kromitzki died and I could marry Aniela I should speedily get well. A disease springing from nerves must be cured through nerves. But she will not be my physician, even if my life is in danger.

I went with Aniela and my aunt to Angeli's studio. The first sitting took place to-day. How right I was in saying that she is one of the most beautiful women I ever met in life, because there is nothing commonplace in her beauty. Angeli looked at her with manifest pleasure, as if he had before him a noble piece of art. He was in excellent spirits, drew the outline with enthusiasm, and did not conceal at all the reason of his satisfaction. "In my profession," he said, "a model like this is very rare indeed. With such a sitter it is delightful to work. What a face! what expression!"

The expression was by no means so charming as usual, because Aniela is a shy little creature; she felt confused, bewildered, and it evidently cost her an effort to keep a natural pose. Angeli understood that.

"It will be easier the next time," he said; "like everything else, one must get accustomed to it." And he repeated several times: "This will be something like a portrait."

He looked also with a pleased countenance at my aunt, who has noble features and a singularly commanding presence. The way she met Angeli was in itself a treat. It was the off-hand manner of the *grande dame*, always in good taste, but evidently not making much of him. Angeli, who is used to flattery and homage, and at the same time a clever man, judged her aright, and I saw he was amused by her demeanor.

We had decided upon a black silk dress, very elegantly made. It shows off Aniela's figure to perfection, its suppleness and rounded curves. I can neither think nor write about it calmly. Angeli, addressing Aniela. repeatedly called her "Mademoiselle." Feminine nature, even an angelic one, has still its little weaknesses. I noticed that my dear love was pleased, and still more so when I told Angeli of his mistake, and he said: —

"But I shall always fall into the same mistake; looking at madame it is impossible not to make the mistake."

And indeed with those vivid blushes mantling in her face she was surpassingly lovely.

On our way out, when a little distance from my aunt, I whispered to Aniela: —

"Aniela, do you know yourself how beautiful you are?"

She did not say anything, but lowered her eyelashes, as she always does in such a case. Nevertheless, I noticed that during the rest of the day there was a shade of unconscious coquetry in her manner towards me. Angeli's words and mine had attuned her to that disposition. She knows I admire her, that never woman was admired more, and it pleases her. I not only admired her, but I said inwardly, rather shouted to myself: "To the deuce with all compacts. I love you without limits and restrictions."

In the evening we went to the opera to hear Wagner's "Fliegende Hollander." I scarcely heard anything at all, or rather, heard and saw only through her. I asked of Wagner: "What impression do you make upon her? Does your music enter her soul and make her inclined to love me? Do you transport her into higher spheres, where love is the highest law?" That is the only thing that interests me. Women perhaps cannot love so exclusively. They always reserve part of their soul for themselves, for the world and its sensations.

27 August.

My aunt expressed a wish to depart. She is anxious to be back at Ploszow, and says that her presence here is not necessary, and that in fact we should get on better without her; that we should not be obliged to consider her and could devote all our time to the portrait. We all protested a little, and maintained that a lady of her years ought not to travel alone. Though reluctantly, I considered it my duty to offer my companionship. I confess that I awaited her reply with a certain trepidation; but the dear old lady said, with great liveliness: —

"Don't think of it even. Suppose Celina should fall ill again, who would look after them, or accompany Aniela to the studio? She must not go alone." She shook her finger playfully at Aniela, and with a frown on her brow, and smiling mouth she added: "I don't quite trust that painter, he looks at her more than his work requires; and she sees it too and is pleased with it, — I know her little ways."

"But aunty, he is not a young man," said Aniela, laughingly kissing her hands.

My aunt muttered: "Little coaxing rogue, he is not a young man, you say? but he pays you compliments all the same. Leon, you must keep your eye on them."

I relinquished the journey to Ploszow with delight, yielding to my aunt's convincing reasons. Pani Celina insisted upon her taking the maid, at least, who had gone with them to Gastein. My aunt refused at first, but consented when Aniela pointed out that they would do very well without a maid in the hotel. She gave orders at once to have her things packed. She is very quick in her decisions and wants to go to-morrow by an early train. I teased her during dinner, saying that she liked her horses better than all of us together. "Foolish boy," she said, "don't talk nonsense;" then forgot herself, and began soliloquizing about the horses. The sitting was a very long one to-day. Aniela posed much better. The face is already laid in.

28 August.

My aunt left us this morning. Pani Celina, who went with us to the studio, could scarcely restrain an exclamation of horror when she saw Aniela's face on the picture. She has no idea about painting and the different phases a picture has to go through, and fancied the face would remain thus. I had to set her mind at rest. Then Angeli, who guessed what was the matter, laughed and said that what she saw before her was only the chrysalis, from which the butterfly would come forth in time.

"I believe it will be one of the best portraits I ever painted," he said; "for a long time I have not worked so *con amore.*"

I hope his words will prove true. After the sitting I went to get tickets for the opera. When I returned I found Aniela alone, and suddenly temptation seized me with the force of a hurricane. I thought if she would come into my arms, now was the moment; and at the very thought I felt myself growing pale, my pulses beat wildly, I trembled and caught my breath. The room was in semi-darkness, veiled by heavy curtains. I made superhuman efforts to conquer the irresistible power that pushed me towards her. It seemed as if a hot wave emanating from her enfolded me, and that she too must feel the same storm in her breast. "I must take her in my arms, kiss her eyes and lips," a voice within me seemed to say, "though I were to perish for it afterwards." She noticed at once my unusual state; there was a momentary terror in her eyes, but she collected herself at once and said quickly: —

"You must be my guardian now in mamma's absence. There was a time when I used to be afraid of you; but now I trust you and feel quite at ease with you."

I kissed her hands and said in a choking voice: "Oh, Aniela, if you knew what is passing within me!"

She replied, with sadness and compassion: "I know; you are so good, and all the nobler."

For a moment I still fought with myself; but she disarmed me, — I did not dare. During the remainder of the day she tried to compensate me for my restraint. Never had I seen in her eyes so much affection and such tenderness. Is this not perhaps the best way, after all? Perhaps in this guise the feeling will grow stronger and conquer her at last. I do not know, I begin to lose my head. But following this road I sacrifice every day my love for love's sake.

29 August.

Something very strange and terrifying has happened. During the sitting, while posing quietly, Aniela suddenly shuddered, her face grew very red and then turned as white as snow. Both Angeli and I were terribly frightened. He interrupted his work at once and asked Aniela to rest; I brought her a glass of water. After a few moments she grew better and wanted to resume the pose; but I saw that it cost her some effort and that she still seemed dazed. Perhaps she was tired. The weather is very hot to-day and the streets are like a baker's oven. We went back much sooner than the day before, and I noticed that she had not recovered her usual spirits. During dinner she grew suddenly very red. Pani Celina asked whether she felt indisposed. She assured us that nothing was the matter with her. To my offer to go and bring a doctor, she replied with unusual vivacity, and with a touch of irritation, that there was no need for it, that she was not ill. During the remainder of the day she was pale, the black eyebrows contracted every now and then, and there was an expression of sternness in her face. She was more indifferent to me than yesterday, and I fancied she avoided my eyes. I cannot make out what it means. I am very restless, and shall not be able to sleep; or if I go to sleep I shall have dreams such as I had before.

30 August.

There is something mysterious going on around me. Towards noon I knocked at the room of the ladies, to let Aniela know it was time to go to the studio; but they were not there. The hotel servant told me they had ordered a carriage two hours before and driven into town. A little surprised at that, I resolved to wait for their return. Half an hour later they came in, but Aniela gave me her hand silently and passed at once into her room. A quick glance at her face told me it was troubled. I thought she had only gone to change her dress, when Pani Celina said: —

"My dear Leon, please go to Angeli and apologize for Aniela; her nerves are so shaken that she cannot possibly sit for him."

"What is the matter with her?" I asked, anxiously.

Pani Celina seemed at a loss what to say, and at last replied: "I do not know; I took her to the doctor, but we did not find him at home. I left my card and asked him to call on us at the hotel; that is all I can tell you."

I could not get anything more out of her. I took a cab and drove at once to Angeli's studio. When I told him that Aniela could not come it seemed to me as if he looked suspicious. Perhaps the troubled expression of my face had something to do with it. It crossed my mind, "Suppose he suspects us to have changed our minds, and that we do not want the portrait any longer?" He does not know us; he might even think that some money difficulties are the cause of my anxiety. To guard against such suspicions, I made up my mind to pay him in advance. When he heard of this, he protested vehemently and said he never accepted payment until the picture was finished; but I replied that I was only the depositary of the sum, and as I might be called away at any moment, I would rather get rid of the trouble. After some more discussion, which bored me, it was settled according to my wish. We agreed that the sitting should take place at the same hour the day following, and in case Pani Kromitzka was still unable to attend I would let him know before ten. When back at the hotel, I went at once to the ladies. Aniela was in her room. Pani Celina said the doctor had just gone away, but did not say anything conclusive; only advised her to keep quiet and avoid emotion. I do not know why, but I fancied I saw again in her face the same hesitation. Possibly it comes only from her anxiety about Aniela, which I can well understand, as I feel the same.

When in my own room I reproached myself bitterly for having been, at least partly, the cause of this; as all this struggle between her love and her duty could not but act perniciously upon her health. Thinking of all this, I had a sensation which might be summed up in a few words: "Better I should perish than that she should suffer." I thought with terror that she would not come down to dinner, as if something serious, God knows what, had depended upon it. Fortunately she did come down; but she still avoided my eyes, and there was the same mysterious something in the air. First she grew confused at seeing me, and then made an effort to be her usual self, but failed. She made upon me the impression of a person that tries to conceal a trouble. She must have been paler too than usual, for though she cannot be called dark she almost looked like a brunette.

I racked my brain to guess what could have happened. Was it anything connected with Kromitzki; and if so, what could it be? Perhaps my money is in danger. The deuce take the money! All I possess may perish, rather than that Aniela should have a moment of anxiety. I must get at the bottom of the mystery to-morrow. I am quite sure it has to do with Kromitzki; but what can he have done? He has not sold another Gluchow, for the simple reason that there is not another to sell.

BERLIN, 5 September.

I am at Berlin, because escaping from Vienna I had to go somewhere. I could not go to Ploszow, because she will be there. I was so convinced that no human power could tear me from her that the very idea of separation seemed to me a wild impossibility. But no! It is always the unexpected that happens, for I have gone away, and everything is at an end. I am at Berlin. I feel as if I had an engine in my head, the wheels of which keep whirring incessantly. This hurts me; but I am not mad. I know everything and remember everything. My physician was right; it is only weak heads that come to grief. Besides, it could not happen to me, because insanity sometimes means happiness.

6 September.

Yet at times I fancy that my brain is bursting bounds. What is there more natural than that a married woman should have children? But to me that natural order seems so monstrous that it well-nigh maddens me. Yet a thing cannot be at the same time in the order of nature and a monstrosity. No brain can withstand that. What does it mean? I understand that those whom fate means to crush are crushed by some great, overwhelming calamity. With me it is different. I am rent asunder by an ordinary, natural event, — and the more natural, the more terrible it is. One contradicts the other. She is not responsible, — I understand that because I am not mad. She is still virtuous, and yet I could have sooner forgiven her any other crime. And I cannot, God knows I cannot forgive you, because I loved you so much. And believe me, there is not another woman in the whole world I scorn so much as I scorn you. For, after all, it comes to this: you had two lovers, one for Platonic love and the other for matrimonial love. There is in me a wild desire to laugh, and at the same time to dash my head against the wall. I had not foreseen that a way could be found to tear me from you; and yet there is one, and it has proved effective.

8 September.

When I come to think that all is at an end between us, and that I have left her forever, I can scarcely believe it. There is no Aniela for me any more. Then what is there? Nothing. Then why do I live? I do not know. It is not out of curiosity to know whether a son or a daughter will be born to Pan Kromitzki. I always think of it as the most natural thing in the world, and my head seems nigh to bursting. It is very strange! I ought to have been prepared for that, and yet the thought never entered my head. I should have sooner expected a stroke of lightning to fell me down. Yet Kromitzki was with her at Ploszow; they were together in Vienna, and afterward in Gastein.

And I put it all down to her nerves, to her deep feelings! What egregious foolishness! Since I could bear to see the two together, I ought to be able to put up with the consequences. Alas, it is not my reason that revolts, it is my nerves that quiver under these consequences. There are people in whom these two forces dwell in harmony; within me they worry each other like dogs. That is another of my misfortunes. How is it I never thought of it? It ought to have struck me that if there were any terrible coincidence, any blow more painful than another, it would be reserved for me.

Sometimes it seems to me as if I were hunted by a Providence that, not satisfied by the logic of facts that contain in themselves a Nemesis, took a special delight in fastening personally upon me. There are many others who love their neighbors' wives, and they do not suffer, because they love less honestly, more thoughtlessly. Is there any justice in that? No, it is not that. There is no self-conscious thought in the ordering of these things; they happen by chance and by virtue of necessity.

10 September.

The thought still pursues me that as a rule human tragedy is the outcome of exceptional events and calamities, and mine comes from a natural event. Really I do not know which is worst. The natural order of things seems to me past bearing.

11 September.

I have heard that a man struck by lightning stiffens, but does not fall down at once. I too keep up, sustained by that thunderbolt that struck me, but I feel myself falling. As soon as it grows dark in the evening something strange takes place within me. I feel so oppressed that it costs me an effort even to sigh; it seems as if the air could not get to my lungs, and that I breathe with only a part of them. During the night, and also in the day, a sudden nameless terror seizes me, — terror of nothing in particular. I feel as if something horrible was going to happen, something worse than death. Yesterday I put the question to myself: "What would become of me if, in this foreign town, I suddenly forgot my name and where I lived, and wandered on and on in darkness without knowing where I was going?"

These are sick fancies. Besides, in such a case that would happen to my body which has already happened to my soul; for in a moral sense I do not know where I dwell, — I walk in darkness, aimlessly, in a kind of madness. I am afraid of everything, except of death. Strictly speaking, I have a strange sensation as if it were not that I am afraid, but as if fear dwelt in me, as a separate being, — and I tremble; I cannot bear darkness now. In the evening I go out and walk in the streets, lighted by electric lamps, until I am thoroughly tired. If I met anybody I knew, I should escape, if to the other end of the world; but crowds have become a necessity to me. When the streets are getting empty I feel terrified. The thought of night fills me with nameless fear. And how long they seem, these nights!

I have continually a metallic taste in my mouth. I felt it for the first time that night when I came home and found Kromitzki waiting for me; the second time I felt it when Pani Celina told me the "great news." What a day! I had gone to ask how Aniela was, when the doctor had seen her for the second time. There was not the slightest suspicion in my mind; I did not understand anything even when Pani Celina said: "The doctor says that those are purely nervous symptoms, and have nothing to do with her state."

Seeing that I did not understand, she said, with a certain uneasiness:—

"I must tell you the great news."

And she told me the "great news." When I heard it I felt the metallic taste in my mouth, and a cold sensation in my brain, exactly as I had felt that evening I met Kromitzki unexpectedly. I went into my room. I remember among other things that I felt an immense desire to laugh. That ideal being, for whom even Platonic love seemed to be impermissible, and who instead of "love" used the word "friendship!" I felt a desire to laugh, and at the same time to dash my head against the wall.

I preserved nevertheless a mechanical self-possession. It came from the consciousness that everything was over and done with; that I must go — that there was nothing for it but to go. That consciousness transformed me into an automaton, doing by routine everything that was necessary for my departure. I was even conscious of keeping up appearances. Why? I do not know, as this did not matter now to me any longer. Most likely it was an instinctive action of the brain, which for months had been trained in concealing the truth and keeping up appearances. I told Pani Celina that I had seen a doctor, and that he said there was something amiss with my heart, and ordered me to go to Berlin without delay, — and she believed it.

Not so Aniela. I saw her eyes dilated with terror, and in her face the expression of a degraded martyr; and there were two persons within me: one who said, "Is it her fault?" and another who despised her. Oh, why did I love her so much?

12 September.

It is almost two weeks since I left. They must be at Ploszow by this time. I wrote to-day a letter to my aunt, because I was afraid she might be uneasy about me and come here to look after me. I am sometimes astonished to find there is still somebody that cares what becomes of me.

13 September.

There are men who lead astray other men's wives, deceive them, and afterwards throw them aside and quietly resume their every-day life. I have never done any such thing, and if Aniela had been my victim I should have wiped the dust from off her path; no human power could have torn me from her. There are greater crimes than mine, but upon me has fallen such a burden that it gives me the impression of an exceptional punishment; and I cannot help thinking that my love must have been a terrible crime.

This is a kind of instinctive fear, against which scepticism is no safeguard. And yet by all moral laws it must be admitted that it would be a greater offence to lead a woman to ruin without love, and do from calculation what I did from a deep love. Surely the responsibility cannot be greater for an immense, overpowering feeling than for a mean little weakness.

No! therefore my love is, above all, an awful calamity. A man free from prejudices can imagine how he would feel if he were swayed by prejudice; so, too, a man who doubts may imagine how he could pray if he had the faith. I not only have the feeling, but it breaks forth into a complaint, almost like a sincere prayer, and I say: "If I am guilty, O God! I have been punished severely, and a little mercy might be shown to me." But I cannot even imagine in what shape that mercy could come to me now! It is impossible!

14 September.

They must have gone back to Ploszow by this time. I still think of Aniela very often, for we cannot wipe out the past; especially when we have nothing to look for in the future; and I have nothing, nothing at all. If I had faith I might become a priest; if I were a man who denies the existence of God I might become a convert. But within me the organs with which we believe are withered, as sometimes a limb withers. I do not know anything except that in my sorrows I do not find comfort in religion.

When Aniela married Kromitzki, I thought everything between us was over. I was mistaken. It is only now I have the full conviction that everything is over; for now we are divided not only by our will and my departure, but by something that is beyond us, by forces of nature independent of us. We are like two parallel lines that can never meet, though we wish for it ever so much. On Aniela's line there will be suffering, but there will be also new worlds, a new life; on mine there is nothing but solitude. She doubtless understands that as well as I. I wonder whether sometimes she says to herself: "It is I who, without intending it, have ruined that man." It does not matter much to me, and yet I should like to know that she is sorry for me. Maybe she will feel a little sorry until her child is born. After that all her feelings will flow into one channel, and, for her, I shall not exist any longer. That also is a law of nature, — an excellent law.

16 September.

I saw to-day on an advertisement in big letters the name of Clara Hilst. I now remembered that she had told me in her last letter that she was going to Berlin. She is here, and she is going to give several concerts. At the time, the news neither pleased nor displeased me. Now, in proportion as my nervous restlessness increases, the sensation grows more distinct, and takes a twofold shape: the thought that she is near acts soothingly on me, but the thought is sufficient, and I would rather not see her; and when I say to myself that I ought to call on her it gives me an unpleasant sensation. Clara has that inquisitive solicitude that wants to know everything and asks questions. She has a strong leaning towards romantic situations, and the firm belief that friendship is a remedy for all evils. For me to make confidences is simply impossible. I often lack the strength even to think of what has happened.

17 September.

Why do I wake up in the morning? Why do I exist? And what do I care for acquaintances or people in general? I did not go to see Clara, because she can have nothing to say to me that could possibly interest me, and it wearies me beforehand. The whole world is as entirely indifferent to me as I am to the world.

18 September.

I did well to write to my aunt. If I had not done so she would have come here. She writes thus: —

"Your letter came to hand the same day that Celina and Aniela arrived. How are you now, my dearest boy? You say that you are all right, but is that really and truly so? What did the doctors in Berlin say, and how long do you think of remaining there? Send me a telegram whether you are still there, and I will come to you at once. Celina says you went away so suddenly that she and Aniela were terribly frightened. If you had not mentioned that the doctor most likely will advise a sea voyage, I should have started off at once after receiving your letter. It is only some fifteen hours by rail, and I feel stronger than ever. The congestions I used to have have not returned. I am very anxious about you, and do not like the idea of the sea at all. You are used to that sort of thing, but I shudder at the thought of ships and storms. Celina is quite well, and Aniela fairly so. I hear that you have been told the news. Before leaving Vienna they consulted a specialist, and he said there was no doubt whatever about Aniela's state. Celina is overjoyed, and I too am glad. Perhaps this will induce Kromitzki to give up his speculations and settle at home. Aniela will now be altogether happy, having an aim in life. She looked rather tired and as if oppressed when she came back, but that may be only the consequence of the journey.

"Sniatynski's child has been very bad with croup, but is better now."

Reading my aunt's letter gave me the impression that there is no room for me among them, especially near Aniela. Even my memory will soon become unpleasant to her.

19 September.

I cannot imagine myself as living a year or two hence. What shall I do? Such utter aimlessness ought to debar one from life. Properly speaking, there is no room for me anywhere.

I did not go to see Clara, but met her in the Friedrichsstrasse. Seeing me she grew pale from joy and emotion, and greeted me with such effusion that it pleased and pained me at the same time. I was conscious that my cordiality towards her was a mere outward form, and that I did not derive any pleasure from the meeting. When she had recovered from the surprise at meeting me thus unexpectedly, she scrutinized my face anxiously. Truly I must have presented a strange sight; and my hair has become much grayer too. She began to inquire after my health, and in spite of my friendship for her, I felt that to see her often would be more than I could stand. I resolved to put myself on guard against this; I told her that I did not feel very well, and was shortly going away to a warmer climate. She tried to persuade me to come and see her; than asked after my aunt, Pani Celina, and Aniela. I put her off with general remarks.

I thought to myself that she perhaps is the only being who would have understood me, and yet I felt that I could not open my heart to her.

Nevertheless I am still susceptible to human kindness. At moments, when those honest blue eyes of Clara's looked into mine with such kindliness and such keen scrutiny, as if they wanted to look into my very soul, her goodness humiliated me so that I felt a desire to weep. Clara, in spite of my effort to seem as usual, noticed that I was changed, and with quick feminine intuition she guessed that I speak, live, almost think mechanically, and that my soul is half dead within me. She left off all searchings and inquiries, but became very tender. I saw that she was afraid of wearying me. She also tried to make me understand that in the tenderness she was showing there was no concealed intention of winning my regard, but only the desire to comfort me. And it did comfort me, but I could not help feeling very tired. My mind is not capable of any concentration, any effort to maintain a conversation, even with a friend. And besides, since the one aim of my life has vanished from my eyes, everything appears to me so empty that I have continually the question in my mind: "What is the use of it? what can it matter now?"

21 September.

Never in my life have I passed a more terrible night. I had a sensation of terror, as if I descended by endless steps into deeper and deeper darkness, full of horrible, indefined, moving shapes. I made up my mind to leave Berlin; I cannot breathe under that heavy, leaden sky. I will go back to Rome, to my house on the Babuino, and settle there for good. I think my accounts with Aniela and the world in general may be considered as closed, and henceforth I will quietly vegetate at Rome until my time comes. Anything for tranquillity! Yesterday's visit to Clara convinced me that even if I wished it, I cannot live with others, since I have nothing wherewith to repay their kindness. I am excluded from general life and stand outside, and though I am conscious of the indescribable solitude, I have no wish to go back. The idea of Rome and my hermitage on the Babuino smiles upon me; it is a pale, sorrowful smile, but I prefer it to anything else. There I spread my wings to fly out into the world, and thither I go back with broken wings,—to wait for the end.

I am writing mostly in the morning, for at night I always descend to those dark regions wherein fear dwells. To-day I shall go to the concert and say good-by to Clara. To-morrow I depart. On the way I may stop at Vienna, perhaps see Angeli, but am not certain. I am never certain how I shall feel, or what I shall do the next day.

I received to-day a note from Clara, in which she asks me to come and see her after the concert. I shall go to the concert because there are so many healthy-minded people there that I feel safer in their midst; and they do not tire me, as they are personally unknown to me; I see only the crowd. But I shall not go to Clara. She is too kind. It is said of persons dying from starvation that for some time before their death they cannot bear the sight of food. In the same way my spiritual organism cannot stand sympathy and kindness. It cannot bear memories either. It is a very small thing, but I know now why that visit to Clara was such a trial to my nerves. She uses the same scent I brought from Vienna for Aniela. I have noticed the same thing before, that nothing recalls to the mind a certain person so distinctly as when one inhales the perfume she is in the habit of using.

22 September.

I have broken down at last. I caught a chill yesterday coming from the concert-room, where the air was very close. I did not put on my overcoat, and when I arrived at the hotel I was chilled to the bone. Every breath I draw gives me a sensation as if my lungs in expanding came in contact with two rows of needles hidden under the shoulder-blade. I feel alternately very hot and very cold. I am continually thirsty. At times I feel so weak that I could not go downstairs. There is no question now about going away ; I could not get into the carriage without help. While writing I hear my own breath coming three times as quick and loud as usual. I am quite certain that but for my nerves the sudden chill would not have done me any harm, but in my present state of nervous prostration I have lost all power of resistance. It is undoubtedly inflammation of the lungs.

I shall keep up as long as I can. In the morning as soon as I felt ill, I wrote to my aunt, telling her I was all right, and would leave Berlin in a few days. In a few days, if I am still conscious, I shall write the same. I asked her to send all letters and telegrams to my banker here. I shall take care that nobody at Ploszow knows about my illness. How very fortunate I said good-by to Clara yesterday.

23 September.

I am worse than yesterday. I am feverish and at times conscious that my thoughts wander, but I have not lain down. When I shut my eyes the border line between the real and the outcome of my sick brain seems to vanish altogether. But I have still control over my senses. I am only afraid the fever will overpower me and I shall lose consciousness altogether.

The thought comes now and then into my mind that I, a man more richly endowed by fate than so many others, who could have a home, a family, be surrounded by loving hearts, sits here lonely and in sickness, in a strange place, with nobody near him to give him a glass of water. Aniela would be near me too — I cannot go on.

14 October.

I resume my writing after an interval of three weeks. Clara has left me. Seeing me on a fair way to recovery she went to Hanover and promised to come back in ten days. She nursed me during the whole time of my illness. It was she who brought a doctor to me. I should probably have died but for her. I do not remember whether it was the third or fourth day of my illness she came here. I was conscious, but at the same time as indifferent as if it were not to me that she had come, or as if her being there were an every-day occurrence. She came with the doctor, whose thick, curly, white hair attracted my attention and fascinated me. After examining me he asked me several questions, first in German, then in French; and though I understood what he said, I did not feel the slightest inclination to answer, could not make an effort,—as if my will-power had been struck down by the disease, as well as the body.

They worried me that day with cupping, and then I remained quiet without any sensations. Sometimes I thought that I was going to die, but this did not trouble me any more than what was going on around me. Perhaps in severe illness, even when conscious, we lose the sense of proportion between great and small matters, and for some reason or other our attention is mainly fixed upon small things. Thus, for instance, besides the doctor's curly hair, I was greatly interested in seeing them push back the upper and lower bolt of the door of the room adjoining mine, which Clara intended to occupy. I remember that I could not take my eyes off that door, as if something depended on whether it would open or not. Presently the surgeon came in who was to look after me under Clara's supervision. He began to say something to me, but Clara motioned him to be silent.

I am still very tired, and must leave off.

16 October.

My nerves have quieted down during that long illness. I have none of those terrors that haunted me before. I only wish Clara would come back as quickly as possible. It is not so much a longing for her presence, as the selfishness of the convalescent, who feels that nothing can replace her tender care and nursing. I know she will not dwell close to me any longer; but her presence soothes me. Weakness and helplessness cling to the protecting power as a child clings to its mother. I am convinced that no other woman would have done for me what Clara did; other women would have thought more of the proprieties than of saving a man's life. Thinking of this, bitterness rises in my throat, and there is one name on my lips — But those are things better left alone, as long as I have not strength enough to think about them. Clara used to sleep fully dressed on the sofa in the room next to mine, with the door open. Whenever I moved she was at once at my bedside: I saw her by night, leaning over my bed, her hair disarranged, and eyes winking with sleeplessness and fatigue. She herself measured out my physic, and raised my head from the pillow. When, in moments of consciousness, I wanted to thank her, she put a finger to her lips as a sign that the doctor had enjoined quietness. I do not know how many nights she spent at my bedside. She looked very tired in the daytime, and, when sitting near me in an armchair, sometimes dozed off in the middle of a sentence. Waking up she smiled at me, and dozed again. At nights she walked to and fro in her own room, in order to keep awake; but so softly that I could not have known it but for the shadow moving on the wall, which I saw through the open door. Once, when she was near me, not knowing how to express my gratitude, I raised her hand to my lips; she stooped down quickly, and, before I could prevent it, kissed my hand. But I must confess that I was not always so grateful. Sick people as a rule are fanciful and irritable; I felt irritated at her being so tall. I felt a kind of resentment that she was not like Aniela; for so long a time I had been in the habit of acknowledging grace and beauty only in so far as they approached the grace and beauty of that other one.

Sometimes, looking at Clara, I irritated myself inwardly by the most singular thought that she is beautiful, not because nature meant her to be beautiful, — not by right of her race, — but by a fortunate accident of birth. Sometimes other beautiful feminine heads made upon me the same impression. These are subtle shades which only very delicate and sensitive nerves can perceive.

There were moments, especially at night, when, looking at Clara's face grown thin and tired with watching me, I had a delusion that I saw the other one. This happened when she was sitting in the half-light, a certain distance from my bed. This delusion was fostered by fever and a sick brain, for which impossibilities do not exist. Sometimes my mind wandered and I called Clara by that other's name, spoke to her as if she were Aniela. I remember it as if in a dream.

17 October.

The banker B. sent me some letters written by my aunt. She asks me about my plans for the future. She writes even about the crops, but nothing about the inmates of Ploszow. I do not even know whether they be alive or dead. What an irritating way of writing letters. What do I care about the crops, and about the whole estate? I replied at once, and could not disguise my displeasure.

18 October.

To-day I received a telegram from Kromitzki addressed to Warsaw. My aunt, instead of sending its contents in another telegram, put it into an envelope, and sent it by post. Kromitzki entreats me to save my own money and his whole future by sending him another twenty-five thousand roubles. Reading this I merely shrugged my shoulders. What do I care now for Kromitzki or my money? Let it go with the rest! If he only knew the reason I helped him the first time, he would not ask me now. Let him bear his losses as quietly as I bear mine. Moreover, there is awaiting him the "great news;" that ought to comfort him. Rejoice as much as you can; have as many children as you like; but if you think I am going to provide for their future, you ask a little too much.

If at least she had not sacrificed me with such inconsiderate egoism to her so-called "principles." But enough of this; my brain cannot stand it, — let me at least be ill in peace.

20 October.

They cannot let me alone, — found me even here. Again for two days I had no peace; again I press both hands against my head to stop that whirring sound in my brain. I think again of Ploszow and of her, and of the solitude that is awaiting me. It is a fearful thing when suddenly something goes out of our life for which we lived exclusively. I do not know whether illness has weakened my brain, but I simply cannot understand various phenomena that I perceive within myself. It seems as if jealousy had outlived my love.

It is a twofold jealousy, — a jealousy not only of facts, but of feelings. I am torn by the thought that the child which is to be born will take Aniela's heart from me, and what is more, and concerns me most, it will bring her closer to Kromitzki. I would not have her now if she were free; but I cannot bear the thought of her loving her husband. I would give all that remains of life if nobody would love her, and she not love anybody any more. Under such conditions life might be endurable still.

21 October.

If what is now in my mind does not save me, I shall again fall ill, or perhaps go mad. I am making up my accounts. Is there anything owing to me from life? Nothing. What is awaiting me in the future? Nothing. If so, there is no reason why I should not make a present of myself to somebody whom that present would make happy. For my life, my intellect, my abilities, — for the whole of my own self I would not give a stiver. Moreover, I do not love Clara; but if she loves me, and sees her happiness in me, it would be cruel to refuse her what I hold so very cheap. I should consider it my duty to tell her what she is taking; worse for her if it does not discourage her, — but that will be her concern.

This plan attracts me chiefly for one reason, — namely, it widens the gulf that separates me from the other one. I will prove to her that, as she has taken her own way, I am able to take mine. Then there will be an end of it. But I am thinking of her still! I notice it, and it puts me into a rage. Perhaps it is hatred now; but it is not indifference.

Pani Kromitzka probably fancied that I tore myself away forced by circumstances; she will see now that it was also my wish. And the thicker the wall I raise up between us, the sooner I shall be able to banish her from my mind. As to Clara, I repeat that I do not love her; but she loves me. Moreover, I owe her a debt of gratitude. During my illness there were moments when I considered Clara's devotedness a piece of German sentimentality, and yet the other one would not have found courage enough for such sentimentality. It would be more in accordance with her exalted virtue to let a man die than to see him without his necktie; this is a freedom reserved for the lawful husband. Clara did not care anything about such things; she gave up for me her music, exposed herself to trouble, sleepless nights, and possibly to the world's comments, and stood by me. I contracted towards her a debt, and am going to pay it. I pay it badly and in bad faith; for I offer to her what I do not value myself, — the mere remnants of what was once a man. But if she values it, let it be hers.

To my aunt it will be a disappointment; it will hurt her family pride and patriotic feelings. Yet, if my aunt could but know what has been lately going on in my heart, she would prefer this matrimonial scheme to that other love; I have not the slightest doubt as to that. What does it matter that Clara's ancestors were most probably weavers? I have no prejudices; I have only nerves. Any casual view I take tends rather towards liberalism. Sometimes I fancy that people professing to be liberals are more narrow in their views than conservatives; but, on the other hand, liberalism itself is resting on a larger basis than conservatism, and more in accord with Christ's teachings; but I am wholly indifferent to both parties. It is scarcely worth speaking or reasoning about them. Real unhappiness shows us the emptiness of mere partisan hair-splittings. Involuntarily I fall to thinking, "How will Aniela receive the news of my resolve?" I have been so accustomed to feel through her that the painful habit still clings to me.

22 October.

This morning I sent the letter to Clara. To-morrow I shall have a reply, or perhaps Clara herself will come to-night. In the afternoon they sent me a second despatch from Kromitzki. It expresses as much despair as a few words can contain. Things seem to have turned out very badly, indeed; even I did not think ruin would come so quickly. Some unexpected circumstances must have intervened that even Kromitzki could not have foreseen. The loss I incur does not make a great difference to me; I shall always be what I was, — but Kromitzki? Why should I deceive myself? There lurks somewhere in a corner of my heart a certain satisfaction at his ruin, — if only for the reason that these two will be now entirely dependent on us; that is, upon my aunt, who is the administrator of the Ploszow estate, and myself. In the mean while I do not intend to reply at all. If I changed my intention it would be to send him my congratulation at the expected family increase. Later on it will be different. I will secure their future; they shall have enough to live upon and more.

23 October.

Clara has not arrived, and up to this moment there is no answer. This is the more strange as she used to write every day, inquiring after my health. Her silence would not surprise me if I thought she wanted even ten minutes to make up her mind. I shall wait patiently; but it would be better if she did not put it off. I feel that if I had not sent off that letter, I should send now another like it; but if I could take it back I should probably do so.

24 October.

This is what Clara writes: —

DEAR MONSIEUR LEON, — Upon receiving your letter I felt so foolishly happy that I wanted to start for Berlin at once But it is because I love you sincerely that I listened to the voice which said to me that the greatest love ought not to be the greatest egoism, and that I had no right to sacrifice you for myself.

You do not love me, Monsieur Leon. I would give my life were it otherwise; but you do not love me. Your letter has been written in a moment of impulse and despair. From the first instant of meeting you in Berlin I noticed that you were neither well in body nor easy in your mind, and it troubled me; the best proof of this is that although you had wished me good-by, I sent every day to the hotel inquiring whether you had gone, until I was told you were ill. Afterwards, nursing you in your illness, I became convinced that my second fear had been also right, and that you had some hidden sorrow, one of those painful disappointments, after which it is difficult to be reconciled to life.

Now I have a conviction — and God knows how heavily it weighs upon my heart — that you want to bind your life to mine in order to drown certain memories, to forget and put a barrier between you and the past. In the face of that is it possible that I could agree to what you ask? In refusing your hand, the worst that can happen to me is that I shall feel very unhappy, but I shall not have to reproach myself with having become a burden and a dead weight upon you. I have loved you from the first time we met, therefore it is nothing new to me; and I have got used to the sorrow which is the inevitable consequence of separation and the hopeless certainty that my love will never be returned. But even if my life be sad, I can weep either with tears in the usual woman-fashion, or through my music as an artist. I shall always have that comfort at least, that when you think of me it will be as a dear friend or sister. With this I can live. But if I were your wife and came to see that you regretted your impulsiveness, were not happy, perhaps learned to hate me, I should certainly die. Besides, I say to myself: "What have you done to deserve such happiness?" It is almost impossible to imagine perfect happiness. Can you understand that one may love somebody with all one's heart in a humble spirit? I can understand it, for I love thus.

What I am going to say seems to me overbold, yet I do not feel it in my heart to give up hope altogether. Do not be angry with me; God is merciful, and the human soul is so athirst for happiness that it would fain leave a door open for it to enter. If you ask me again in half a year, a year, or any time in life the same question, I shall consider myself rewarded for all I have suffered, and for the tears I am shedding even at this moment.

CLARA.

There is within me something that is keenly conscious and can appreciate every word of this noble letter. Not a syllable is lost to me, and I say to myself: "All the more reason for asking her again; she is so honest, simple, and loving. But there is also that other self, very tired, who had all the strength taken out of him, who can give sympathy but no love; because he has staked his all upon one feeling, and sees clearly that for him there is no return.

28 October.

I am quite certain that Clara will not come back to Berlin; and what is more, that when she went away it was with the intention of not coming back again. She wanted to avoid my gratitude. I think of her gratefully and sadly, and am sorry she did not meet a different man from me. There is such an irony of fate in this! But what is the use of deceiving myself? I am still yoked to my memories. I see before me Aniela, as she appeared to me at Warsaw, as I saw her at Ploszow and Gastein; and I cannot tear myself away from the past. Besides, it has absorbed so much of my strength and life that I am not surprised at it. The difficulty is, not to remember. Every instant I catch myself in the act of thinking about Aniela, and I have to remind myself that she is changed now, that her feelings will be going, have gone already, into another direction, and that I am nothing to her now.

Formerly I preferred not to think of my wrecked condition, because my brain could not stand the thought; now I do it sometimes on purpose, if only to defend myself against the voice that calls out: "Is it her fault? and how do you know what is passing in her heart? She would not be a woman if she did not love her own child when it comes into the world, but who told you that she is not as unhappy as you are?" At times it seems to me that she is even more unhappy, and then I wish for another inflammation of the lungs. Life with such a chaos of thoughts is impossible.

30 October.

With my returning health I am gradually drifting back into the magic circle. The doctor says that in a few days I shall be able to travel. I will go hence, for it is too near Warsaw and Ploszow. It may be one of my nervous whims, but I feel I shall be better and more at rest in Rome on the Babuino. I do not promise myself to forget the past; on the contrary, I shall think of it from morning until night, but the thoughts will be like unto meditations behind cloister walls. Besides, what can I know of how it will be? All I know is that I cannot remain here any longer. I shall call upon Angeli by the way; I must have her portrait at Rome.

2 November.

I leave Berlin, I renounce Rome, and go back to Ploszow. I wrote some time ago that Aniela is not only the beloved woman, but the very crown of my head. Yes, it is a fact; let it be called by any name, — neurosis, or an old man's madness; I have got it in my blood and in my soul.

I am going to Ploszow. I will serve her, take care of her, do for her what I can; and for all reward let me be able to look at her. I wonder at myself that I fancied I should be able to live without seeing her. One letter from my aunt brought out all that was buried within me. My aunt says: —

"I did not write much about us, because I had nothing cheerful to tell you; and as I am not clever at disguising things, I feared I should make you uneasy, knowing that you were not well. I am in terrible anxiety about Kromitzki, and should like to have your advice. Chwastowski showed me his son's letter, in which he says that Kromitzki's affairs are in a deplorable state, and that he is threatened with legal prosecution. Everybody has deceived him. He suddenly received orders to deliver a great quantity of goods, and as the appointed term was very short, he had no time to look into things and see whether everything was as it should be. It turned out that all the goods were bad, — imitations, and second and third rate quality. They were rejected; and in addition Kromitzki is threatened with a trial for defrauding the agency. God grant that we may be able to prevent this, especially as he is innocent. Ruin does not matter, provided there be no disgrace. I am altogether at a loss what to do and how to save him. I do not like to risk the money I intended Aniela to have, and yet we must not let it come to a trial. Tell me what to do, Leon; for you are wise and will know what is expedient in these matters. I have not told Celina anything about it, nor Aniela, — and I am very anxious about Aniela. I cannot understand what is the matter with her. Celina is the worthiest of women, but she always had exaggerated ideas about modesty, and has brought up Aniela in the same way. I do not doubt that Aniela will be the best of mothers, but now I am quite angry with her. A married woman ought to be prepared for consequences, and Aniela seems to be in despair, as if it were a disgrace. Nearly every day I see traces of tears in her eyes. It torments me to see her looking so thin and pale, with those dark rings under her eyes and ready to burst into tears at the slightest provocation; and there is always an expression of pain and humiliation in her face. I have never in my life seen a young woman so distressed at her situation. I tried persuasion and I tried scolding, — all in vain. Perhaps I love her too much, and in my old age am losing my former energy; but then she is such an affectionate creature! If you only knew how she asks after you day by day, whether a letter has arrived and if you were well, when you will be going, and how long you mean to stop at Berlin. She knows I like to speak about you, and she makes me talk for hours. God give her strength to bear all the troubles that are awaiting her. I am really so concerned about her health that I positively dare not give her any hint about her husband's position. But sooner or later it must come to her ears. I have not said anything to Celina either, because she is troubled about Aniela, and cannot understand why she should take her position so tragically."

Why? I alone in the world understand and could have answered that question, — and that is the reason I go back to Ploszow. It is not her position she takes tragically, but my desertion. My despair she is aware of, the sundering of those ties that have grown dear to her from the time when after so much suffering, so many efforts, she contrived to change them into ideal relations. Only now I enter into her thoughts, into her very soul. From the moment I came back to Ploszow there arose a struggle between duty and feeling in that noble heart. She wished to remain true to him to whom she had promised her faith, because her spiritual nature abhors impurity and falsehood; and at the same time she could not help being drawn to the man she had loved with all the fresh feelings of her young heart, — all the more as the man was near her, loved her, and was supremely unhappy. Whole months had passed in that struggle. At last there came a moment of peace, when the feeling had become a union of souls so pure and unearthly that neither her modesty nor her loyalty could take exception to it. This is the reason of her unhappiness; I am reading now her soul as an open book, — therefore I go back.

I also now see clearly that I would not have left her if I had had a complete certainty that her feelings would outlast all changes in her life. The mere animal jealousy that fills my mind with rage because another has rights over her which are denied to me would not have been sufficient to drive me away from the one woman who is all the world to me. But I thought that the child, even before it was born, would take possession of her heart, draw her closer to her husband, and blot me out of her heart and life forever.

I do not delude myself even now, for I know that I shall not be to her what I have been, nor what I might have been but for the combined forces of circumstances. I might have been the dearest and only one for her, attaching her to life and happiness; now it will be quite different. But as long as there is a glimmering spark of feeling for me I will not leave her, because I cannot; I have nowhere to go.

Therefore I return; I shall nurse that spark, fan it into life again, and get some warmth from it for myself. I am reading again my aunt's words: "If you only knew how she asks after you day by day, whether a letter has arrived, and if you were well, when you will be going, and how long you mean to stop at Berlin," and I cannot fill myself enough with these words. It is as if I had been starving, and somebody had given me a piece of bread. I am eating it, and feel as if I could cry from sheer gratitude. Perhaps God's mercy toward me is beginning to appear at last. For I feel that I am changed; the former self has died in me. I shall not revolt against her will any more; I will bear everything, will soothe and comfort her; I will even save her husband.

4 November.

After thinking it over, I remain two days more at Berlin. It is a great sacrifice for me, because I can scarcely contain myself in my impatience; but it is necessary to send a letter to prepare her for my coming. A telegram might alarm her, as also my sudden arrival. I have sent off a cheerful letter, winding up with a friendly message for Aniela as if nothing ever had happened between us. I want her to understand that I am reconciled to my fate, and that I come back the same I was before I left her. My aunt must have counted upon my coming on receipt of her letter.

WARSAW, 6 November.

I arrived this morning. My aunt awaited me at Warsaw. At Ploszow things are a little better. Aniela is much calmer. There is no news from Kromitzki.

The poor old aunt met me with a horrified exclamation, — "Leon, whatever has happened to you?" She did not know I had been so ill, and protracted illness alters one's appearance; and my hair has grown quite gray on the temples. I even thought of darkening it artificially. I do not want to look old now. My aunt, too, had changed very much, and although it is not so long since we parted, I found a great difference in her appearance. Her face has lost its familiar determined expression, though her features have grown more immovable. I noticed that her head is trembling a little, especially when she is listening with deep attention. When with some inward trouble I inquired after her health, she said, with her usual frankness, "After my return from Gastein I felt very well; but now everything seems to go wrong, and I feel that my time is coming. We Ploszowskis all end with paralysis, and I feel a numbness in my arm every morning. But it is not worth talking about; it will be as God ordains."

She would not say anything more. Instead of that we took counsel together how to help Kromitzki, and we resolved not to let it come to a criminal prosecution if we could help it. We could not save him from ruin, as this would have involved our own ruin, which, if only in consideration for Aniela, we must avoid. I made a proposition to settle Kromitzki here, by giving him one of the larger farms. God knows how my mind recoiled from the very thought of his being always with Aniela, but to make my sacrifice complete I had made up my mind to swallow the bitter draught.

My aunt offers one of her farms, and I am furnishing the necessary capital to establish him, which, taken together, will be Aniela's dowry. Kromitzki will have to pass his word not to embark in further speculation. But before that can be done we must get him free, and for that purpose we are going to send out an able lawyer with instructions and ample means.

When we had finished our consultation I began to inquire after Aniela. My aunt told me, among other things, that she was very much changed, and her former beauty almost gone. Hearing this, I felt the more pity for her. Nothing will be able to turn my heart from her. She is the very crown of my head. I wanted to start off at once for Ploszow, but my aunt said she felt tired, and wanted to pass the night at Warsaw. As I had told her about my having had inflammation of the lungs, I suspect she remained on purpose so as not to let me travel in bad weather. It has been raining since morning. Besides we should not have been able to go, as Kromitzki's affairs must be dealt with at once.

7 November.

We arrived in Ploszow at seven in the evening. It is now midnight, and the whole house is asleep. Thank God, the meeting did not excite her much. She came out to me with hesitating step, and there was fear and shame in her eyes; but I had vowed to myself to meet her as if we had parted yesterday, and take care to avoid anything in the nature of reconciliation, anything to remind her that we had parted under unusual circumstances.

When I saw her coming, I put out my hand, saying cheerfully,—

"How do you do, dear Aniela? I have been longing to see you all, and it made me put off my sea voyage for another time."

She understood at once that such a greeting meant reconciliation, peace, and the sacrifice of myself for her sake. For a moment there passed across her face a wave of such emotion that I felt afraid she would lose command over herself. She wanted to say something and could not; she only pressed my hand. I thought she might burst into tears, but I did not give her time, and continued quickly in the same tone:—

"What about the portrait? The head was finished when you left Vienna, was it not? Angeli will not send it soon, because he said to me it would be his masterpiece. He will want to exhibit it in Vienna, Munich, and Paris. It is lucky I asked him to make a copy, otherwise we might wait a year before we got it. I wanted a copy for myself."

She was obliged to fall in with my humor in spite of all the emotions that worked in her breast, especially as my aunt and Pani Celina took part in the conversation. In this way the first awkward moments were tided over. Everything I said was intended to divert our attention from the real state of feelings. I kept on in the same strain all the evening, although at times I felt the perspiration breaking out on my forehead from the effort. I was still weak after my recent illness, and all this told upon me terribly.

During supper Aniela looked at my pale face and the gray hairs. I saw she guessed what I must have suffered. I spoke about my Berlin experiences almost gayly. I avoided looking at her changed appearance, so as not to let her see that I had noticed it, and that the sight moved me deeply. Towards the end of the evening I felt faint several times, but I fought against it, and she did not see anything in my face except calmness, serenity, and boundless affection. She is very keen-sighted; she knows, perceives, understands things very quickly; but I fairly surpassed myself,—I was so natural and so much at my ease. Even if there be still any lingering doubt in her mind as to my submission, she has none as to my affection and her being to me the same worshipped Aniela.

I noticed that she seemed better and evidently began to revive in the warmer atmosphere. I had indeed reason to be proud of myself, for I brought at once an appearance of cheerfulness into a house where dulness had reigned paramount. My aunt and Pani Celina appreciated it keenly. The latter said frankly when I wished her good-night:—

"Thank Heaven, you have come. Everything looks different at once with you in the house."

Aniela, pressing my hand, said shyly, "You will not go away soon, will you?"

"No, Aniela," I replied; "I will not go away again." And I went, or rather fled, to my room, because I felt that I could bear the strain no longer. There had been such an accumulation of misery and tears in my heart during that evening that I felt half choked. There are small sacrifices that cost more than great ones.

8 November.

Why do I repeat to myself so often that she is as the crown of my head? Because one must love a woman more than life, consider her as the crown of life, if he does not leave her under circumstances like these. I am perfectly aware that mere physical repugnance would have driven me from any other woman; and since I remain here the thought occurs to me again that my love must be an aberration of the nerves, which could not exist were I a normally healthy specimen of mankind. The modern man, who explains to himself everything by the word "neurosis," and is conscious of all that is going on within himself, has not even the comfort which a conviction of his own faithfulness might give him. For if he says to himself, "Your faithfulness and perseverance are signs of disease, not virtues," it adds one bitterness the more. If consciousness of all these things makes life so much more difficult, why do we take so much care to cultivate it.

To-day, by daylight, I noticed how much Aniela is changed, and my heart was torn at the sight. Her mouth is swollen, and the once so pure brow has lost its purity and clearness. My aunt was right, — her beauty is almost gone. But the eyes are the same as those of the former Aniela, and that is enough for me. That changed face only increases my pity and tenderness, and she is dearer to me than ever. If she were ten times more changed I should love her still. If this be disease, I am sickening with it, and do not wish to get well again; I would rather die of this disease than of any other.

9 November.

A time will come when under changed circumstances she will recover her beauty. I thought of it to-day and at once asked myself what would be our relations towards each other in the future, and whether it would make any change. I am certain it will not. I know already how it feels to live without her, and shall not do anything which might make her cast me off. She will always remain the same; I have now not the slightest doubt that I am necessary to her life, but I know also that she will never call the feeling she has for me by any other name than great sisterly affection. What matters the name? it will be always the ideal love of one soul towards another; and that is lawful, because permitted to brother and sister. Were it otherwise, she would be in arms against it at once.

In regard to this I have no illusion whatever. I have already said that since she changed our mutual relations into ideal feelings, they have become dear to her. Let it remain thus, provided they be dear to her.

10 November.

It is an altogether wrong idea that the modern product of civilization is less susceptible to love. I sometimes think it is the other way. He who is deprived of one lung breathes all the harder with the remaining one; we have lost much of what makes up the sum of life, and are endowed instead with a nervous system more highly strung and more sensitive than that of our ancestors. It is quite another matter that a lack of red globules in our blood creates abnormal and unhealthy feelings, and the tragedy of human life rather increases therefore than grows less. It is increased for the very reason that, whereas the former man in his disappointments found consolation in religion and social duties, the modern man does not find it there. Formerly character proved a strong curb for passions; in the present there is not much strength in character, and it grows less and less because of the prevailing scepticism, which is a decomposing element. It is like a bacillus breeding in the human soul; it destroys the resistant power against the physiological craving of the nerves, of nerves diseased. The modern man is conscious of everything, and cannot find a remedy against anything.

11 November.

There has been no news from Kromitzki for some time; even Aniela has not heard from him. I sent him a telegram to inform him that a lawyer was coming out to him to set his affairs straight; then I wrote to him, — trusting to chance that he may get the letter; for we do not know where he is at present. No doubt the telegram and letter will find him in time, but where or when we do not know. The elder Chwastowski has written to his son; perhaps he first will hear something as to how matters stand.

I spend whole hours with Aniela, with nothing to disturb us. Pani Celina, who knows now about Kromitzki's position, asked me to prepare Aniela for any news she might be likely to receive. I have already told Aniela what I think in regard to her husband's speculation, but only from a personal point of view. I told her even that she ought not to take it to heart if he lost all his money, which after all might be the best thing that could happen to him, as then he might be able to settle to a quiet, practical life. I set her mind at rest as to the money I had lent him, and said that was all right; I also told her something of my aunt's plans for their future. She listened with comparative calmness and without showing signs of emotion. What most gives her strength and comfort is the consciousness that so many loving hearts are near her. I love her now beyond all words; she sees it, — she reads it in my eyes, and in my whole manner towards her. When I succeed in cheering her up, or call forth her smiles, I am beside myself with delight. There is at present in my love something of the attachment of the faithful servant who loves his mistress. I often feel as if I ought to humble myself before her, as if my proper place were at her feet. She never can grow ugly, changed, or old to me. I accept everything, agree to everything, and worship her as she is.

12 November.

Kromitzki is dead! The catastrophe has come upon us like a thunderbolt. God keep Aniela from any harm in her present state. To-day came a telegram to the effect that, accused of fraud and threatened with imprisonment, he has taken his life. I should have expected anything but that! Kromitzki is dead! Aniela is free! But how will she bear it? I have been looking again and again at the telegram, to make sure I am not dreaming. I cannot yet believe my own eyes; but the signature, "Chwastowski," vouches for its truth. I knew it could not end well, but I never supposed the end would be so speedy and so tragic. No! the thought never crossed my mind.

I feel as if I had received a blow on the head. If my brain does not give way now, it can bear anything. I once helped Kromitzki, and latterly I have done what I could for him, consequently I have nothing to reproach myself with. There was a time when from my whole soul I wished him dead, — that is true; but it is all the more to my credit that I helped him in spite of that. And death has overtaken him, not in consequence of anything I did, but in spite of it. And Aniela is free! Strange, though I know it, I cannot believe it altogether. I am as if only half conscious. Kromitzki to me was a mere stranger, moreover the greatest obstacle in my way. The obstacle is removed, therefore I ought to feel a boundless joy; and yet I cannot, dare not feel it, — possibly because a fear of the consequences for Aniela is connected with it. My first thought when I received the telegram was: "What will happen to Aniela? How will she bear the news?" God guard her! She did not love the man, but in her present state a shock may kill her. I am thinking of taking her away from here.

What a fortunate thing that I received the telegram in my own room, and not in the dining-room. I do not know whether I should have been able to control my features. For some time I could not recover myself from the sudden shock. I then went to my aunt, but did not show her the telegram. I said only: —

"I have had bad news about Kromitzki."

"What has happened?"

"You must not be shocked, aunty."

"They brought him up for trial, — is that it?"

"No, it is worse; he is brought up for trial, but before a higher tribunal than ours."

My aunt winked with both eyes vigorously.

"What do you mean, Leon?"

I showed her the telegram. She read it, and without saying a word went to her prie-Dieu and buried her face in her hands. After a short time she rose from her knees and said: —

"Aniela may pay for it with her life. What is to be done?"

"She must not know anything until after the child is born."

"But how can we prevent it? It will be in everybody's mouth; the papers will discuss it. How can we keep it from her?"

"Dearest aunt," I said, "there is only one way. We must have the doctor here and ask him to prescribe for her a change of air. Then I will take her and Pani Celina to Rome. There I can keep all news from her. Here it would be difficult, especially when the servants come to hear about it?"

"But will she be able to bear the journey?"

"I do not know; it all depends upon what the doctor says; I will send for him at once."

My aunt agreed to my proposal. It was really the best thing to do under the circumstances. We resolved to take Pani Celina into our confidence, in order that she might further our plan of departure. I saw all the servants, and gave strict orders that all letters, papers, and telegrams should be brought direct to my room, and nobody approach the young lady with any news or gossip whatever.

My aunt was terribly shocked. According to her views, suicide is one of the greatest crimes anybody can commit; therefore with the pity for the unfortunate man, there was a great deal of horror and indignation. "He ought not to have done this," she said over and over again, — "especially now when he expected to become a father." But I suppose he might not have received news of that. During the last few weeks he must have been in a state of feverish anxiety, travelling from one place to another as the entangled position of his affairs drove him.

I dare not condemn him, and will confess openly that it has raised the man in my esteem. There are some men who, justly accused of fraud and wrong-dealing, and sentenced to imprisonment, take it easy, and pass their time in prison gayly drinking champagne. He did not do that, — he preferred death to disgrace. Maybe he remembered who he was. I should have less sympathy with him if he had made away with himself merely because he had failed; but I suppose even that would have been a sufficient motive for him to do so. I remember what he said about it at Gastein. If my love be a neurosis, then most undoubtedly his feverish desire for gold is the same. When this one aim went out from his life, this one basis slipped away from under his feet, he saw before him, perhaps, a gulf and a desert such as I saw when alone at Berlin. And what could hold him back? The thought of Aniela? He knew we would take care of her; and besides, — who knows? — perhaps in a dim way he felt that he was not necessary to her happiness. I did not think he had it in him; I had not expected from him so much energy and courage, and I confess that I judged him wrongly.

I had put down my pen, but take it up again because I cannot sleep; and besides, while writing my thoughts flow more evenly, and I do not feel my brain reeling. Aniela is free! Aniela is free! I repeat it to myself and cannot encompass the whole meaning. I feel as if I could go mad with joy, and at the same time I am seized with an undefined dread. Is it really true that a new life is dawning for me? What is it? Is it one of Nature's tricks, or is it God's mercy at last for all I suffered, and for the great love I bear in my heart? Perhaps there exists a mystic law which gives the woman to the man who loves her most in order that a great, eternal commandment of the Creator should be fulfilled. I do not know. I have a feeling as if I and all those near me were carried away by an immense wave, beyond human will or human control.

I interrupted my writing again, because the carriage I sent for the doctor has come back without him. He has an operation on hand and could not come, but promised to be here in the morning. He must remain with us at Ploszow until our departure, and go with us to Rome. There I shall find others to take his place.

It is late in the night. Aniela is asleep, and has no foreboding of what is hanging over her, what a complete change in her life has taken place. May it bring peace and happiness to her! She deserves it all. Perhaps it is for her sake God's mercy is showing.

My nerves are so overstrung that I start when I hear a dog barking in the distance, or the watchman's rattle; it seems to me as if somebody were bringing news and trying to get to Aniela. I make an effort to calm myself, and explain away the strange fear that haunts me, by the state of Aniela's health; I try to be convinced that but for this I should not feel so uneasy. I repeat to myself that my fear will pass, as everything passes, and afterwards there will be the beginning of a new life.

I have to familiarize myself with the thought that Kromitzki is no more. Out of this catastrophe springs my happiness, such happiness as I dared not hope for; but there is within us a moral instinct which forbids us to rejoice at the death of even an enemy. And moreover in death itself there is an awful solemnity, — those who speak in presence of it speak in hushed voices; that is the reason I dare not rejoice.

13 November.

All my plans are shattered. The doctor came this morning, and after examining Aniela, announced that there could be no question of any long journey for her, as it would be positively dangerous. There seem to be some irregularities in her state. What a torture to hear his professional jargon, when every word he utters seems to threaten the life of the beloved woman. I told the doctor the position we are in, and he said that between two dangers he preferred the lesser one.

What troubled and angered me most was his advice to tell Aniela, after due preparation, about her husband's death. Alas! I cannot deny that from his point of view he is right. "If you are quite sure," he said, "that you can keep it from Pani Kromitzka for some months to come, it would certainly be better to do so; but if not, it would be advisable to prepare her mind and then tell her; for if she receives the news suddenly there may be another catastrophe."

What is to be done? I must establish a quarantine around Ploszow, not let a paper or letter come in unknown to me, instruct the servants what to say, and to keep even their features under command.

What an impression news like this makes upon every one; I had an illustration in Pani Celina, to whom we had to tell the truth. She fainted twice, and then went off into hysterics; which almost drove me frantic, because I thought she would be heard all over the house. And yet she was not fond of her son-in-law; but she too, I suppose, was mostly afraid for Aniela. I am strenuously opposed to the doctor's advice, and do not think I shall ever agree to it. I cannot tell them one thing,— that Aniela did not love her husband, and that for that very reason the shock will be more terrible to her.

It is not merely a question of sorrow after the death of a beloved being, but of the reproaches she will apply to herself, thinkiug that if she had loved him more he might have clung more to his life. Empty, trivial, and unjust reproaches, for she did everything that force of will could command, — she spurned my love and remained pure and faithful to him. But one must know that soul full of scruples as I know it, to gauge the depth of misery into which the news would plunge her, and how she would suspect herself, — asking whether his death did not correspond to some deeply hidden desire on her part for freedom and happiness; whether it did not gratify those wishes she had scarcely dared to form. My hair seems to rise at the very thought, because it is his death that opens a new life for her; consequently it will be a twofold shock, — two blows to fall upon the dear head. This, neither the doctor, my aunt, nor Pani Celina can understand. No! she ought not to be told until after the event.

What a misfortune that she cannot go away! Here it is difficult, almost impossible, to guard her. She will read in our faces what has happened. The least word, the least glance will rouse her suspicion, and she will fancy all sorts of things. To-day she was surprised by the sudden arrival of the doctor Pani Celina told me she had inquired why he was sent for and whether she was in any danger. Fortunately, my aunt, always ready for any emergency, said that it was the usual thing in such a case to call in the doctor from time to time. Aniela has no experience, and believed her at once. How shall I be able to persuade the servants not to look so mysterious? They already guess that something is the matter, from my warnings and cautionings, and they will know all about it in time. I cannot dismiss them all. The frequent telegrams are enough to excite their curiosity. To-day I had another telegram from Chwastowski at Baku, with the inquiry what he is to do with the body. I replied that he should bury it there for the present. I asked the elder Chwastowski to take it to Warsaw, and sent a money order by telegraph. I do not know even whether such an order can be sent from Warsaw to Baku.

To-day I looked through the papers. In two of them there was a paragraph about Kromitzki's death. If that is young Chwastowski's doing, he must be mad. The servants know everything. Their faces are such that I am surprised Aniela does not suspect something During dinner she was cheerful and unusually lively. The doctor's presence is a great relief to me. Kromitzki is nothing to him. He engages Aniela's attention, makes jokes, and teaches her to play chess. Pani Celina, on the contrary, reduces me to despair. The merrier Aniela grew, the longer and more funereal became her mother's countenance. I spoke to her about it rather sharply.

14 November

We are all at Warsaw. They told Aniela that hot-water pipes were to be laid in all the rooms at Ploszow, and so, to avoid the general upset and discomfort, we all intended to go to Warsaw. The drive tired her very much; but I am glad we are here, for I can rely upon my servants. The house is a little in disorder. A great many pictures are already unpacked. Aniela, in spite of being tired, wanted to see them, and I acted as cicerone. I told her that it was my greatest wish to be at some time her cicerone at Rome, and she replied, with a shade of sadness: —

"I, too, often dream of seeing Rome, but sometimes I think that I shall never go there."

Her words caused me a twinge of anguish, for I am afraid of everything, even presentiments, and am ready to see in every word a forecast of evil.

"I promise you shall go to Rome and stop there as long as you like," I replied cheerfully.

It is strange how easily human nature adapts itself to a new position and exercises its rights. Involuntarily I look upon Aniela as my own, and guard her as my property.

The doctor was right. We did well to come to Warsaw, — firstly, because in case of any sudden emergency there is help at hand; secondly, we are not obliged to receive visitors. At Ploszow we could not have avoided that, as it is impossible to turn away a visitor from one's own gates; and probably a great many would have come with condolences. Finally, at Ploszow there existed already a mysterious, heavy atmosphere, in which my efforts to give the conversation a light and cheerful turn appeared unnatural. I suppose this cannot be avoided even here, but Aniela's mind will be occupied with hundreds of little sensations, and be less observant of any slight changes in her surroundings than she would be at Ploszow. She will not go out often, and never alone. The doctor orders exercise, but I have found means for that. Beyond the stables there is a good-sized garden with a wooden gallery near the wall. I will have it glazed, and in bad weather Aniela can walk there. It is a terrible strain, this continual anxiety hanging over our heads.

15 November

How did it happen? How the slightest suspicion could have entered her head I cannot understand. And yet it is there. To-day, during breakfast, she suddenly raised her eyes, looked inquiringly at all of us in turn and said —

"I cannot quite make it out, but I am under the impression that you are concealing something from me."

I felt myself growing pale, — Pani Celina behaved most fatally; only the dear old aunt did not lose her presence of mind and at once began to scold Aniela: —

"Of course we are hiding something, and did not like to tell you that we consider that little head of yours a foolish one. Leon said yesterday that you would never learn to play chess, as you had no idea about combination."

I breathed more easily, and getting hold of the clue began to make fun of her. Aniela seemed satisfied for the moment, but I am quite certain that we have not dispersed her suspicion, and that even my cheerfulness may have seemed artificial to her. My aunt and Pani Celina were thoroughly frightened, and I was in despair; for I saw how fruitless would be our endeavors so keep the thing from her altogether. I fancy that Aniela suspects we are keeping from her some bad news about her husband's financial affairs; but what will she think if week after week passes and she does not get any letters from him? What can we tell her; how explain the silence?

Towards noon the doctor came. We told him what had happened, and he repeated what he had said before, that it would be better to let her know the truth.

"Naturally Pani Kromitzka will be getting anxious at not receiving any letters, and thence will draw the worst conclusions."

I still tried to avoid extreme measures and said that this anxiety would prepare her mind for the news.

"Yes," replied the doctor, "but anxiety prepares the organism badly for an ordeal which even under more favorable circumstances would not be an easy thing to bear."

Perhaps he is right, but my heart quakes with terror. Everything has its limits, and so has human courage There is something within me that protests desperately against this, and I am afraid of the voice which says, "No."

The ladies have almost made up their minds to tell her to-morrow. I will have nothing to do with it. I had no idea one could be afraid to such an extent. But it is a question concerning her.

16 November.

All was well until evening, when suddenly hemorrhage set in. And I had said no! It is three o'clock at night. She has fallen asleep. The doctor is with her. I must be calm — I must. It is necessary for her that somebody in the house should preserve his presence of mind — I must.

17 November.

The doctor says that the first phase of illness is progressing according to rules. What does that mean? Does it mean that she will die? The fever is not very great. This seems to be always so the first two days. She is quite conscious, feels out of sorts and very weak, but suffers little. The doctor prepared us to expect that the fever would increase gradually up to forty degrees; there will be great pains, sickness, and swelling of the feet — that is what he promises!

Let there be at once also the end of the world! O God! if that is to be my punishment, I swear I will go away, never to see her again in life, — only save her!

18 November.

I have not seen her. I sit at her door almost bereft of my senses; but I do not go in, because I am afraid that the sight of me will make her worse and increase the fever. At times a horrible idea crosses my mind that I am going mad and might kill Aniela in a fit of insanity. That is the reason I force myself to write, for it seems to me that it is the best way of keeping my senses under control.

19 November.

I heard her voice and her moans through the door. In that illness the suffering is terrible. According to the doctor it is the usual sign, but to me it seems blind cruelty! My aunt says she clings round her neck and her mother's and asks them for help. And nothing can be done, nothing! Continual sickness, the pains are increasing, the feet are quite swollen. The doctor says nothing, but that it may turn out all right, or may end badly. I know that without him! The fever is at forty degrees. She is always conscious.

20 November.

I know it now. Nobody told me, but I know for certain that she is going to die. I have all my senses under control, I am even calm. Aniela will die! Last night, sitting at her door, I saw it as clearly as I now see the sunlight. A man in a certain condition of mind sees things which other people with less concentrated minds cannot see. Towards morning something passed within me which made me see how it would end; it was as if a veil had been torn from my eyes and brain. Nothing now can save Aniela. I know it better than all the doctors. And that is the reason why I do not resist any longer. What good can it do either to her or to me? The sentence has been pronounced. I should be blind if I did not perceive that some power as strong as the universe is parting us. What this power is, what it is called, I do not know. I know only that if I knelt down, beat my head on the floor, prayed, and cried out for mercy, I might move a mountain sooner than move that power. As nothing now could part me from Aniela but death, she must die. This may be very logical, but I do not consent to part from her.

21 November.

Aniela wished to see me. My aunt took everybody out of the room, thinking she wanted to recommend her mother to my care, and this was really the case. I saw my beloved, the soul of my life. She is always conscious; her eyes are very bright and her mental faculties excited. The pain has almost ceased. All traces of her former state have disappeared, and her face is like an angel's. She smiled at me, and I smiled back. Since yesterday I know what is awaiting me, and it seems to me as if I were dead already; therefore I am calm. Taking my hand in hers, she began to speak about her mother, then looked at me as if she wished to see as much as she could of me before her eyes closed forever, and said: —

"Do not be afraid, Leon, — I feel much better; but in case anything should happen to me I wanted to leave you something to remember me by. Perhaps I ought not to say it so soon after my husband's death; but as I might die, I wanted to tell you now that I loved you very, very much."

I replied to her: "I know it, dearest;" and I held her hand and we looked into each other's eyes. For the first time in her life she smiled at me as my betrothed wife. And I wedded her by vows stronger and more lasting than earthly vows. We were happy at this moment, though overshadowed by a sadness as strong as death. I left her only when we were told the priest had come. She had prepared me for his coming, and asked me not to grieve at it; she had sent for him, not because she thought she was dying, but that it might do her good and set her mind at rest.

When the priest had left I went back to her. After so many sleepless nights she was tired and fell asleep; she is sleeping now. When she wakes up I will not leave her again until she falls asleep again.

22 November.

She is very much better. Pani Celina is beside herself with joy. I am the only one who knows what it is. There was no need for the doctor to tell me that it means paralysis of the bowels.

23 November.

Aniela died this morning.

ROME, 5 December.

I might have been your happiness, and became your misfortune. I am the cause of your death, for if I had been a different man, if I had not been wanting in all principles, all foundations of life, there would not have come upon you the shocks that killed you. I understood that in the last moments of your life, and I promised myself I would follow you. I vowed it at your dying bed, and my only duty is now near you.

To your mother I leave my fortune; my aunt I leave to Christ, in whose love she will find consolation in her declining years, and I follow you — because I must. Do you think I am not afraid of death? I am afraid because I do not know what there is, and see only darkness without end; which makes me recoil. I do not know whether there be nothingness, or existence without space and time; perhaps some midplanetary wind carries the spiritual monad from star to star to implant it in an ever-renewing existence. I do not know whether there be immense restlessness, or a peace so perfect as only Omnipotence and Love can bestow on us. But since you have died through my "I do not know," how could I remain here — and live?

The more I fear, the more I do not know, — the more I cannot let you go alone; I cannot, Aniela mine, — and I follow. Together we shall sink into nothingness, or together begin a new life; and here below where we have suffered let us be buried in oblivion.

THE END.

www.ingramcontent.com/pod-product-compliance
Lightning Source LLC
Chambersburg PA
CBHW011349010726
47494CB00008B/2236
* 9 7 8 1 5 8 9 6 3 3 0 1 8 *